ARISE MY LOVE
AND COME
AWAY WITH ME

Arise My Love And Come Away With Me

Wendell R. Ware

AuthorHouse™
1663 Liberty Drive
Bloomington, IN 47403
www.authorhouse.com
Phone: 1-800-839-8640

© *2012 by Wendell R. Ware. All rights reserved.*

Book Cover Design: Michelle Beaulieu

This book is based on a true story. No part of this book may be reproduced, stored in a retrieval system, or transmitted by any means without the written permission of the author.

Published by AuthorHouse   05/21/2012

ISBN: 978-1-4685-8656-5 (sc)
ISBN: 978-1-4685-8658-9 (hc)
ISBN: 978-1-4685-8657-2 (e)

Library of Congress Control Number: 2012906951

This book is printed on acid-free paper.

Because of the dynamic nature of the Internet, any web addresses or links contained in this book may have changed since publication and may no longer be valid. The views expressed in this work are solely those of the author and do not necessarily reflect the views of the publisher, and the publisher hereby disclaims any responsibility for them.

To Doey

Arise My Love And Come Away With Me

Arise my love
And come away with me.
Arise my love
Come fly with me.
Arise my love and
Spread your wings again
We are cleared to fly again
The sky is ours again.
Come fly with me
And be my love again.
Come fly with me
And be my love again.

Inspired by "The Song of Solomon"

Prologue

An elderly man sat in his bedroom before the fireplace thinking dark thoughts. Mentally he closed the book of his life. There was nothing left to see or live for. For almost a year the ashes of his love, Gloria, his wife of sixty-two years, lay cold and buried in a dark, damp cemetery plot. All that was left was a slender thread to the past that raced through his mind searching for moments worth remembering. There were quite a few. In his mind a soft whispering voice said, "Remember me? Do you remember me?"

"Yes, I remember you, Doey. For more than seventy years you have lived within my heart and shared the memory of my long life. Could I forget you? Never! You have been with me always. You have traveled the world with me. Yes, I remember that once we flew in a moonlit dream. You have always been my love. You were my first and only love . . . and then you left me."

Last night I dreamt I went back to the old Chapel Hill Airport. The light from a three-quarter moon spread its glow through a mist that covered the land. I was alone. Before me lay the ravages of time, as I stood in front of Hangar 2. The hangar door stood half open. Nature found it a handy place to store trash that fled before the restless wind, and was reclaiming the land that once belonged to her. The terminal was vacant and locked. The tower had been infested with bats. The runways were cracked and broken allowing weeds a convenient place to sprout. A tattered wind sock hung listlessly from a short post between the runways. Only the footprint of Orville and Wilbur's Diner remained to remind people that once a popular place to dine was gone.

As I was standing there reliving the past, I watched the downwind leg and final approach of a twin-engine Douglas DC3. The color and markings identified it as a United States Air Force plane. The wheels of the plane gently touched the runway, rolled out, and headed for Hangar 2. There was no sound. Two people stepped from the plane and started walking towards me. They were Red and Doey. They stood there calling, but I couldn't hear what they were saying. They turned and started back to the plane. I ran after them calling their names, but they and the plane faded from sight. I was alone again in an alien world that I knew so well. The dreams will not release me from the past. Those actors, in the history of the war years that spanned the days of World War II, are mostly gone now. I'm left to tell my part in a time that was. There is still much to tell and so little time. We have had our brief moment upon the stage of life, and now it's time to move on.

I awoke in my home in California, shaken and exhausted by dreams of a frightening long-ago and far-away past.

Chapter 1

New Beginnings

On May 21, 1927, Charles Lindbergh flew a single-engine Ryan monoplane, *The Spirit of Saint Louis,* across the Atlantic Ocean to Paris, France. The lapsed time was thirty-three and a third hours. I was nine years old.

It was the same year that I retired my cowboy suit and stabled my broom for a horse in the garage, and declared that I was going to be an aviator. Instead of playing cowboys and Indians, my playmates and I donned aviator helmets bought at the Kress Dime Store, and with outstretched arms zoomed and swooped around the neighborhood, making our version of an airplane's engine noise in flight.

Mother, alarmed at my ardent interest in aviation, countered with a plan of her own. I had shown a mild interest in music, but it was just a small flame that threatened to be no more than a flicker. Together, my parents conspired to change the direction of my future. For Christmas that year, I received a violin, one of Sears Roebuck's best. I believe it cost nine dollars. For the world I wouldn't hurt their feelings, but when they saw me strumming the violin like a guitar, they knew their son would never play first chair in the string section in the New York Symphony Orchestra.

Mother was not discouraged. She had offered piano and violin lessons. They were her favorite instruments, not mine. A few weeks later my dad said that he was sorry that I had no interest in music "but your mother and I . . ." I stopped him and said that I did like music, but I had no interest in taking piano or violin lessons, "those are girls' instruments!" He asked me what I would like. "I'm not sure," I said. "I think that I would like to play a trumpet or trombone."

"You're not big enough to play a trombone," he said. "I'll talk with Mr. Fitch. He runs the Fitch Band School of Music. We'll have a talk with him and maybe you can make up your mind."

A few days later he said, "We have a meeting with Mr. Fitch on Saturday. I want you to pay close attention to what he says and ask any questions you may have. It's a big decision for you to make. Mother doesn't want another fiasco like the one we had with the violin."

"What does 'fiasco' mean?" I asked.

"It's an ignominious failure," he said.

"What's 'ignominious' mean?" I asked.

"It's an unexplained failure," he replied

"Oh?" I said.

"Oh! Look it up!" Dad replied impatiently.

I liked the sound of the word and rattled it around in my mind for a few days looking for a word to go with "fiasco" to make a sentence. The closest I could come up with was the word "nuance." "Fiasco of the nuance" sounds high tone, but I never found a way to use it. Oh well, I suppose it was an ignominious failure.

During the summer we built model airplanes of balsa wood and rice paper. Rubber bands extending from the tail to the nose of the plane connected to a balsa wood propeller providing the power for them to fly. Mostly they just crashed, leaving nothing more than a heap of irreparable parts and a reminder of the two or more weeks of our time spent building them. At the public library we found a book written by F.B. Evans that contained diagrams of every part of a single-engine plane, with words supplied by Orville and Wilbur Wright.

We learned why our planes crashed and what we could do to make winners of our failures. We learned about pitch, roll, and yaw, and spoke in terms of dihedral and torque, and why weights and balance were so important. We spoke in a language that we called "Airplane."

We read stories of World War I flying aces that had replaced our heroes of yesteryears, Tom Mix and Ken Maynard, with stories of Eddie Rickenbacker, who destroyed 21 German planes and became America's ace of aces. After the war, Rickenbacker, a member of the famed 94th Hat-in-the-Ring Squadron, became president of Eastern Airlines. Frank Luke gained ace fame by destroying German planes and balloons. His name lives on to identify an Air Force base in the city of his birth, Phoenix, Arizona.

When I was ten years old I started hanging around the Albert Whitted Airport. After church one Sunday, I begged my mom and dad to take me to the airport. It wasn't an easy sell. I had to do a lot of begging, but with a sniffle or two, and promises made that even an accomplished politician couldn't keep, I carried the day . . . I thought.

Our auto, an Oldsmobile touring car, changed directions and headed to the Bay Front Airport. My sisters, Irene, age 14, and Ruth, age 13, had other plans for a day that did not include the airport. I thought their arguments were flawed, and in a loud argumentative voice let them know how much I didn't like silly old girls.

"One more word out of any of you, and we go home. Now, calm down or you will stay in your rooms for the rest of the day." When my dad spoke like that, it was an honest-to-gosh non-negotiable edict. Mom added her soothing voice, with logic that we all understood, and utter silence from the back seat reigned. We drove down Second Street south to Beech Drive, and Dad parked the car at the curb. Before me, lay the most beautiful sight in the entire world.

Along the margin of St. Petersburg's strip of Tampa Bay lay the airport named for Albert Whitted, whose father was one of the pioneer developers of our city of sand and palmettos. Albert, his son, was a U.S. Naval flight instructor stationed at Pensacola, Florida.

One unfortunate day he was flying over an area designated for flight training, teaching a cadet how to recover from stalls on take-offs and landings, when a stay wire on one of the wings of his biplane snapped. The plane, about a hundred or so feet in the air, rolled to the left and crashed into a field at the end of the runway. Albert was killed, but the student lived to fly again.

Along the south boundary of the field stood two hangars; one for airplanes and another giant hangar for the Goodyear blimp *Mayflower* that, along with the tourists, spent the winter here. There was an attached single-story office building that one day would become the home office of National Airlines Inc.

I started walking along the fence to where a small crowd had gathered to watch, as two men were preparing to take their place in the cockpit of the Ford tri-motor passenger plane. The passengers were probably tourists adding one more experience to their winter holiday to take north with them.

I watched as the plane taxied to the east west runway and turned east into the wind. I could see the pilot and co-pilot as their hands moved easily about the cockpit adjusting dials and flipping switches. I could only imagine what else they were doing; but I did know that their hands, eyes, and hearts knew the magic of flight.

I watched spellbound as the three roaring engines pulled the plane faster and faster down the runway. The wheels of the plane were, like dipping a toe into bath water to see if it's too hot or too cold, cautiously testing the air for the right moment to break the bonds of earth. The plane found that precise moment and, like an aviation expression of the day, "climbed like a home-sick angel" into a beckoning sky.

When the plane disappeared into that bright Sunday morning sun, my imagination took flight. I had loosened one of the ties that bound me to the earth. I heard my father say, "Let's go!" With visions of flight safely locked away in my memory, I followed him to the car.

"Well! It's about time," my sister Irene said.

"Hush," my mother said, as we started for home.

I had no time for a debate with my sisters, I just said, in a civil voice, "I'm sorry." It was the moment I knew that the wonderful days of childhood were coming to an end. I started by giving my sisters the same respect that I gave adults. It took time to learn new ways to get what I wanted, and the transition was not easy. I also increased the scope of my reading to include history, and, most especially, I became a habitual Saturday visitor to the Albert Whitted Airport.

Chapter 2

George Baker

George "Ted" Baker was a five-foot-nine muscular man carrying a weight of one hundred and eighty-one pounds. He had dark brown hair and eyes that were always searching for the next rung up on the ladder to success. As a partner of an automobile and airplane leasing company, he sat in the lobby of a Chicago hotel reading the Sunday Tribune. He was there to repossess a Cadillac sedan that was leased to a Mr. Samuel Jones, a known member of a Chicago gang. The monthly payments on the car were two months past due.

For just a moment, however, Mr. Jones was completely forgotten as an article in the newspaper pointed the way to a new and exciting future. While the new future beckoned, Mr. Jones slipped from the elevator and disappeared through a side door into the alley where the Cadillac was parked. Ted finished reading the article that told that all airmail flights had been grounded for safety reasons, and there was to be a complete reorganization of the nation's airmail routes. The article called for responsible companies to bid for segments of a grid of routes that covered the country. The last rung on Ted's ladder to success lay before him. Without further thought of Mr. Jones, Ted left the hotel committed to starting a new career.

He convinced his good friend and partner Lew Bower that their future success did not lay in the leasing business, but rather as owners of an airline. Ted had recently learned to fly and he was confident that he and Lew could bid for a segment of the airmail routes. They owned two single-engine Ryan aircraft that had been leased to a Chicago businessman. The planes had been used to fly illegal liquor from Canada to a seldom-used field on the southwest side of Chicago. The cargo was consigned to a customer whose well-guarded person and name was Al Capone. When Ted and Lew discovered that the planes they owned were being used to import illegal booze, they cancelled the lease and had two used Ryan aircraft on their hands.

The Ryan was kin to the *Spirit of St. Louis*, flown by Lindbergh. Until 1932 the United States Army Air Force had carried the mail. In severe winter weather, obsolete airplanes that were not built to fly in such weather often crashed, causing loss of life. Compounded by the lack of pilot training to fly under such conditions was enough to "stay these couriers from their appointed rounds." Those were the reasons given for grounding the airmail service and implementing a new government program that would turn that service over to civilian companies.

The government would step aside and solicit bids from newly formed organizations for sections of a new air route system that covered the nation. When the bidding was over, Ted was awarded 109 miles of route, the shortest in the country, connecting St. Petersburg and Tampa with Daytona Beach. It was a segment of air miles that Eastern Airline's president, Eddie Rickenbacker, declined to include in their winning bid for the entire east coast from Miami to Maine. It was a decision that he would live to regret.

The dollar and thirty cents in Ted Baker's pocket represented his total net worth; the name of his new airline, National Airlines System, represented his total optimism. For Ted, the 140-mile route was really more than he could afford, but he had his foot in the door. With help from his partner and a Wall Street firm, he organized his new company and prepared the two used Ryan planes for duty. His calling card was soon printed proclaiming him to be the President of National Airlines System. Spread across both sides of the planes were the words National Airlines, a name that in no way described an airline with a short mail route and two obsolete airplanes with a passenger capacity of only two. Even with a full load and both planes constantly in the air with paying customers, the odds of survival would still be doubtful. Without the expansion of planes that could carry more passengers, and a generous cash infusion, the future looked grim. But, with the addition of optimist Ted Baker to the equation, survival was assured.

A couple of investors with money to risk gave credibility to the airline's future. National soon purchased two used Stinson monoplanes from Western

Airlines, each with a passenger capacity of ten, and the Ryan aircraft were history. In time, the network of routes would grow to honor the name that would become not just national, but international, with many destinations in the United States and Europe.

Chapter 3

Chance Meeting

A hot August sun spread a blanket of heat over St. Petersburg that tested the young woman's will to continue. Her name was Sally Weatherford. As she walked by a park, trees with leaves that fanned the air created an oasis of cooling relief as she paused for a moment before a monument. Slowly, she read the names of local men who had died in the trenches of France in "the war to end all wars."

Sally was a visitor to St. Petersburg. She had graduated from the University of Virginia with a master's degree in English and a minor in history. For almost a year she had searched for a position in academia. She followed every lead in her home area, but none were successful. She didn't want to live on inherited money, as her father had. Even though it was family money that had put her through college, she now wanted to earn money from any job that would pay for an independent life and not compromise her Episcopal morals. Sally recently extended her search radius to include Florida.

Standing there, she heard a woman's voice say, "Are you a visitor to St. Petersburg?"

She turned to the woman and replied, "Yes, I'm visiting from Virginia. I'm hoping to make my home here if I can find a job."

"Good luck," the woman said, as she continued into the park in search of a bench where she could rest. Her name was Maggie McGregor. She was the owner of a small lunchroom across the street from the Albert Whitted Airport.

A rumor, with more truth than doubts, said that a new airline would soon become a reality and the Whitted Airport would become its home base. With that glimmer of promise, Maggie decided that the time was right to transform her rundown lunchroom into a real restaurant. Red-checkered tablecloths would cover the bare tables. A candle and a vase with fresh flowers would be added for the dinner patrons. The bare walls, including the suggestive picture of a Hollywood screen queen, would be replaced with suitable pictures of aircraft and notables in the aviation world. Over the doorway there would be an airplane propeller. She was even thinking of live piano music. But first she would call Mr. Reeder, the franchised dealer of Wurlitzer's Music Company that leased jukeboxes, and find out what it would take to have one installed in her diner.

All morning she had been shopping for items that would address her dream of the future for turning Maggie's Diner into an eating emporium. She had a cook and a waitress, but the waitress named Zelda came to her from a basement bar in Gulfport where sailors gathered to spend their money on beer and sexual favors. At least Zelda was dependable, even if she was a little crude, and Maggie decided she'd keep her as she looked for someone with a little more class. The problem was she needed to attract someone good enough that she could afford.

Maggie looked down the path and saw the young lady she had just spoken to approaching. As the girl came near, she said to Maggie, "I looked for an empty bench, but they are all taken. May I share yours?"

"Certainly," Maggie replied, as she moved her packages closer, making room on the bench.

"It's beastly hot," the girl said, with a hint of British accent on the word "beastly."

"Yes, it is," Maggie replied. Her hair hung in waves around her shoulders and her bright brown eyes, with crow's feet, reflected the charm and satisfaction of the flawed world she knew. She was wearing a sleeveless dress with a soft color of summer green. She was on the tall side and slim.

Arise My Love And Come Away With Me

The young lady was tired, hot, and in a pensive mood. For today, she had given up her search for a job and now sat on the bench in the shade of a green oasis in the middle of the city. Bells from the church tower across the way tolled the hour. She gave little notice of the petite lady who sat on the other end of the bench. Maggie looked at the young lady and said, "It's very warm for April."

Sally replied, "I could tolerate the heat if I could just find a job . . . any job that would provide a living wage. I have searched everywhere. I came to St. Petersburg on a rumor that a man named George Baker may be hiring for his new airline. I have twice been to his office in the Times Building, but I got the same answer: 'Mr. Baker is too busy to talk with anyone now. If it's about a job, see Mr. Wieland, but he's out of town and won't be back for two weeks.' I know that I'm just getting the run around. If I could just talk with Mr. Baker . . ." Sally's voice trailed off to almost a whisper saying, "If I don't find a job by the end of the week, I may as well go home."

Sally's words touched a soft spot in Maggie's heart. Maggie put her packages on the ground and moved over closer to Sally, picked up her hand, and said, "My name is Maggie, Maggie McGuire. What's yours?"

Sally began to smile, and said, "You are very kind, Maggie. My name is Sally Weatherford, and I'm sorry if I disturbed you with my theatrics."

"Oh, that's alright," Maggie said. "We all experience a little disappointment every now and then. Come with me. All you need is to cool off and have lunch. I know just the place, and you will be my guest."

"That's very nice, Maggie. I can still pay my own way, at least for a few more days. I do appreciate your offer for lunch and a cool place to rest and talk."

"Then come with me," Maggie said. They walked to the curb, where a Dodge coupe was parked. Maggie opened the passenger side door. "Get in" she said, "We're not going far."

Fifteen minutes later Maggie pulled up to the curb before a neat little building that added class to the neighborhood. There was a sign above the door to the diner that let people know that it was Maggie's Diner. Across the street was the Albert Whitted Airport, and on the far side of the airport was Tampa Bay. Maggie's Diner was not only a place to eat, but also the meeting place for most people who had anything to do with aviation.

Maggie led the way to her office in the back of the dining area. At a table near her office sat three men in deep conversation. She paused there and said, "Are you still complaining about the food, Joe?"

"Yes, but it doesn't do any good. My wife keeps telling me that I need to keep coming back until you get it right. Red and Sam here aren't married, so they can do as they please. Except on rare occasions Red brings his lunch in a paper sack, and Sam, well, he'll eat anything."

Red chuckled and said, "Say the word, Maggie, and I'll throw the bum out."

Maggie turned to introduce Sally. "This is Sally Weatherford, a new friend of mine from Virginia. And, Sally, I've told the complainer, Joe Bailey, several times, that I would pay him to stay away, but he just smiles and orders another slice of homemade pie."

"It's nice to meet you, Joe. You don't look like a complainer to me," Sally said.

"I'm pleased to meet you as well, Sally," Joe replied.

Maggie placed her hand on Red's shoulder and said, "This is Red Hederman, the only sane one in the group."

Red nodded his acknowledgment and said, "The truth is, Sally, we all love Maggie, and from the whistles and cheers I hear in the background the guys approve of you too. I hope that you will visit Maggie often." Sally smiled shyly. With the introductions over, Maggie and Sally disappeared behind the door to Maggie's office.

Like a model in a dress salon, Sally had been appraised by every pair of eyes in the room. She was a neat, trim, slim young lady of twenty-three years.

Her face was shaped like a valentine. Golden hair fell in waves around her shoulders. Her sparkling eyes were as blue as the bluebells of Scotland, and her voice was soft and lyrical, reminding one of an educated Southern Belle.

Once settled in her office, Maggie turned to Sally and said, "It looks like you have made quite a hit with my customers. I've been thinking about adding another waitress. What do you say you come to work here for now, and if that other job comes through you can make a decision what you want to do at that time?" Sally, relieved to have her dilemma solved, immediately agreed to take up Maggie's offer.

Chapter 4

My Reverie

My dad—my hero—knew of my secret love for flying. On my tenth birthday, December 12, 1928, he said, "Come with me." To my mother he said, "We're going for a birthday ride, and we'll be back soon." And with that we were off on a quest that brought my life a step closer to the path I chose to follow. We drove down Fifth Avenue north to Beach Drive, turned south, and parked in front of the Goodyear blimp hangar.

"Follow me," Dad said, as he led the way to the field.

Just off the runway sat a beautiful red and white Waco biplane. The soft morning sun surrounded the plane with a halo of dazzling light. Every step took me closer and closer to what certainly was the holy grail of aviation. The two men who stood by the plane were pilots.

My dad said, "Mr. Hederman?"

"Yes, I'm Mr. Hederman." Mr. Hederman was six feet tall and slim, with close-cropped red hair. He wore a long sleeve blue shirt and pants to match.

"Mr. Hederman, I'm John Cary. We had a brief conversation about the importance of today." Dad placed his hand on my shoulder and said, "This is my son Wynn. Today is his birthday. He's ten years old and wants to learn to fly, even if it takes all day. Can you help him?"

"I believe I can," Mr. Hederman replied. He shook hands with my father and put his hand on my shoulder and said, "I'm pleased to meet you, Wynn. Just call me Red, everybody does. I think you will make a fine pilot." He introduced us to the man next to him. "Joe Bailey is also a pilot and my partner. He's here to help me start the engine and answer any questions you may have."

Red turned to my father and said, "I think that you'll be more comfortable in the shade by the hangar. You'll find a chair and a Coke in the cold box in the office. Joe will tell you how easy it is to fly and bore you with how he won the air war in Europe." Joe laughed and shook hands with Dad.

"Come with me, son," Red said, as he led the way to the Waco.

As he helped me into the front cockpit and strapped me in, I was told not to touch or move anything. "The front cockpit," he said, "contains a duplicate of all the instruments that are in the back cockpit. When I move the joystick or rudder in the back cockpit I also move the same in the front cockpit. Just follow me on the controls and think of this as your first flight lesson."

Joe stood in front of the plane and called to the pilot, "Switch off." Red checked to make sure that the switch was off and called, "Switch off." Joe pulled the prop through a couple of times then called, "Switch on." Red flipped the switch to the on position and called, "Switch on." Joe checked to make sure that the area was clear then called, "Contact," and pulled down on the prop. The engine came to life and settled into a steady beat. We taxied to runway 90 and took off into my future.

We flew west across the city to the Gulf of Mexico and then north along the coastline to the little town of Clearwater. We then flew east to Tampa and south along the coast of Tampa Bay. Across the bay I could see the little towns of Bradenton and Sarasota. Too soon the flight was coming to an end. The summer sunrays were slanting towards the east leaving little patches of shade across the land.

Our plane banked east into the wind and started its slow descent to the east-west runway of the airport. I could see from horizon to horizon. Could the world be any larger? I knew there was more to see beyond that distant horizon—and to see it, I must learn to fly.

Now I knew two pilots. One named Red, another named Joe. Both would become important to my future. Eventually, Red would teach me to fly and become a close friend for life.

On the way home we stopped at a root beer stand for lunch. I asked Dad what I would tell Mom. He said, "If she asks, and I'm sure she will, tell her the truth," and a banned subject would be mine to explain.

When we arrived home, Mom asked if I was enjoying my day. "Yes" I said. "We had lunch at the root beer stand."

"And before that?" Mom asked. I stammered, tried to speak, and turned red in the face.

Dad said, "What he's trying to say is that he had his first flight in an airplane."

Then the words poured out. "Oh Mom, I wanted to tell you, honest I did, but I didn't know until we got to the airport that I would get to fly in a plane. You should have been there," I said excitedly. "It was the best present I've ever had."

"I'm glad you told me," Mom said, "but I already knew, and I'm glad you got to go up in a plane. Now that you've done it, you won't ever have a reason to fly again."

Later I asked my dad how she knew. "I don't know," he said, "but mothers know everything!"

If I had no chores on Saturdays or after church on Sundays I would pedal my bicycle down to the airport and walk around pretending that I belonged. If I got too close to a plane, someone would yell, "Hey, kid, get away from that plane!"

I would always visit Red Hederman and Joe Bailey. They even permitted me to touch the plane and look into the cockpits. On one visit I noticed a splatter of mud on the sides and bottom of the Waco's fuselage. I said to Joe,

"If you have a bucket and a sponge I can remove that dirt." Joe looked at Red and Red nodded.

"There's a sponge and a bucket in the back of the hangar, and there's a hose over there by the soft drink container. Let's see what you can do," Joe said.

I swelled with pride as I walked out to the plane carrying a sponge in the bucket and dragging a hose. I was trusted with the most important job in aviation. An hour later the plane sparkled in the morning sun.

Red said, "How much do we owe you?"

"Owe me? Nothing," I said.

"It's lunch time," Joe said. "Wynn and I are going over to Maggie's for lunch. Watch the store, Red. This is routine," he said to me. "Red brings his lunch in a paper sack. Let's go, Wynn."

Could life be any better than this? I thought. I know two pilots and they call me by my name and I'm going to have lunch with one of them. We walked toward Maggie's in silence. I searched my mind for something to say in "airplane" talk, but could think of nothing.

I had never been in Maggie's before. Joe led the way to a table in the back where Major Paul Mulzer was sitting. Sometime later I was told that Paul was a reserve pilot in the United States Army Air Force. As we approached the table, Paul said, "Over here, Joe. I saved a place at the table for you and Sam Hughie. He should be along in a minute or two."

"Thanks, Paul," he said. "I brought my friend with me. This is Wynn Cary."

"Welcome, kid," Paul replied.

Paul spotted Sam Hughie as he walked through the door and signaled Sam over. As he took a seat, Paul said, "This is Sam Hughie, and," turning to Sam, said, "the kid's name is Wynn Cary. Sam just got his limited commercial license and the kid is in Joe and Red's maintenance department." That sounded pretty important to me. Quickly I looked around the room to see if anyone could see how important I was. No one looked; they just kept on talking and eating.

"Well, we haven't hired Wynn," Joe said, "and how do you know what he did for us?"

Paul answered, "I saw him washing the Waco." I just sat there with nothing to say. I could hardly wait to tell Dad that I had lunch with three pilots!

With lunch over, Joe and I got up to leave. I told Maj. Mulzer and Sam Hughie that I was glad to know them, "And now that I'm in the aircraft maintenance business, please remember me when you need technical advice on aircraft maintenance," I offered, "anything that can be solved with a bucket of water and a sponge!" They laughed and promised they would call me for an estimate.

As I peddled my way home, I felt that I had shed the uncertainty of the past and took my first step into the future. I studied the mannerisms, the walk and talk of the older guys, those grownups of fifteen years or so. Those had to be the golden years of life. What came after that was mostly downhill and not worth the worry.

Chapter 5

Home

1929 marked the end of an era. The banks, credit markets, and greed stretched beyond their limits and could no longer support the basic building blocks of the economy. The tower of Wall Street tumbled down. Overnight, bankers, brokers, and investors became have-nots and competed for their places in the nation's soup kitchen line with the blue-collar workers.

Christmas that year was similar to all the others. We had a big tree with a star on top that touched the ceiling. The tree filled the house with the piney smell of the forest and the aromas from mom's kitchen added a touch of Christmas magic and created a delicate scent that would put the best French perfume in distant second place. Through the clear night air, a far bell could be heard answering the mellow tones from the bells of our church. The only things missing were the Bible story of the first Christmas and Charles Dickens' *A Christmas Carol.* Those were reserved for the twelve days of Christmas. Each night of the twelve days, my dad read a portion of stories, ending on Christmas Eve.

My sisters, Irene and Ruth, were appointed tree and house decorators. I was not given a part to play, so I joined Dad and sat on the sidelines eating popcorn and watched as the house turned into a Christmas card. Mom came in with a tray of hot chocolate and gingerbread.

Dad said, "I have a new Christmas story titled "The Littlest Star." If you like it, maybe we'll include it in our future Christmas celebrations." Mom pulled up a chair, and we children settled around him and sat on the floor. Before he started to read, he said, "We will call it 'A Christmas Carol for the Carys'."

Wendell R. Ware

"The Littlest Star"

Many long eons ago, give or take a millennium or two, when the Lord was still a young God and the Earth was still a pile of space junk, aimlessly bumping its way around, in a far and forgotten corner of the Celestial Empire called Heaven. A curious event occurred. God became bored with the endless darkness in a far corner in one of His Worlds and some changes were in order. It was time to implement His Grand Plan, which called for the construction of a facility large enough to contain a few animated objects in His own image. It would be a small beginning, and if it worked out, He was thinking of calling them men and women. They would have a self-generating mechanism that would automatically, and not without some physical enjoyment, replenish the species without becoming a tedious bother to Him.

But first, He would need light; lots of light, to accomplish what He allowed would take six days. A simple job, to be sure, but no need to bump around in the dark doing it, when light was a command away. With that, He turned His thoughts into action. He scooped up a handful of gravel, and like a catapult, His mighty arm flung the gravel far into the void about Him. One very small pebble slipped from His grasp and fell "plunk" at His feet. The others arched true to their predetermined positions in space. Upon God's command, "Let there be light," they marked their position with a dazzling array of light so beautiful that a special word would be needed to describe them. Light, being a noun, was not enough. They deserved a better description. As God pondered His first step in celestial improvement, a tiny voice was heard to say, "They look like stars, for surely the light is a winking, blinking, dazzling star light." God looked down and saw the tiny pebble at His feet emanating a most pleasing, icy blue light, whose luminous quality, though pleasing, was hardly bright enough to be much use far out in the void.

"'Stars', that's a nice name," God said, as he stooped and picked up the pebble. He turned it this way and that way, admiring the pleasing glow that radiated from the bit of rock.

"What are you doing here?" roared God. "You should be up there," pointing to the countless glows and the twinkling radiance. "What did you call them?"

"Stars," cried the small voice.

"'Stars' you say? I like that. But what are you doing here and not out there where you should be?" God said.

"You let me slip out of your grasp and I fell to the ground," said the small pebble.

"That's ridiculous," God said. "I make no mistakes, unless letting you talk is one, but don't get too sassy or I will turn you into gravel."

"Oh, I won't," said the Littlest Star. "I'll be ever so quiet . . . and I'll only shine at night . . . and I will stay close to you at all times . . . and I'll follow you around and . . ."

"And I'll turn you into gravel," said the Lord. "Fine gravel, if you say one more word," roared the Lord.

The Littlest Star shook so hard from fright that her light flickered and almost went out.

"Oh, come now," God said, "I was only teasing. I had planned to let you be a star all along, might even make you a 'Star' star, even give you a name. I know, I'll call you 'Stella' and if you get the hang of glowing and glimmering like a star, I might, just might, mind you, let you shine for the people on Earth."

"What are 'people' and what is 'Earth'?" asked the little pebble.

"At the moment it's a blueprint in my mind. When I work out the details, I'll let you know. Until then, get up there, little Stella, with the other stars, and light up that area that's just southeast of that bright star, Ursa Major, the one that looks like a bear." With that, God placed the pebble in the palm of His hand and turning into the direction of Ursa Major, blew his breath lightly across the pebble, sending her arching upward and outward to her assigned position in the galaxy.

"What's a 'blue print'?" Stella asked, her voice echoing faintly as she swooshed outward and upward into a Heaven of stars, leaving a streak of starlight to mark her progress.

"You ask too many questions," replied God. As He turned away, His mind filled with the plans to create a prototype, for a species to be called humans, but first He would need a place to contain them. He certainly wouldn't want them for neighbors, at least not right away. They would have to prove themselves worthy before He would offer to share His Heaven. As He scanned the horizon looking for a likely spot to commence construction, His eyes spotted a very large black rock, where no stars shined. "I'll tuck this experiment

out of sight behind that rock and on the other side of beyond. It will be the place where worthy people will go after they serve their time on Earth and earn the right to live there forever, with every creature comfort."

God liked to think of the Grand Plan that He carried in His mind as the 'Experimental Area Residence Terrestrial Humans', or 'Earth,' for short. He had toyed with the idea for the past two or three eons, and now that He had invented light, it was time to implement the plan.

Early the next millennium, God, with Stella leading the way, picked a path around the Milky Way and the black hole to the other side of beyond. When they arrived at the construction site God set about the task of creation. His pre-plans were right on the money. In six days, He had finished the land, sea, sky, sun, moon, stars, planets, plants, animals, and one man that He called Adam, and a female that He called Rib . . . a name that Adam changed to Eve just as soon as God, with Stella in the lead, disappeared behind the black hole from whence they came.

For the first few years, conditions on Earth were sublime. The living was easy and propagating was considered a work ethic. Then the little world they knew started to come apart. It all started when Eve ate an apple and got them tossed out of their home called Eden. Then Cain slew Able . . . a real no, no, and it seemed that things just went downhill from there. God wasn't at all pleased. In fact, He was downright put out. All along He had planned to bring a few of the better humans to Heaven, and give them the title of 'Angel', an honor that would now have to be deferred until His contingency plan could be tested.

What was needed, He decided, was a boss, someone the people could trust and look to for leadership; someone to interpret the moral code necessary to achieve the status of Angel. That someone would be His son. He would send Him to earth with no special privileges. He would learn the earthlings' business from the ground up, and in time become the only agent to approve passports into Heaven, on the other side of beyond.

And so, on a cold dark night in December of an uncertain year, God sent the brightest and most trustworthy star in His Heaven . . . a star called Stella, to light the world and lead the Wise Men to a place called Bethlehem of Judea, where a child named Jesus, His son, was born in a stable, to a Virgin named Mary.

The plan to save the world and salvage a few souls wasn't perfect . . . wasn't meant to be. God runs an equal opportunity Heaven; everyone has a chance. Like the "Littlest Star" that made good. They must try harder.

The End

Chapter 6

Youth

I'm not sure that I ever believed in Santa Claus, but to create the proper atmosphere for Christmas, I pretended that I did, and Mom and Dad pretended they believed me. I wanted a bicycle, a couple of books by Zane Grey, and a book titled *A World of Aviation*.

I was fairly sure of the bicycle and the Zane Grey books, but if Mother had a say, it would be for Santa to leave a note saying, "Sorry, but the book *A World of Aviation* is out of print."

Immediately following Christmas that year was the end of the secure life that I was accustomed to, and the beginning of a new life. It was the year my father died of a heart attack and my world collapsed.

My dad, measured by a bank account or a successful business career, was not a paragon of success. I never found that important. He was a romantic, he liked poetry and read Shakespeare and knew who Voltaire was. At Christmastime he read Dickens' *A Christmas Carol* to my sisters and me, and, best of all, he spoke "Airplane"; and when the time was right, he introduced me to flying. He was, and is still, my hero.

On Saturdays and Sundays, rich tourists from the North lined up at the airport to pay for a twenty minute ride over the city. Most of the people like me, who didn't have the money, just stood and watched the plane and the Mayflower blimp come and go.

Almost every time I showed up, I'd lean my bike against the fence near Maj. Mulzer's Ford tri-motor plane. He would find time to come over to the fence and say, "Hi, kid, how about running over to Maggie's and getting us a Coke?" Today was such a time. He came to the fence, smiled, and slipped me a dime through an opening in the fence, and with the speed and alacrity of an Olympic sprinter, I was off to Maggie's on a very important mission.

Cold drinks and candy were sold through a window in the side of Maggie's Diner. The window was open. I could see Sally, the waitress who served our table the day I had lunch with Joe, Sam and Maj. Mulzer. She was sitting behind the cash register. She swiveled her chair around, looked at me, and said, "Hi there, don't I know you?"

"You're Sally, aren't you?"

"Yes," she said, "You have a good memory. What can I do for you, Wynn?"

"How do you know my name?" I replied.

"Whenever I see a good-looking young man," she said, "I find out who he is and I remember his name. You were having lunch with Joe, Sam, and Maj. Mulzer one day and I waited on your table."

I blushed and stammered, "I would like two Cokes, please."

She set two Cokes on the window counter and said, "It's a pleasure to serve you, Wynn."

"Thank you," I replied. "Is it alright for me to call you Sally?" I asked.

"Of course," she replied. "We are old friends. I've been selling you Cokes for a long time." She paused for a moment as if searching for the right words and then continued. "If you should see Mr. Hederman, would you please ask him to call me when he can? I've been out of town for a few days and told him that I would call when I returned, but we're asked not to use the phone here. He'll know where to call."

"Yes," I said, "I'll tell him as soon as I deliver the Cokes. Have you known Red long"?

"Yes," she said, "I have known Red for almost a year. Last week he was driving me home from work and we drove by your house. You and your father were on the porch. You were sitting on the steps with an open book in your hands and your father was lying on the porch swing. Red said, 'That's Mr. Cary and his son Wynn.'"

I said, "Just as soon as I deliver Cokes to Maj. Mulzer, I'll tell Red to call you."

After completing my mission to Maggie's I hurried over to the hangar and delivered Sally's message to Red. Other than "Thanks," he made no effort to add to what I had just learned.

The next Saturday, Maj. Mulzer asked if I was still in the aircraft maintenance business. "Yes sir!" I replied.

"The tri-motor plane in the hangar is up for a tune-up," Maj. Mulzer said. "And I think it's time for the interior to be cleaned. Next Sunday morning I'm flying down to Miami and I want the plane to look good inside. If you're still in the business, you might like to look at the job and give me a price."

"Oh, yes, sir," I said, "I'll take the job."

"Don't you think that you should see what it requires before you answer?"

"Well, yes, sir. When it's convenient for you to allow me to go inside the plane, I'll take notes of what I think should be done, and of course I will listen carefully to be told what you would like for me to do. I go to school, and on Saturday and Sunday mornings I go to church. They are the only days that I have any free time, but there will be plenty of time for me to complete the job," I said.

"We'll find a time that's suitable, kid. You do have a name, don't you?"

"Yes, sir, it's Cary, Wynn Cary." He was teasing me. He knew my name.

"Okay, Mr. Cary," Maj. Mulzer said, "if you can spare the time, I'd like you to accompany me on the last flight of the day. Then you'll be able to see what I might have missed when I describe the work to be done."

I couldn't believe what I was hearing. I would get paid to fly in the Ford tri-motor plane. Surely, I misunderstood. I stammered a reply, "Maj. Mulzer, did you mean that I could go with you on the last flight of the day?"

"Yeah," he said, "but only if you can spare the time."

"Thank you, sir. Yes, I'll be there."

There were five passengers including me on the last flight of the day. From a seat in the back of the plane I could see that the floor mat needed cleaning and the covers on the seat headrests would need washing. The windows needed to be cleaned on the inside and out. I figured that I could take the headrest covers home and wash and iron them. The floor mat and windows would take about an hour. When we landed, Maj. Mulzer asked if I had seen enough to price the job.

"Yes, sir, I have. If you will allow me to take the headrest covers home, I'll wash and iron them and have them back the same day. I will also clean the floor mat and wash the windows inside and out. I priced the job at one dollar and seventy-five cents. You have already paid me one dollar which leaves a balance of seventy-five cents."

"Fair enough," Maj. Mulzer said. "But the ride was in payment for all the times that you crossed the street to get me a Coke."

"That time was not for sale," I said. "I owe you for the ride in your plane. I priced the entire job at seventy-five cents."

"Done," he said.

I discussed the job with my friend Eldon Thompson, and the Aircraft Maintenance Company was in business. Eldon Thompson was one of my best school friends. About a year after his father died, his mother Lillian met Robert Harlow at St. Petersburg's Pasadena Golf Club. Their meeting resulted in a marriage that took place in New Haven, Connecticut, where Mr. Harlow lived. He was the first president of the Professional Golfers Association and also managed Walter Hagan.

Eldon Thompson signed on as vice president in charge of buckets and sponges. He was a scant five feet tall. His mop of unruly brown hair hung in front of wide-set dark brown eyes that searched his world for amusement.

Together we finished the job with time to spare. I gave Eldon a quarter. Eldon and I stood by the runway and watched *our* plane, the Ford Tri-Motor, break free from the ground and take up a heading for Miami. We watched until the plane faded from sight. We had fallen into a routine that seldom changed. Any spare time would find us hanging around the airport.

One Saturday morning I was walking around the airport looking for work. When I approached Hangar 1 I heard someone call me. It was Stan Ford, a propeller mechanic. "Come here, kid. I'll give you a nickel, if you will go to maintenance and get me a gallon of prop wash. I have just finished work on this propeller and it needs to be cleaned."

"Mr. Ford, you know my name is Wynn Cary, not Kid," I said with a smile. "I'll be glad to get the prop wash for you." I picked up the bucket and headed for maintenance. Harold Smith was behind the tool cage.

I sat the bucket on the floor and said, "Stan Ford in Hanger 1 sent me to get a bucket of prop wash."

Harold replied, "Jim Johnson was here not more than an hour ago. He got the last two buckets of prop wash we had, but he only needs one. I'm sure he'll let Ford have one of them."

I thanked him and started walking towards Jim Johnson's operation, which was a couple of hundred yards beyond Red and Joe's operation. Of course I stopped to say hello.

Red said, "What's with the bucket? Do you have another plane to wash?"

"No," I said. "I'm going to Johnson's place to get a bucket of prop wash for Stan Ford."

"Wynn," Red said, "there's no such thing as liquid prop wash. Prop wash is the turbulence that comes from the tips of the wings from the plane in front of you. So, when you're taxiing for take offs or landings, never follow too closely behind the plane in front of you because you may not be able to control your plane. Stan is just having a little fun at your expense." Red shook his head and smiled. "Here's what we're going to do. Fill the bucket half full of water and take it back to him. Tell him a half a bucket was all that I had. Tell him he owes me thirty cents for the prop wash, and you a nickel for getting it for him."

After that, Red and Joe's operation near the blimp hangar became my headquarters. Sam Hughie had a four-place Stinson with a 425 hp Jacob's engine and he was now a part of their operation. By now, most everyone on the field had learned my name!

Chapter 7

A World Expanding

In 1932 Franklin Delano Roosevelt became our thirty-third president. He said in one of his fireside chats, "We have nothing to fear but fear itself." It was a good slogan, but it didn't remove the fear of not having a job and what an uncertain future would bring. That summer, Chicago put the finishing touches on their "A Century of Progress" extravaganza, and invited the world to come and see their World's Fair.

In 1934, our high school bandleader, Joe Lefter, told me that he had recently received notice from the Regional Headquarters of the Boy Scouts of America. He had been recommended by their committee to organize a Boy Scout band to represent the southern region of Florida, Georgia, and South Carolina at the upcoming Boy Scout's World Jamboree to be held in Washington, D.C., the first two weeks of July. They requested that the band's membership be limited to First Class Scouts.

Joe believed he could meet that requirement by recruiting members from the high school and the Junior Chamber of Commerce bands.

"Would you like to be my assistant?" he asked me one afternoon. "You are a Scout, aren't you?"

I thought about an answer to a question that promised undreamed travel to places beyond the boundaries of my small town and sheepishly replied, "Well, not exactly."

"What do you mean, 'not exactly'?" Joe asked.

"I'm not a Boy Scout, Joe, not even a Tender Foot, their lowest rank, and I'm 16 years old. That's pretty old to start scouting. Not only that, I don't have the uniform or the money to buy one. On the other hand, I would really love to be your assistant."

"I need some help, Wynn. Don't worry about the scout rank or uniform, I can fix that. You are now an honorary First Class Scout. We'll send the band up on the train and you and I will drive to D. C. in my car. I really need you, Wynn; don't let me down. We have a little more than a month to assemble as many Scouts as we can find who own and can play an instrument. Then we need to practice. It will mostly be Sousa marches, easy stuff. I'm counting on you to help me pull the band together. Sound your A, and let's get started."

"That sounds great, Joe. I'll run it by my mother. If she agrees, you have a helper."

I couldn't wait to get home and tell Mother the wonderful news. All my life I had never been out of St. Petersburg. Well, I had been to Clearwater, about thirty miles up the coast. There wasn't much there, not even a dot on the map to mark its existence. As far as I was concerned, it didn't even rate mentioning. (Years later I was reminded of my hasty judgment. Today many rank Clearwater as one of the top tourist destinations in the world.)

Mother took her time examining every facet of what she considered a momentous decision. She prayed and consulted God before giving her okay; God found nothing wrong with the plan, and by morning my life was completely changed. I was introduced to a life that included unlimited travel, education, and a rich choice of life's endeavors to follow.

In June, a band of Boy Scouts representing Region Four took the train to Washington, D.C. and Joe and I followed in his car. We drove all night and arrived in plenty of time to rest before the opening of the Scout's World Jamboree.

Our camp was at the foot of the Washington Monument. Next to us were the Scouts from Nazi Germany. Nearby was the information tent where news of the day was broadcast by Lowell Thomas and Gabriel Heatter whose opening remark, on almost every broadcast, was, "Ah yes, there's good news tonight!"

In the evening, campfires marked the campgrounds of ours and other Scout groups from around the world. Colonel Theodore Roosevelt Jr., Teddy Roosevelt's son, entertained us with tales of the west. He spoke of Tom Mix and Mark Twain, both of whom he knew.

One evening, to our surprise, a Ford touring car pulled up to our camp circle. He introduced the driver—his uncle, President Franklin Delano Roosevelt, President of the United States—and his dog. Our band rose to the occasion and played several numbers, ending with "God Bless America."

A decade later, Col. Roosevelt would lead his command ashore and die of a heart attack near Normandy, France on July 12, 1944.

The next evening Joe and I went to a movie. We walked into a beautiful, ornate movie palace. When the audience found seats of their choice, the lights began to dim, and then fade away. For a few moments we sat there in the dark of night. Then like the sunrise, the room became gradually lighter, soft music filled the air, and the master of ceremonies began to speak.

"Good evening ladies and gentlemen of our listening nation. I am speaking to you tonight from the proscenium of the Palladium Theatre in Washington, D.C., where from out of the night, the NBC Red Network and Maxwell House Coffee are pleased to bring your way the *Major Bowes Amateur Hour.*" The red curtains, hiding the stage, began to open, revealing Major Bowes standing behind a table containing a microphone and a wheel, much like the ones used in the gambling games of a western movie saloon. The MC introduced the host, and *Major Bowes Amateur Hour,* featuring stars of tomorrow, was on the air.

Major Bowes took his seat behind the table, spun the wheel, and said, "Around and round she goes and where she stops nobody knows." As the wheel turned it made a clicking noise like something pliable was stuck between the turning blades. The numbers on Major Bowes' wheel were related to the performers on the program.

It came to a stop on a number that identified a young man named Frank Sinatra, the singing leader of a trio that had won first place the week before. He looked to be about five feet nine or ten inches tall and to weigh about a hundred and ten pounds. Skinny? Yeah, he cast a very thin shadow. He wore a blue serge suit. On his head was a snap-brim felt hat that he hoped would make him look older than sixteen. When the show ended, Frank Sinatra was declared the winner, and a new star was born.

Along with scouting activities were side trips to many of the historic places in and around Washington, D.C. Our journey into the historic past began with the seemingly endless steps to the top of the Washington Monument. Only the legs of youth could survive the constant walking required to visit those places of beauty and historic values of the past.

We toured the tidal basin and stopped at the Lincoln Memorial to thank Abraham for saving our nation. The words, chiseled into the marble wall of his memorial, expressed the thanks of the nation: *In this temple, as in the hearts of the people for whom he saved the Union, the memory of Abraham Lincoln is enshrined forever.*

We, the Boy Scouts of America, were some of the inheritors of a well-planned journey into the heart of American history. We viewed the Ford Theatre where Lincoln was shot and across the street where he died.

Many books have been written about our nation's capitol, and the men and women whose services have become so important to our country, but this trip taught me that just reading the printed word, was not enough. To come alive, history had to be viewed from the perspective of visiting the places where history was made; sight and sound were essential to retaining those memories of the long ago past. After paying our respects to many of the historic places in and around Washington, we visited Mount Vernon, the estate of George and Martha Washington.

The last stop on our Washington tour was to visit the National Cathedral where Joe and his wife Ruth had been married several years before. Joe and I then headed back to St. Petersburg, while the band travelled home on the train.

Chapter 8

Brother, Can You Spare a Dime?

1936 . . . . Franklin Delano Roosevelt, our thirty-second president, was running for his second term against Kansas Governor Alf Landon . . . After three years of hot, dry weather, the soil of the plains and the Midwest gave up their last drop of moisture and turned into fine dust . . . A sprinter named Jesse Owens had a field day annoying Hitler and the 'super race' at the 1936 Olympics in Berlin . . . In Atlanta, Georgia, Margaret Mitchell finished the "Great American Novel," *Gone with the Wind.*

The world had fallen upon evil times. The good and the bad competed for attention. Foreign names worked their way into the lexicon and minds of people vying for support. Hitler, Mussolini, Churchill, Roosevelt, and Chamberlain readily come to mind. It was the year that Edward, Prince of Wales, soon to be King Edward VIII, defender of the Church of England, which did not recognize divorce, gave the throne to his brother George, and married the twice-divorced Baltimore belle, Mrs. Wallis Warfield Simpson. They left the soil of England on a honeymoon that included a stopover in Berlin, where they learned the stiff-armed Nazi salute.

St. Petersburg was a small city in Florida, nestled between Tampa Bay on the east and the Gulf of Mexico on the west. It was a tiny speck on the world map, but it was the world that I knew. I was seventeen years old, 6'2", and weighed 172 pounds. My hair was brown, my eyes blue, and I had a ruddy complexion. I was a little suspicious of that word "ruddy" and looked it up in the dictionary. It was a good word. It even suggested that I was in good health. I liked English, but music was my only A subject. I liked school, but I just didn't have time to study, and I couldn't spell worth a damn. I could write a fairly good theme paper, but we weren't assigned enough of those to make a difference in my grade average.

I thought that I might like to become a journalist, but that would require college, and anything that required money was placed in the "Dream-on" file. I was advertising manager of my school paper, which was a competitive position that was awarded to the student who sold the most advertising for the first month of the school year.

It wasn't much of a contest. I had an unfair advantage. After school and all day on Saturdays, I worked at the Arthur Johnson Clothing Company where many of the merchants bought their clothing. In making sales, it was easy for me to include a few reasons why supporting the school paper was a great opportunity for them to show their support for the school, and at the same time, increase their business. Within a couple of weeks we had enough ads for the entire year. The salesmen in the store started referring to me as the "Ace" salesman, and I thought I was.

My downfall came a few days later when Harley Neat, the manager of the men's suit department, decided the time had come to test my salesmanship in the real world. "Selling advertising for the school paper," he said, "is not the same as selling clothing to a man whose only purpose for coming into the store is to look, and maybe buy. He can, at his convenience, look, buy, or walk out. He's not ready to find himself in a public arena without an option to say 'No.'

"A few people in the store, even Mr. Johnson, paused to listen while you told John Harris, president of the City National Bank, why he should support the high school's paper with an advertisement. If he said "no," the next day he would find a paragraph in the local newspaper calling him a money-grubber without civic pride. He couldn't chance that, and so he bought a six-inch, two column space, for bank copy, to be run for a year in every issue of your school paper. 'It's for a good cause,' he said to those who paused to listen. Yes, Cary, that was a good sell, but now we'll see if you can *really* sell!"

It was mid morning when a lady walked into the store. Mr. Neat had a short conversation with her, and then turned to me. "This is Mrs. Dawson," he said, and then to her he said, "and this is Mr. Cary. He will show you to the suit department." I glowed with pride and confidence as I escorted Mrs. Dawson through the store. Along the way she paused to look at shirts and ties. She stopped, for a moment, and leaned on the counter with her head down.

"Are you alright, Mrs. Dawson?" I asked. "Would you like to sit down?"

She turned a troubled face to me and tearfully said, in a voice that was almost a whisper, "My husband has just died and I have come to buy a suit in which to bury him." In a second my pride and confidence faded.

"Would you like to lie down and rest for awhile?" We had a room that was equipped for such emergencies. She thanked me and said that I was a nice thoughtful young man, but she would like to finish her shopping and go home.

Thirty minutes later she had purchased a blue serge suit, a white shirt, and a light blue tie. Almost as an afterthought I told her about the sale. "And in addition," I said, "for only ten dollars more, you can get an extra pair of trousers to go with the suit. Alterations and delivery are free." She nodded her head in agreement, placed her hand on mine, and once again said that I was a very nice young man. I rang up the sale on the cash register, gave her a copy of the signed sales slip, and with a voice to match the occasion, I once again expressed sympathy and walked with her to the door. With mixed emotions of sorrow and elation, I had made my first suit sale.

Mr. Johnson, who owned the store, thought I handled the sale with the tact and the solemnity that was required; but when he found that I had sold a suit with an extra pair of pants, he questioned my line of reasoning that required two pairs of pants in which to bury a man. He pointed to the telephone and suggested that, before the day was out, I call the lady and tell her that I had made a mistake, and that a refund would be made for the charge for the extra pair of pants.

When I thought Mrs. Dawson had had time enough to get home, I called and apologized for the crass mistake I had made in even suggesting she purchase the extra pair of trousers, and asked that she please accept my apology. "The charge has been removed and you will receive a company check for the overcharge," I explained. She thanked me for being so honest and thoughtful. We talked for two or three minutes longer, and I was made to feel that Mrs. Dawson and I were friends. My ego, which had hit bottom, was back on track. The word was still out as to whether I belonged in the suit department. Although I was no longer referred to as the "Ace" salesman, I was known by other names.

For the moment my interests were music and flying. I still liked to hang around the airport and dream about becoming a pilot. I liked girls, but I did get a little edgy when I found myself alone with one. At home, I learned never to bring the word "flying" into any conversation. To Mom, the word "flying" was a synonym for "death."

"There is no practical use for flying," she would say. "For every ounce of good it does, there's a pound of grief."

"You should learn a useful profession. If you could get a job with the Post Office, you wouldn't have to worry about a depression. Postal workers have good careers for life. I hope you will consider what I am saying."

"Oh, I will," was always my respectful reply. She failed to remember that some mail was delivered by air, and I didn't bother to remind her. I had already made the connection and moved the U.S. Air Mail Service up to head the list of possible careers.

Chapter 9

Come Fly With Me

In the summer of 1936, my dream of flying yearned to be realized. Bit by bit, as finances permitted, I added time in the air to my logbook. By mid December I had the eight hours of instruction required by the government before a license could be issued. My next flight would be to fly before an agent of the Civil Aeronautics Agency, who would approve or disapprove of my fitness to be issued a solo license—but that would be a few weeks in the future.

On a cold Saturday morning, I took my last flight with my civilian instructor, Red Hederman. I arrived at the airport at 8:45 a.m. for instruction in the care and use of a parachute. Red and the CAA inspector, M. Huchins, watched as I took off, flew the pattern, and landed.

As I started my take-off run, I realized that I carried nothing that would ward off danger. No four-leaf clover, no magic charm or lock of hair from the girl I took to high school dances. Anything would do, but I had nothing. Then I thought of a passage from the "Song of Solomon" that my dad had read to me when I was a child. I chose a few words from that, and when I gently eased the joystick back and the wheels of the Cub left the ground, I silently said a line from the poem. Did I believe the chosen talisman that I used would ward off danger? No, not really, but why take a chance?

It only took a few minutes for the 40 horsepower engine to power the plane to the assigned altitude and fly the assigned pattern. My ego then took over the landing. I flared over the threshold and a few seconds later the wheels and tail skid together, gently touched the ground and rolled out, making a perfect three-point landing. That's kin to making a hole in one on a golf course with the first ball you ever hit. I would have to rethink my belief in that talisman.

On January 27, 1937, I soloed at the Albert Whitted Airport in St. Petersburg, Florida. I taxied back to the hangar and expected a "Well done!" from Red. Instead, he said, "Thanks for bringing the plane back in a repairable condition." I did get a handshake and a pat on the back from Inspector Huchins, who issued a temporary solo certificate which would permit me to fly solo until a permanent license was issued.

I had earned the right to hang out with other pilots and was invited to join an all pilot club that included my instructor Red Hederman, Sam Hughie, Maj. Mulzer, and Ted Baker, president and founder of National Airlines. It was one of the moments that changed my life. My instructor became my life-long friend, and aviation was in my future.

In March, I received my solo license # 60621 from Director of Commerce Inspector, Robert R. Reining, and the next upward move in aviation, a Private License, seemed as remote as an unreachable star.

Chapter 10

Who's Afraid of the Big Bad Wolf?

On the far horizon war clouds were gathering over Germany. Adolph Hitler and Nazism were on the rise, and the world stood by and watched as a maelstrom of death swept over mankind.

There was little doubt that war in Europe was a certainty, but the college students that year had little interest in world affairs. Their ears were more attuned to Benny Goodman and Tommy Dorsey. On Friday nights their feet kept time to the music of Paul Harper and his collection of musical misfits. There were only six members in our band: Paul Harper, our leader, played bass; Bill Shartzer played drums; Bill Nelson, trumpet; Tom Manning, guitar; Tom Gregory played trombone, and I played clarinet. Our motto was: "If you can hum it, we can play it."

A week or so before the Christmas holidays I got a job selling Christmas trees, and I could envision many ways that freedom from daily classrooms could put my future endeavors on a fast track. It made sense to me to give up school and get a full-time job. Maybe I could become a full-time salesman for the Arthur Johnson Clothing Company. That was one possibility.

I knew I could become a full-time painter at my uncle's Gregory Hotel. At most hotels, paint and varnish was a year-round job. Becoming a full-time painter held no appeal for me. It was stoop labor when you varnished floors, and if you were required to paint from a ladder or scaffolding two or three stories high, it would be helpful to have the agility of a circus high-wire performer, which I didn't have.

It was several days later, while I was down on one knee nailing a stand on a Christmas tree, that I heard a voice say, "Wynn." I looked up and saw my high school English teacher standing there. Her usually soft southern lyrical voice exploded in my ears like a lightning strike in a summer storm.

With a very weak voice I replied, "Hello, Miss Parker."

"Stand up when you speak to me," she said sternly. I dropped the hammer and stood before her. In a voice closer to normal, she said, "What are you doing here, and why have you missed the last three days of school?"

"I've quit school," I said.

"Does your mother know?" she asked.

Before answering, I weighed truth against a lie. It was the mental equivalent of flipping a coin to get the answer you wanted. Then I thought of my mother, and knew I was headed for a losing toss. "No, Miss Parker," I replied meekly.

"It's an honest answer," she said, "and no more than I expected. Now let's go in and tell your employer that this will be your last day. Your mother thinks that you have been in school. In the meantime, here are the lessons you've missed. No one needs to know more."

"Thank you, Miss Parker." I resigned my job, and the more I bridged the lost days of my formal education, the more the dreams of my recent future began to fade.

I attended my last high school function, the Senior Prom. That night climaxed twelve long years of organized study that seemed to have had no end, but as I looked back to the beginning of my first day in grammar school, it was no time at all.

After the prom, my date, Betty Moran, a freshman in the local college, and I attended an all-night obligatory party that marked the end of youth. We now thought of ourselves as adults, and had earned the right to stay up all night and smoke and drink, if so inclined. There were no smokers in our

Episcopal Church trained crowd, and only a few of us sipped beer from a bottle. Before the sun came up we took our dates' home, and faced the first day of our new lives.

That summer, my mother's worry about my flying increased. On July 2nd, the news of Amelia Earhart missing and five hours overdue at Howland Island flooded the airwaves. Navy planes and ships were dispatched to search for her, but to no avail.

Chapter 11

Skylark

In early September 1937, Betty Moran and most of my high school friends left to attend out of state colleges, and I enrolled in the local college. Betty enrolled in the University of North Carolina. It was the beginning of a strange new life. To pay my way, I was living at my uncle's hotel, painting rooms, varnishing floors, and working after school and all day Saturday at the Johnson Clothing Company.

When I returned to the hotel after my first day of college, my uncle came to my room on the third floor. I was changing into my painting work clothes. "Stop right there," he said, "you're fired." I couldn't believe what I was hearing. He had always been the calm, helpful person in my life, the one I always turned to for help and advice. He taught me the meaning of inculcate. To him, honesty and hard work were a formula for a good reputation. "From now until you decide to move on, you've earned the right to free room and board!" my uncle declared.

From the first day at college, the future replaced the past. My hotel painting and varnishing days were over. I was still working part time at the Johnson Clothing Company, which was within easy walking distance from the college. This provided me with many additional hours of work to my schedule.

Red and I were returning from a flight to Orlando, he had called me the night before, and said: "I'm going to Orlando tomorrow, would you like to go along? We'll be back by three in the afternoon." I hesitated for a long moment before answering. I had just started my first year of college at the St. Petersburg College and wasn't sure I could, in the first week, spare the time.

"Well," Red said, "there will be some time during the flight that you can log."

"Sure," I quickly replied, "free is good. You did say free, didn't you?" I started asking who, what, when, where, and why questions.

Red cut me off and said, "You ask too many questions. Time off is 7 a.m., don't be late."

I was on time and as our plane left the ground, I silently said my line of verse that was to keep us out of harm's way. "Now that we're in the air and heading for Orlando," I said, "don't you think it's time to tell me why?"

"In time," Red replied.

We arrived at the Orlando McCoy Air Force Base with time to spare. On the downwind leg for landing, Red got the green light from the tower and turned on the base leg and lined up for our final approach. Over the threshold, with power reduced to a whisper, we floated to a landing and rolled out.

Quickly, Red cleared the runway and taxied to a large hangar with a two-story office building beside it. On the other side of the hangar was the tower with a sign on the top that directed pilots of planes with two-way radio communications to "transmit on 3105 KC listen 219 KC's."

Most civilian planes at that time had neither transmitters nor receivers and depended upon the red and green lights system from the tower for communications. At ten to nine we joined five other pilots who were on the same mission, and were escorted to the second floor offices of the building to the Civilian War Contract's Office. We were seated around an office table when Major John M Beckley entered. "Good morning, gentlemen." He sat down at the head of the table. "Thank you all for coming. Each of you has replied to a letter, containing a rather lengthy questionnaire, requesting your help in establishing flight schools at major universities."

At the end of two hours all questions had been answered. I put a period at the end of my notes and tucked my notebook into my shirt pocket. Red had a signed paper in his possession, appointing him to the head of the military-sponsored flight program at the Chapel Hill Airport in North Carolina.

Red paid ground service for refueling, and as he climbed into the plane, he said, "Pre-flight it." I did a walk-around looking for any external problems that might require attention. I watched as Red ran the controls through; they were all working fine. I checked the pitot tube's air intake hole, making sure it was free of anything that could prevent the altimeter from giving a proper reading. I unscrewed the gas cap and stuck my finger in the tank to make sure ground service had refueled the plane. They had. The plane was ready to fly. Making sure the power switch was off, I called, "Switch off."

Red echoed the call and replied, "Switch off."

"Switch on," I called.

Red turned the switch on and repeated, "Switch on."

"Contact," I said.

"Contact," Red replied. With one downward pull of the prop, the engine came to life. For a moment I stood there looking at Red. For the first time it dawned on me that he had moved over to the co-pilot seat.

"Get in," he said, "don't just stand there looking confused. Get in and take me home. I'll be in charge of the flight training programs for the University of North Carolina and Duke University at the Horace Williams Airport in Chapel Hill," Red told me.

"That's great news, Red. I wish I could go with you."

"Maybe you can," he said, "but not now. When you finish at St. Pete's College, you might think of the University of North Carolina at Chapel Hill."

By the time we reached St. Petersburg, I knew that I was but a transfer away from completing my studies there. Two years later I transferred to the University of North Carolina.

Chapter 12

I've Got A Pocketful Of Dreams

It was Saturday, September 2, 1939. I arrived in Chapel Hill with my clarinet, logbook, and a bag containing my clothing. My junior year at the University of North Carolina was to start Tuesday, September 5th. My first chore was to find a place to stay.

I was standing outside of the student union building, looking at a bulletin board covered with listings of rooms for rent, and making notes of those that looked promising. I heard a voice say, "Are you looking for a place to stay?"

"Yes," I replied.

"My name is Bob Lovell," he said. "I have a place that I'm sure you will like. Follow me."

"I'm Wynn Cary," I replied. I asked the monthly cost of the room, and if it covered all utilities. He said it did, and he gave me a price that was a little more than I felt comfortable with, but I said, "Lead on. It won't hurt to look."

He picked up my bag and started to walk. I followed him to 126 Fetzer Lane, where I found my home in Chapel Hill. It was an old and well cared for house, which was built in the late eighteen hundreds. For several years, it had been the home of Professor Fetzer and his three boys who lived, taught, and attended classes at the university, after whom the house was named.

The house was alive with sounds of music and chatter that were coming from the second floor. We entered and walked a few steps down the hallway to a large cheerful living room. On a table against a far wall, a portable jukebox turned a disc, releasing the sounds of a love that had somehow gone wrong. A dancing couple moved and swayed with the tempo of the sentimental tune. As the music came to an end, and the next record fell into place, I recognized it as a Glenn Miller recording of "Moon Love." Bob Lovell, recognizing it as competition, turned the machine off. The dancers looked quizzically at him.

"This will only take a minute," Bob said. He placed his hand on my shoulder, saying, "This is Wynn Cary. He's from Florida, and this gorgeous creature, Wynn, is Carolyn Perry. She goes to Duke, wherever that is. Her derelict dancing partner is Harry Woods. He's a Tar Heel and hangs out here. That loud noise you hear coming from upstairs is our football-playing housemates, doing whatever football players do when they're not playing football. I know it sounds weird, but that's part of education. The female voice you hear belongs to Helen Lind. She's a Tar Heel and also Phil Clay's girlfriend. Phil plays left end on our football team, and tempting as it may be, never ask Helen for a date unless Phil and the team are out of town. You might say that Phil's a mite protective of Helen."

I acknowledged the introductions and said, "I'm not sure, but I think I might like it here."

Carolyn was gorgeous. Her shoulder length, raven black hair, and sparkling dark eyes with a touch of cat green set her apart from the merely beautiful. She was wearing a close-fitting white jersey with blue letters on the left side of the blouse that spelled Duke University. Her blue pleated skirt was made for displaying her long slender legs. On her feet she wore the obligatory penny loafers and bobby sox. Yeah, she definitely deserved the adjective "gorgeous."

Harry Woods was perfectly at ease with one of the campus glamour queens. He was six feet tall, give or take an inch. His blue eyes looked out with amusement upon a world of college life and fun. Harry was wearing a white shirt, a tie of Carolina blue and gray slacks. When we shook hands, I somehow knew that we would become friends.

Later, I would learn that Harry's charm and wit, like wealth, placed him in a select class, the kind that attracted beautiful girls. Of course, having a dimpled chin like Cary Grant was an added attraction.

With my years of working in a men's clothing store, I had formed a habit of looking at the quality of clothing and the coordination of colors. Harry and Carolyn passed the test. They were expensively dressed in the expected college fashion. They knew, as most students did, how to speak correct English, but the slang of the day was not only tolerated, but demanded by the student population. "Groovy man, gimme some skin."

At the conclusion of the introductions, Bob turned the record player back on and I followed, as he led the way through the door at the end of the room, and said to me, "Welcome home, Wynn." He paused a moment, then looked at me and said, "You don't snore, do you?"

"Nope," I replied.

"Good," he said. "If you snored, I was going to put you upstairs."

The Fetzer house became my home. I shared a room with Bob, a law student, and Leon Barns, a junior studying chemistry. There were three football players who lived upstairs whom I was yet to meet.

Harry Woods was a sometimes resident in the other downstairs bedroom. He and Bob would become my best college friends. They were Beta Theta Pi fraternity brothers, but found more liberty by living part time at the Fetzer House. You might say they had dual memberships and were wealthy. Tomorrow I would enroll for classes and look for Red Hederman.

By 9 a.m. the following morning I was a registered member of the junior class of 1939. I asked directions to the airport and was on my way to find Red. I had my private license and a little less than 80 hours logged. My goal was to add another 20 hours. To do so would require flying about nine hours a month. That was a lofty goal requiring more than just a little luck and money than I could count on.

At the airport, I asked where I might find Red Hederman. I was told that Red was with a student, but should be back in thirty minutes. I walked across the room to the operations desk and asked if there was a plane available for an hour. I removed my license from my wallet and said, "I'm Wynn Cary." I waited to see if Sam remembered me.

"Sam Hughie," he replied. "Just file a flight plan and Baker Adams 6-5 is yours." Sam looked up at me and said, "I'll be damned, if it isn't Wynn Cary. You were about ten years old when we met. You were at Maggie's with Joe Bailey and Paul Mulzer. Red said you would show up one of these days. He will be glad to see you, Wynn. Welcome aboard!"

I looked at Sam and said, "Thanks, Sam. I remember the day we met. That was eight or nine years ago, and a lot has changed since then. I knew that you and Red were here, but what's happened to Joe Bailey and Paul Mulzer? I haven't a clue."

"Well, Joe and Paul have been recalled into the Air Force. Joe is a lieutenant colonel stationed at the Santa Ana Army Air Force Base in California, and Paul is a colonel at Maxwell Field in Alabama."

"I expect to be here for the next two years," I replied. "We will have plenty of time to talk about the good old days. You, Paul, Red, and Joe were my heroes. You could all fly, and the closest I could get to a plane was with a bucket of water and a sponge."

He laughed and said, "How much time do you have?"

"Not much," I replied. "I have my private license and a little less than 80 hours logged. I would like to fly for an instructor's rating by the end of the year. Any flying I do here, I have to pay for. I'm not eligible for the flight school."

"Yeah," he said. "When Red's request for more planes is honored, we send our pilots to Lock Haven, Pennsylvania, where the Cubs are built and they fly them down. The number of students who remain in the program after the first month dictates the need for more or less planes. Forty percent of those who enter will either drop out or wash out. Maybe Red can use you to help out. It's just a thought. Red's with a student now, but I know that he will be glad to see you. When you finish your flight, check the debriefing room. That's in the office building to the right of the hangar as you go out."

"Thanks, 'hero,' I expect to see more of you. I'll check back when I finish my flight."

Baker Adam 6-5 was a Taylor Craft. I walked around the plane looking for any damage that should be reported. None was found. The Taylor Craft had a 65 hp engine and was a first cousin to the 65 hp Cub. It was an easy plane to fly and easy to forgive any mistake a pilot could make. It was one of two planes stressed for advanced flight maneuvers.

I watched three Cubs in the air. One was on base leg turning final. The landing was two-to-one in favor of a crash. Three times the Cub's wheels reached for the ground before coming to a halt. Slowly the plane turned off the runway and meandered its way back to the hanger.

Once more an instructor had earned his keep. At the ramp, the instructor and his student deplaned and stood talking for a moment, then turned and walked to the debriefing room. I couldn't hear the conversation, but I could see that the student belonged in a beauty pageant and not in the back seat of a Cub. I watched as Red and the beauty disappeared behind the door of the debriefing room. She was probably a student here at the university and had joined the flight program. Mentally I placed finding out her name at the head of the long list of things to get done.

In the meantime, my plane was waiting and it was time to move on. I taxied to the runway and waited for a green light from the tower to signal that the runway was mine. It was. Quickly I taxied into position, applied full power, and at the point of rotation, silently recited a short phrase, words that I mumbled on my first flight lesson and every flight since.

I climbed and leveled off at 1500 feet and flew out to an area set aside for beginner flight training. A thousand feet below I spotted a smokestack that would serve as a pylon that could be used as a reference point in flying figure eights. I followed with a series of maneuvers that I had only watched others do. I added my version of a wingover, rolls and loops to my repertoire of avionic maneuvers. The recovery from stalls and spins at take off and approaches to landing were beginner's maneuvers of which I already had some knowledge.

My allotted time in the air was about over. I throttled back and dropped the nose of the plane just below the horizon mark on the climb and descent indicator. With the tower in range, I waggled the plane's ailerons to signal that Baker Adam 6-5 was in range for landing. I got the green light and turned base.

On the final approach, with the nose of the plane up and the power reduced, I flared over the threshold, and seconds later the wheels of Baker Adam 6-5 touched the ground and rolled out. I taxied back to the parking area, and the Hobbs meter in the plane confirmed that I could add another hour to my logbook.

Now that one of the minor things had been accomplished, it was time to check the list and get to the important things! Number one on the list was 'What's-her-name'. Where did she live? Did she have a phone number? But first, how do I meet her? An education can be so perplexing.

I went to operations and closed my flight plan and started asking questions about the girl who all agreed was a beautiful dream, but whose name no one knew. Next I went to the instructors lounge and asked if Red was still on the field. Sam's answer was, "No. He left with his last student. He was gone before I could tell him that you had arrived."

"Where were they going?"

"I don't know," he answered.

"Do you know her name?" I asked.

"Yes, I think he said it's Dorothy Brooks. She joined the flight program last semester. She survived ground school and has been back a week early this year to prepare for the flying part of the program. Just wait until you meet her. She's friendly and easy to get to know. Every pilot on the field, married or single is in love with her, and none have more than bragging rights to having a Coke or coffee at Orville and Wilbur's with her. Even then, she probably insisted on paying for her own drink. Red introduced her as Doey, I believe. I'm not even sure it was Dorothy. I was too busy just looking. I know she's been through ground school and had her first flight lesson today. If she can fly as well as she looks, she will have her wings in a week . . . if she doesn't already have them," Sam replied.

"What do you mean by that?" I asked.

"Oh, it's something that just came to mind. You know like . . . well, she looks like the angels made and assembled every part of her. She looks like how every woman wishes she could look."

"Wow! Sam. You sound like her press agent."

"Hell! Even without a wife and two kids, all I could do would be to wish that I could be her flight instructor. That bastard Red, even with the good looking girlfriend he has, he knows her name, address, and phone number, and at this very moment, he's probably somewhere on Franklin Street in a bar telling her that a martini or two is good and essential for keen eyesight . . . but I don't think that Red is anymore than a friend." He paused and looked at me intently. "What's your interest in her? Whatever it is, just stick to your studies and flying. Before you graduate we will probably be at war, and the government will do all the thinking for you. Just forget her. You wouldn't have a chance anyway. She's been groomed for the country club set . . . probably even knows what a finger bowl is for."

I thanked Sam and came away knowing that he was probably right. I walked over to Red's office, sat down, and waited for his return, and thought about my future with Doey, a girl that I hadn't even met.

Chapter 13

April Played the Fiddle

Mr. John Brooks lived in Terre Haute, Indiana, and had come to Durham hoping to talk his daughter out of the flying course. Her mother had lost sleep over their daughter's reckless decision to risk her life on a whim. "Flying is for men," she said. "The university has no business enticing girls into such a dangerous and worthless program. John, go there and tell her to either drop out of the program or come home."

"Now, Dorothy," he said, "I know you don't mean that. Doey is 21 years old. If she's not suited for the flying program, she will know it and drop out, but I will go down and do what I can. You and I know she won't abandon law school."

John boarded the overnight train to Durham. After dinner he spent an hour in the club car reading the Chicago Tribune and listening to Edward R. Morrow reporting the evening news from London. German tanks and their air force invaded Poland's boundaries and annexed the conquered territory for themselves. Early the next morning, the train pulled into the Durham station.

From his room at the Blue Devil Inn, he called the Tri Delta Sorority House and asked to speak with Doey Brooks. During his patient wait he was able to filter out a background of girls' chatter and heard a voice calling, "Doey, telephone." After three attempts and no answer, the voice said, "I'm Carolyn Perry, Doey's roommate. I'm sure she's somewhere on campus, and if you'll leave your name and telephone number, I'm sure she'll call you."

Arise My Love And Come Away With Me

"Thank you, Carolyn, I'm Mr. Brooks, Doey's' father. I'm staying at the Blue Devil Inn. Ask her to call me at 789-927."

"I will, Mr. Brooks. I thought it was you, but I wasn't sure. I'll tell her the moment she comes in. Is Mrs. Brooks with you?"

"No, she didn't want to make the trip, and thank you for remembering her, Carolyn. If time allows, maybe you can join us for dinner tonight."

"I would like that, Mr. Brooks."

"Goodbye for now, Carolyn." He hung up the phone and closed his eyes for only a few seconds, and time flew backwards. Once again he was standing in the chapel on the campus of the University of Chicago. Dorothy Weatherford was by his side. His best friend, Doctor Glen Leland, whom only the day before received his diploma certifying him to be a doctor, stood beside him. Glen was his best friend. Dorothy had no relatives, and John's father was there to give the bride away. A year later Doey was born.

The telephone rang, returning John to the present. He opened his eyes, picked up the telephone, and said, "Hello."

"Daddy!" Doey said, "You sound out of breath. Has something happened at home?"

"No, sweetheart. All is well at home. Your mother wanted me to come and have a little talk with you. Are you free for lunch?"

"Yes, I am. Mother called last night and said that you were coming down to talk with me about flying. If it's alright, I'll come now."

"I'll wait for you in my room," John replied. While waiting, he reviewed the scanty aviation knowledge he had to support his case. This would not be an easy one to win and he knew he had to be diplomatic. Doey would never enter a program just for the fun of it. There had to be a logical reason for adding flying to her legal education.

55

John heard the knock on the door. It was Doey. She had come well prepared to obtain a postponement of her case until her father had an opportunity to talk with Maj. Red Hederman. In the meantime, she said she would not drop aviation from her course of study. "Daddy, I know I should obey you and Mother, but I want to learn to fly. I want to be a pilot."

"Doey," he replied, "I have no rebuttal. You may have it your way, but only for now. This is a family matter and for the moment I have lost, but your mother will make me try again. For now, if you and Carolyn are free for dinner, let's meet here at seven. I have a return ticket to Terre Haute tomorrow morning."

"Thank you, Daddy. We'll be here."

Doey was an only child, but never pampered. Movies, radio, and reading were the staples of her entertainment. The daring deeds of pilots who flew the oceans or around the world joined her list of interests. Law and aviation would be her career.

Aviation was her introduction to a new life, but she would remain at Duke University in the School of Law. That would please her mother and father, and flying would please her. She smiled and thought of herself as a "Legal Eagle."

At 10 a.m. Saturday morning Doey reported to Red Hederman in the airport's ready room. She was there to begin her flight training and was eager to get started. Red sat at his desk, going over progress reports he received from the ground school. When school started last year, seven women signed up for the course. It was now September 10th and only three women remained. The aviation school had an enrollment of 31 students. Twenty-two completed the course. Miss Brooks led the class with a straight "A" average. The next highest score was Harry Woods with a "B plus" average.

Well, she had survived ground school, and maybe I have misjudged her, Red thought. I suppose someone from Park Avenue, or wherever, can fly a plane, but she belongs in Hollywood, he thought, and made a mental note to add her name to his instructor's column. He wasn't surprised to learn that Dorothy Brooks was an A student. She never missed a class and was always on time. She read and retained every scrap of information pertaining to class instructions.

"Have a seat," Red said. "I just have to make an adjustment in the scheduling and we'll be ready to go." Quickly he checked the names on the chalkboard. Dorothy Brooks was his student. He placed the papers in a file, dropped his pen on the desk, and said, "Okay, Miss Brooks, your first flying lesson is waiting."

Chapter 14

The Beta Four Plus Two

Back at the Fetzer house I settled in for the afternoon with a book of CAA questions and answers on how to become a flight instructor. With any luck and a bit of hard study I hoped to turn the effort into an instructor's certificate by Christmas. I had about four months to reach that goal. Meanwhile, I had to make some money. Help from home was barely enough to cover my room rent and flying. I had to generate a little more cash to maintain solvency.

A few weeks later, I received a pledge card from the Beta Theta Phi House and an invitation to dinner. My sponsor, of course, had to be Bob Lovell or Harry Woods, both of whom were Betas. I told them that I appreciated the honor, but I didn't have the money to cover fraternity expenses. Harry said, "No problem. You have a clarinet, Lovell plays drums, and there are two other pretty good musicians in the Beta house who play trumpet and guitar. I'm sure that we could put together a good quartet and play for inter-fraternity dances. Until we get recognition, Bob and I will fund your expenses. Bob will forgo your rent here, and I will advance the balance of the money you need until the band is organized and we play our first gig. This is not charity; it's what I see as a good business proposition."

"We have tried before," Bob Lovell said, "but failed, primarily for the reason that we had three bosses, all with a different agenda and it takes more than three to make a quartet. Bob and I have heard you play, and we think we have found the fourth man. You'll be doing us a favor, not the other way around."

"It sounds great, Harry," I said, "but what's in it for you? I can't accept your charity."

Harry said, "My job will be to get gigs for the band. I'm head of the Entertainment Committee of the Inter-Fraternity Council. I'm responsible for obtaining music for the dances."

I slept on the proposal and agreed to attend the Beta dinner, providing I'd have an opportunity to meet the other two musicians here at the Fetzer House. I suggested it might be helpful if they bring their instruments and a couple of scores for trumpet and clarinet.

Saturday morning, Harry showed up with Bill Reeder, who had his guitar, and John Harper, Paul Harper's brother, who brought his trumpet. When they settled down, I thanked them for coming and told them that I was not a very good musician. "Harry told me that you are both good musicians. Until I have a rehearsal and play a couple of numbers, I'd like to be sure that I won't embarrass myself or you. Then you can decide whether I'm good enough to join your group. Why don't we play a couple of the scores you brought?"

I ran a chromatic scale a couple of times to warm up, and played a few bars of Cole Porter's "Begin the Beguine." Bill passed out the sheet music, and we all started with a beat and time of our own. Without thinking, I stopped and said, "Hold it! Let's get it together. The music is written in four-four time. Just for kicks, why don't we play it that way? *Pianissimo* now." I counted the beat, "one, two, three, and four" to establish a time, and softly we played Artie Shaw's version of the song, which became one of the most popular songs of the Swing Era. We played several more numbers, and then paused for a rest.

"What do you think, Harry?" Bob asked.

"I think we need a name for our band and to decide who will be the leader," Harry replied.

I said, "I'm more concerned with an honest report on how we sounded. Anyone can be the leader."

A dozen or more students had gathered to listen to the music. Harry turned and said to them, "What's your verdict? Can you dance to their music or should we just keep trying?" They all tried to speak at once. There was a jumble of words, but all seemed positive.

"Thanks," Harry said. "This is our first practice and it's too soon to know when we will be open for business, but we will do everything possible to prove you right."

Harry turned back to us and said, "Before we continue, let's vote for a leader by a show of hands."

"We already have a leader," Bill said. "It's Wynn. Let's get on with the practice."

We needed a name and a theme song to identify our group. We played several tunes, and by a show of hands "Deep Purple" became our theme song. Next, a name. With no agreement on a name, Harry finally said, "Why not The Beta Four? With a name like that we will never play at The Glen Island Casino or the Hollywood Palladium, but on campus we'll get instant recognition."

Harry was quick to remind the brothers that having a band named for the fraternity entitled them to sponsor the first dance. In addition, for a three-hour dance, the cost to the fraternity would be sixty dollars. I looked at Harry and thought he had lost his mind. Sixty dollars, for three-hours work? He must have made a mistake. We, the band, were ready to play anywhere for twelve dollars and cut Harry in for ten percent. Jim Henry, president of the Betas, looked around the room and asked for a show of hands for those who approved of the price. To my amazement, all hands were raised. I learned a valuable lesson: When you want something accomplished, get an agent and be prepared to pay him well.

Hell Week was over, and I was a Beta pledge. I remained at the Fetzer House because it was where we practiced, and where our instruments and music were stored. Until our band was known on campus, I would delay moving to the fraternity. I still thought of the Fetzer House as home.

Lovell said, "You are within easy walking distance to the fraternity house. You are now the fifth member of the fraternity, who has hang-around privileges here. Harry and I, and now you, are Betas. Leon and Phil belong to other fraternities, and they spend as much time here as they do there. There's a bunk bed upstairs that you can use anytime you want. I spend most of my time here because I'm the caretaker. When I'm not here, Harry's in charge."

"That's good to know," I said. "If I ever find myself flush with cash, I'll pay for the hang—around privilege. If you and Harry hadn't come up with the plan to organize a band, I would still be looking for a job."

Harry said, "A band of our own would work. After all, didn't Kay Kyser and Hal Kemp get their start here on the campus of the University of North Carolina? Maybe the charm will work for us too."

A week after forming the band Harry announced, "We have our first gig at the Beta House in two weeks." Before we ever performed, The Beta Four became The Beta Four Plus Two when Jeff Stanley and Tom Gregory joined, adding a trombone and sax to our band. We had many hours of late night practice. By the end of two weeks, we were beginning to play the notes with the feeling required to make the music come alive.

The day before our big debut, the Beta dining room was cleared of tables and turned into a ballroom. The familiar keg of beer, the primer for all Beta parties, had sat overnight in a basement tub, packed in ice. All other festive food and drinks would be available, but beer was the drink of choice.

The night of our Beta debut, we had tuned our instruments and stood by the piano talking about our program. We discussed the latest *Down Beat* songs of the week. We were sure to get requests for some that we didn't have sheet music for, and picked those tunes that we had heard and could fake without the music.

John Harper said, "Let's get a beer."

"No drinks!" I replied. "We were not invited to the party. We're here to play music. When it's over, we can all go to the Fetzer House, where Harry has beer on ice waiting for us."

"It's survival time," Harry said.

We sat in our places behind the music racks. I quietly said, "Our future depends on this moment."

The band came alive with the opening tones of "Deep Purple," bringing dancers to the floor. In my imagination I heard Mitchell Parrish's beautiful lyrics sung by a lovely young girl that fronted our band. Yes, we need to add a singer, was my silent thought.

More than occasionally, I could see dancers remove brown pint bottles from their coat pockets and offer their dates a sip. Mostly, they refused.

By midnight, we played "Goodnight, Ladies" and our first gig was over. We heard enough encouraging words, enthused by both drunk and sober voices that we knew our band would survive.

Chapter 15

Betty Moran

Bob Lovell invited me to dinner at the Beta House. "Bring your clarinet," he said. Everyone at the house had a hundred stories to tell, mostly about girls, dances, and beach parties from the summer. At 5 p.m. we were about talked out, and took time to get ready for dinner. At 6 p.m. we assembled in the dining room where we heard more stories of real and imagined deeds.

No one was interested in how many shirts, socks, or neckties I had sold for the Arthur Johnson Clothing Company, how many floors I had varnished, or walls I had painted as payment for room and board at the Gregory Hotel.

What little time I had for myself was squandered on that "dangerous flying hobby," which my mother kept reminding me would come to no good. She relented a bit and offered this bit of advice: "Son," she said, "if you must fly, be sure that you always fly low and slow." I don't know where she got that advice, but it seemed to placate her nerves and we remained on loving terms.

Dinner at the Beta House always ended in singing. Bill Reeder brought his guitar and I brought my clarinet. For an hour or more we played the latest tunes to the accompaniment of the worst cacophony of voices on campus. By 8 p.m. most of the brothers were off to sorority row making dates for next weekend's football game.

On Sunday I was invited to the Tri Delta House for lunch by my girlfriend from Florida, Betty Moran. She was good looking, belonged to the "in" crowd, and was fun to be with. It was assumed that we were a couple just waiting to tie the knot and make our actions legal. So what's my problem?

After lunch Betty wanted to walk in the arboretum, the botanical gardens that rivaled the beauty of the gardens at Kew near London. Silently we walked along a pathway with trees, shrubs and flowers that were native to foreign lands, but now added a background of beauty for a love that found other paths to follow. "There's a bench," she said, "let's rest awhile."

Betty had a troubled mind and it had something to do with me. Was she expecting me to marry her? Oh, we shared many romantic moments, but I wasn't prepared to even remotely consider marriage. If not that, what? I held my breath and waited to hear what her mind wanted to share with me. She started to talk.

"Wynn, I struggled all last summer, trying every way I could think of, to put words together that would not destroy the beautiful friendship that we have shared. Most of all, I don't want to hurt you. We have shared a relationship that I shall always treasure. There were times that had you asked, I would have joyfully said 'Yes' to that all-important question and let you slip a ring on my finger. But you know and I know that was not to be. I turned down every request for a date that conflicted with our being together. I was sensitive to your needs, but I think our relationship has run its course. My only hope is that we can still be friends."

Our campus romance was over. I couldn't have written a better script with the words she used and the tonal inflection that conveyed a feeling of mutual love and respect.

"Yes, we can be friends, Betty. If I'm replaced in your affections by a summer's romance, I would like to know his name. You have been honest with me, and, yes, there is hurt, but the hurt is not all mine. Together we share that. I would like to be as honest with you as you have been with me. In a different way, I have come to the same conclusion. My schedule of classes, music, and flying leaves little or no time for social activities. It isn't fair to expect you to spend an evening sitting on the sidelines listening to me playing while you tap your toe waiting for someone to ask you to dance. It's true that you never miss a dance, but your date with me offers nothing but a beer and a couple of dances to the jukebox music at Egan's bar, then the evening is over. The schedule that I'm trying to keep, rules out a social life. Expecting you to live by my schedule is not fair to you. Yes, we can be friends, and with a touch of jealousy, I may even come to like whoever you date."

Our talk had loosened the knot that bound us together, and I told Betty of my feelings for a girl I had seen, but never met. I placed my hand on hers and looked into her brown eyes where a tear threatened to fall, and said, "Hello, my friend."

At the next Saturday night dance, Betty introduced me to her new boyfriend Don Pierce, a senior in the School of Law. They met during summer vacation in Highlands, a little town near Ashville, in western North Carolina.

Now I was free to divide my attention between playing and looking through the crowd for a glimpse of 'What's-her-name'. There were dozens of good-looking girls, but not a *gorgeous* one in the bunch. For me it was a lackluster evening.

For Betty it was a winning situation. She was free to accept any date without considering me, and she was always given the choice of being included in any college function that I attended. When the dance was over, Harry Woods, his date Carolyn and I ended the evening at Egan's, where we danced to jukebox records and drank illegal beer from UNC mugs.

Chapter 16

First Illegal Student

Sunday morning Harry and I went out to the airport. Harry had signed up for the flight school and was eager to get started. I told him it would probably be several weeks before he got his first flight lesson. Until then he would spend time in ground school learning why and how an airplane could fly. Nonetheless, he was eager to fly and was willing to pay for the use of a plane, if I would fly it. Of course I would. I'd never turn down a free hour in the air.

There was a crowd at the airport, mostly visitors. We checked in at operations. Sam Hughie was in charge of the operation's desk for the day. Sam was filling out a report. He looked up when I spoke. "Sam, we need your help."

"Ok, what can I do for you, Wynn?"

"We need a plane for an hour. What about Baker Juliet 9?"

"Baker Juliet's gone for the weekend and won't be back until noon tomorrow. All of our planes are in the air. Nothing will be available for the rest of the day. Sorry."

"Is Whiskey Sour available?" I asked. *Whiskey Sugar*, commonly called *Whiskey Sour* among the pilots that flew her, was a Stinson aircraft, classified as "high performance," which at that time included any aircraft with an engine rated 300 horsepower or more.

"Well, yes, it's available," Sam replied. "If you have the right answer to two questions, the sky machine is yours by the hour."

"And what are the two questions?" I asked.

"The Stinson's hourly rate is four times the cost of a Cub, which makes it exactly $25.00."

I checked with Harry. I knew the extravagant life style he supported and was not surprised by his quick "Okay, let's do it." Harry's college expenses came under miscellaneous items and were automatically stamped approved. His father was legal counsel to the American Tobacco Company.

"What's the next question?" I asked.

"Are you certified to fly it?" Sam questioned.

My logbook recorded thirty minutes of flight instruction in *Whiskey Sugar 1-4* and a note in my log book, signed by my instructor, Red Hederman, indicated that I was checked out and qualified to fly the Stinson. I got my wallet out and pulled the CAA certificate of competency and handed it to Sam.

Twenty minutes later, after running through the checklist and finding the avionics and flight instruments in the green and behaving as they should, I released the brakes and taxied to the assigned runway 0-9-0 and held short. At the blast fence, I ran the engine up to 1000 RPMs and checked for a drop in the magnetos readings. There was none and .75 per was the maximum allowed. If it were more than that, I'd have had to return to the hangar and report the finding to the maintenance department. The engine was performing as it should. I held short of the runway reduced power, and waited for the tower to give me clearance.

My headset was alive with static, but cleared the moment the tower controller spoke. "Whiskey Sugar 1-4," he said, "you are cleared into position and hold." I released the brakes and rolled into position for takeoff and held. A few seconds later, a Lockheed 9 flared over the marker and rolled out.

Runway 9-0, 2R was clear. The tower voice came alive. "Whiskey Sugar 1-4, you are cleared for takeoff."

"Whiskey Sour rolling," I replied, and pushed the throttle to the firewall. With one eye on the air speed indicator, I waited for the right moment to ease the yoke back, and release Whiskey Sugar into the beckoning sky. I murmured my line of poetry, and at eight hundred feet I throttled back, closed the cowlings to one half open and eased into a gentle climb. When the altimeter reached a thousand feet I leveled off and Harry became my first *illegal* student.

The hour I had planned for him was nothing more than a basic orientation flight. I would not be an instructor, but would answer any question that any passenger might ask. With a scan of the instruments, I paused and explained the function that each played in flight. Harry was a good listener. He asked intelligent questions and filed the answers away in the notebook of his mind.

I tapped the climb, descent, and bank indicator, sometimes referred to as the *slip slide and mush* indicator, and explained the needs they filled in visual or instrument flying. "Watch the little airplane on the face of the instrument, Harry. It will mimic any change I make with the controls; it will follow. It's like monkey see, monkey do. At the moment our plane is flying straight and level, the little icon is on the black line that represents the horizon, and the little black ball below the plane is centered, floating in a liquid encased behind a small rectangle of glass. When the icon senses any change in the plane's movement, no matter how small, the icon plane and the black ball will follow."

I went through a small series of climbs, descents, and banks. The little plane and black ball followed every motion. Then I dropped the nose, and with the coordination of yoke and a touch of the left rudder, put the plane in a gentle downward spiral.

"Watch the movement of the little plane in the climb and descent instrument. It mimics our movement. If you do nothing, you will hit the ground. That would ruin your whole day. If the weather is so bad that you can't see the horizon and you become disoriented, don't panic and don't look for help outside of the cockpit. Help is right in front of you. You and the little icon plane, working together, will instantly cure vertigo and restore your confidence. Feed in a little right rudder and at the same time, ease back on the yoke until the wings of the icon are level with the horizon and adjust the throttle to any setting above stalling speed. You must be careful for the reason that you can stall at any speed. The lesson to be learned is to trust your instruments."

The Hobbs meter in the plane reminded us that it was "time to pancake," which was slang for "time to land."

Chapter 17

I Dream Of You

In early October, our band, the Beta Four Plus Two arrived at the Beckley Auditorium to play for a dance sponsored by the Inter-Fraternity Council. The routine was to arrive thirty minutes before a gig, set up the music stands, and make sure that each had the right music arranged in sequence to be played. Of course, there would be requests for numbers that we didn't have music for, but we could fake it. Then Joe would tap the key of A on the piano, the note the band used to tune their instruments.

At the coatroom, dancers were shedding their coats and hats. Others were moving down the aisle to claim a seat at tables near the bandstand. I stood in front of the band, my back to the dancers. With clarinet in hand, I watched the hands of a clock on the wall count down the last few seconds to eight o'clock, and I whispered "one, two, three, four" to establish a beat and time. I then turned to face the crowd, and on a down beat the band opened with "Deep Purple," a song made famous by Larry Clinton and His Orchestra featuring Bea Wain. The number became our theme song and identified us as the Beta Four Plus Two. We were not professionals, nor union, and not very good, but by new band standards we filled a gap that was frequently filled by the professional touring bands of Tommy Dorsey and Benny Goodman, and singer Frank Sinatra, and the singing group known as the Pied Pipers. We were booked for a Christmas-week dance that would mark the start of our holiday break.

From my vantage point on the podium, I could see cigarette smoke beginning to rise. It marked a tribute to those movie stars who couldn't finish a scene without lighting another cigarette. Here in Chapel Hill, we were surrounded by friendly tobacco companies, which kept *The Daily Tar Heel,* the university newspaper, solvent by running daily ads showing that to be successful, like the movie stars, college kids must smoke.

I scanned the crowd as I played. I knew many of the students. I spotted most of my fraternity brothers with their steady dates, some stags, and a few who were obviously with someone's roommate, who fell into that class known as the luck of the draw. Couples moved to the floor to join the happy feet of young America, as they danced and swayed to the beat of a drum.

We had just finished playing our first set. Dancers lingered around the bandstand talking, singing, and asking questions that could be answered with a simple yes or no. It was the general jumble of English that sounded more like the mumbling of a Zulu speaking to a Mombasa native. The band members and I were about to "take five." I started to leave for the break when I heard Harry's voice.

"Hang on a minute, Wynn. I want you to meet one of my dates." I was not surprised to hear he had two dates at the same time; Harry always played one-upmanship. When I turned, I found myself looking down into the sparkling blue eyes of the girl who had stepped out of the Cub several weeks earlier. I couldn't believe my good luck.

"This is Doey Brooks," he said. "Doey is a student at—I'm sure you will pardon the expression—Duke University. She is Carolyn's roommate."

"Of course I know Carolyn. She spends so much time at the Beta House that I think of her as our housemother." Then with a smile, I turned to Doey.

"I'm very glad to meet you, Doey. I remember seeing you several weeks ago at the airport. Are you in the flying program?"

"Yes," she said. Of course I knew that, but it was the first thing that came to mind.

"Well, Doey, my break is about to be over, and the music must go on. So good to meet you," I said.

Just as I was about to leave, she said, "Do you know 'Stairway to the Stars'?"

"Yes. It's Glenn Miller's hit song."

Harry broke in to say, "Wynn, when the dance is over, why don't you join us at Egan's."

"Thanks, Harry, I would like that." I could have leaped over and kissed him.

Egan's was a student hangout on Franklin Street where Joe Egan, the barkeeper, sometimes defied the state law that prohibited students under the age of twenty-one from taking a friendly sip of brew.

It was time for the second set to begin. For the first number we played "Stairway to the Stars." Doey sat out the dance, and as I watched, I could see her lips moving in time with the rhythm of the song. I watched intently as a guy from Sigma Chi interrupted Doey's reverie, and asked her to dance. I silently supplied the words for her answer: "Wait until this number ends." The words may not have been exact, but they were close enough, because he sat down and impatiently tapped his toe to the beat of the music.

Not until the number ended did they move to the dance floor. When they danced by the podium, Doey looked in my direction, smiled and said loud enough for me to hear, "Thanks for the Stars." I acknowledged by moving my clarinet up and down, and played on.

They danced away, and a short time later someone tapped Sigma Chi on his shoulder and cut in. Protocol gave way, and Doey had a new partner. I watched as they returned to her table. I could see Carolyn. She was there with someone I didn't know. I do know that I had a very short, but important conversation with Doey. I now had a name and knew where she lived.

At eleven o'clock we played "Goodnight, Ladies." The doors were opened. An orderly crowd anxious to get on with the evening moved like lines of penguins toward the sea.

We collected the music books, returned our instruments to their cases, then folded and stored the music stands. I asked Bill Reeder if he had no other plans, would he take my instrument back to the Beta House. He said he would and I was on my way across the campus to Franklin Street.

Inside Egan's, the dim light reduced my vision to a point where I could only identify where voices were coming from. Most were telling me that they enjoyed the dance and the music was great. "Thank you," my standard reply, didn't come close to expressing the satisfaction I felt.

As my eyes were slowly adjusting, and led by Harry's voice, I moved across the room, and sat down next to Doey. Harry said, "We're having Coke in a mug. It's special. Try it, you'll like it." Harry caught the eye of a waitress named Jean. "Four more of the same," he said. The waitress knew the tip she would get and hurried along to fill the order.

Doey said, "Please, I haven't finished the first one yet, and that's my capacity. Just make it three." Harry changed the order to three, and he and Carolyn excused themselves and got up to dance.

I turned to Doey and said, "I think it's wonderful that you're in the flying program. I think it's a little intimidating for most girls. Flying is fun, but it must offer more than fun to be included in a college curriculum."

"Yes," she said, "I agree with what you say. I only wish my mother could agree. She sees no future for a woman in aviation, and hopes that I give it up."

"Do you think you will?" I asked.

"Not a chance" she replied.

"I saw you land after flying one of your first lessons."

"It was my third hour of instruction. Pretty bad, wasn't it?" she said.

"Oh, no. On my solo flight, my instructor said 'Thanks for bringing the plane back in a repairable condition." He paused, then said, 'Are you sure you want to continue flying?'"

"I don't believe that," she said. "Red and I had just finished the lesson for the day when we saw a pilot flying an acrobatic routine. We delayed returning to the field for a few minutes to watch, when he said 'That's Wynn Cary, he's a natural pilot.'"

"You can't believe anything Red says," I replied. "Sometimes he gets confused and makes statements that are no more than a version of a faulty truth. The truth is there is no better pilot than Red. He has more time in the air than he has on the ground. He's the only pilot I know who can land on the sea and walk to shore. If you will fly with me, I will try not to prove him wrong."

"Have you known Red long?" she asked.

"Yes, a long time. Red gave me my first flight lesson when I was ten years old."

"You're kidding. You've been flying since you were ten years old?" Doey remarked.

"No, when I was ten, the flight was a birthday gift from my father. Red was my instructor, and for several years after that I just hung around the airport dreaming of becoming a pilot. That was in St. Petersburg, Florida, where I grew up. My father died when I was eleven, and I lost the only support I had for flying. By the time I was seventeen I realized that Mother was making life decisions for me, and it was not easy to openly defy her. She was firm in the belief that music and flying were not in my best interest. To her, flying was unsafe. And music? 'Well,' she said, 'you sure can't call songs with names like 'Inka Dink Doo' and 'Jeepers Creepers' music. It's just a fad. Music just isn't stable enough to base a future on.'

"When my sisters left home, Irene enrolled in the nursing school at the Baptist Hospital in Atlanta, Georgia, and my younger sister Ruth was enrolled in the Mound Park Hospital School of Nursing in Florida, my mother gave up our rented house and we moved to live in a hotel owned by her brother in St. Petersburg. I lived there for two years while I went to college and learned to fly. It was as necessary as breathing. With bits and pieces of time, I accumulated enough hours to solo and that brings us up to this moment."

It was nearing the end of the evening and I turned to Doey and said, "I hope there will be another time when we can talk about you."

"Thank you, Wynn. The next time Carolyn invites me to accompany her to Chapel Hill for a dance, I'll tag along and maybe we'll find time to talk again. I will fly my fifth lesson next Saturday morning. If you're there, I would like to fly with you."

"Look for me. I will be there. Before you go, would you like to dance?"

"Yes," she said.

The music playing was "The Very Thought of You." We moved to the floor and I took her in my arms. As we floated across the floor she softly sang the words. Her voice was sweet and low with a tonal timbre that would please an angel.

"Have you had vocal training?" I asked.

"No, nothing special. I sing at home in our church choir and in the Duke Glee Club."

"You have a beautiful voice."

"Thank you," she replied.

"When the song comes to an end," she said, "let's play another." I slipped a nickel into the slot of the jukebox, and Glenn Miller had two dancers for "Moonlight Serenade". I held Doey a little tighter, and felt completely at ease with the way she fit into my arms. When the dance was over, I clung to her longer than propriety required.

Mechanically, the turntable of the jukebox had moved into position and Harry James and His Orchestra played the music, while Frank Sinatra sang the words to "From the Bottom of My Heart."

As we returned to the table, we overheard Carolyn commenting to Harry, "It looks like Doey and Wynn have the makings of a couple." I wondered how Doey would react to that.

"I couldn't help but hear what you said, Carolyn," Doey said. "You always wait until I'm within hearing distance, then you make the same remark. You do it every time I look in the direction of a man. If I followed your advice, I would have been arrested for bigamy a dozen times." Doey turned to me and said, "I'm sorry, Wynn. Carolyn is the matchmaker of the Tri Delta House and thinks it's her duty to tie the knot that binds every couple. She keeps poor Harry in a trance. We're all friends," she added, "and I hope that you will join us."

"Oh, I will." Then, without missing a beat, I faced Doey and said, "Will you marry me?" It was taken as a joke, and everyone laughed.

Doey had an assortment of smiles to fit any occasion. Her mind searched for one that fit, and came up with the enigmatic smile of the Mona Lisa. She sighed and left me with the knowledge that one semi-date barely qualified me to ask for her hand. Nonetheless, I took those moments to mean that my life *might* be moving in the right direction.

Harry said, "Drink up! It will soon be time to go." To me he said, "Carolyn and Doey have to be in no later than midnight, or they'll turn into pumpkins. That's the law." I knew the campus restrictions, so we got up and joined the exodus with the others.

The evening was ending. It had been an unforgettable day for me. I finally met the golden-haired beauty.

When we arrived at the Tri Delta House, Harry, with his knowledge of moonlight madness, cautiously parked under some trees that provided protection from the light of a harvest moon.

Doey and I thanked him for a grand evening, and for being so protective of Carolyn. We got out and left the car to the accomplished lovers. My silent thoughts were, envy, envy, envy as Doey and I made our way to a bench in a patch of moonlight near the entrance to the Tri Delta House and sat down.

To open a meaningless conversation, I said: "Hi, honey, do you come here often?"

She played along with the inane conversation, and replied, "Oh, my yes, quite often. My dates and I always park in the dark until we hear the housemother's voice saying, 'in one minute, girls, the door will be locked. Hurry, now.'" The monologue was a perfect imitation of a girl chewing gum, and speaking a language that I believed belonged in Brooklyn.

Time was in short supply and was close to running out. I raced the clock to its midnight deadline, and asked as many questions as I could.

"How long have you known Carolyn?" I asked.

"Carolyn has been my roommate since I was a freshman. From the day she met Harry her life has centered on him. He's all she talks about. When Harry comes to Duke, we double date. When she turned down dates with her many boyfriends, they formed a club and started wearing black armbands."

"You're kidding," I said.

"No, I'm not," she replied. "There was a picture in the Durham paper of seven boys, all wearing black armbands; they were in a back room of a Durham bar. On the wall behind them was a banner, which read, 'Carry, We Carry the Torch for You'. "

I recognized the play on words. Harry often used Carry for Carolyn, and I apologized to Doey for questioning her black armband report.

"You said 'we.' Do you have a boyfriend?"

"Well, yes," she replied. "Joe was coming with us tonight, but he has a test Monday and needs the time to study. I decided to stay on campus, but Carolyn insisted I come with her. She said it was time I make some new friends. I'm so glad I came. Harry made sure that I wasn't just someone who couldn't get a date. I've had a wonderful time and I loved your music."

"Thank you. I hope you will come back. We play almost every weekend. I'll be looking for you. Other than the dance and a beer at Egan's, I don't have much to offer. I do have Saturdays. That's the day I fly. I'll be there this Saturday to watch you fly for your solo ticket."

What an idiot, I thought. Joe gave up a date with Doey to study? I wanted to ask if Joe was the one and only boyfriend, or what position he held in her life. Whatever it was, Joe would have to go.

Harry and Carolyn arrived. There were traces of lipstick on Harry's collar, and a silly grin on his face. Carolyn was surprised by our "know it all" glance and said, "Who me?" Again Harry kissed Carolyn goodnight.

I was holding Doey's hands. \She said with a solemn voice, "I enjoyed the evening, Wynn. Don't forget Saturday!"

"I'll be there," I said, as I collected the usual light kiss on the cheek, which goes with a first time introduction. Harry and I watched as time counted down the last few ticks to midnight, and the girls turned and disappeared behind the door. One of the best days of my life was over and a new one was about to begin.

Later, at the Beta House, Harry and I compared our version of the evening. Harry wanted to talk about a future with Carolyn, and for the moment, I was satisfied with knowing I had met 'What's-her-name', a girl named Doey.

Chapter 18

Doey Gets Her Wings

It was Saturday, the tenth of October 1939. The Chapel Hill Airport was a busy place on weekends, mostly with people who had nothing to do, and the airport was an interesting place in which to do it.

Doey's ground school and flying was from 9:00 to 10:30 a.m. I knocked on Red's office door and hearing the word "enter," I walked in. Red and Sam were seated at a table discussing flight schedules. When I showed up, I got some "know-it-all" looks from them. Sam stood, and with a flourish took out his wallet, removed a one-dollar bill, and handed it to Red.

"What's that all about?" I asked.

"Pull up a chair, Wynn. Sam and I have been discussing flight schedules. I bet Sam a dollar that within the next ten minutes you would knock on the door. Sam took the bet, and five minutes later, by that clock on the wall, you knocked."

"How did you know I would knock?" I asked.

"Today Doey flies for her solo license," he said. "Everyone on the field knows that, except Sam and you just happened to come along, ha! I was sure that you would be lurking somewhere in the background. And the clincher was when Doey came by earlier and asked if I knew where you were. She's somewhere on the field with her mother and father."

Red slipped the dollar back across the table to Sam and said, "I'll bet ten dollars that Doey aces the flight." There were no takers. To me he said,

"Don't just stand there, go find Doey and tell her that I'll be at the flight line in ten minutes. And tell Joe that there is an airport ordinance that prohibits undocumented civilians from going onto the field. That's a law." I started to leave. "Hold it, Wynn. You've just barely met her, and now, like her mother, you're concerned about her flying safety? She's the best student I've had in a long, long time, and until she gets her private, I don't want anything to get in her way."

"That's quite a speech, Red. I'm on your side. I want the same thing," I replied.

"Well, what are you doing standing around here for? Go find her mother and try to convince her that flying is safe." He smiled and waved me out the door.

The first place I looked was the debriefing room. Charlie White, one of the instructors, was there checking a flight schedule for the week ahead. He looked up when I entered.

"Sorry to interrupt," I said, "I'm looking for Doey, have you seen her?"

"Yes," he said. "Doey and her parents left here not more than five minutes ago. She was looking for you. If I were you, she would only have to glance over her shoulder to find me. I would follow her anywhere."

"Thanks for the advice, Charlie. I'm glad you're not me."

"I think you will find her with her parents," Charlie said. "They came down from Terre Haute to watch her fly. They're out there somewhere. In fifteen or twenty minutes she's scheduled to fly for her solo ticket."

I found Doey walking toward the flight line with a couple that I thought might be her parents. They stopped and turned toward me when I spoke. "I'm here to see you ace the flight test, Doey."

"Oh, I'm glad you came, Wynn. I knew you would. I'd like for you to meet my parents. This is my mother and father, John and Dorothy Brooks. They have come to see me solo." Turning to me, she said, "This is my friend,

Wynn Cary. He's a pilot, and I'm sure he can answer any question you want to know about flying."

Mr. Brooks took my extended hand. He had a firm grip and a friendly smile. "I'm pleased to meet you, Mr. Brooks, and you, Mrs. Brooks," I said. Mrs. Brooks held out a soft hand. Her beautiful blue eyes came alive with a smile, so much like Doey's. I took her hand in mine. "I am pleased to know you, Mrs. Brooks. I haven't known Doey very long, but I have known her instructor, Red Hederman, for a very long time. He's one of the finest instructors there is. To quote him, 'Doey is truly one of the best students I have ever instructed.'"

We moved on to the flight line, and Doey proceeded onto the ramp before Hangar 1, where Red stood by the plane she would fly. For a few minutes she stood listening to Red as he imparted a few more words of wisdom before releasing one of his "birds" about to leave the nest and fly.

After a minute or two of conversation, Red, apparently satisfied with the question and answer session, moved to the front of the plane and stood near the propeller and called, "Switch off."

From the rear cockpit of the plane, Doey looked, to make sure the switch was off, and called, "Switch off."

Red pulled the prop through a few times to prime the engine, and then called, "Switch on."

Doey flipped the switch to the on position and called, "Switch on."

Red called, "Contact," as he pulled the prop down and the 65 hp engine came to life, and Doey was on her own. He turned and walked to the sidelines, and joined us. "She'll do fine," he said to Doey's parents. "She's a good pilot."

Doey called ground control for taxi instructions. "Ground control; Charlie Alpha 2-9 on the ramp at Hangar 2 taxi for takeoff."

"The tower clears Charlie Alpha 2-9 to 9-0 and hold."

Doey acknowledged with "Charlie Alpha 2-9 to runway 9-0 and hold."

At the blast fence she held the breaks, powered up, and checked the magnetos for a drop in revolutions. There were none. She called the tower and said, "Chapel Hill Tower, this is Charlie Alpha 2-9, holding runway 9-0, ready for takeoff."

"Tower to Charlie Alpha 2-9, taxi into position, you are cleared for takeoff."

She lined up with the white stripe that runs down the center of the runway. The weather report indicated a 15 mph wind out of the south. She looked at the windsock. It indicated the wind had shifted a bit west of south, but a tip of the right wing into the wind and a touch of the rudder and stick would take care of that. A few stratus clouds floated in the blue sky. The weather couldn't be better.

Standing back from the edge of runway 1-8 Right, was John Chamberlain, a Civil Aeronautics Inspector. He was here to grade Doey on flying competence. From his vantage point, he could watch Doey's take-off and landing. In his left hand he held a clip board and a CAA booklet on flying. In the lapel of his neat brown suit was a small enameled image of a parachute and caterpillar. Not many would recognize it as a small, but a very exclusive, club emblem that required no money or standing in a community to join. Membership was open to all who flew and made a let down to earth by way of a parachute. The parachute at that time was made of silk, and the caterpillar supplied silk. One of the noteworthy members was Charles Lindbergh.

John's limp was a daily remembrance of an onboard fire in the cockpit of a plane he was flying in France in 1921. His price for membership in the club was a few broken bones and a permanent limp that served as a daily reminder that the price of admission was high.

Doey was flying a 65 hp Cub, one of the new trainers equipped with a two-way radio. She turned the communications switch on and listened to the latest broadcast of local weather and altimeter report for the field. A few moments later a plane flared over the runway marker and floated, like

Arise My Love And Come Away With Me

a feather, a third of the way down the strip, and lightly touched the runway and rolled out.

A voice from the tower came alive in Doey's headset. "Charlie Alpha 2-9 you are cleared for take-off." Quickly she acknowledged, applied full power and climbed to the assigned altitude, then flew a left hand pattern around the airport.

On the second lap around the field, when abeam the tower, she called, "Chapel Hill tower, Charlie Alpha 2-9, abeam the tower for landing."

The tower acknowledged. "Charlie Alpha 2-9, you are cleared to runway 1-8 Right. Continue downwind. You are number two to land." She continued downwind and saw a Cessna turning base leg. When it turned final, her head set came alive with landing instructions from the tower. "Charlie Alpha 2-9, you are cleared to land."

"Roger, Charlie Alpha 2-9," Doey replied. She turned base leg, and at the right moment a little left yolk and rudder, and lined up on course for the final approach. She dropped the nose of the plane and eased the throttle back. Over the threshold the engine, starved for fuel, was barely ticking. Slowly with backpressure on the yoke and a hand on the throttle the nose of the plane came up, and the wheels gently touched the ground. Doey increased the power and taxied clear of the runway, and back to the ramp where her parents, Red, and I waited. She turned engine power to idle cut off. The prop turned a couple of times, using the last drop of fuel in the system, and stopped. Doey stepped out of the plane with a smile. The deft hands and mind of a *solo* pilot had guided Charlie Alpha 2-9 home.

She hugged her mother and softly said, "It's really safe, Mother. Please don't worry. I promise to be very careful." Her mother hugged her, smiled, and softly said something that brought a happy ending to a moment that was so important to Doey. She put her arms around her father and thanked him for his support and understanding. Red got his share of praise for being her instructor, and John, the CAA inspector, assured her that her solo license would be in the mail, and for now she was cleared to fly solo with a temporary license.

"I saved you until last," she said to me. "You are a good friend, a good pilot, and I enjoy dancing to the music you play." With that, she kissed me lightly on the cheek.

For the first time I thought of Joe, Doey's friend, and remembered that Red said undocumented visitors were not permitted on the field. Quickly I checked along the fence where many people were standing, but not knowing what Joe looked like, maybe he just got tired of waiting and went back to Durham. Well, it was a hopeful thought.

Her father started taking pictures. He took one of Doey by the plane, Doey and Red by the plane and one of Doey and me by the plane. We were looking at each other and laughing at something that Red said. Then Mr. Brooks asked a stranger if he would take one of all of us, including John Chamberlain. With memories of the occasion safely recorded in John's camera, we were ready for the next event of the day.

Red announced that the Round Table, at the Orville and Wilbur room was reserved to celebrate Doey's solo flight, and that we were all invited.

As we were leaving the field, Joe showed up, out of breath. He looked like he had just finished a hundred yard dash. He was apologizing to Doey with a line that got no sympathy from her. Each time the name Emily was used in their whispered debate, Joe's position needed more than a quiet reply to hold his losing position.

Quietly, Doey asked Red if she might invite Joe Ridley, her friend from Duke, who had come too late to see her fly. Red glanced at me and hesitated a moment, and said, "Why certainly you may."

It was easy to see that Joe enjoyed a somewhat close friendship with Doey and her parents. They were a group within the group. Doey introduced Joe to me and John Chamberlain, and then moved with Joe to join her mother and father.

As a group we walked across the street to Orville and Wilbur's. Doey and Joe were quietly talking and gesturing with their hands in a way that I could only hope meant that their campus-born friendship had ended. I thought of Betty Moran and how peacefully we had drifted apart.

Red shrugged his shoulders and looked sympathetically at me. Discouraged? Who me? No! But I did hope that Doey had no more "friends" to muddy the waters of romance, but that was not to be.

Doey had a following of male friendships maneuvering to be her number one escort. They had the advantages of going to the same university, sharing classes, and attending the same school functions, including campus dances.

They were sharing their third year of college life with her, and I had barely made her acquaintance. I was a late entry, and late though I was, I vowed to be the winner.

The Round Table provided seating for sixteen people. Each place was numbered. Place number one was reserved for the inductee. Red, acting as president, was here to host the luncheon. He sat next to Doey, the honored solo pilot. Red was seated on her right. Sam Hughie, John Chamberlain, and I were on her left. Mr. and Mrs. Brooks, and Joe were seated on Red's right. There were six vacant seats between Joe and me.

My eyes and mind bridged the vacant seats with thoughts that didn't include Joe. The sound of Red's voice interrupted my reverie. When luncheon was over, Red stood and walked the few steps to the lectern that faced the table where he placed a scroll tied with a pink ribbon.

"It is always a good moment," Red said, "when an instructor says to his student, 'You have learned, and now it's time to leave the nest and fly. You can now expand your life into a new dimension. You will never run out of sky in which to roam, and the land below will be in constant change. You will never reach the horizon; it is forever out of reach. Fly as fast as you can, in any direction, but you will never get there. In time you will learn how to read the weather, and to fly by the rules, which are there to guide you. In time of need, trust your instruments, for they will see you safely through the roughest day and the tumult of the darkest night. If you follow the rules, flying is safer than driving a car through busy traffic.'" He looked at Mrs. Brooks when he said that. Doey looked at her mother and smiled.

"Doey," he said, "your parents and friends are here to share this day with you." He paused a moment, then invited Doey to come to the lectern and stand beside him. "Doey, I'm proud to have been your instructor. You have taken the first step into the world of aviation. The knowledge of flying will be an asset in any endeavor that you wish to follow. And, if I may, I would like to read the words on a scroll that you will long remember and treasure.

The Chapel Hill Flight Training Center
Chapel Hill, North Carolina
Know Ye by These Present

That Doey J. Brooks, having proven herself mentally unstable, physically cross-controlled and spiritually eager to meet her maker; and WHERAS she had conscientiously driven her instructor to that dreaded disease known as extremis doubtfulitis, AND WHEREAS said condition has so caused said instructor to abandon hope that further instruction shall do any good; THEREFORE the first named party above has been allowed to exercise her

FIRST SOLO FLIGHT

Said flight having been perpetrated in a P.T.17

IN GRATEFUL APPRECIATION for having brought the plane back, in repairable condition, she is herewith an accredited member in good standing of:

The Imperial Order
of the
Bold Eagles

Doey laughed as she accepted the scroll and said, "Thank you, Major Hederman. I know that flying solo is only the first step in my career, which I hope will combine flying with a law degree from Duke University. With you as my mentor, I'm sure to find a cure for my mental instability, and I do promise to find a cure for my cross-controlled emotional condition. With your help, Major Hederman, my business card, after my name, can bear the legend, 'Dorothy J. Brooks, the Legal Eagle.' And I thank all of you," Doey said, "especially my mother and father, for caring enough to watch, as I broke the bonds of earth."

After the applause, Red pointed to the roster of names on the wall that listed thirty-seven pilots that had been inducted into the Imperial Order of the Bold Eagles. The thirty-eighth name to be added would be Miss Doey J. Brooks.

Doey's father invited me to have dinner with them that evening at the beautiful Carolina Inn dining room. My idea of dining out was eating at Big John's hot dog counter in the local bowling alley. So for more than one reason, I gladly accepted.

Chapter 19

Back To the Future

I had reason to remember the days that I worked for Arthur Johnson's Clothing Store in St. Petersburg, Florida, and was thankful that they provided me with a top of the line wardrobe, with accessories, at a token price that even I could afford. They reasoned that I would attract the attention of high school and college students, who would spend their clothing dollars somewhere, and it might just as well be at the Johnson Store. I went from rags to riches and the students were a little suspicious about where I got the money to dress so smartly. Harley Neet, the store manager, made daily suggestions on what I should wear. I was always a little uncomfortable showing up at school every day, wearing something different. The students quickly caught on and made my life miserable. They would step aside and bow to me as I walked down the hallway. Once the members of my English class stood until I was seated, and then they sat down. It was all in fun and thankfully they soon tired of the game. However, they did start spending their clothing dollars at Johnson's. This experience held me in good stead for my college days. I was one of the best dressed students on campus and it filled me with confidence.

I borrowed Harry's car and drove to the Carolina Inn, the only place on campus that a student was permitted to drive. I parked and walked in. Doey was standing in front of the fireplace talking with a young man whom I didn't know. As I approached, she saw me and smiled. I heard her say, "Here's Wynn now."

My mind raced to the only scenario possible. My plans for the evening with Doey had just been sidetracked. Well, maybe not. A silent thought doesn't rattle easy, "Watch it, boy. Think positive!"

"Wynn, I would like for you to meet my friend, Carl Robinson. He's majoring in English Literature at Duke. Carl, this is Wynn Cary. He's in the Economics' School here at Chapel Hill." I acknowledged Carl and shook his outstretched hand that had a weak grip and a damp palm. Just the idea of him touching Doey was appalling.

"I told Carl," she continued, "that my parents would be here tonight. He came to see me solo today, but was held up in traffic and missed the big event, so he took the opportunity to see them here. I asked him to stay for dinner, but he said, 'Some other time.'"

Good answer, I thought. Now I knew the names of two of her boyfriends. How many more could there be? I was well-trained in manners, so I smiled and extended my hand. I told Carl that I was glad to know him and hoped to see him again, but that was a lie. We shook hands, and as we did, for one brief moment our eyes locked, and we knew then that we would meet again.

At six, Doey's mother and father came down and joined us in the lobby. I told Mr. and Mrs. Brooks how nice it was to see them again. "I thought you were leaving," Mr. Brooks said to Carl.

Mrs. Brooks said, "I wish you would change your mind, Carl, and stay for dinner." Carl looked at Doey and said that he was very sorry to have missed her solo, but he couldn't stay. He had a commitment in Durham, but was looking forward to seeing them sometime during the Thanksgiving break. "You are always welcome, Carl," Mrs. Brooks said. Carl shook hands with Mr. Brook's and gave Mrs. Brooks the obligatory kiss on the cheek, but lingered much too long holding Doey's hand and kissing her cheek.

It was obvious to me that given the right location and lighting, Carl had, at least tried, to do better than that. Carl looked at me and said, "Pleased to meet you, Wynn." We exchanged a few more insincere words, and he turned and walked to the exit.

John led the way and we followed into the dining room. We were seated near the grand piano where a music student was playing "The Way You Look Tonight" from *Swing Time*.

Mrs. Brooks filled the void of table conversation and said, "John, Carl is such a nice boy. You could have been a little friendlier and insisted that he stay for dinner."

"Now, Dorothy," John replied, "Carl is alright, and he is Doey's friend. I'm sure he is sorry that he missed her solo, but I didn't want to spend the evening listening to Doey and Carl come to terms with, 'I didn't.' 'Yes you did. If you had left earlier you could have, etc, etc.' Besides, Carl will be home for Thanksgiving, and by then, today's conversations will be history, and there will be plenty of time for them to fill you in on all the blank spots."

I interrupted and said, "I hope you will forgive my interruption in a family discussion, but Doey did ask him to stay. I'm afraid it's my fault that he didn't. I had reminded Doey that at seven thirty we had another college function to attend, and being the gentleman that he is, he didn't want to interfere. Having two guests on such short notice, with different agendas, can create a problem, especially when time is part of the equation."

Doey looked at me and with a quizzical smile said to her mother and father, "I had completely forgotten the meeting until Wynn reminded me in the lobby. It is important that I attend."

"What is the meeting about?" Mr. Brooks asked. Again Doey looked at me for an answer. "It's a meteorology class that deals with the adiabatic lapse rate of heat in an up slope fog, and how it affects the weather during various phases of the moon. It's important for pilots to understand that."

Mr. Brooks looked at me with a knowing smile. "Well, you can't afford to miss a lecture as important as that," he said with a wink.

Mrs. Brooks just nodded her head as if she knew all about the weather and the four phases of the moon and said, "Oh, I see."

I was about to change the subject to something that I knew absolutely nothing about, when mercifully, our student waiter, with a pleasing smile and voice, approached the table and pointing to one of the two nametags on his white linen jacket said, "My name is Fungus." The other, more believable nametag contained the name, Jimmy Johnston, and like the opening deal in a black jack game, he flipped menus around the table. I opened mine and exclaimed, "Black Jack!" He looked at me and smiled. He paused to get our attention and said, "We have specials tonight." We listened to the recital of specials that needed to be sold before they were overrun with age. He looked around the table for a prospect. There was none.

"While you wait, may I get you something to drink . . . coffee, tea, soft drink?" he asked, as he handed the wine list to John. Doey and I opted for a soft drink, leaving the alcoholic beverages to the more accomplished drinkers. Mr. Brooks ordered something that was red and came in a dark bottle with a label that mentioned France. When the waiter returned with the drinks, Mrs. Brooks asked if he was a student, and what he was studying.

He said with a grin, "Yes, I'm in the school of music. I'm majoring in the triangle. Do any of you play?" he asked. It was obvious that he was having fun at our expense.

"I do," I said, "I'm studying the didgeridoo, and Julliard is the only music university that offers the course. I'm there on a bowling scholarship."

"A didgeridoo, you say? I don't believe I know much about that, but I am a good bowler. Maybe I could transfer to Julliard?" he said with a smile. "Would you like to order now?"

"I've never heard of a didgeridoo or whatever it's called," Mrs. Brooks said.

Fungus interrupted and said, "I believe it's an instrument that is featured in the reed section of the New York Symphony Orchestra." That brought a knowing laugh from all.

"It is a musical instrument," I said, "but certainly not one used in any orchestra. To my skimpy knowledge, a didgeridoo is an Australian Aborigine's instrument, which is similar in looks to a Swiss Alpine horn that produces a tone for which there is no known use."

Fungus served an excellent dinner to a background of soft piano music of show tunes, classical music, and an original line of entertaining conversation.

I thanked Mr. and Mrs. Brooks for including me for dinner and wondered if Doey had anything to do with the invitation.

In the lobby, Doey reminded her parents that we had a lecture to attend and that she would see them at eight o'clock in the morning for breakfast. We walked her parents to the elevator, and again I thanked them.

Chapter 20

The Moon Flight

When the elevator door closed, Doey turned and said to me, "I didn't know we had another class to attend. What is it?"

"Don't you remember?" I replied. "You said the next time we had a full moon we would fly."

"Oh yes, I remembered, but I wasn't sure you did."

"Tonight we have a full moon, and today you earned your solo license. You have slipped the bonds of earth. Now let's fly in the high un-trespassed sanctity of space. Are you ready to aviate?"

"I thought you had forgotten. And where is the high un-trespassed sanctity of space?" she asked.

"It's beyond the moon, and beyond the stars. It's just the other side of beyond. It's where the angels fly. One day I will take you there," I said. I helped her into the car and we were on our way to the airport. I had reserved the Stinson for this evening. The plane was now equipped with a two-way radio. This would make communicating with the ground and tower easier, and would add to flight safety.

Paul Henry was running the operations desk. As we approached, he said, "I see by the check-out log that you're flying tonight." He slipped a flight plan across the desk for me to fill in the blanks and sign.

"Thanks, Paul," I said. "This is Doey Brooks. She's in the flight program and just soloed today."

"Pleased to know you, Doey. Congratulations, and now that you're a solo pilot, I'll have the pleasure of seeing you more often."

"Down boy," I said to Paul as he handed me the key to Bravo Juliet 1-9.

Doey smiled, "I'm pleased to know you, Paul."

"Have a good flight," he replied.

The dim light in the hangar cast our moving shadows before us and merged them with the shadow of the Stinson, the only plane near the hangar door. Together we moved slowly around the plane, checking the free movement of the ailerons, rudder, and elevators. Doey ran her hands over the propeller blades to make sure there were no nicks large enough to possibly cause trouble. I checked the fuel to make sure it had been topped off, and then checked the pitot tube, to make sure that the small hole in the side of the plane, which directed the flow of air into the navigation system, was not clogged.

Without the free flow of air through the tube, the altimeter, rate of-climb, and air speed indicator would not work properly. There was a heater in the head of the tube to keep it clear of ice. We kicked the tires, got in, and closed the doors. I inserted the key into the power slot, and was ready to call ground control for taxi instructions.

I looked at Doey and asked, "Ready?"

"Let's fly," she replied.

"Now," I said, explaining the new radio communications, "when you call ground control for taxi instructions, you'll also get a brief local weather report for the area and the altimeter setting for the field. The report also includes other information that may change by the hour." I turned the communication switch on and we listened to the current report, which was information Tango. I then switched to ground control and said, "Ground control, Bravo Juliet 1-9, on the ramp at Hangar 2. Taxi for take-off, we have Tango."

"Bravo Juliet 1-9, ground control clears Bravo Juliet 1-9 to runway 1-8 Right and hold."

"Roger," I replied. "Bravo Juliet 1-9 to 1-8 Right and hold." At the blast fence I held the brakes and powered up. When the hand on the rpm meter reached 1000 rpms I checked the magnetos for a drop. There were none. My hands moved about the instrument panel in a busy and familiar way. Carburetor heat in; directional gyros checked; flaps up; beacon lights on; transponder on standby. All instruments and suction gauges in the green. Altimeter set for field elevation. One radio was set to the tower frequency, the other tuned to the 330 radial from Chapel Hill VOR.

I slipped my feet to the rudder pedals, and Doey watched as I ran the controls through to make sure that nothing impeded their smooth action. All was ready. The preflight and engine run up was complete. Our plane was found fit to fly. I called Chapel Hill tower and said, "Bravo Juliet 1-9 holding short 1-8 Right, ready for take-off."

"Bravo Juliet 1-9, the tower clears Bravo Juliet 1-9 into position and hold."

I repeated, "Into position and hold. Bravo Juliet 1-9."

We taxied into position, and lined up with the white stripe that divided the runway. The first plane to cross the runway threshold was a DC3. We waited expectantly for the tower's call. A fleeting shadow of a Beach biplane flared over the marker and rolled out. When it cleared the runway my headset buzzed with a cacophony of sounds that live in the atmosphere to confound the hearing of man. Then the runway was ours. "Bravo Juliet 1-9, you are cleared for takeoff."

'Bravo Juliet 1-9 rolling," I replied. The throttle was advanced to the firewall, and the white line that divided the runway streaked beneath the aircraft as we ran with it to a point about 800 feet ahead. The yoke stirred, and then came alive in my hands. At 70 mph indicated, and with a gentle backpressure on the yoke, the wheels of the plane found the right moment and remembered how to fly. At rotation, I silently recited my one line of poetry. Not to do so would test the wrath of Saint Elmo. I eased the power setting to 75 mph after checking the sky for other planes in the area, we made an into the wind departure. We were cleared, and I set a course for northeast.

I expected that this flight with Doey would be special. The feeling persisted. Maybe it would come later. Doey looked at me and said, "As we took off, you were saying something to yourself. What is it that you were saying?"

"It's nothing," I said. "It's just a few meaningless words."

"Would you tell me what they are?" she asked.

"It's kind of silly," I replied.

"I would like to know," she insisted. "If it's personal, I'm truly sorry that I asked. Please forgive me."

"No it's not personal or private. It's just something the flying fraternity started doing a long time ago. I think it started with the Wright brothers. They carried a token piece of the wing fabric from their first plane with them when they flew. I'm not sure that anyone, including them, knew why they did, but from then on, pilots have carried on the practice. A lucky something or other has become the thing to do. I think that any object or saying can be your lucky charm. Mine is a line of poetry, and not to say it could lead to an unhappy ending. Do I believe that it wards off danger? No, not really, but why take a chance? It may be superstitious, but for my protection I carry a line of poetry in my mind, which my father read to me when I was a child. I have never forgotten it. It's always there. I silently recite it every time I fly, or even if I'm with someone else who is doing the flying. At rotation I silently repeat the phrase: Arise my love and come away with me. If I carried something that I believed to be magic, I might lose it, and if I forget my line of poetry, I shouldn't be flying."

Doey looked at me as I repeated the words, and said, "It's beautiful, may I use it too?"

"Of course you may." It was the first of many things that we were to share. The Chapel Hill Airport fell away and the altimeter started measuring our distance from the earth. We were at six hundred feet and climbing. At fifteen hundred feet we leveled off. I closed the engine ventilators to one half open and engaged the autopilot. A cloud drifted over the face of the moon and the land beneath us was covered with a cold October sky. Doey zipped up her flight jacket, and I turned the cabin heat up a notch or two.

"That's just a little unimportant cloud whose pathway got in the way of the moon," I said. "In a few minutes it will drift on." Like the opening of a Broadway play, the cloud curtain slowly drifted away revealing the stage of Earth lit by the light of a full moon. In the sky a profligate heaven had hung out its treasure of stars. It was a scene so lovely that words alone could not describe its beauty.

We were flying through diaphanous clouds, on a pathway which one could only believe was the approach to heaven. "Westward, look!" she said. Across the distant horizon, a million or more light years away, the Milky Way reflected the subtle colors of millions of stars, standing like sentinels across the sky, guarding the treasures of God.

"It's so beautiful!" Doey exclaimed. "It's all you said it would be, and more." We flew on through the high pristine sanctity of space, gazing at the light from stars that ceased to be more than a millennium ago. As we flew a twenty mile course around a panorama of stars, our view was in constant change. As our plane changed position, it brought beauty, not only of the sky and world we knew, but of a sky crowded with millions and billions of stars and planets that stretched from here to a horizon that faded from the sight of the most powerful microscope fashioned by man.

"Our first step," I said, "is to place a man on the moon, and one day we will. One day a man will walk on the moon and fly beyond that far horizon. It may take a millennium or so, but it will happen. That's my belief." I removed my headset and handed it to Doey, then swung the yoke over to her position. She was now the command pilot. "The plane is yours," I said.

Doey moved her feet to the rudder pedals, turned off the automatic pilot, sometimes referred to as George, and flew the plane through a short list of maneuvers. Satisfied with the plane's obedience to her touch, she returned the plane to its original altitude and direction, and re-engaged the automatic pilot. With her right hand resting on the yoke, she dropped her left hand into her lap. Gently, I picked it up and moved closer. She turned and looked at me and smiled. We flew on in silence.

Our flight in the moonlit sky was coming to an end. Doey returned the control back to me and I set a course that would take us back to the airport. Mentally I checked the landing procedure, and the radio compass pointed the way home. On the ground I taxied back to the hanger where we sat and talked about a future that maybe we would one day share.

Doey deftly turned any conversation which impinged on her private thoughts to something less private. I did, however, believe that I had attained a status of boyfriend. We got out of the plane and stood in its shadow and talked about what tomorrow would bring. I reminded her that she had a breakfast date with her parents at 8:00 a.m. "I'm curious to know what your parents thought about my using an obvious lie for an excuse to leave early and take you with me. If the topic comes up, and I think it will, please tell them that I will never again use a lie to attain a gain."

She said, "I knew that we didn't have a lecture on the adiabatic lapse rate in an up slope fog, and I knew about the full moon. I really wanted to fly with you, but if they ask, I will tell them the truth. Even if the topic is not mentioned, I will tell them what you've just told me."

Testing my boyfriend status, I drew her to me. We shared a kiss, or two, or three, maybe four or more. I'm not sure, but I knew that I had a replacement for Betty Moran, and without Doey's commitment she had gained a permanent place in my heart.

I drove Doey to the Tri Delta House and I parked under the trees where the dark was the antidote for too much moonlight. It was a known fact that too much moonlight would wrinkle the soul. Ask any coed, and she will tell you that a measure of darkness, at the end of a date in the light of the moon, is necessary. I didn't know this, but went along with the thinking and acted in

Arise My Love And Come Away With Me

a manner that helped our friendship mature. Best of all, Doey didn't seem to mind. At midnight we said goodnight at the Tri Delta door, and I walked to the Fetzer House where Harry would be waiting with his list of questions.

At 8:00 a.m. Doey was back at the Carolina Inn. She called her parents room and told her mother that she was in the lobby. "We'll be right down," her mother said. A few minutes later, they were in the dining room, talking and sipping coffee as they waited for their Eggs Benedict.

"Did you enjoy the lecture last night?" her father asked. "I would like to know more about the adiabatic lapse rate of heat in an upslope fog."

"Oh, Daddy," she said, "there was no lecture last night, but Wynn had told me about flying in the light of a full moon. Last night the moon was full, and there wouldn't be another one for a month. He told me to tell you how sorry he was in using that deception. He urged me to tell you and Mom the truth. He knew it was wrong, and so did I." She paused a moment and then said, "He will never tell you a lie again, and he's very honest and trustworthy. He had learned a valuable lesson of honesty. It's the keystone of a good reputation."

"You think a lot of Wynn, don't you?" her mother said.

"Well, yes I do. He's a good friend, a good pilot, a good musician, and he has good values," she replied.

"What does he play besides the didgeridoo?" her father asked, smiling.

"He plays a clarinet and has a band that plays for inter-fraternity dances."

"How long have you known him?" her mother asked.

"Only a month," she replied. "Maj. Hederman speaks very highly of him. He's known him and his family since Wynn was ten years old. I overheard a conversation he was having with Wynn. Wynn said he was not going home for Thanksgiving. He planned to stay on campus to study. I had planned to ask you if I might invite him to have Thanksgiving with us. And Mother, don't start thinking that I'm in love with him. He's just a good friend, and I'm really sure that you and Daddy will like him."

Her mother listened with interest. "How did you meet?"

"I met Wynn at a dance that Harry and Carolyn invited Carl and me to attend. Carl couldn't go. He had a theme to write for his English literature class, so I just went along with Carolyn. I knew there would be a stag line. Harry was dancing with me. When the music stopped and the band took a five-minute break, Harry said, 'Come with me, I would like for you to meet my roommate.' I was surprised when I looked up and saw Wynn standing on the podium. I didn't know his name, and I had only seen him once before, at the airport. I had no idea that he was in the flying program or played in a band. Harry introduced us and invited Wynn to join us after the dance at Egan's, a student hangout in Chapel Hill. Wynn was a perfect gentleman. We talked about flying, and he asked me if I would like to dance, and at a quarter to midnight, he and Harry took Carolyn and me to the sorority house.

"He did say he was glad to meet me," Doey continued, "but other than the few flights we've had together, and his offer to fly me on a moonlit night, which we did last night . . . and Mother, it was so beautiful! It's a different world up there, but it must be seen on a night when the moon is full."

"I have a ten thirty meeting with Maj. Hederman," John said, "and I don't want to be late." Breakfast was served, and talk about Doey's friend was put on hold. "Let's eat," her father said. "We'll talk about your friend later."

With breakfast over, they went into the lobby and sat by the fire. There was a moment of silence. Then John said, "Doey, when you wrote to tell us of your class enrollment, you included aviation as an elective, a subject of which we have no depth of knowledge. Of course we know that the word 'aviation' refers to a broad industry that covers many areas and that offers wonderful opportunities, so my meeting this morning with Maj. Hederman is to learn more about the industry. It would be helpful to know what part interests you. Your mother and I can find nothing in flying that would help a lawyer."

Arise My Love And Come Away With Me

"Daddy," she said, "when I sent my schedule of classes to you and Mother I didn't include more than the name, 'aviation,' for the reason that at that time I didn't know anymore than you and Mother. I was hoping that it covered the entire field of aviation, with knowledge and training to become a pilot. I'm glad that you've come to talk with Mr. Hederman. I'm sure it will help you, mother, and me to share and expand our knowledge. I do want to become a pilot, and I assure you that I will be a lawyer, but a war is on its way and I want to be ready. I'm assured that women will not be sent anywhere in harm's way and that the war will end. I believe that what I learn, and what I will do in aviation, will give me more opportunities in the future. I'm terribly sorry if you thought that I would keep anything from you. More than my life, I love you and Mother, and for now I need your help."

The meeting ended without a word from Dorothy, but her grim look silently spoke her troubled thoughts. John kissed his wife, hugged Doey, and headed for the door. He paused there and said, "Don't forget we will have dinner here at seven tonight. Don't be late." Doey told her mother that she had an afternoon law lecture, but she would be on time for dinner.

"Carolyn and I stayed at the sorority house last night," Doey said. "We have Harry's car and we have plenty of time to study and get to Durham in time for the class."

"Are you sure that you're allowing enough time for studies?" Dorothy asked. "You seem to be spending a great deal of time with flying, and your new friend Wynn. When do you have time to study?"

"Mother, please don't worry. Flying is like any other course. It's scheduled, and like any other course there is homework. And I've never had what you might call a date with Wynn. We do attend flying class together, and I've met him a few times at dances, but I was with Carolyn and Harry. I do attend law classes with other boys, but that doesn't mean that they are any more than friends. Wynn plays for the dances and doesn't have time to date, and I'm not at all sure that he would invite me to anything more than an occasional flight with him. I was surprised when Daddy invited him to have dinner with us."

She considered her next words carefully before she spoke. "At the end of the flight last night, I suppose I did, in a way, encourage him to kiss me. It was really no more than to thank him for taking me to a sky that I had never seen before. Now you know the whole story, a story that I'm sure wouldn't shock a Puritan. I do hope that you and Daddy will let me invite him to have Thanksgiving with us."

Chapter 21

John Meets Red

At ten thirty, John Brooks arrived at Maj. Hederman's office. The door was open and he walked into an office that, in his mind, would contain nothing more than a calendar with a picture of a Hollywood pinup queen in a provocative pose, a clock on the wall that probably didn't keep time, and a waste basket overflowing with trash.

John was pleased to find that he was wrong. There was a clock on the wall. He glanced at his watch then back to the clock. He was surprised to find that they were only a few ticks apart. Instead of a provocative picture on the wall, there were several framed letters and a diploma from the University of Texas. Next to the diploma were his flying credentials that authorized him to fly anything with wings.

He heard the door close and turned to see a six-foot man with close-cropped red hair. He was dressed in tan shirt and tie, low cut brown shoes, tan pants, and a United States Air Force brown leather jacket. On the left side of the jacket was an identification patch with the name Maj. R.J. Hederman. The R was for Richard, but after a short time acquaintance with anyone, he became known as Red. Red's dark blue eyes scanned the room, a smile lit his face. He was in charge of flight training. "I'm sorry to be late," he said, looking at his watch.

"I'm John Brooks, Doey's father," he said as he shook Red's hand. "I'm pleased to meet you again Maj. Hederman." Their firm grip and smiles set the stage for a congenial meeting. "While waiting, I took a moment to view your very impressive career. If you don't mind my asking, what was your major at the University of Texas?"

"Aeronautical engineering," Red replied. "And you?"

"I'm a product of the law school at the University of Chicago."

With introductions over, Red moved behind his desk and invited John to take a chair. "I'm sorry that I was a bit late for this meeting, but a time schedule in this job is extremely hard to keep. You have come to discuss your daughter's inclusion in the flying program, is that right?"

"Yes, Maj. Hederman," John said.

"Since we are involved in the same problem, it would save time if you call me Red."

"It's a point well taken, Red. Call me John," he said, and a new friendship was born. For more than an hour they discussed the place for women in aviation.

Red said, "I have read Doey's ground school report. She leads the class in every subject, with nothing but A's. She is eager to learn, dependable, and shows no sign of distress when faced with a quick decision. Those are traits that we are trained to look for in students. Physical and mental alertness to support the desire to fly are basics. We will not let a student go beyond a point where, in our judgment, they cannot safely go. I'm your daughter's instructor. She leads the class in flying. She just flew her solo rating. She understands the plane's limitations, and never tries a new maneuver before learning what the consequences of a mistake could be. In my opinion, she was born to fly."

He paused for a moment and then continued. "There is a war on the way and every man and woman trained for the military will be needed. When the war is over the jobs in aviation, as well as all industry, should be plentiful. It's a sad thought that it will take a war, a loss of life, and the total destruction of many countries of the world to achieve peace and order, but it will end a ten-year depression, and bring an era of peace and prosperity that the world badly needs. Aviation, I believe, will be one of the leaders in our recovery.

"Airlines from around the world will profit by the inclusion of the new innovations, which will be necessary to create aircraft that can stand the rigors of war. Given the same time period, such improvements could never happen in peacetime. I understand that your daughter is enrolled in the School of Law at Duke."

"Yes," John replied. "And that's where her mother wants her to be. Even if she thought flying was safe, she can find no connection where the knowledge of flying could be any help to a lawyer." He paused to gather his thoughts, and added, "I'm sorry to say that I can't come up with a reason not to support my wife's contentions."

Red said, "When a man runs for the Presidency of the United States, he makes many promises. Some promises he knows he can't keep, but the votes he gets for those promises are what gets him elected. President Roosevelt ran for another term. One of his promises was to keep America out of war, but I believe, as many do, that's a promise he won't be able to keep. We will be forced to take sides."

Red went on to say, "Fifty thousand airplanes are being built, with more to follow. The plants are working around the clock producing ammunition and clothing for our military. For the past ten years our work force has been idle, and now there are more jobs than there are men and women to fill them. The depression is history, and the workplace is vibrant again, with men building military camps, airfields, and shipyards to receive, train, and arm the first draftees.

"By the end of the war, the world will take a deep breath and utter a sigh of relief. They will be faced with converting a wartime economy into a peacetime economy. Your daughter, with a background of law and aviation, will be well positioned to take advantage of becoming a counsel to one or more of two hundred countries that will have aspirations of sharing the world's transportation and cargo business. Today, a law firm that can include a lawyer that has a background in aviation is generally believed to have a better grasp of international law than one that hasn't. The same will be true when peace follows the war that is coming."

"Thanks Red," John said. "You have made a case that I have no reason to doubt. I do have one more question, which seems to be important to my daughter. She wants to invite one of your acquaintances to join us in our home for Thanksgiving. Would you care to give me your character rating of Wynn Cary?"

"Certainly," Red said. "I have known Wynn and his family for many years. As you are proud of your daughter, his family and I are proud of Wynn. He is truthful, sensitive, and ambitious. I would trust my life and checkbook with him. Your daughter shows good judgment of character; it will be your good fortune to share your day with him."

"Thank you, Red. My daughter does have good judgment of character, but I would like to keep this conversation between us."

"What conversation?" Red replied.

John smiled and said "I hope to meet with you again."

When John arrived back at the Carolina Inn he had considered every possible reason why Doey should not invite Wynn to be a guest for Thanksgiving, and failed. Maybe he was a little over protective of Doey. She thought and acted like an adult. She had good values and was honest and dependable. And then he remembered Red's final words: 'It will be *your* good fortune, to share your day with him.'

John felt reasonably sure that Dorothy would not object to having a weekend guest for Thanksgiving, but he knew there was no way to convince Doey to drop the flying part of the aviation program. He went up to his room and walked in. Dorothy was asleep in a chair; there was an open book on her lap. He leaned over and kissed her forehead. She awakened with a start, and it took her a moment to remember where she was. She threw her arms around his neck and drew him closer, and said, "Have you forgotten how to kiss?"

"No," he said, "and I'm glad to know that you haven't forgotten how to be a hussy. My father told me about women like you."

"My mother," she replied, "warned me about men like you, and said you only wanted to get me in bed."

"Your mother was so right, but it took all summer to accomplish what should have required no more than a date or two. I even had to say that I loved you and couldn't live without you, and you believed me, and something weird happened—I believed me, too."

"We did have a beautiful wedding, didn't we?"

"Yes, my darling, we did. You are still an angel in the kitchen and a hussy in bed." He picked her up and carried her into the bedroom, and with a backward kick, closed the door.

Chapter 22

Dorothy Weatherford

Dorothy awoke from a deep dream of peace. She lay there thinking about a beautiful past that now had a bridge to a future that boded nothing more than the unspeakable horrors of war. Doey was sure to have a part in that maelstrom of evil. She knew that she was losing her daughter to a world without compassion, and decided then that she would not make the way harder for her by insisting that she drop flying from her schedule. For Doey to carry out her plans for the future, she would need the complete support of her parents.

This trip to Chapel Hill was like another day of vacation. It was a day off from the busy regimen of church charities, civic affairs, and what she missed most—her home, and the endless work in the flower garden she loved. It was a day when her memory slipped back in time.

She was Dorothy Weatherford, twenty years old and a senior in the University of Chicago's School of Arts and Science. It was a day that she would never forget. She received a telegram notifying her that her mother and father had been killed in an automobile accident in Charlottesville, Virginia, her hometown. Other than an elderly aunt and uncle, she was alone.

Jean Gruendler, her roommate, made the train reservations to take her home, and wanted to accompany her. Dorothy thanked her, but insisted that she would be alright, and she wanted to go alone.

Her family's lawyer, Henry Holt, and his wife Cheryl were at the station to meet her when the train arrived. Henry picked up her bag, placed an arm around Dorothy, and led her to his car.

On the way home Dorothy wanted to hear more about the accident. He told her all that he knew. "Your mother and father were coming home from a movie. It was about nine p.m. and the streets were dry and visibility was good. At an intersection, your father had the right of way, and as he was crossing, a drunk driver who was speeding and going the wrong way on a one-way street, hit their car head on. The drunk sustained minor injuries and is now behind bars awaiting trial.

"Dorothy," Henry said, "I have been your family's lawyer for almost forty years, and you and your parents are among my very best friends. I want you to know that you don't carry this loss entirely alone. I know that this is not the time to talk shop, but you should know that your dad left everything to you, and that's considerable. I will attend to the legalities concerning the estate and stay in touch with you. Whatever you need please let Cheryl, or me know. Call day or night; we're here to help."

"Thank you," Dorothy said. "I'll remember that." Henry pulled the car into the driveway, and together they walked to the front door. As she was putting her key in the lock, the door opened and a tearful Aunt Betsy Weatherford drew her into her arms.

Through sobs, she heard Henry say, "I'll call you tomorrow." She nodded her thanks, and walked into the home that she knew and loved. Tears of the tragedy filled her eyes.

A few days later she said a tearful goodbye to her parents at the cemetery, and left the legal matters in Henry's hands. Henry and Cheryl accompanied her to the train station, and gave her a basket filled with things to eat and a book to read. Dorothy thanked them and made sure that they had her campus address in Chicago.

Henry and Cheryl hugged Dorothy, and assured her that they would take care of her aunt and uncle, and the legal matters. "I will keep in close touch with you," he said. Henry helped Dorothy and Cheryl onto the train and led them to Dorothy's coach and private room. They made every effort to move the conversation into the promise of tomorrow. Dorothy clung to a past that was gone.

A Pullman porter in charge of Dorothy's car came down the aisle and asked if he could do anything to help. Henry said, "Yes, this young lady is going to Chicago. I would like for you to attend to her every need." He pulled his wallet from his pocket and removed a ten dollar bill and tore it in half. He gave the porter one half and Dorothy the other, and said to Dorothy, "If you get good service, give your half to him when you are safely off the train in Chicago."

The porter had never received a tip larger than a dollar before, and just the thought of a ten dollar tip quickened his step and put a smile on his face. He looked at Henry and Dorothy and said "Thank you, Miss. My name is Dave. I am pleased to serve you. Just touch your call button there, the one under the window, and I'll be here."

"Thank you, Dave," she said.

They heard the conductor say, "Last call, all aboard!" It was time to say goodbye. Cheryl and Henry quickly hugged and kissed Dorothy, and again assured her that everything would be taken care of. "Just stay well," Cheryl said. They left the train, and watched as it got under way.

They could see Dorothy watching them as they waved goodbye. Dorothy sat there reliving the recent events. At the cemetery, she had watched as her parents' coffins were lowered into the ground. She felt part of her life was going with them. She now had no ties to anyone that was close to her. She was desperately alone. The world around her was an endless sea of sorrow.

Where was the compassionate God which she prayed to every night since childhood? For the first time in memory, she stopped praying. She wanted to believe what Sister Mary Lucas and Father Kilpatrick told her, but they were wrong. What was the point that God had in removing her parents from her life? In some way she felt that it was her punishment, for the way she lived her life. Through the train window she watched as the cities and towns raced past and in sorrow knew that she must adjust to a new page of life.

At seven, she answered the call for an early dinner and followed other travelers to the dining car. The tables were full, and she was about to return to her room. She was stopped and told that they might find a place for her if she didn't mind sharing a table with someone. She said that would be alright. She was led to a corner table near the kitchen, where a young man was seated at a table for two. When asked if he would mind sharing his table, he was more than agreeable to have dinner with such a good-looking girl.

He stood and said, "It will be my pleasure, please sit down. My name is John Brooks."

"I'm Dorothy Weatherford," she replied.

John couldn't believe his luck and figured she was probably married or engaged, and would probably get off at the next stop down the line. "Where are you headed?" he asked.

"Chicago," she said.

"Do you live in Chicago?"

"No, I live in Charlottesville, Virginia."

"I live in Terre Haute," he said. "I was in Charlottesville on business, and now I'm on my way back to Chicago."

"Are you a lawyer in Chicago?"

"No," he said, "I'm a senior at the University of Chicago Law School. What do you do in Chicago?" he asked.

"I'm a senior at the University of Chicago's School of Arts and Science."

John smiled and said, "I'm very glad to know you, Dorothy."

When the train reached Chicago, Dave received the other half of the ten dollar bill, and John invited Dorothy to share a cab to the university campus. As they parted, John said, "Now that we are friends, may I call you sometime?" She knew that she had not been good company on the trip, and was surprised that he wished to call.

111

Dorothy willed her memory to return to the present. Today was like one of those days when she accompanied John on a business trip, or when they were on vacation, but never in her memory had she spent an entire day in bed. She was always up at seven. She had no tolerance for sloth, and then she thought of John. Today was a surprise and what a wonderful, restful day!

With evening coming on it was time to shower and get dressed. At 6:30 p.m. Doey arrived, called her parents from a house phone, and announced that she was in the lobby. "We'll be right down," her father said and hung up. Doey sat down in a secluded corner where she could watch the elevators.

This morning when her mother seemed to imply that she was in love with Wynn, she assured her that she was not. "He's only a friend," she had said. All day the words came back, and like an echo they seemed to say, "Your mother knows. Your mother knows. My mother knows what? Your mother knows that you are in love with Wynn." Her mind rejected that and replied, "You stay out of this; my mother doesn't need your help."

Doey heard the elevator doors open. She waved to her parents and said, "Over here."

"We're a few minutes early," her father said, "but let's go in." John gave his name to the maitre d' and said, "If it's possible, we would like to be seated at one of Jimmie Johnston's tables."

"Certainly sir, there is a vacant table near the piano. Will that be alright?"

"That will be fine," John replied.

At the table they were surrounded by a soft blend of table talk and the beautiful piano music of Debussy's "Clair de Lune." "The music," Dorothy said, "reminds me of the last time your father and I were in New York. After dinner one night, we went to the Rainbow Room at the top of Rockefeller Center. As we walked in, Eddy Duchin and His Orchestra were playing their theme song, "Clair De Lune." It was so beautiful."

"Yes, Dorothy," John said, "it was a wonderful night, but you provided the beauty." John leaned over, picked up his wife's hand, and kissed it. "It was a wonderful evening, Dorothy," John said. "I saw envy in the eyes of men, as they watched you pass by."

"Oh John," she said, "We're in public, and that's our daughter sitting there, and all these people, what will they think?"

By way of an answer, John pulled Dorothy's chair closer, put his arms around her, and the diners who watched sighed and vicariously shared the kiss that followed. Dorothy just sat there with a smile and whispered, "Oh, John, I do love you." The piano's music had changed in tempo, and slowly joined the moment in time with a promise of "I Love You Truly."

Fungus arrived at the table with a tray containing three glasses of champagne. "It's from the manager," he said. John picked up the card which read, "Please accept our thanks. There will be no charge for the dinner or champagne." John quickly wrote a message of thanks to the manager.

"Daddy, did you talk with Mr. Hederman this morning?" Doey asked.

"Yes, we had a pleasant and enlightening talk. He's a gentleman who excels in words that even a layman can understand. He has a passionate belief in what he is teaching, and he's able to answer any question without notes or references to books. He speaks as if he wrote the manuals, and I wouldn't be surprised to find that he did. Just knowing that the knowledge you will take with you when you leave Duke with a law degree, will be a great assistance to your career. Flying will not be required, but you will have the experience of flying, where others may not. You will be buying a place at the head of the line, where a law firm needs a lawyer with aviation experience."

We were interrupted by a voice that said, "Welcome back to the Fungus café, the providers of good food and grog. May I bring you something else to drink while you peruse *la carte de jour?*" Fungus passed the menus around, and to Doey he said, "Are you a student here at Chapel Hill?"

"No," Doey said, "I go to Duke."

"Well," he said, "maybe it's not too late to transfer to Chapel Hill, it's a better school. My name isn't Fungus, its Jimmie Johnston. I believe I had the honor of serving you once, have I not?"

"Yes, you have. Do you know Harry Woods and Wynn Cary?" Doey asked.

"Yes," he said. "Harry and I are members of the Inter-Fraternity Council, and Wynn plays for our dances. I, however, am always working on weekends." He looked at Doey's father and asked, "Are you ready to order, sir?"

"Yes, my wife and I will have the same thing, roast beef, medium rare, baked potato with butter and chives, and a green salad."

"And you?" Fungus asked, turning to Doey.

"I would like a shrimp salad, crab cakes, a baked potato with everything on it, and hot tea with the dinner."

"Thank you, your majesty; I hasten to carry out your wishes. Do you have a name?"

"Yes, my name is Doey Brooks, and these are my parents, Mr. and Mrs. John Brooks."

"We are happy to be here again, Jimmy," Dorothy said.

Jimmy replied, "It is my pleasure to know and serve you again, and thank you for choosing my table. Whenever you are in Chapel Hill, please remember that you are always welcome at The Fungus Café."

Daddy ordered a bottle of red wine and a soft drink for Doey. Doey continued the conversation by asking how his meeting went with Red Hederman. "Splendid," he said. "Red acquainted me with a part of aviation that I never knew. There was no talk about flying as a recreation. Within a year or so aviation will, to a great extent, replace much of the business that trains, trucks, and buses now dominate as a primary way to travel, send mail, or ship cargo. It will become the center of a new worldwide industry. There will be a network of airplanes flying to every corner of the earth. Just think, from here to England in less than a day, and a few years after that, planes will be flying nonstop to every country around the world.

"The more a lawyer knows about aviation, including hands-on flying, the better his or her chances will be to aid in the development of international laws, which will be needed by those countries who survive the devastating war that is eminent. That's where you, Doey, as a lawyer, may play an important role.

"Red told me that Germany has more aircraft by far than France, England, and the United States combined. With aviation's ability to export war to any place on earth, the surviving country with the largest fleet of aircraft will dictate the peace. The only country capable of that now is Germany. The world is getting smaller and there is no place too far that a plane of destruction can't reach. If Hitler has his way, and I think he will, he will redraw the map of the world to include the lands of other countries that will cease to be." John lifted his glass of wine and took a sip.

"If that happens," John continued, "Germany will become a country to be listened to with laws that will make international changes. Before this year is out, I'm sad to say, the world will be faced with war. And when that happens, Red said airplanes will be foremost in the defense plans of the world. Red believes that women in aviation will not fly in harm's way, but may be used to fly aircraft from the manufacturers, such as Boeing, Lockheed, Douglas or Northrop to airfields within the military bases in the United States." Satisfied that he had said all he needed to say on the subject, John asked, "Is there anything else on the agenda to discuss?" He paused and looked at Doey, and then at Dorothy.

"Yes," said Dorothy, eager to turn the conversation away from women and aviation, she turned to Doey and said, "We would be pleased to have Wynn be our guest for Thanksgiving. Your father and I have separately come to the same decision."

"Thank you," Doey said, "I'm pleased with your decision."

John and Dorothy looked at each other with knowing glances, and smiled. When dinner was over John left Fungus a generous tip, and waited to have a word with the pianist to thank her for the music and the part she played when he kissed his wife. He laid a folded tip on the keyboard and returned to his table.

As they left the dining room, John followed his wife and daughter, the two people he loved most in the world, and thought of all the tomorrows to come, and how they would change the lives of his family. Since 1929 the world was held tight in the grip of the depression. "I know that you have to get back to Duke, but the evening is still young," he said while leading Dorothy and Doey through the lobby where a cheerful fire added a touch of beauty and romance.

"I don't suppose we will see you before Thanksgiving," Dorothy said. "We will expect you the day before Thanksgiving or sooner if your schedule changes. I will send Wynn an invitation and we will be very pleased to have him for our guest."

Doey kissed her parents goodbye and thanked them for inviting Wynn. Then, as an after-thought, she said to herself, he may have other plans. They said goodbye in the lobby. Dorothy's parting words to Doey were spoken softly, "Please be ever so careful when you fly. We love you, Doey."

Chapter 23

College—Airport

My college activities and cost of flying had reached a point where my income from home and music gigs could not support my meager lifestyle. More and more, my friends Harry Woods and Bob Lovell were paying for my meals and extra college activities. I would have to cut back on flying and maybe give up my fraternity life. I reviewed two possible ways to remedy my dilemma. We could raise the cost of our dance music to seventy-five dollars, or I would write a letter to my uncle and ask for a loan of one hundred dollars per month. I opted for the loan. I carefully wrote a letter filled with the best economical terms that I had learned, and asked if he would consider a loan. I would pay any percent of interest that I could realistically afford.

I had also mentioned my problem to my economics professor. His business approach was simple. "Why not ask the university to loan you two hundred dollars. I think you are good for it, and you wouldn't have to repay it until after you graduate." That same day I went to the office of student affairs and timidly approached the matter of a loan. I expected nothing more than a polite turn down, but when my request was listened to, I was asked to wait a few minutes. At least I thought my request was being considered.

Then the wait was over. With a few strokes of a pen I signed my name and received a check for two hundred dollars. A week later I received a letter from my uncle that contained a hundred dollars, and an assurance that I would receive a hundred dollars each month until I graduated. He also said he would not loan me the money, for the reason that he didn't have time to prepare the note. "It's much easier," he said, "to give you the money."

I will always wonder what part my economics professor had in removing the gloom of debt that I had always considered normal. I wrote a letter to my mother and told her that her monthly check was no longer needed. I gave her all the reasons, along with a hundred dollar check.

At an opportune moment, and with my new financial status, I raised the price per gig to seventy-five dollars. Without objection, the new terms were agreed to and I was no longer burdened with a life that reluctantly accepted the generosity of others.

Saturday morning Doey had a 10 a.m. flying appointment with Red. She arrived early and went in search of him. The first stop was his office, but he wasn't there. She checked with Sam in operations. "Red and Wynn just left here," he said. "They were going to Hangar 2. I think you will find them there."

On the way Doey paused to watch a plane on its final approach. She walked on to the hangar, where Red and I stood watching as the plane's wheel's lightly touched the ground, rolled out, and taxied toward Hangar 2. The plane, a twin engine AT 11 with military markings, slowly edged closer to the hangar and stopped.

Doey thought that it might be Colonel Anderson, whose job it was to check the progress of the government-funded flying program. That would account for Red being there to welcome him. She arrived in time to say hello to Red and me and to tell Red that she was on time for her flight lesson.

She watched as an attractive young female pilot stepped out of the cabin door of the plane, shaking her head and running fingers through her dark brown, shoulder length hair, which hung loosely around a face that men, and even women, would find attractive. She was wearing military coveralls with wings, and a name tag that identified her as First Lieutenant Jane R. Austin in the Woman's Air Force Service. As she spoke, she removed dark sunglasses and tucked them into a sleeve pocket.

"I'm Lt. Austin," she said. "I'm in the service of delivering planes to where they are needed. This one comes from Wichita, Kansas. Can you tell me where I might find Maj. Red Hederman?"

Red replied, "I'm Maj. Hederman. I'm in charge of the flight program here." Turning he said, "This is Miss Doey Brooks and Mr. Wynn Cary. Miss Brooks is attached to the flight program, and Mr. Cary is a pilot."

She smiled, acknowledging the introductions, then turned to Red and asked, "Are you *the* Red Hederman, the one whose name always comes up whenever pilots find time to talk about the past?" Red modestly nodded his head. "I'm honored to make your acquaintance, Major," she said, and then reached into the plane for a briefcase full of papers.

Doey and I just looked at each other puzzled, not knowing the depth of the man we knew and respected as a mentor and a friend. The answer would have to come from someone else who had knowledge of Red's past.

Red said to Lt. Austin, "I know you have a bundle of papers that must be signed before releasing the plane to us. Let's go to my office and take care of the paperwork."

Red turned to Doey and said, "Our flight will have to be rescheduled for tomorrow." He then asked Lt. Austin how long she would be here.

"Until morning," she replied. "I'll be picked up at 6 a.m., and fly to San Diego for another assignment." She returned to the plane and removed her parachute and travel kit. "Lead the way," she said.

Red picked up her parachute. Lt. Austin said, "Thank you, I'm used to carrying my equipment, but I have just completed a night flight of five hours with strong headwinds all the way. I'm tired and I do appreciate your help." As we walked toward his office, Lt. Austin said, "I'm booked into the Carolina Inn for the night. Is it near here?"

"Yes, it is," Doey said. "When you are through with the paperwork, I'll be pleased to take you there."

"Oh, that won't be necessary," the lieutenant said. "If there is transportation, I'll find my way. All I want now is a place to sleep."

"There is the Blue and White shuttle bus that stops at the curb outside the terminal," Doey said. "It's supposed to make one round trip each hour, but they seldom keep that schedule. Mostly you call them and wait to be picked up. I can take you there in fifteen minutes. Here or on the way, I would like to ask you one question, and I assure you that our conversation will not take more than two or three minutes. I would like to become a ferry pilot and do what you are doing, and even if you have nothing to say, I will save you an hour of sleep."

"Thank you for your interest, Doey. Of course I will help you. I have information in my flight bag that will give you everything that you need to know, and I will accept your kind invitation to drive me to the Inn."

"Maj. Hederman," said Doey, "I'll be in Hanger 2 or the debriefing room. Please call me when you're through here."

Red answered with a nod of his head. "Check with me later about tomorrow, for a time to fly."

I looked at Doey and said, "I'm glad that your flight has been postponed. The day before yesterday, Red checked me out in the new Beech Craft, and again this morning we went through basic maneuvers. When we landed he got out and told me, 'Take it around the field.' He signed my logbook, and now I'm qualified to fly a plane that is a step up from the Stinson." As we walked into the hangar, I asked, "Will you fly with me?"

"Yes, but now I have a question," Doey said.

"And that is?"

"I asked my parents if it would be alright to invite you to Terre Haute for the Thanksgiving break."

I was stunned and thrilled! I told Doey that I would go home with her, but I had previously told my mother that I would remain on campus to study. I couldn't do both, and now an invitation from Doey's mother added more guilt than I knew how to handle.

I had made the decision to remain on campus over the holiday, to study and try to understand the subject of economics, which is like trying to pick up a drop of mercury between your thumb and forefinger. It's not possible.

I explained to Doey, "I may fail the course if I don't study, but yes, my favorite flyer, I am grateful to you and your parents for the invitation." Doey turned her head and looked at me with those beautiful blue eyes. I reached and pulled her into the hangar, where prying eyes and ears could not see or hear my acceptance of the most wonderful invitation of my life. To show my appreciation, I knew that I could come up with some tired old words to fit the occasion, but I didn't have time for that, so what else could I do? I kissed her. In what way was I taking advantage of her? To stop my advances all she had to do was say "Please don't," or "Can't we just be friends?"

"Doey," I said, "I may be wrong, but it has occurred to me many times that I'm in love with you. I hope that we are more than just friends."

She just smiled and said, "I'm beginning to believe you when you say that you love me."

I received Mrs. Brooks' invitation to join them for the holiday. Now I was faced with a dilemma. My dilemma needed answers, which I didn't have. I called Mother that evening and told her my problem. "Please, dear," she said, "I will be just fine. We will have Christmas together, and, God willing, all three of my children will be home. You know how disappointed I am, but I do have Ruth and Irene coming home, and we will be with Uncle Adam's family. I did have a very lonely feeling when you told me of your decision to remain in Chapel Hill for Thanksgiving, but things change, and I'm so thankful that you won't be alone. You have written such glowing letters about Doey. I know that one day we will meet and you must accept Mrs. Brooks' invitation. I would not like to think that you were alone at Thanksgiving. I'm so glad that you told me."

"I love you, Mom. Once more you have helped me out of an awkward situation. I will spend the entire Christmas holiday with you." We said goodbye, and with a clear conscience, I wrote Mrs. Brooks and thanked her for the invitation.

A week before Thanksgiving, Harry and I invited Carolyn and Doey to be our guests at the Thanksgiving football game between the Duke Blue Devils and the Tar Heels of North Carolina. After the game there would be a formal dance.

Harry was in charge of transportation. He picked Carolyn and Doey up at the Tri Delta House and arrived at the Fetzer House in time to hear our weekly band practice. For some time, we had talked about adding a girl singer to the band. The girl must be pretty, petite, and able to sing. There were always female students with nothing better to do with their Saturdays than hang around and listen to the music. We found several who filled the petite and pretty requirements, but none who could sing. There were a few who could sing, but they looked more like overweight truck drivers with hairy legs. One girl filled all of our requirements, except we had yet to hear her sing. Her name was Helen Lind. Bob Lovell said she could sing, and that her only problem was stage fright.

I asked her if she would like to try out for the job. She said she would like to but knew that she was not good enough. "Well, we're not very good either. Maybe we can help each other become better. We are about to play "Stardust." Do you know the number?"

"Yes," she replied.

"What's your key?" I asked.

"F," she replied.

"We'll play an eight bar introduction in four-four time. Here's the music, Helen. We need you to make us look and sound good."

With Helen standing in front of the band, we played every note with such feeling that there was a moment of silence from the onlookers as they moved closer. We played three or four numbers. Now we had a singer and Helen had a job. Harry, our manager and agent, mentally made a note to raise the price of gigs to cover Helen's pay, plus ten percent for him.

Harry, always the showman, introduced Helen to Carolyn and Doey, and said, "Carolyn Perry, Doey Brooks, this is Helen Lind. Helen is the new singing "Queen of Swing." She is the star performer of the band that, for now, goes by the name The Beta Four Plus Two. For an hour or more we played some new tunes, and the "Queen of Swing" proved that she could sing.

Chapter 24

Football—Dance

The football game was played in Wallace Wade Stadium at Duke University in Durham. Duke was favored to win, but North Carolina's quarterback, Lalane, and blocking back, Dunkel, were not familiar with that prediction and created what was called an upset.

After the game, we walked with the girls to the sorority, where they would rest and pretty up for the formal dance at eight o'clock. We would meet again at six for dinner, after which we would attend the dance, where Glenn Miller and His Orchestra would play for our listening and dancing pleasure.

That night, Harry and I walked into the Tri Delta house and displayed our tuxedoes, like paid models, and claimed our American beauties. Glenn Miller's theme song, "Moonlight Serenade," filled the air with the beautiful soft sound of music. Early dancers gathered around the podium tapping their toes in time with the sound of the slap base fiddle and the beat of the drums that were keeping time for the reed and brass sections. The floor was becoming so crowded that holding on to your partner and moving in time with the music was difficult. We bumped into Carolyn and Harry and had time to exchange a few words.

Harry said, "After the dance, wait for us in the lobby. We're going to The Danziger for a night cap."

I looked at Doey. She nodded her head and I said to Harry, "Okay, we'll be in the lobby." A few dance steps took us in different directions.

I felt a tap on my shoulder and a familiar voice said, "May I cut in?" I paused and turned in the direction of the voice. It was Joe, Doey's sometime Duke Boyfriend. My first thought was to say "buzz off." Instead, I moved off the floor and kept a keen eye on them, and waited for the number to end. During the pause between numbers, I tapped Joe on the shoulder and said, "May I cut in?"

The music started, and after a few seconds or two, a voice from someone that neither Doey nor I knew, tapped me on the shoulder, and said. "May I cut in?" Again I waited on the side for the next break in the music, and again I tapped on the shoulder and asked if I could reclaim Doey. With a smile to Doey and a mock bow to me, he left the floor, only to be replaced by another dancer who said, "May I cut in?"

"I'm sorry," I said, "but we are just leaving." We looked at the stag line and there were Joe and his cronies, laughing at what they thought of as a triumph.

Doey said, "I will never forgive Joe for this."

What a beautiful end to a miserable dance, I thought. Now Joe would be a candidate to join the Black Armband Club for Doey. We sat at our table, listening to the music. The evening was coming to an end. "Let's get something hot to drink," Doey said.

I got our coats and a couple of coffees in paper cups, and we headed for the terrace. It was a move made without a thought. We could hear the music, and hesitated at the door and stood listening to "All or Nothing At All" by Frank Sinatra.

A three quarter moon hid behind clouds that kept the terrace in darkness. We were alone. We sipped our coffee, and stood in silence. After a few moments, I placed my cup on a nearby table and Doey handed me hers. No words passed between us. On impulse I placed my hands on her shoulders and said, with a confidant voice that I had never felt before, "Doey, I'm in love with you." Time stood still, and what seemed to me an eternity, silence replaced my hope with doubts that left nothing more to say. I felt a moment of rejection, and when she removed my hands from her shoulders, my heart stood still. Clearly I had lost. Maybe we could still be friends. Slowly her hands moved upward, and around me. No words were spoken. The dark clouds hiding the moon mist drifted by, leaving a soft light that marked the pinnacle of my life. Her face tilted upward and we were just a kiss apart. Then a long passionate kiss said more than words could say. Our future was sealed, and our commitment was bound forever.

We left the terrace with minds reeling with dreams worth keeping, and headed for the lobby to look for Carolyn and Harry. They were in a double line that moved slowly to the coat check counter. Twenty minutes later we were in Harry's car heading for Chapel Hill and Danziger's on Franklin Street.

"Harry, it's cold back here," Doey said from the back seat of the car.

Carolyn said, "Put your arms around her, Wynn. That will help warm her up."

"He's doing that, Carolyn, but I'm still cold."

"Turn the heat up, Harry," Carolyn said.

"It's all the way up," Harry replied.

"What you need is a nip of Old Crow. It's guaranteed to make you forget the cold." He passed the bottle over his shoulder saying, "Wynn, you had better have a wee sip yourself."

I took the bottle and said to Doey, "Do as Harry says. Just think of something worth toasting, maybe like your future."

Doey tilted the bottle and said in a voice so low that only I could hear, "To our future." I took the bottle, and took a small swallow and repeated what Doey had said.

"What was that?" Carolyn asked.

"It's none of your business," Doey said.

Arise My Love And Come Away With Me

I passed the bottle to Carolyn and asked, "Won't you and Harry join us?" Harry turned onto Franklin Street and a couple of minutes later we arrived at Danziger's.

Harry requested a table in the corner where the light was dim. It was so dim that the prices on the menu were difficult to read. A cheerful waiter came to take our order. His name was Jack Palance. He spoke to Harry and Carolyn as old friends, and Harry introduced him to Doey and me.

Much of Jack's prime time was spent acting in college plays. It was said that he spent so much time at The College Play House, called "The Sound and The Fury," that his mail was delivered there.

Acting was his love. Restaurant waiter and prizefighting were only the enablers that helped keep him barely solvent. He was a serious student, but the study of acting kept him focused on Hollywood. Many years later the world would know him as a Hollywood actor, who was cast as a gunfighter in many western pictures. One picture that will bring Jack into focus is the role he had in the classic western, *Shane*. Jack took our dinner orders and turned to leave. He knew Harry was a big spender who left good tips, but first, he and Harry were good friends.

To us Harry said, "Forget the prices. This night is my treat. When we started this semester I knew Carolyn and barely knew Doey, and we had no knowledge of Wynn. Now here we sit, four strangers that have become good friends." Harry turned to Jack and said, "Bring us four cups of your special beverage. It's the one that features a cherry."

"Right away, Harry," he said. "I'm sure Doey and Wynn will like it."

"A cup of what?" Doey asked.

"It's called a Manhattan," Harry said.

When we left the restaurant we had another drink, or I should say a sip of Old Crow from Harry's bottle. We were on our way to Egan's, just two blocks away, so Harry made a U-turn on Franklin Street. The sound of a siren alerted us that the campus cop, who was parked nearby, was pulling us over. He stopped us, not for drinking, but for making an illegal U-turn. He said, "Follow me."

We followed him to the campus police station, where we were sure to be reported to the dean of our school for a sentence to fit the crime. At the station we stood before the desk of a sergeant who gave us the standard lecture. His desk sat on a platform about two feet above the floor so that he could look down upon us.

I was standing closest to the desk so that he could barely see me. Carolyn and Doey were standing close to Harry, who had the bottle of Old Crow in the pocket of his topcoat. He realized that if they found the bottle on him, we would all be in real trouble. So with Carolyn standing close, Harry slipped the bottle to her. She passed it to Doey and Doey slipped it to me. If we were caught, I would be the one to answer to the dean.

I noticed that the sergeant's desk sat a few inches off the raised platform, and wondered if there was enough clearance to hide the bottle under the desk. It would be a tight fit, but it was the only hope I had. Carefully, I slipped the bottle under the desk without anyone noticing. The lecture ended and we were dismissed.

When we walked out to our car, Harry said, "Where's the bottle?"

"Under the sergeant's desk," I replied sheepishly. Everyone laughed as we got into the car and drove off.

Chapter 25

The Trip to Terre Haute

Thanksgiving break was upon us. Harry and I found Carolyn and Doey waiting for us at the Tri Delta House. Harry drove us to the Durham train station and parked. We entered the station, which was beginning to fill with students on their way home for the holiday, and we found a table by a window. Harry excused himself and went to the lunch counter and returned with coffee.

"This looks serious," Carolyn said to Doey. "You have known Wynn for a few months, and today you're taking him home for the holiday?"

Doey blushed. "You know that's not so, Carolyn. When I found out that Wynn decided to remain on campus, I invited him to have Thanksgiving with my family, and nothing more. And while we're on the subject why didn't you and Harry invite him to have Thanksgiving with you?"

"We did," Harry said. "He turned us down and said that he was going to remain on campus to study. I think he owes us an explanation." He turned to me and said, "Speak up, Wynn. Why did you turn us down?"

"Well, it's this way," I said. "Doey has a dog named Brindy, a Scotty, who just happens to live in Terre Haute. I know it sounds a bit weird, but that's the way it is. I'm going to visit Brindy."

Carolyn smiled and said, "We love you, Wynn. Now Doey, tell us the real reason why you invited Wynn to go home with you." Before she could reply the loudspeaker announced that the train for Terre Haute was in and now ready to board. I looked at my watch. It was ten minutes past six in the morning. The train was on time.

"Doey," Carolyn said, "I have known you since your freshman year, and you have never invited any man into your home to spend even a day, much less a weekend with you, until you met Wynn. Harry and I want to know why?"

I broke in and said, "I've already told you why, Carolyn. If you're not satisfied with that answer, would you believe that for some mysterious reason I have received an invitation from Mrs. Brooks to be their guest for Thanksgiving? I do not know who, what, when, where or why, but you do know that I want to be with Doey."

Harry picked up our bags and escorted us to the steps of the train, where we hugged, kissed, and said our goodbyes. Carolyn would be going with Harry to Winston Salem to be with Harry's family for the holidays.

Doey and I boarded the train and walked a few steps down the aisle to our compartment and sat down. Through the frosty window we could see Harry and Carolyn standing in the cold gray break of day, waving, until distance removed them from our sight. I shed my hat, coat, and gloves and helped Doey out of her Arctic coat, and placed them with our bags above our seats. I looked down at Doey, and a warm feeling of contentment settled around me. I sat down beside her and said, "What is the real reason that you invited me to go home with you for Thanksgiving? I hope that you share my reason for accepting the invitation. It would have been lonely on campus thinking about you. For whatever your reason may be, I am thankful to be sitting here beside you."

Doey gave me her Mona Lisa smile and said, "I know why and so do you. I will never tire of hearing you say 'I love you.' I'm beginning to believe it. We have . . ." she paused, and with a pensive look said, "we have a lifetime before us, and a war to win." The thought of war brought with it the realization that there may not be another time or place. I picked up her hand, and in silence we sat there letting our minds run free with thoughts of what might be.

It was a long train ride, but our conversation seemed effortless and the time passed quickly. Before we knew it, the train began to slow. Through the window I saw street lights with halos that added a holiday touch, and a sky full of falling snow. Sounds that only a train can make while moving into a station rivaled the voice of the conductor, who shouted, "Terre Haute! Terre Haute, Station!" The passengers rushed about trying to be first in line when the exit doors opened.

"Keep your seat," I said to Doey. "There's a better way to leave the train."

"I agree," she replied. "Stepping off the train is better than being pushed off."

I got our belongings down from the overhead rack and helped Doey into her coat. At the door, with bags in hand, we stepped into the snowy November chill. Doey scanned the crowd looking for her father. I heard someone call her name, and I pointed to the calling voice.

"It's Edward. In this weather, I expect Daddy is waiting in the car."

"It's good to see you, Miss Doey," Edward said. "Welcome home."

"It's good to be home, Edward. Is Daddy in the car?" Doey asked as she turned to introduce me. "This is Mr. Wynn Cary. He has come to spend the holiday with us."

"Welcome, Mr. Wynn," Edward responded. "I have heard the family speak of you and I'm pleased that you have joined us." He picked up our bags and said, "Miss Doey, your father has been detained at his office and will see you at home."

We followed Edward to the parking lot where their Chrysler station wagon would take us to their home. I opened the rear door and followed Doey into the back seat. On the way home, Doey said to Edward, "Please drop the 'Miss'. For more than twenty years I have been Doey to you and you have been Edward to me. It's too late to change now."

I chimed in to say, "Edward, I would be pleased if you would just call me Wynn."

"Thank you, Wynn," he replied.

Light from a three-quarter moon lit our way through the frigid evening air. Along the way we passed through an area of parkland. Doey said, "At the top of the incline, the park ends and we will be less than a mile from home. When you and I fly, we silently repeat a line from your special poem. When I come home, I have always repeated a line from my special song 'Back home again in Indiana'."

"It's beautiful and appropriate," I said. "May I use it too?"

"Of course, I knew you would say that."

At the top of the hill, we silently murmured, "Back home again in Indiana." I squeezed her hand and kissed her forehead. In the rearview mirror I detected a smile on Edward's face.

Edward turned into a circular driveway. Every light in the two-story house was lit, spilling its glow onto a mantel of new snow. The door opened and standing there to greet us were Mr. and Mrs. Brooks and Edward's wife Anna. Joyful greetings were exchanged and I received more than my share of attention to let me know that I was welcome. We were standing in the entrance hall. To the right was a staircase which rose to the second floor. A crystal chandelier hung from the middle of the ceiling to a few feet above a round dark table with an oriental vase filled with colorful flowers.

Doey and I followed her parents to the library. We had just sat down when we heard a yelp coming from the stairway. With short legs hitting on all four, like the soft rhythm beat of a drum, Brindy, wagging his tail and with barks of love, greeted his mistress, who had finally found her way home. Doey patted her lap and instantly Brindy jumped up and started covering her face with kisses. I could see that I had a serious competitor.

Mrs. Brooks said to us, "I know that you would like to freshen up after your long trip. Dinner will be served at seven-thirty. Take your time and come down when you are ready. Edward, please show Wynn to the guest bedroom."

I followed Edward to the second floor, where he opened the door to my room. With my permission, Edward unpacked my suitcase and hung up my clothes in the closet. He turned the bedside lamps on and they cast a soft glow over the beautifully furnished room. I thanked Edward and he left closing the door behind him. I showered, shaved, and dressed for the evening in gray slacks, white shirt, and a black tie. I slipped on a black sport jacket and returned to the library where Mr. and Mrs. Brooks were listening to the war news broadcast from London. A few minutes later, Doey and Brindy appeared in time to hear Murrow say, "Good night and good luck." Doey came and sat down next to me.

"You two make a handsome couple," Mrs. Brooks said. Doey was wearing a pale blue cocktail dress that accentuated the beauty of the girl I loved. On a scale of one to ten, she was an eleven.

Doey's parents were seated on the sofa in front of the fireplace, where a kaleidoscope of colors danced and swayed to the soft background music of Mozart's concert in A Flat Major. Lamps spread a glow that completed the tranquility of the room. Mr. Brooks offered us a drink, cautioning us to always drink responsibly.

Edward came in and announced that dinner was ready. Brindy led the way to the dining room. I helped Mrs. Brooks and Doey into their chairs and took my place across the table from her. We bowed our heads as Mr. Brooks offered a word to God, thanking Him for a day that brought us together and for the abundance of food on our table. Together we said, "Amen."

Edward served a leafy green salad, oysters Rockefeller, medium rare roast beef, asparagus, and baked potato topped with sour cream and chives. Into our wine glasses Edward poured a Cru 1 Margaux red wine that was so good, I instantly became addicted to a wine that I could never hope to afford. I looked at Doey and wondered if, given the opportunity, I could ever give her a life like this. The look on her face assured me that I could. Our dinner conversation centered on the war in Europe. It was real and it was sure to involve us. It was difficult for me to speak of our involvement without bringing flying into the discussion.

The next morning, Doey was showing me around the house. We went up to her room, where I asked and listened as she answered my many questions about the people in the pictures on the wall. I felt a pang of jealousy when I asked her about the boy with her in one of the pictures. They were standing in swimsuits on the beach in front of her summer cottage at Macatawa. Doey looked so beautiful in a two-piece swimsuit that she bordered on breaking the public decency laws. He had the build of a quarterback on a high school football team, and the looks to go with it. I compared that with a mirror image of me, and felt that I was holding a losing hand. The smiles they shared spoke of a summer love. I was certainly outclassed in looks, but could he play a clarinet and fly a plane? That wasn't much of an accomplishment, but it was all I had. Pointing to the boy in the picture, I asked "Who is that?"

"Oh," she said, "that's George Ellis, a neighbor here in Terre Haute. His family also has a summer home at Macatawa. Our families have been friends forever. George and I have been friends since grammar school. You'll meet him. He's enrolled in the Wharton School of Economics at the University of Pennsylvania."

Oh goody, I thought. I could feel a touch of resentment that settled around my heart. I paused at every picture and pennant on the wall that included Doey. She paused a moment at every question to let her mind gather the facts, and then answered with a soft lyrical voice that assured me that I, for the moment, was her companion of choice.

There were only two other pictures with 'What's-his-name' and Doey. One was of a grammar school celebration, where Doey and George were dancing around a maypole. The other one was taken of the two of them on the back lawn of the Brooks' home. They held Easter baskets filled with chocolate eggs and Easter bunnies. He was too young to be a threat. So is a disease, when first discovered, too harmful to be a threat, but it grows with age. Keep your eye on that kid, was my thought.

Doey challenged me to a game of rotation pool, so we descended into the cellar game room. There I was awed by the extent of the extravagant collection of items that even professional clubs do not offer their members. Doey picked up the cue ball and set it about a foot from the bottom edge of the table's cushion. "Grab a cue," she said. "We will each shoot the cue ball at the other end of the table where it will rebound and return to this end of the table. The one whose ball is closest to the cushion on this end wins the right to break the rack of balls. You are my guest so you shoot first."

"Am I allowed to test the resilience of the cushion?" I asked.

"Sure. Take as many test shots as you like."

I selected a cue and applied chalk to its tip and hit the ball with just enough speed to send it to the other end of the table and return where it lightly struck the rail cushion and rolled back about two inches from the edge.

Doey said, "You've played this game before!"

"I do what I can to earn a few bucks when I need money to fly," I replied with a smirk.

"What shall we play for?" she asked.

"If I win, you will play the piano and sing; and if you win, I will do anything you ask of me for the rest of the day."

"It sounds like you intend to win," she said.

"Male pride," I replied.

Doey took aim and hit the ball hard enough to send it into the cushion where it rebounded and rolled back to the end of the table and came to rest an inch from the cushion. "You're either lucky or a pool room hustler. It's your break," I said.

The break scattered the balls leaving a choice of shots. In about ten minutes, except for one ball that clung to the lip of a corner pocket, the table was clean. My shot barely touched the ball and it dropped into the pocket.

"Well," I said, "that's one that I didn't deserve to win, but I'll take it. Rack 'em up. It's my break." Doey was intensely competitive. To her the world was a jigsaw of puzzles, and it was her job to solve them all. We played four more games. Our final score was three to two. The game was over. "You owe me a song," I said.

We walked to the piano. She sat down and played a few chords and said, "I wish you had your clarinet." A few feet from the piano was a set of drums, base, cymbals, and a snare with sticks and a pair of brushes. I had never played drums and knew nothing more than the importance that a good drummer is to a band.

Doey played a few notes strung together with the pleasing sound of chords that introduced "A Fine Romance." "Hold it one second, Doey. Let me play along with the brushes. They will add a soft background to the music. Just start and I'll jump in somewhere along the way." Doey replayed the introduction and established a time.

At the chorus, her voice added a lovely touch that made the music come alive, and softly the brushes added a bit of color to the musical picture. We played several other numbers ending with "Stardust."

We heard applause and looked up to find Mrs. Brooks standing at the foot of the stairs. "It was beautiful," she said, "I'm sorry to interrupt, but it's time for lunch." As she turned to go, Doey said, "Thank you, Mother, we'll be right up."

"Doey," I said, "you have a beautiful voice. I would like you to be a guest vocalist at one of our dances."

"Oh," she replied, "I'm not good enough for that."

"I'm not good enough to play in a band either," I said, "but we all hang in there together. It gives the illusion that we know what we're doing. You can sing and you're beautiful and I love you, and it's time for lunch."

Anna's luncheon was special for Doey and me. Edward served a bowl of Boston chowder and cheeseburgers with pickles, onions, and relish on the side. For dessert we had hot apple pie topped with vanilla ice cream. Doey's parents opted for a different luncheon that included a glass of Burgundy wine.

During lunch I told Mr. and Mrs. Brooks how beautiful their home was, and said that I had never been a guest in a house so beautiful, that its picture belonged on the cover of *Better Homes and Gardens* magazine. "It is truly a classic, and I am privileged to be here."

"Thank you, Wynn. We're very glad that you are here to share our Thanksgiving holiday," Mr. Brooks said. "Dorothy and I are only the caretakers. The house was built more than one hundred years ago when land was almost a gift. It's big for the reason that Great, Great Grandfather Brooks had a big family. There have been no changes to the original structure of the house, and only a few minor changes have been made to the interior. Most of the furnishings are antique. If he could walk into his home today, among his surprises would be the telephone, radio, electric lights, plumbing, and the automobiles. Otherwise, the house would be pretty much as he left it. The barn is large enough to stable five horses and a sleigh. All this is land that once belonged to him. Doey," he said, "perhaps you'd like to show Wynn the names that are carved on the walls of the stable tack room."

"I plan to do that, Daddy, but for now we plan to go to the Rex to see *Love Affair* starring Irene Dunne and Charles Boyer. After the movie we will stop at the record shop to buy Judy Garland's record. Mother likes the song "Over the Rainbow".

"Aren't you trying to do too much for one day?" Doey's mother asked.

"I don't think so," Doey replied. "We'll be home by three and our reservation for dinner is at seven. We may even have time to see the carvings in the stable."

"Just be very careful driving," her mother said. "I know the roads have been cleared of snow, but there are still patches of ice."

"Don't worry, we will," Doey said. "Please excuse us."

I stopped by the kitchen on the way out to tell Anna how much Doey and I enjoyed the special lunch she had prepared. Edward met us at the front door with our coats and hats. "I have started the car and turned the heater on," Edward said. "Drive carefully."

"I will," Doey replied.

Doey was driving carefully, especially on the uphill grade. However, with the icy road conditions, the car slid backwards and ended on the opposite side of the road. We sat there and watched other cars creeping by.

"What did I do wrong?" she asked.

"Nothing," I replied. "You just hit some ice. In fact, the chains on your car broke up the patch of ice, making it a little safer for the others to follow."

Calmly, Doey started the engine, put the car in low gear, and cautiously eased into the traffic. "That might be true," she said. "Let's try it again." Without a problem we topped the hill and were now on level ground.

We parked in front of the drugstore and walked across the street to the Rex Theater. We were standing in line inching our way to the ticket booth when I heard a male voice say, "Hey, Doey, we didn't expect to see you until tomorrow." The man looked at me and with an outstretched hand said, "Hello, I'm George Ellis."

"He's the one you asked me about—the one in the picture, remember?" Doey said.

"Hello, George," I said as I took his hand in mine.

George then introduced Jane Gaynor. "She's in Arts and Science at the University of Pennsylvania. Jane and I are going bowling. Why don't you come with us? You can see this movie anytime."

Jane's beautiful face, shaped like a heart, was surrounded by curly chestnut-brown shoulder-length hair. She had deep blue sparkling eyes, and a friendly smile. The long, heavy Burberry coat that hung from her shoulders could not hide her curvaceous shape. She wore a fur-lined hat with ear flaps, not beautiful, but warm. Jane said, "Yes, please come with us."

Doey looked at me and said, "Shall we?"

"Of course," I said. I took Doey's hand and we followed Jane and George to the bowling alley.

Jane was first to bowl. She came up with a gutter ball and ended with a spare. George left one pin standing. At the end of four games, Doey was declared the winner. Jane was a close second. George and I tied for last place. When we left the bowling alley, George whispered to me and said, "You weren't trying, were you?"

"Neither were you," I replied. We walked across the street and stood talking in the bright sunshine of a cold November day.

"It's too cold to stand here and talk," George said. "I think we should go to the Malt Shop for a hot drink."

"Good thinking, George," Doey said. "Lead on."

The Malt Shop and the hot chocolate provided the right setting for the frigid day, and a meeting place for longtime friends. Doey and George shared the memories of their life's friendship that now included Jane and me. George looked at his watch and said, "Oh my, it's already time for us to go. He paid the bill and once more we stood outside in the cold November air.

"We'll see you tomorrow for Thanksgiving dinner," Doey said. "Come early."

"Of course," George replied. "Our families have had Thanksgiving dinner together as far back as I can remember."

"That's true," Doey said. "And wouldn't it be nice, if the four of us carry on that tradition?"

We said our goodbyes and I was relieved to know that George was happily occupied and would be no threat to my amorous pursuit. On the way home we stopped at the record shop and then the floral shop, where I bought a corsage for Doey to wear at dinner that evening.

Chapter 26

Thanksgiving 1939

The sun had thawed the ice and the blue sky, with a few stratus clouds, promised a good day for Thanksgiving. On the horizon, however, I could see a touch of darkness forming. Before entering the house, I said to Doey, "I don't think we should mention the car sliding on the ice."

"I was about to say the same thing," she replied.

We walked into the library where Doey's parents were playing a card game and listening to music. "We're back," Doey said.

"Did you have a nice time?" John asked.

Her mother added, "Did you enjoy the movie?"

"We didn't go," Doey said. "We met George and his girlfriend Jane and went to the bowling alley instead; where Wynn and George, I'm sure, let Jane and me win. We went to the Malt Shop with them and had hot chocolate. After that we stopped at the record shop and brought this present for you, and now here we are."

"Well, thank you," Dorothy acknowledged.

"Would you like for me to play your new record?" Doey asked.

"That would be wonderful."

While Doey and her mother were talking, Mr. Brooks said to me, "I have something in the morning room that you might like to see." I was curious and followed him.

When we entered the morning room he closed the door and said "Wynn, I was just coming from the stable when I saw a car sliding backwards down the hill and ending up on the wrong side of the road, and it looked very much like our car. Who was driving?"

"Yes," I replied, "it was your car." To protect Doey I wanted to say that I was driving, but I felt sure that he knew that Doey was behind the wheel and I didn't want to get caught in a lie. "Doey was driving," I said, "and I know that had you been there you would have been pleasantly surprised at the way she handled the situation. We were almost at the top of the hill when we hit a small patch of ice. The back wheels lost traction and the car began to slide backwards. Doey showed no signs of panic. She made the right movements with the wheel and brakes and guided the car to a safe landing. I was very proud of her calm approach to a problem that could confront anyone. We decided not to mention the incident, for the reason that it was minor and we didn't want to alarm her mother. I hope that we made the right decision."

"In my opinion, you did. Shall we return and listen to Dorothy's new record?"

"Yes," I said. "If we are asked why we left the library, I would like to leave the answer to you."

"I can handle that," he said.

When we walked into the den, Mrs. Brooks said, "What are you two up to?"

"As Doey would say, that's our little secret, but if you must know, I was showing Wynn our family book of autographs."

"What did you think of the book, Wynn?" Dorothy asked.

Arise My Love And Come Away With Me

While I couldn't tell the truth, I hoped to bring closure to the troubling question by telling a partial truth. "I would like to spend more time with the book, but time is short and I may have to wait for another opportunity." Let's see them get around that answer.

At six o'clock Doey and I were ready to leave for the club. I wore gray slacks, a white shirt, a dark blue sport coat, and a paisley tie. Doey wore a lavender evening dress and her pearls. The white corsage was the right touch. Her mother said, "You two look beautiful. Have fun and drive carefully."

"We will," Doey said, as she kissed her parents.

Edward was at the door with our coats, and told us he had started the car and turned the heat up. "Have a good time."

"Thank you, Edward," I said.

A little less than thirty minutes later, we were greeted by Dodd, the maitre'd. "Welcome, Miss Brooks."

"Good evening, Dodd. This is Mr. Cary. He's with us for the holiday."

Dodd nodded to me and said that he was glad to meet me. "We have reserved a table for you and your guest by the bandstand. I was just following your father's instructions."

"When did you see Daddy?" she asked.

"About a week ago your mother and father were here for lunch; but I spoke with him about an hour ago." We followed Dodd to the table. Dodd said to Doey, "I'm sure that you know Vince. He will be your waiter tonight."

"Of course, Vince and I have been friends for seventeen years."

Vince looked at Dodd and said, "I've known Doey since she wore pigtails and would only order a glass of milk and a peanut butter and jelly sandwich for lunch or dinner, if she could get away with it. Did Mr. Brooks tell you to put her at my table?"

"As a matter a fact he did," Dodd answered. "Please enjoy the evening and give my best to your parents." He turned and went back to his stand where people were waiting to be seated.

"Can I get you something to drink?" Vince asked as he gave us our menus.

I looked at Doey and said, "Manhattan?" She nodded. "Two, if you please."

"Right away," he replied.

While waiting for our drinks, like a blotter, my mind absorbed the image of my beautiful Doey and the soothing sounds of the orchestra playing "I Didn't Know What Time It Was". It was a moment to remember. I heard Doey say, "Come back to me. Where are you?"

"Sorry, I was busy taking mental pictures of you surrounded by the music." Vince brought our drinks and set them before us. We raised our Manhattans and toasted to our future. "May it last from this moment on."

"Just remember, forever is never too much time," she replied.

"Would you like to dance?" I asked.

"I'd love to." The band was playing "Sunrise Serenade".

We returned to the table when the band took a break, and I gave Vince our dinner order, which included an entrée of medium rare roast beef, baked potato, and a green salad. For dessert we chose chocolate mousse and coffee. We were down to dessert when we heard the band start to play.

We moved to the dance floor and I took her in my arms. It took only a moment to establish a step in time with the music. Doey looked up at me and smiled, then closed her eyes and moved as if she was in a peaceful sleep. I pulled her a little closer and whispered, "Now where are you?"

"I was thinking of you and the night we met. If Harry had not asked me to dance, I may never have met you."

"Yes," I said, "and if you had gone to another law school, I wouldn't have met you; but that didn't happen. We did meet and here we are, two people wishing that this night would never end."

"We have a lifetime before us," she replied, "and we will dream together and every day will be one worth remembering."

At eleven thirty the orchestra played "Goodnight, Ladies". We joined the revelers and headed for home. Cumulus clouds heavy with snow, riding a wave of cold air, were precursors of a gathering storm. Feeble light filtered through a break in the clouds. A romantic drive in the light of a full moon changed the scenario. Like lanterns, the lights of the car ran before us showing the way home.

When we arrived, we parked and talked of the war on the horizon, that each day moved closer. At the door, she handed me her key and said, "Keep it, I have another." We walked in and softly closed the door.

"There's a light in the library. Your dad is probably waiting up for you."

"I don't think so," she said. "My father trusts me, and I trust you. Anyway, if he didn't trust you, we wouldn't be here." We sat on the sofa and watched as the flickering light of the embers in the fireplace turned to ash.

"Doey," I said, "many times I have told you what you mean to me. You are my one and only love, but I don't believe that I have ever asked you to be my wife. I would like to correct that omission and ask. Will you marry me?"

"You didn't have to say that. I knew that you would get around to it. You know the answer is yes. You are also my one and only love."

"How do you think your parents will react?" I asked.

"I don't know. I think they like you. I know that Anna and Edward do, and even if they all say they don't, it wouldn't matter to me. It's you I love and you that I will marry, but it would be nice to have them on our side."

I looked at my watch and said, "Happy Thanksgiving. It's two o'clock, and four hours past bed time." We walked up the back stairs where we paused in the hallway to share a goodnight kiss. I watched as she disappeared into her room and closed the door.

Sleep evaded me. I lay in bed dreaming of a future with too many possibilities. I had nothing to offer Doey in the way of the luxurious life to which she had become accustomed. I still had a year and half before the university would release me to an uncertain future. Every day, like the sun, the threat of war rose higher over the rim of the world. On a table beside the bed was a radio. I turned it on to listen to a recap of the day's news, but it was not good.

It was November 23, 1939. I was up at six with a mind overflowing with more problems than answers. I went down the back stairs to the kitchen where Anna was mixing something in a bowl. She looked up. "Good morning. Did you and Doey enjoy your evening at the club?"

"Yes, thank you, Anna, we did. Where is Edward?"

"He'll be down soon. Mr. Brooks arises at six. Edward goes up to make sure that he's up and dressed. It's a routine that Mr. Brooks and Edward have kept for many years. Mr. Brooks has breakfast at six thirty, and at seven he's off to his office. Of course, on holidays like today, he takes the day off. When Edward returns, I will tell him that you would like you're coffee in the morning room."

"Yes, please. You have a good memory, Anna."

While waiting for the coffee, I read the local paper. The headlines were grim. The news that followed settled many of the doubts that haunted me. It was clear that a long war was awaiting my future and my life with Doey, a life that would not begin until after the war.

Edward walked in with a pot of coffee and set the tray on the table between two chairs. "Shall I pour your coffee?" he asked.

"Yes, please."

I looked up when I heard Mr. Brooks say, "Pour one for me too, Edward. Good morning, Wynn. Did you and Doey enjoy the club last night?"

"Yes, we did. It was a wonderful evening," I replied.

Mr. Brooks settled in a chair before the fire, then said, "Doey's mother and I see very little of her since she started college. We miss her very much." He paused. "I'm so pleased that she has so many good friends. Every week she writes to us and recently your name is mentioned in every letter. More and more her spare time revolves around the dances that she attends where you are playing or the days and nights that she flies with you. It's easy to see that her intrusion into your life must stop."

"Mr. Brooks, I encourage her to come to the dances and to fly with me. I assure you that I am an honorable man. If there were any advantage to be gained, it would come from my intruding into her life. When we are together, we speak of only of the coming war and our future. She knows that for now I have nothing more than my devotion to offer." I hesitated. "I have said more then I intended. I'm sure that Doey will speak to you and Mrs. Brooks. I know that it is my responsibility to make a case that hopefully will satisfy you both regarding our intentions. Doey wanted you and her mother to be the first to know what we are prepared to do. I know that this conversation is somewhat out of sequence, and I respectfully ask, and would be greatly relieved, that Doey learns nothing of this conversation until after we find the right time to talk more about my interest in your daughter."

"You have made a good case," Mr. Brooks said. "I will keep this conversation private and we'll talk again later."

"Thank you, Mr. Brooks." I poured a little more coffee into our cups and we sat by the fire as we spoke of the day ahead.

Mrs. Brooks and Doey, led by Doey's Scotty, Brindy, entered and shut the door behind them. We exchanged morning greetings. Doey kissed her father and then came to me and said, "Good morning, darling," and kissed me. We had never shown any visible affection before her parents before, and I was relieved when she said that she just had a talk with her mother.

She sat down and said, "Daddy, I want you and Mother to be the first know that Wynn has asked me to be his wife, and I told Wynn that I wanted to talk with you first. He objected, saying that it was his responsibility to speak with you. I know that we have only known each other a little less than three months." She paused to gather her thoughts, and then she continued. "After one month and a flight in the moonlight with him, I knew that I was in love. Last night Wynn asked me to be his wife. All I could say was, 'What took you so long to ask?'

"I was awake most of the night worried that I was making a mistake in talking with you before Wynn did. If you had any objections I wanted him to know what they were. I know now that I was wrong, and I apologize to you and Wynn for being out of line. I just wanted him to know in advance what my parents might say." Turning to me she said, "Knowing that I will be your wife, Wynn, and whatever the outcome of your talk with my parents may be, I will never back down. I hope that you and my parents can forgive me."

"Of course, I forgive you, Doey, and as long as it's understood, when you become my wife, you are my responsibility. I want only the best for you. In the beginning it's understood that a degree in economics and aviation can't give us what we may want, but it will give us what we need. The only wild card is what the war may do, but we can't change that."

Mr. Brooks said, "I think that you and Doey have made your case. What do you have to say, Dorothy?"

"What more is there to say but welcome to the family, Wynn. I only hope that you won't rush into marriage. You both have a little more than a year to finish college."

I stopped her there with the assurance that there would be no more than talk of marriage before graduation, and possibly until after the war that was coming. Doey said to me, "Let's just leave the decision of before or after the war until later." I agreed.

"I have just one more thing to say. If you are to join our family, Wynn, please call me John."

Mrs. Brooks added, "Call me Dorothy; and, Wynn, I do have a question. Why did it take you three months to say that you loved my daughter? I met John on a train. We were on our way from Virginia to Chicago, and one month later we were married."

"I saw Doey get out of a plane and walk with her instructor into the debriefing room. I was about fifty yards away, and yet I knew, even then, that I was in love with her. It didn't take me three months, but it took a month to find her. Why don't you ask your daughter why it took two months to discover that she was in love with me? I was playing at a dance when my roommate, Harry Woods, came to the bandstand and introduced me to Doey. It was interesting to learn that she was enrolled in the Duke School of Law, and that meant she was intelligent as well as beautiful. It would have been a little more convenient if she had enrolled at UNC, but that too was not important."

My love for Doey was no longer a secret. I wanted everyone to know of our future together. After breakfast we went in search of Anna and Edward and found them standing in the doorway to the kitchen whispering as we approached. "What are you smiling and whispering about?" Doey asked.

"We're smiling about something Anna heard when she went up to make the bed in your room. The door to your parent's room was ajar and she couldn't help but hear what you and your mother were talking about. She quickly retreated, knowing that you and Wynn would be married. She heard the wonderful news. You know that Anna would never reveal even a word that is spoken here in confidence," Edward said.

"Please, Doey," Anna said, "you know that I would never pry or take advantage of any words spoken in our house. Whatever I hear stays here. Your mother and father always tell us what they want us to know, especially if it's important, and oh my, what I heard is ever so important. I hope that you won't tell them that we already know. I'm sure that they will find the right moment to tell us."

"We won't tell them," Doey said. "We just came to tell you ourselves. You and Edward are part of my family, and of course we wanted you to know." Doey and Anna put their arms around each other and hugged, smiled, and even wept a little.

"We're going to the stable," Doey said. "I want Wynn to see the carvings on the wall."

"It's freezing outside," Edward replied. "Be sure to bundle up good. The weather is changing fast and it may be snowing before you return."

At the coat room we found an assortment of cold weather gear and started the short walk to the stable, about three or four minutes from the house. Along the way we passed three trees with arrows painted on signs that pointed toward the house.

"What are the arrows for?" I asked.

"Have you read 'Snow Bound'?"

"Yes." I said. "It's a very long, epic poem by John Greenleaf Whittier that describes how fatal a day like this could be. Just change a word or two and the poem describes this very day." I changed the month from December to November and quoted the only verse that I could remember: "The sun, that brief November day rose cheerless o'er the hills of gray and darker circle gave at noon, and paler light than waning moon.' Now I know what the arrows are for. To lose your way in a blizzard could cost your life. The arrows point the way from the stable to the house." At the stable we watched, through the window as the fair weather prediction for today dissolved into a troubled dark purple sky, with its gift of snow

"I don't think that we will have to depend on the arrows to show us the way home today," Doey said, "but the ceiling and visibility are approaching zero, and depending on the condition of roads and the snow plow, we may not be able to leave at six in the morning, as we planned."

Doey started relating the story of the names on the wall. "I don't know who most of the people were, but their names have been researched and entered into the family list of early visitors. If you are interested, you may read all about them in the family's book of autographs. I'm sure that you will recognize the names Lindbergh, Harvey Firestone, and Thomas Edison. My parent's names are on the wall and when I was seven or eight years old, I asked why my name wasn't there. My father said, 'When you grow up and meet the man you love, he will carve your names on the wall.' 'When will that be?' I asked. 'You will know,' he said. Our names may never be known, but we will be listed in the Brooks Stable of Fame."

The oldest name on the wall was William Allen, dated 1765. Next to a wooden peg on the wall an antique harness hung with the name Freemont 1766 beside it. Another carving let us know that once a British soldier stood here and carved the name John Clancy and the date 1769. From 1765 to 1937, all the names, including the Brooks', who had called this place home, were found on the wall. The book of names was kept up to date by the family in residence.

"I would like to see our names carved on the wall," Doey remarked.

"What a wonderful thought, Doey, but the wall is paneled in very hard oak, which has become as hard as petrified wood. To carve our names and date may require more time than we have now, but it will be done. With a pencil I wrote our names and date, November 30, 1939, on the wall beside the window. I spotted a knife lying on the window sill and picked it up. I started carving Doey's name.

Edward came to tell us that our Thanksgiving guests had arrived. We put the name carving on hold and followed him through heavy snow to the house. In the library we found George Ellis, his parents, and Jane Gaynor talking with Dorothy and John, while "Day In-Day Out" played in the background. In the fireplace a blazing fire added warmth and beauty to the cheerful background of music for a dark, cold fall day.

Jane said, "Thank you, Mrs. Brooks, for allowing me to share this day with you and your family. I'm glad that I had the good judgment to accept

George's invitation to his home for this Thanksgiving holiday. Meeting all of you makes it very special."

"Any friend of George's is always welcome here," Dorothy replied.

George saw us as we entered the room, and said to me, "Dorothy told me that you and Doey are really pool hustlers. Let's go down to the pool room and rack up the balls."

George looked at Doey and said, "When we were ten years old I asked you to marry me. When I was eleven or twelve years old, I gave up and settled for you becoming my best friend. For all years past, and years to come, I will think of you as my best friend. I have brought Jane home to meet my family and yours. She is the girl that I have waited for. You, your family, mine, and Wynn, are the first to know. I'm sure that when the time is right, you will let us know who the man in your life is, Doey. The odds are ten to one that you already know."

"George," Doey said, "your friendship has always been special to me. Thank you for those beautiful words, I will remember them always."

"So will we," George Sr. added. Dorothy and George's mother Ann sat there wiping tears from their eyes. John and I sat there with contented smiles.

"Right on, George, a wonderful speech," I replied.

Doey said, "Let's get on with the day."

George led the way to the cellar door and paused on the steps leading down to the recreation room. I watched the expression on Jane's face as her eyes scanned the room that featured so much. "Wow! It's beautiful!" She exclaimed. "It's like seeing an entire home without walls. Not only is there a pool table and a bar, there is a living room with a fire in the fireplace, beautiful chairs, tables, a sofa, a piano, and a dance floor. What's behind that black door?"

Doey laughed and told George to open the door. George obliged. He stepped in and flipped a switch which lit a wine cellar and tasting room. There were two tables; each table could accommodate six wine tasting experts, who could sit, sip the wine, and speak in esoteric terms of nose and all the subtle aromas found in the wine. Until I could afford a vintage wine, I would have to leave the wine dissertations to the experts. I think that it was Mark Twain who said, "We're all ignorant . . . but not about the same things."

My introduction to fine wine was when I discovered that one bottle could be worth more than I could make in a month playing my clarinet. I have never acquired a taste for wine, unless it's a First Cru Rothschild, but that would require a loan from a bank!

Beyond the wine tasting room, dim lights lit a room of wine racks containing hundreds of bottles of wine, heavy with an accumulation of dust. "If you are now satisfied with the mystery of what's behind the door, let's play pool," Doey said with a laugh.

We played five games of rotation pool. Jane and George were declared the winners. Doey and I paid off with a few musical notes on the piano and a whisk or two of the brushes on the symbol snare drum, and a tap or two on the cymbals. I asked if Jane or George played the piano.

George said, "Jane does, she's ready to play a piano concert in Carnegie Hall, only they don't know that she's ready."

"This is Carnegie Hall, "Doey said as she stood, and made an exaggerated bow then moved aside. Jane took her place at the piano.

I spoke into a make believe microphone and said, "Good evening ladies and gentlemen of the listening audience. We're speaking to you this evening from Carnegie Hall in New York City. NBC is proud to bring, for your listening pleasure, the "Concerto No. 3" for the piano by Ludwig van Beethoven, played by the world famous pianist, Miss Jane Gaynor, accompanied by the New York Philharmonic Orchestra. Miss Gaynor is taking her place at the piano. George Ellis, concert maestro of the New York Philharmonic Orchestra, raises his baton, and with a down beat, Miss Gaynor begins to play."

Jane's rendition was flawless. She was, in our opinion, ready to play Carnegie Hall. When she concluded the concerto, Doey said, "You had better sign her up, Wynn, to play in your band."

"No," I remarked, "it would be like throwing mud on a rose!" Jane, of course, was the rose.

"Do you have a band, Wynn?" Jane asked. I nodded. I was too overwhelmed with her talent to speak. "What instrument do you play?"

"Clarinet and sax," I said, "but not very well." She played a tremolo of chords and smoothly picked up an eight-to-a-bar boogie woogie beat. We all applauded, and said, "More! More!"

Jane played and Doey sang most of the songs listed on *Down Beat's* list of songs of the week. I added a touch to the music's background by sweeping the brushes across the drum head and cymbal in time with the music. George stood in awe, listening to the talent of the girl he thought he knew.

"I didn't have the vaguest idea," he said to Jane. "I knew that you had a piano, and I have a piano. All I can play is chop sticks, and not very well."

"I got a scholarship to Julliard, but I opted for Princeton where I also was offered a music scholarship. If I had accepted the offer from Julliard, I wouldn't have met you." In that hour we formed a friendship that would last a lifetime.

Edward came down with a tray of appetizers and coffee and set the tray on the low table in front of the fireplace. We sat and changed our conversation from the carefree words of youth, to a new language called "war talk." Our teachers were Hitler, Chamberlain, Churchill, Mussolini, Roosevelt, and the Emperor of Japan.

It has been said by some, whose youth is growing short of days, let their minds take refuge in the past, to a time that was. I must admit that's true.

The organized killing started in 1939 when Hitler fashioned a reason to go to war with Poland. Neville Chamberlain, the Prime Minister of England, flew to Munich, Germany, hoping to lead Hitler down a path to compromise. When he returned to England, he stepped from the plane waving a paper with Hitler's signature. The paper spoke of peace in our time. The crowd, there to welcome him home, surrounded him and cheered. "Good old Neville, we knew he would find a way out!"

In Green Park, men, stripped to the waist, were digging trenches. They had put up a sign saying, "Westminster Strip Tease." The sun of summer covered London with a blanket of mild and soft weather.

And then there was war—but only in Poland. A stunned moment of disbelief fell over the land and around the world. Death, in a black shroud, smiled. For us, our world of wine and roses abruptly ended.

Our youth was threatened. Maybe we would find it in another place and at another time, but we had crossed the Rubicon, a point of no return, and there was no turning back. Time and place can exist only once, and then it moves on.

Jane said, "Do you think there will be war that involves us before we graduate?"

George replied, "Our government is busy building camps and airfields, and as the projects are ready for use, they will be turned over to the military. A few facilities have already been finished and are ready for use, but those students who have a year or less may be given an opportunity to complete their education, before induction."

"Do you have anything to add to that Wynn?" Doey asked.

"Not much," I said. "I would like to finish school before I'm called, but if we become involved in Hitler's war, and I believe we will, I believe that our part will mostly revolve around supplying England with the tools to fight. France has the Maginot line and the largest army on the continent. England will need help, but only in armament.

"For the last five years, Winston Churchill has been warning that if war is declared, England cannot hide behind her mighty navy. Their air force is made up of four or five hundred obsolete planes that cannot compete with the thousands of planes that Germany has or is building, even though the Versailles treaty was suppose to prevent Germany from building them. But nothing in the treaty prevents Germany from building gliders and flying them at sports events. And nothing prevents Messieurs Schmitt or Hinkle from designing engines. Put an engine on a redesigned glider frame and you have an airplane. Any glider pilot with minimum training can fly an airplane.

"German engineers are unencumbered with an accumulation of old aircraft technology dating back to the end of World War I. Red was telling me that for the past twenty years their engineers have worked in secret developing new technology used in the production of a superior air force that now commands the air over Europe.

"Germany is on a wartime economy. Everyone has a job. They have conquered the depression, and as the world stands by and watches, they are building a war machine capable of destroying the world. There are reports that they have built extermination camps where Jews, gypsies, and others who may be obstacles to their plan are put to death. It's pretty hopeless.

"England and France had signed a treaty to come to the aid of Poland, if she were attacked by Germany or Russia. They cannot, however, honor that pact, with nothing more than their navy. They don't have enough force to support their pledge."

I paused and reflected, "At least it's comforting to know that the ones we love will be protected by two oceans."

Edward came to tell us that dinner was almost ready. We put our war talk on hold and went upstairs. Brindy was lying on his back in his bed basket on the raised hearth. His head hung over the side, his eyes were closed, and his four paws pointed towards the ceiling. He was giving his version of a dead bug. Doey sat on the hearth beside him. He was surrounded by the family he loved.

Jane and George stood at a window watching the snow as it altered the looks of the landscape. I sat in a chair in front of the fireplace surrounded by the heads of two families, asking and answering questions that were nonintrusive and easy to answer.

Mrs. Ellis asked about my school and what my major was. When I said economics, George Sr. said, "My son is also studying economics. John told me that you are a pilot."

"Yes," I replied. "I fly a little." I looked at Dorothy, and quickly moved the conversation in another direction. Edward entered to tell us that dinner would be served in ten minutes.

We followed the aromas, emanating from the kitchen, to the dining room where a table for eight was beautifully set with Wedgewood china and more silver than the miners in the Comstock Lode could mine in a week. Brindy suddenly awakened and headed for the kitchen where he knew that Anna would fill his bowl with food that he seldom got, but this was also Thanksgiving for him.

After the ladies were seated, John took his seat at the head of the table. Place cards put me on John's left. On my left was Jane. Next to her was George Sr., and Dorothy was in her place at the foot of the table. On her left was Ann. Next to her was her son George Jr. who sat next to Doey. The circle was complete.

John said, "I would like to read a prayer that was written by Voltaire in the seventeenth century. When he wrote this prayer, he was imprisoned in the Bastille for speaking and writing treasonous words against the monarchy. It is a prayer for all times." John cleared his throat and began to read as we bowed our heads.

"To thee, God of all creatures, of all worlds, and of all ages, I address my petition. Thou hast not given us hearts so that we may hate one another, and hands that we may slay one another. Grant that the trifling differences in the clothes which we cover our frail bodies, in the inadequate tongues we speak, in our absurd customs, in our, imperfect laws, in our meaningless convictions, grant that all these trifling distinctions which appear so vastly important to us and are so insignificant in Thy eyes, grant that they may not become tokens of hatred and persecution. Grant that men may learn to abominate and outlaw tyranny over souls as they abominate and outlaw robbery and violence. And if wars may not be avoided, grant at least that we may not hate and tear on another in the midst of peace, but that we may employee our existence, in a thousand tongues yet in one united feeling, from Siam to California, in praising Thy goodness which has given us the brief moment that we call life.”

When the prayer ended, eight “Amens” echoed from around the table, and we looked expectantly as the kitchen door opened. Edward came in and poured white wine into our glasses.

John rose and said, “For the past nineteen years, Dorothy and I have spent most of our holidays with Ann and George Ellis. They are our closest and dearest friends. We always expected our children, Doey and George, would one day announce their wedding plans. For whatever their reasons may have been, it was not to be. God had other plans. Only this morning, He revealed them to Dorothy and me. Doey and Wynn have declared a future together. Dorothy and I are pleased with that decision; however the condition of the world today makes it very difficult to plan for tomorrow. I want you to know, Doey and Wynn, you will always have our support. The fondest hopes that Dorothy and I have is that you will each find a career to follow here in Terre Haute, although we know that's unlikely.

“You have lived through a devastating depression, only to enter a new life of hate, fear, and war. The radio and newspapers prepare us for the world of tomorrow that is to come. Knock on any door and you will find their conversations are laced with words of war supplied by William Shirer from Berlin and Edward R. Murrow from London. Along the rim of the world war clouds are forming.

“You have a little more than a year and a half of college, and by then you, Doey and Wynn, and Jane and George, will take your first step into a future ruled by the laws of war. We love you and will pray for you. Now, I say, Happy Thanksgiving.”

George's father stood and added his reply to John's remarks. “George confirmed to Ann and me that he and Jane have plans for a future together.

No date has been set, but Ann and I are very happy to welcome them—as we welcome Doey and Wynn—into our lives."

The Thanksgiving dinner had a solemn but wonderful beginning. Anna and Edward stood in the doorway smiling. Together, they served the first course. Edward carried the turkey, the symbol of Thanksgiving, on a silver platter and set it before John to carve. The dinner included turkey, dressing, hot rolls, mashed potatoes, gravy, sweet potatoes, cranberries, green peas, and carrots. For dessert, a choice of chocolate, Angel food cake, pumpkin, cherry or mincemeat pie, followed by coffee, tea or milk.

An hour later eight satisfied diners gave their thanks to Anna and Edward, moved into the living room, and sat by the fire. Thanksgiving Day was coming to a close. The clouds had dropped their cargo of snow and, pushed by the wind, had cleared the sky, revealing the light from a bright harvest moon. Edward had cleared the Brooks' walk from the door to the road, and from across the street, the walk from the road to the Ellis house was cleared by the Ellis house man.

We stood in the foyer shaking hands and saying our goodbyes. I liked the part where I shook George's hand, and kissed Jane. Doey got in the way, so I kissed her, too. Doey said, "You didn't have to do that, I live here."

"Oh, so you do. My mistake," I said. "I'll take it back." I kissed her again and said, "Now are you satisfied?" The guests left as Brindy was barking and wagging his tail. He took the lead and showed us the way to the library. There, Edward and Anna were cleaning up the clutter of newspapers, glasses and cups, and returning books to their shelves. Soon the room was in pristine order. Edward asked if there was anything more that he or Anna could do.

Dorothy said, "Not for the moment, Edward. Doey and Wynn will be leaving on the six a.m. train for Durham. Would you please make sure they are up and ready to go?"

"If we want anything more," John said to Edward, "we will take over the kitchen and forage for ourselves. I would like for you and Anna to take the rest of the evening off."

"Thank you," Edward replied. "Please call me at any time if you need anything. I have checked with the station, and they assured me the train will run on schedule. In any event, I will have them up and out on time."

"Thank you, Edward," I said. They were treating Doey and me as children. We knew the drill that required us to get up and catch an early morning train.

"It's been a wonderful Thanksgiving, Mother. I can't remember a better one."

I moved next to Doey, put my arm around her, and agreed, "Neither can I."

For three hours, or more, the four of us filled the room with words that ended with question marks. The way was made easier for me to answer from the status of being recognized as Doey's fiancé; and it was understood that only a few lines on a marriage license stood between the day Doey and I would legally belong together. Doey and I both knew that the moment that bound us forever was that first night that we flew in the moonlight. Our love was more secure than a page of endless lines upon some legal document.

Finally, John looked at his watch and said, "Hey, it's almost eight o'clock. Is anyone hungry?" Brindy heard the magic word "hungry" and happily showed us the way to the kitchen. An hour later, with our hunger sated, John said, "Mother and I are going up to our room. Don't you and Wynn stay up too late; you must be up at five." They walked up the back stairs and we went back to the library and sat on the sofa watching the fire consume the logs.

I called my mother and told her about Doey and me. "We're going back to Chapel Hill early in the morning and I will call you from there, where we will talk as long as you care to listen. I hope that you, Ruth, and Irene had a good Thanksgiving."

"Thank you, dear, we did. I'm so pleased that you and Doey found each other. Red and Sally were with us for the holiday. They will be leaving tomorrow for Maryland. One day we will all be together again. I love you, Wynn."

"I love you too, Mom." I waited for her to hang up. I sat there for a moment wondering why Red was going to Maryland, and what part Sally had to do with the trip. Then I returned my attention to Doey and said, "How do you feel, now that your parents have discovered what they already knew about us?"

"I'm relieved to know that you took advantage of our new status and kissed me in front of them," she said.

"Good gracious," I said in mock surprise, "I did that?"

"You sure did!" she exclaimed. "If you did it once it should be easier to do it again."

"Doey, my love, I just might do it again." It's easier to eat one potato chip and stop, than it is to kiss beautiful Doey once and stop.

"How about right now?" she said. I obliged without hesitation.

We sat on the sofa, watching the flames in the fireplace flicker, and listening to soft music coming from the Glen Island Casino on the shore of New Rochelle, New York. The music playing was "Do I Love You?" by Cole Porter. We ended the evening discussing love, marriage, and a year and a half of school yet to come.

Shortly after midnight we declared our Thanksgiving Day a complete success. I walked Doey up to the door to her room where I kissed her goodnight. She opened the door and said, "I love you so very, very much, Wynn. I wish that I could ask you in. At another place and time, I will."

"We have a lifetime before us," I replied.

Chapter 27

The Train to Durham

We were up at five a.m. and downstairs with our bags, ready to go. Brindy followed us into the morning room and lay down close to Doey's bag. A few minutes later John and Dorothy came in. John was dressed and said that he would see us off, and then Edward would drive him to the office. Dorothy said that she would say her goodbyes here.

Edward came in to tell us that breakfast was ready. "We should leave here in twenty minutes. Your bags are in the station wagon. I will be in the library waiting for you."

After we had eaten our breakfast, we gathered in the library long enough for Anna to give Doey a box of Thanksgiving leftovers to see us through the day. I thanked Anna, stooped down and spoke a few words to Brindy, and as a family of six we moved to the front door. For a moment we stood in silence. I hugged and kissed Dorothy on both cheeks and thanked her for the very best Thanksgiving that I could remember, and for trusting me with Doey's future. With tears in their eyes Doey and her mother spoke their words of love. Doey said a few "I love you" words to Brindy, and Edward said, "It's time to go."

Anna stood by the door with a box in her hand which she handed to me and said, "Now that you are a member of our family, I wish you and Doey the best of life ahead and a safe trip to Durham. Now I know that you will come again. Please make it soon."

I opened the door to a future with Doey and sat beside her in the back seat of the car. The drive to the station was slow. We arrived with only a few minutes to spare. At the station John spoke a few words of advice, ending with "Wynn, take care of my daughter."

"I will," I said, "with my life."

From the loudspeaker we heard "All aboard!" At the train I thanked Edward for his devotion to the family, and to me as a friend. Doey kissed her father, and together, with baggage in hand, we boarded the train. Through the window of our compartment, we could see John and Edward waving. The train started to move.

After placing our bags on the rack above our seats we removed our coats and hung them up. My first act was to kiss my bride to be. "Doey, do you know how very much I love you?"

"Yes," she replied, "I know that you do. However, in a moment when I was not thinking clearly, I promised Mother that we would not speak of marriage until after graduation, but waiting until after the war is too long. We must have another talk with her."

"We will," I said. "But for the moment, I'm happy just to know that we will be together from now until the end of time."

At noon, the receiver in our compartment came alive with an announcement that this was the first call for lunch. Doey laid her book aside, stood, and raised the table at the window. She reached for Anna's survival kit of food and placed it on the table and said, "Lunch will be served in two minutes." She removed paper plates, napkins, cups, plastic knives, forks and spoons, and set containers of whatever she found in the survival kit, in the space available on the small table.

I watched as Doey arranged the first meal of our commitment to a long life together. "There's a note," she said, and handed it to me to read.

Dear Doey and Wynn,

We want you to know how pleased, Edward and I are to know that Wynn will become a member of our family. We pray for you every night. Come back to us soon. We love you.

Anna and Edward

By the minute, the train sped closer to Durham. Doey said, "Before we left for Thanksgiving I asked Carolyn and Harry to have dinner with us when we returned. They'll meet us at the train. It's time for me to pretty up," and with that she disappeared. When she returned, she stepped out of the cubicle refreshed and glowing. "Your turn," she remarked.

There wasn't much that I could do to change my appearance, so I washed my hands and face and joined Doey.

The wheels screeched as the train began to slow down, emitting great puffs of steam as it came to rest in the Durham station.

With coats, hats, and baggage we left the train.

Chapter 28

Carolyn and Harry

Carolyn and Harry were there to meet us. We went through the expected routine of hugging and all talking at once. It was the mark of good friends meeting after an absence of many months, except we had only been separated by four days. In our case, we knew that our friendship would be with us for life. Youth would permit us the certainty that we would all grow old and die together of old age.

We spoke once more of Thanksgiving, and agreed that it was the best ever. Then Harry led the way to his car and we trailed along. Harry said, "Carolyn tells me that you bums are springing for a free dinner. Where are we going? All that I can get out of Carolyn is 'It's a secret.' It's time to let me know where to go."

Carolyn said, "Take us to the Durham Country Club."

When we arrived, Paul, the door man, opened the car door and greeted Harry, Carolyn, and Doey like old friends. Harry introduced Paul to me and said, "This is Wynn Cary. He heard that someone here is handing out free dinners and wants to get in line."

Paul said to me, "I've known these people for several years and I've never known them to miss a free meal. Just remember, 'free' is just a word, and free is always too expensive!"

I liked these people. They were honest, dependable, friendly, and they moved through life guided by logical and independent reasoning. They made their share of mistakes, but too few to matter. I was pleased to be counted as one of their friends, but what's the secret that Doey was about to tell us?

Paul opened the door and we entered the plush lobby of the country club and checked our coats and hats. Doey spoke to the maître d' saying, "We have a reservation for dinner."

"Yes, Miss Brooks, your table is waiting. I will show you the way. Please come with me."

"Thank you," Doey replied.

Standing at the table, a waiter named Sam, who obviously knew Harry, Carolyn and Doey for a long time, greeted them as friends. "Good evening, Sam," Doey said. "You know Miss Perry and Mr. Woods," and turning to me said, "and this is Mr. Wynn Cary."

"I'm glad to make your acquaintance, Mr. Cary."

"Thank you, Sam."

"What may I get for you?" Sam asked as he passed the menus around.

Harry said, "Manhattans would be nice."

"For everyone?" he asked.

"Yes," Harry said.

"If you don't mind the coffee cups, along with a coffee pot and a glass of crushed ice, I'll see what I can do. If anyone should ask, I can say that you ordered coffee and I can also say that you must have brought the Manhattan mix with you."

"You are a scoundrel, Sam," Harry said.

"I like that, Harry," Sam said with a big smile. "Say some more nice things about me." Sam left, giving Doey time to reveal her secret.

Arise My Love And Come Away With Me

Harry said, "You're on Doey. What's your secret?"

"This is something that we will share only with you and Carolyn." Doey lowered her voice and said, "While Wynn and I were home, Mother said to me that Wynn was the only man that I had ever invited to be an overnight guest, and that I must be very fond of him. I told her that when I learned that Wynn planned to remain on campus for the holiday and study for an upcoming test, it was then that I thought of inviting him to spend the Thanksgiving break with us.

"Mother said, 'Your father and I have known for some time that you are in love with Wynn. We expected that you would ask to invite him for Thanksgiving, but we didn't have a clue that he is in love with you.'

"I told her that 'we didn't come to ask for your or Daddy's permission for us to marry. I just wanted you to know more about Wynn. He has told me many times that he loves me, and I know he does. I assure you that I'm in love with him. The uncertainty of war makes plans for a future impossible. Until last night the word marriage has never been mentioned, but I'm sure that when the time is right he will speak with you about our future. Wynn has always been a gentleman and treated me with great respect, and last night he asked me to marry him. I want you and Daddy to know this.'

"Mother and I went down to the morning room where we found Daddy and Wynn in conversation. They looked up as we entered. Wynn stood and said good morning, and before I sat down, I said, 'Good morning' to Daddy, then I kissed Wynn and said 'Good morning, darling.' It was the first time that I had shown any affection for Wynn in front of them.

"Daddy said, 'Wynn, she just made your case.' My mother said she hoped that I would tell you what I had told her and I said that I would."

Carolyn looked at Harry and said, "I told you so. Doey took Wynn home to meet the family and they came back ready to be married."

"It's not that way at all, Carolyn. I went home with a mistaken idea that I would, without Wynn's knowledge, talk to my mother and father first, to learn of any objections they might have so that I could tell Wynn what they were. That was as far as I intended to go. I talked to Mother first. She thought Wynn was a very nice young man, and if he loved me as I did him, then after graduation, in a year and a half, they would have no objections to our marriage.

"I was already sure of my love for Wynn, and his love for me. I knew that if I wanted the moon, somehow he would find a way to get it, and whatever anyone might say; Wynn and I will always be together . . . forever. We will tell them when we intend to make it official, but we wanted you, our dearest friends, to know. That's our secret."

"It's beautiful," Carolyn said. "Harry and I will keep your secret."

Sam arrived with the pot of coffee, four cups, and a glass of crushed ice. Harry calmly divided the crushed ice into the four cups. He removed the screw tops of the four small bottles of Manhattan mix and poured it into the cups. Then he removed another bottle from his coat pocket that contained four cherries, with their long stems still attached. He placed one in each cup and passed them around. He put the empty bottles into his coat pocket, raised his cup, and said, "Here's a toast to our good friends, Doey and Wynn, and a secret that we will keep." We took a sip and set the cups down.

I raised my cup and said, "To our caring friends, Carolyn and Harry, and to our uncertain futures, may they treat us kindly. We touched cups and the sound of clicks put an extra seal on our friendship. Harry motioned for Sam to come and take our orders for dinner.

Sam said, "While you mixed the Manhattans, I closed my eyes. I want to be able to say, if I'm ever a witness at your trial, that I didn't see you mix those alcoholic drinks at a table I serve."

Harry chuckled, "Coward. It is my opinion that the law that prohibits serving alcohol to students is illegal. It's true that we are not twenty one, but they don't know that. They seldom ask us for evidence of age. Until they do, I will serve as my own bartender." Sam took our order.

We would remember remarks that were made during dinner that would serve as a reference point for Doey and me when we spoke of our youth as nineteen-year-old college students. And as the night progressed we became nineteen-year-old adults. From that point on there was no turning back. The uncertainty of adult life was to become our path to follow. Doey and I would use this night as a reference point that separated the world we knew from a world of violence that would change our lives forever. We would recall this night often, and I would recall days that she would never know.

When dinner ended, Doey signed the bill that would be sent to her father for payment. Harry and I drove Doey and Carolyn to their sorority house in time for them to slip through the door before the clock struck twelve.

Chapter 29

Sunday Outing

Thoughts of Doey replaced a successful day of music, and my economic books became my evening entertainment. Sunday morning at eight I called Doey to ask what her plans were for the day.

"I was about to call and invite you and Harry to be Carolyn and my guests for the ten o'clock service in the chapel, and luncheon later at the club. I hope you have no other plans."

"We had other plans . . ." I was about to continue and say, "But they can be changed." Doey broke in to say, "Such a short romance. I guess that I will have to call one of my Duke boyfriends. Maybe Joe Ridley could find time to escort me to chapel. If not I can probably find another man, but I don't have time, and it's you I love. Won't you please reconsider?"

"Well, you are expecting a lot on such short notice, but I did promise your father that I would look after you, and the promise I made is forever. When we are a hundred years old, ask me then if I still love you, my answer will still be, 'forever is such a short time.' You will still be my sweetheart, my darling, and I will still adore you. I have a pocketful of those words. They are special and I only use them when I'm talking to a very special girl. I think that our conversation is causing Harry to cry. Hang on for a second or two and I'll ask him."

Harry took the phone and said, "I heard enough of that drivel and I think that I heard the name Carolyn mentioned. Yes, whatever it is, I'll go. Tell Carolyn that we will be on our way in twenty minutes."

We were a little late when we walked into the crowded chapel and found seats in the back. The chaplain was speaking of a caring God who, in every war, is claimed by both sides. In World War I, the German military claimed that God was with them. To prove it, the belt buckles of their soldier's uniforms were adorned with the engraving 'God's with us.' In World War I, our Doughboys prayed to the same God and claimed that He was on their side. On November 11, 1918, in a railway car in Paris, God delivered his verdict. The Allies won . . . but the peace was short. Nineteen years later, Germany has rearmed, and threatens any country which stands in the way of their conquest of the world. At the end of an informative sermon, we believed that God was with us.

As the days of peace grew shorter, the dark shadow of war, like an ink blot, spread across the lands of Eastern Europe. Hitler found the reason he needed for war and invaded Poland. The peaceful days of 1939 had ended.

The future of our generation was changing. It was so gradual that, at first, it was little noticed. The threat of war brought out the best in people. Newspapers and radios broadcast the words that helped form our opinions. The churches grew in attendance, as the threat of war drew closer.

Monday morning my economics grade was posted. I got a B. I called Doey and said, "How are you fixed for free time?"

"I have classes until eleven," she said. "After that I'm free for the rest of the day. I can take the shuttle bus and meet you in Red's office at twelve thirty. How did you do on your test?"

"Better than I deserved," I said, "I got a B."

"I too have more than I deserve; I have you. Together we'll have a long lifetime and when we're ninety, we will fly to our home beyond the moon to the other side of beyond, where we will live forever," she said.

"You really do believe there's a place on the other side of beyond?" I questioned.

"Yes I do, but only because you told me there was. It was on our first flight in the moonlight."

"I really called to invite you and Carolyn to our band rehearsal. It will be at the Fetzer House Saturday morning at nine a.m."

"We'll be there," Doey said.

Saturday morning, we met at the Fetzer House for practice. Carolyn and Doey were talking with Helen, as members of the band ran random scales, producing sounds in a key that could be called "the loud key of confusion." To the musician it's called "warming up."

Harry and I finished our conference; the musicians were in their places. I picked up my clarinet and said to Paul, "Give us an A, Paul." We tuned our instruments to the clean tone produced by the A key of the piano.

After an hour practice, I said, "That's a wrap, fellows. For once, you sounded like real musicians. I'm very proud of you. You make us all look and sound good . . . and Helen what's left to say? You leave no room for improvement. We are all very proud of you. Don't do anything silly like have an accident or get sick. We have no replacement for any of you. Tonight we play for the Inter-Fraternity dance. Please be on time."

The band broke up with a feeling of high satisfaction. They seemed to know that at least once they played like a well-seasoned team of musicians. With the exception of Bob's drums and the piano, they placed their instruments and music books in a room across the hall. Once again a peaceful quiet settled over Fetzer House, but not for long. Harry placed a stack of platters on the jukebox and the music of "Make Believe Ballroom" filled the air. "Let's dance, Carolyn." Harry said.

"What does this remind you of?" Bob asked me, as we watched Harry and Carolyn dancing.

"The first time you, Harry, Carolyn, and I met, and if I hadn't been talked into staying here, I wouldn't have pledged Beta, or have a band, and worst of all, I probably wouldn't have met Doey. In a way I owe it all to you and Harry."

Harry asked, "Why don't we go to Danziger's for lunch?"

Bob replied, "Doris is here from Mt. Airy. We had planned to go to the Carolina Inn, but Danziger's sounds great. What about you and Doey?" Bob asked.

"We can't," I replied. "Doey and I are going to the airport for lunch with Red. We plan to be back by three. And thanks again, Harry, for the use of the car."

"Just drive carefully. Remember, you have a band and dance tonight, so don't be late."

Driving to the airport I put my arm around Doey and drew her nearer to me. She removed my arm and said, "I love the touch of your hands and want to be close and know that you love me, but when we're driving or flying, you must have both hands free."

I removed my arm and said, with a smile in my voice, "You're already a nag. You are as bossy as any woman that I've ever known."

"I don't doubt that," she said. "But I want you to live a long, long time, and I will always try to keep you safe. And, by the way, I'm not a nag."

"Okay," I said. "It's a bad choice of words. What I meant to say was, 'Thank you, my love.'"

We parked in the lot next to the terminal and went in search of Red. We stopped at operations and asked where we might find him. Sam Hughie said, "Red is at a thousand feet over the practice range with a student that's on his first flight lesson. He should be down in twenty minutes. He's flying the new P.T. 17, the only one we have now. He and the student will stop in the debriefing room for a short time. Why not wait there or in his office?"

"Good thinking, Sam. Why don't you come to lunch with us?"

"I've just come on duty" Sam said. "I'll be here for an hour. Then I have a student to fly with. This is a lousy way to earn a living, isn't it?"

"Sam," I said, "you're a pilot and you wouldn't have it any other way, and you know it. You have at least one student who speaks very highly of you."

"Are you talking about Harry Woods?"

"Yes," I said. "Harry's a big fan of yours. He thinks that you taught the birds how to fly. How's is he doing?" I asked.

"Harry is among the best students that I have trained," Sam said. "He thought he was ready to solo after his second lesson. He's quick to learn, and never forgets anything of importance. Show him a new maneuver and he's ready to show you a better way to do it. He's not reckless; he just has a quick mind that stores scraps of useful information that he can recall instantly when it's needed. He will make a good instructor, or more likely a fighter pilot. I hear that Lockheed is coming out with a new fighter, an aircraft they call the P38."

"That's good," I said. "And when Red comes in, tell him we're at Orville and Wilbur's."

"Will do," Sam replied.

Our table in the corner by the window was taken, so we spent a little time in the pilot's room looking at trophies and pictures on the wall. We moved counter clockwise around the room. One of the new pictures was of Will Rogers and Wiley Post. Words below the picture touched on Post's round-the-world-flight and the deaths of Rogers and Post at Point Barrow, Alaska in August 1935.

At the sound of Red's voice our picture tour of the Pilot's Room ended. We turned to see Red standing in the doorway. "Sorry I'm late," he said.

"You're not," I replied. We ate a quick lunch and discussed the latest flying techniques. After lunch, we left and headed back for the evening event. The band played beautifully and the crowds were bigger than ever. It was a great send-off for the holidays.

Chapter 30

Holiday Approaches, Off to Terre Haute

December 19, 1939, the moon and stars over Chapel Hill began to fade, as a scratch of light, which appeared across the eastern horizon, began to widen and let the sun in. We stowed our baggage in the trunk of Harry's car, and put our gifts to Doey's family on the back seat.

Harry drove us to Durham and parked near the Tri Delta House. A lighted Christmas wreath, hanging over the door, was a guide to the lobby where a cheerful fire blazed. We scanned the room, looking for our passengers, and were about to have them paged. Then, with one more look around the room, Harry spied Doey and Carolyn in a gaggle of girls, in the far corner of the room, talking.

Harry called Carolyn's name. She looked up in our direction and called, "Over here!" As we drew near I heard her say to Doey, "They're here." Several greetings like Merry Christmas and Happy New Year echoed around the group of students. I added my holiday greetings and Harry, smiling, said, "Bah, Humbug!"

Doey and Carolyn were wearing identical white blouses with collar and cuffs trimmed with small embroidered green Christmas trees. Their dark green ski pants clung to the tantalizing forms of the two beautiful girls. Draped around their shoulders were Woollen scarves of red and green. They were ready for the weather, or skiing, or both. We picked up their luggage and they followed us to the car.

Doey said that she had called Edward and asked him to meet us at the depot with the station wagon. "We had planned to take a taxi home from the station," she said, "but I knew that we had too much baggage for a cab." We had touched all bases and were headed for home plate, Terre Haute.

We arrived at the train station early enough to find a table by the window where the first act of the season was to exchange gifts with Carolyn and Harry. Their gifts to us would go under the Christmas tree in Terre Haute, to be opened Christmas morning.

Fate had brought us together, and our regard for each other grew stronger every day. A feeling of forever love went with the gifts. The usual crowd of students were milling around, waiting for the time they would board the train for Christmas at home.

At the lunch counter, I bought four cups of coffee and returned to the table and sat down beside Doey. Through the frosty window, I could see the train sitting there emitting small puffs of steam, like a horse that had just run a claiming race at Belmont. A light snow was falling. In a few minutes we would be boarding the train. It would complete a picture, which one would expect to see on the cover of *The Saturday Evening Post*, painted by Norman Rockwell. The name, of course, would be, "Going Home for Christmas."

The loudspeaker announced that the train was now ready to board. We spoke briefly of our impending New Years' trip to Florida to visit my family. Harry said it was his year to spend Christmas with Carolyn and her family. The two families lived only a few miles apart, so they expected to spend time with both.

The loudspeaker broadcast a few moments of static and then a voice said for the second time, "All aboard!" Harry and I picked up our bags and followed Doey and Carolyn to the train. They carried the gifts for our Terre Haute family.

We walked down the aisle and entered our compartment. When we got settled, Carolyn said, "I wish that Harry and I were going with you to Florida. Have a wonderful Christmas and New Years Eve."

"Let us know when you will return, and we'll meet you," Harry added.

"We plan to return to Durham the day before classes begin," Doey replied.

Harry said, "It's time to get off the train, Carolyn, or we'll be on our way to Terre Haute."

Through the window of our compartment, we could see Carolyn and Harry standing in the falling snow waving goodbye. The train began to move and slowly they faded from sight.

I helped Doey out of her coat and hung it beside mine. She removed her Christmas hat, scarf, and mittens and handed them to me. I placed them with the bag of Christmas gifts, and then sat down at her side. I drew her to me and like the one who invented love, wrapped her in my arms, and kissed the closed lids and long lashes that covered her sparkling blue eyes. She looked at me, smiled, and said, "I could never want more than you and your love. Now I have a family in Florida. I hope they like me."

"How could they not like you? They will love you as I do. I made train reservations to Florida and I must pick them up no later than the 23rd, or they'll be cancelled."

"Don't worry about that," she said, "Daddy's law firm handles the railroad's legal work. Someone in his office will take care of it."

"Doey, you and your family continue to surprise me. It's doubtful that I will ever be able to meet the high living standard that you are used to. We will not live on charity from your family. When the war is over, there is a law partnership in your father's firm waiting for you. I will not be humiliated by handouts from your family. You have a reason to walk away from me. Financially you are already a success. It must be understood that whatever success we have must be earned."

"Darling, I will never, never leave you. I know how hard you have worked. I've come to understand your way of life, and I want to always be part of it. I know how easy my life has been, and I have never wanted for anything. My parents have always been there for me. Now we have three families, we must include Anna and Edward and be there for them."

Doey continued, "You may think that my family is perfect in every way. Well, we're not. We can count as many black sheep on our family tree as anyone. In time you will hear about them. Daddy had a younger brother named Robert. He enrolled at the University of Chicago, where my father was a Phi Beta Kappa and president of his fraternity. Robert, of course, became a pledge brother of the fraternity. Unfortunately, he had discovered alcohol in his senior year of high school, and by his freshman year in college, he had become an accomplished drinker. One night he stopped in a bar near the university that only sold beer and wine.

"It required only three Berghoff beers before fantasy began to take over and he imagined himself to be president of a bank. Loudly he called to the bartender and said that he wanted another Berghoff. The bartender was at the other end of the counter and was slow to answer. Robert raised his voice and pounded his empty beer bottle on the counter, loudly demanding another beer.

"'Sir, I think that you've had enough,' the bartender said. 'Why don't you leave quietly and go home.' It was then that the Jekyll and Hyde persona within him began to emerge. He was being ignored. Loudly he said, 'I can' . . . That's as far as he got. A strong bouncer grabbed his arm, escorted him to the door, and threw him into the street. Robert picked himself up and looked for something to throw. He found nothing, so he yelled obscenities until the police came and took him to jail. At two in the morning Daddy went down and bailed him out. The desk sergeant gave Robert a stern lecture about his conduct. He was released, but Daddy was mortified by his behavior. Robert protested that they had no right to call the police. Daddy told him that he had no right to get drunk and disorderly and took him back to the frat house.

"Robert was jealous of Daddy's success. I'm sure he tried to overcome his dependence on the bottle. He blamed Daddy when he was not asked to join his fraternity, and left college and went to work in the bank, where he let nothing stand in the way of drinking and having a good time. My father and grandfather tried many times to help him."

"That must have been tough on your father," I said.

"It was. Grandfather wanted Daddy to follow him and become president of the bank, but that was not to be. One night, shortly after my grandmother died, Grandfather called Daddy and Robert to the library to discuss their futures.

"Before coming down from his room, Robert fortified himself with a drink for courage. He went down to the library and sat in a chair by the sofa, dreaming of his life to come. He believed his brother would live and work in Chicago. With him out of the way, he would become president of the bank and live in the tax-free family home. He knew that he must stop drinking.

"Grandfather had told Daddy that Robert would not become the next president of the bank. He would be offered a position in the bank, but not one that required daily knowledge of money and banking. He would be no more than an employee. Grandfather worried that Robert's drinking and slothful way of life would only end in losing the bank and the house and land that our family has owned for two centuries.

"Daddy knew then that his future belonged in Terre Haute. He agreed to open his office in Terre Haute and look after the bank's legal needs, but it would not be possible for him to become president. He asked that he be appointed to the board of directors and that Grandfather sell fifty one percent of the bank stock to First National Bank. That way, we would always have an interest in the bank.

"While Daddy listened carefully to what his father was saying, Robert was daydreaming. The president's desk in the bank, and the only key to this house, were all he needed for his future. He heard his father say, 'Pay attention, Robert. Did you hear what I have just said?'

"Once more Robert was told that part of the bank would be sold, and that Daddy would be appointed a member of the board of directors. He and my dad would receive equal shares of bank stock. In addition, Daddy would receive a salary for managing the family's portfolio."

"What happened to Robert?" I asked.

Arise My Love And Come Away With Me

"He died in California when I was twelve years old. I have only seen his picture. He is buried in the family cemetery."

"You're right, Doey, I guess all families have their trials."

On the small desk in our compartment was the latest issue of the *Daily Tar Heel*, the campus newspaper. Like a magnet, our eyes were drawn to the disturbing headline news. War was moving closer, and the war was all important to our future.

"Every day," I said, "the war is moving closer. Now that France has fallen, England stands alone. Winston Churchill was called to Buckingham Palace by King George, and asked to form a government to replace Prime Minister Chamberlain. The next day, when Churchill stood in the House of Commons and made his first speech as prime minister, he got a standing ovation and the people of England were his to lead.

"England needs help. The world is falling apart and Hitler is picking up the pieces and adding them to Germany, and Churchill looks to us for help. At the moment we have nothing much to give. Air fields and barracks are under construction, I'm told, and as they are completed for use, the draftees will fill them. Our president and his cabinet are just looking for ways to help England and for a reason to declare war. And when they do, our main act will be to supply England with food and ammunition to stay alive. Somewhere along the way, Doey, you and I will find our place to help."

"Yes," she sighed. "There is a big detour in our future."

At noon we had a light lunch in our compartment; then walked back to the club car where we read, and listened to the radio. We spoke of our life ahead, where the life we knew would end—and an uncertain future would begin.

On the way back to our compartment, we stopped in the observation car and watched the winter scenery fly by. "This movie keeps repeating itself," I said. "The scenery never changes. The train stops every now and then and the cast of characters on the train get off and a new group gets on. Why don't we go back to our room where we can read a book, work a crossword puzzle, or, better still, I can make love to you?"

"You wouldn't dare," she said, with a mischievous smile.

"I'm beginning to take issue with your mother and our religious teachings."

"I'll lock you out," she said, giggling.

"So lock me out. I have the only key."

"We wouldn't have time," she said, as she put her arms around me. "We will soon be in Terre Haute and I would never lock you out."

It wasn't long before the conductor announced, "Terre Haute!" When the train rattled, bumped, and shrieked, I knew, by the sound, that we had arrived. Like a herd of cattle breaking out of a holding pen, the rush was on to see who would be first to leave the train. I called a porter to help with our luggage.

When our bags were safely on the platform I tipped the porter and started searching the crowd for Edward. Doey spotted him first. He was coming pushing a two-wheeled baggage cart. When he drew near, he saw us and smiled. "Welcome home," he said. We shook hands and Doey kissed him enthusiastically on the cheek. We loaded the baggage and packages onto the cart.

"I can see why you needed the station wagon," Edward said. "This load would never fit into a taxi. Your father wanted to come, but it was too cold. Miss Dorothy was able to talk him out of it."

A light snow began to fall. The station and street lights cast their filtered Christmas greetings upon the land. We loaded the station wagon with our luggage, and were on the way to Doey's home.

Light from stars and a half moon broke through diaphanous clouds, adding their glow to the beautiful Christmas scene. At the top of the hill,

Doey and I whispered, "Back home again in Indiana." A few minutes later Edward turned into the curved driveway, I kissed Doey, and we were home.

"Take the packages with you, I'll take care of the rest," Edward said. I grabbed two suitcases and Doey picked up the packages.

"You bring the other two bags, Edward. We can make it in one trip."

Chapter 31

Christmas with the Brooks

The branches of the small spruce tree by the door hung heavy with snow. It shared its Christmas lights with the glowing holly wreath that hung on the door that opened as we approached. We entered quickly and left the cold outside. John and Dorothy greeted us with hugs and kisses.

A small Christmas tree sat on the round table in the foyer, and bright green holly garland with red berries looped its way up the banisters to the second floor. Brindy, with a red ribbon around his neck, barked for attention. Doey picked him up and scratched behind his ears as we followed Dorothy and John to the library. Along the way we stopped for a few moments to see the living room that Dorothy and Anna had transformed into all the splendor of Christmas.

There was the family's Christmas tree in all its glory! The angel's wings atop the tree touched the twelve-foot ceiling. Below the tree a blanket of cotton snow was visible and surrounding that, a growing pile of gifts. Doey added our gifts to those under the tree. The grandfather clock in the foyer struck ten. It was December 21, 1939, and the radio was tuned to a program of Christmas music. From the fireplace a cheerful fire blazed in greeting. We sat by the fire talking about today and what we would do tomorrow.

We asked about George and Jane and if they had arrived. Dorothy told us that George and his family had been invited by Jane's parents to spend the holidays with them, but they would be home for New Years.

"It's too bad," I replied. "Doey and I will be in Florida. That reminds me, John, Doey told me that someone in your office can confirm our trip to Florida and pick up the tickets. I hate to ask you, and before I do, I need your assurance that this will not cause you any more work than a phone call to your office. In this envelope there is a confirmation of the train route and the cost. The envelope also contains a check that I've signed to cover the cost of the tickets. I had planned to pick them up at the Durham Station before we left, but I didn't allow enough time to stand in a long slow-moving line. If, for any reason this cannot be done, I'll understand."

John replied, "Doey has already told me the problem, and I can assure you that it will only require a call to the office. We have a young man there whose only job is to run errands and take care of problems like this." With a smile and a thank you to John, I relaxed. I was learning a new way of life.

Edward brought a tray of gingerbread and hot chocolate and set it on a table before the fireplace. Dorothy thanked him and said, "It's been a long and busy day, Edward. Let's start tomorrow with breakfast at eight thirty, and call this day over."

Edward replied, "If there's anything more that I can do, please call me." He turned to Doey and asked, "Shall I take Brindy with me?"

"Yes, please," Doey replied.

Edward went to the Christmas tree and softly spoke Brindy's name. He awakened, and like the hundred percent watch dog that he was, got up and stretched, yawned, and to make sure that nothing threatening was gaining on him or his family, he turned in a circle a few times and found nothing to alarm him. Once again, he had kept his family safe. He was a good watch dog and protector. He flattened a few gift boxes that got in his way as he left his warm bed, and followed Edward out of the room.

John stood and said, "It's past our bedtime, Dorothy." To us he said, "We're so very glad that you're home."

We walked with them to the stairway where Doey kissed her mother, and once again I thanked them for the invitation to be their guest for Christmas. As they started up the back stairway, we returned to the living room. Before sitting down, I turned the radio on to hear the latest news bulletin, and sat down on the sofa beside Doey. The voice of an announcer was saying: "From the Palomar, at Third Street and Vermont Avenue, in the city of Los Angeles, California, NBC brings, for your listening and dancing pleasure, the music of Jimmy Dorsey and His Orchestra, featuring that singing sensation, Miss Helen O'Connell."

We sat on the sofa listening to primetime music. We were alone, wrapped in an atmosphere of hope, and too much in love to say goodnight. The grandfather clock in the foyer struck twelve.

"It's been a long day, darling. I think it's time for us to hit the road to dreamland. This will be a busy day." We walked up the back stairway and stood in the hallway before the door to Doey's room. I kissed her and started to speak, but she interrupted.

"That wasn't much of a goodnight kiss to build a dream on."

"Have patience, my love. That was only the warm up," I whispered, and a long passionate kiss sealed our day with a thousand tomorrows. She opened the door to her room, and said, "Goodnight, or rather, good morning, darling."

At six thirty I was up, took a shower, and dressed for a day in the snow. I wore a white shirt and a pair of Woollen Carolina Blue trousers, and carried a heavy blue pullover sweater with a white UNC logo. The sweater could withstand an Alaskan blizzard. I walked down the stairway to the foyer and back down the hall past the sunroom to the kitchen. Anna and Edward were there. We exchanged "Good mornings."

"Would you like some coffee, Wynn?" he asked.

"Yes, I would," I replied.

"Mr. John said that you and Doey might go for a sleigh ride this morning."

"Yes, that sounds like a good way to start the day."

186

"The coffee will be ready soon. I'll bring it to you in the morning room," Edward said.

In the morning room, I turned the radio on and stood at the window looking at a calm crystal day. In the east, rays of sunlight broke through a stratum of gray clouds. "What would our weather be today?" was my silent thought. A meteorologist would say, "It's too soon to tell." As long as Doey was near, any weather was beautiful.

How could I have known that golden-haired beauty with the sparkling blue eyes would choose me to be her life's companion? How lucky can I get? I heard Edward come in and I turned, but it wasn't Edward. It was Doey and Brindy. Quickly I moved to her side and said, "Good morning, darling. Did you sleep well?"

"Yes, I did," she replied. "Except for waking up and not finding you beside me, I did."

"One day I'll spend every day and night close to you."

"Yes," she replied with a wistful smile. "One day."

I pulled her to me. We were just a kiss apart. I heard the door open and Dorothy entered. She stood there a moment and said with a smile, "Ah ha! Caught you! How long has this been going on?"

"Not long enough, Dorothy," I replied. "Give me just a moment to complete what you so rudely interrupted, and then I will say good morning." At the conclusion of the long, long kiss, I walked over to Dorothy, who was now seated by the fire, kissed her cheek and said, "Good morning."

"I believe that you're in love with my daughter."

"What in the world gave you that idea? I treat all my girlfriends the same way."

Doey entered the conversation saying, "I'm not worried, Wynn. You told me that I was your only love, and I believe you."

"Now, Doey, I have always considered you my number one girlfriend; however, with Dorothy as a witness, I want you to know that as long as we live, there will never be another woman in my life. You are my only love. You are my number one, for always."

Edward arrived with a pot of coffee and poured some for all of us. John entered and asked us what our plans were for the day.

"We would like to hitch Buckshot to the sleigh and make tracks in the snow," Doey replied.

"There's a dinner dance at the club tonight and Dorothy and I hope that you both will join us."

"Oh, yes," Doey replied, as she looked at me. I nodded my head. "We will be pleased to go."

Edward came in and invited us to a buffet breakfast. Brindy barked his acceptance of the invitation and showed us the way to the breakfast room. We stood by the buffet in a circle holding hands. With bowed heads, John thanked God for what we were about to receive. We sat at the table eating and speaking of the activities for the next few days.

At the conclusion of breakfast, Edward came in to tell us that Buckshot and the sleigh were in the portico ready to go. I zipped up my coat and helped Doey into hers. With gloves, hats, and colorful scarves, we were ready to make tracks in the snow. John, Dorothy, and Edward stood watching as we reached the top of a ridge and disappeared from view. Buckshot slowed to an easy walk, then stopped.

"What could be better than this, Doey?" I asked.

"A flight to the un-trespassed sanctity of space," she replied. "I will always remember that night and flight in the light of a full moon at Chapel Hill. That's when I knew I was in love with you."

"My most wonderful memory of you is the night we met," I told her.

"The difficult part of our lives is yet to come," Doey replied.

"I'm afraid you're right. Each day the war comes closer, and each day we lose a little more of our freedom. With humiliating threats and the reality of war, Hitler forces countries to become living space for his new order, Germany. They say he has established death camps for the Jews, whom he has decided have no right to live, and Japan is focused on conquering all of Asia. The world is at war. You and I may be allowed to finish college, but we will become part of the military soon. We are living the very last days of our freedom, Doey.

"Someday the war will end and we will come home, and with good intentions, the winners and losers will kiss and make up. Then the world cycle for war or peace will be renewed, and there will be another war . . . When will we ever learn?"

She looked at me with tears in her eyes. I held her close and kissed away the tears. "Doey, my love for you will never die. You will be with me always as I will be with you."

She snapped the reins and Buckshot began to walk. I took Doey in my arms and said, "There will be days ahead that will try our ability and mental strength to go on, but we will survive those days. One day the war will end and we will have earned our right to a peaceful life."

We crossed the bridge to the other side of the frozen river and turned north towards home. On the way, we stopped at The Tavern, where Doey gave Buckshot his expected apple. We lingered at a table in the bar, over mugs of hot apple cider. When we left, dark clouds were moving across the sun and a fine sifting of snow was beginning to fall.

By the time we arrived home, snow had covered our tracks and our day in the sun was over. We curry-combed Buckshot and gave him a measure of oats. Then we entered the house and went in search of Dorothy and John. They were in the library listening to Christmas music and playing gin rummy. They looked up as we entered. Dorothy said, "I was afraid that you would be caught in a snow storm."

"No," I said. "It's just a little local weather disturbance. The sky is already beginning to clear. Except for the snow, this is Florida weather." I smiled when I said that.

"I forgot to mention that tonight's dance is formal," John said.

"We'll be ready, Daddy. What time will we leave?"

"At six thirty and no later than seven," he said. "Be sure to bring warm wraps."

"After lunch we're going down to the basement 'Play House,' to play a few tunes," I said. "We have reserved two first row seats on the aisle for you. We hope you can come."

"Thank you," John said. "After lunch Dorothy and I had planned to go Christmas shopping, but we certainly can't miss your concert." Dorothy and John followed us down to the Brooks' 'Play House' and took their seats.

I picked up the mike, and said: "From the concert hall of the Brook's Playhouse, we bring your way the beautiful voice and piano music of Miss Doey Brooks, accompanied by Wynn Cary and his clarinet. This program is for your listening and dancing pleasure."

For an hour we played, and Doey sang almost everything on today's and yesterday's charts. We opened with "Begin the Beguine" and ended with "Ramona". Dorothy and John got up and danced as Doey softly sang their songs. We got a standing ovation and they thanked us for a wonderful afternoon.

At six-thirty John and I sat by the fire in the library and waited for our dates. When Dorothy and Doey arrived, they looked like a picture on the cover of *Vogue* magazine. John and I stood and admired the vision. Dorothy asked, "How do we look?"

John replied, "As I grow older, you stay your same beautiful self. How do you do it? It looks as though you and Doey are twins."

I quickly chimed in saying, "In every way, you are both beautiful."

From their golden hair and sparkling blue eyes, down to their dancing slippers, they were a vision of loveliness. Their black silk long-sleeve gowns showed a hint of cleavage and clung to every curve of their bodies. Single strands of pearls adorned the necklines. At the wrists, bracelets of matching pearls completed their dress. Mother and daughter could easily be mistaken for twins. The only difference was the ring on Dorothy's left hand, which marked her as a married woman, and was a reminder to me to give Doey an engagement ring. I put my arm around Doey's waist and said "If it wouldn't spoil your make up, I would kiss you and say how much I love you."

"You would do that, with my parents in the room?"

I looked around the room and said, "I don't see anyone. Where are your parents?"

She looked around the room and said, "I don't see my parents either, so kiss me." When we looked up her parents were standing there, smiling.

At ten to seven, Edward came in to remind us that it was time to go. "Miss Dorothy's car is in the driveway. I left the car running and the heat is on." At the door he gave us our coats, hats, and scarves and said, "It may be cold, but it's a beautiful moonlit night. Drive carefully. It's the season that appeals to drunks."

"Thank you, Edward," John said. "Please don't stay up for us. We will be careful." Doey and I sat in the back seat holding hands and watching a three-quarter moon as clouds drifted by.

John pulled up in front of the club and the parking attendant opened the doors. We got out and John traded the car keys for a claim check. Dodd, the maitre d', greeted us all by name. I was surprised when he remembered mine. "I hope you all have a Merry Christmas. I have you booked for Vince at table number 7."

"Thank you, Dodd," John replied. "Our Christmas celebration starts here, as it has for many years."

I saw John slip a small envelope into Dodd's hand. I had an opportunity to thank him for remembering my name. He smiled and said, "Remembering the names of future club members is an important part of my job, Mr. Cary."

When Vince saw us coming down the aisle, his face lit up like a ray of morning sunlight. In the background, Larry Clinton and His Orchestra were playing, "My Reverie," with Bea Wain singing the beautiful melody.

After we were seated, Doey started tapping her toe in time with the music. She was ready to dance. The bottle of Dom Perignon, that John had ordered was cooling in the ice bucket and ready for pouring. John gave the order and Vince filled our glasses. John raised his glass and said, "To Doey and Wynn, a Merry Christmas and a safe and enjoyable trip to Florida. We will miss you."

"Thank you, John," I replied. "We wish the same for you and Dorothy. We would love to be with you for a New Year's celebration, but it's time for Doey to meet my family. I know they will love her, as I do."

We sat there sipping champagne, listening to the music, and talking when Doey declared, "It's time to dance." We followed Dorothy and John to the dance floor. We stepped into the crowd and moved with the rhythm of the music, and blended into a kaleidoscope of color. She closed her eyes and laid her head on my shoulder. I held her a little closer, kissed the top of her head, and whispered, "Doey, I love you." At the end of the set we returned to our table where Dorothy and John were waiting for us.

"Dorothy," I said, "would you like to dance?"

"Yes," she replied, "but none of that jitterbug stuff."

I led her to the floor and bowed like they did in the seventeenth century. I took her hand and we danced to the music in time with the beat of a jitterbug drum. Thirty minutes later Dorothy said, "I have learned steps and movements that I could only watch younger dancers do. Dancing will never again be the same. For now, I need to rest."

Arise My Love And Come Away With Me

When John and Doey returned to the table, Dorothy said, "Doey, you must teach your father a few new steps. He thinks that college kids still dance the Lindy Hop and wear Coonskin coats." To me, Dorothy said, "Wynn, I really enjoyed our dance. I hope you'll ask me again."

"Dorothy," I replied, "anyone who looks and acts like Doey gets my attention."

John signaled to Vince that we were ready to order. He passed the menus around and said, "Mr. Brooks, we still have several bottles of wine in your locker."

"Yes, Vince, I know. There are a few bottles of vintage 1889 Rothschild Haute Bryon. Uncork one and let it breathe a little of the smoke in the air. Smoke won't help, but the last breath it had was forty years ago. It needs a little time to adjust, but it's the best we can do. When it's ready, bring four glasses."

We gave our dinner order to Vince and waited to be served. I looked at Doey and said, "It looks like we're in for a treat."

"Yes. For all of Daddy's life, wine has been his hobby. You have seen our cellar. It's full of hundreds of bottles of first cru wines, and other wines from around the world. It's an asset. Unlike the market, it always seems to increase in value. I don't think he has ever sold a bottle."

"Well," I said, "it's the only wine that I have really liked, but it's too expensive for me to ever become addicted. I suppose that we will have to adjust to an occasional bottle of beer."

"The only addiction I have is for you. I need nothing more. Well, maybe we should have an airplane. We will need to fly in the moonlight occasionally."

"I don't need an airplane, Doey. All I need is you. An airplane of our own is a long, long dream away."

Vince served a gourmet feast and the wine and music made the night one that I will never forget. Larry Clinton's music beckoned. We answered with

193

bodies that swayed with the rhythm of the music and feet that moved in the timing thump of a base fiddle. The memorable night ended as John slipped a small envelope to Vince.

From the cloak room, the hat check girls redeemed our coats and hats. After a few last words with friends, the sounds of "Merry Christmas and Happy New Year" filled the air.

On the way home, the lights from the car, stars and a bright moon lit the way. As we entered the house, I looked at the grandfather clock in the foyer; it was twenty minutes to midnight. "Dorothy and I will leave you here. We're going up to bed."

Dorothy added her bit. "Don't stay up too late."

"We won't," Doey said. "We want to hear the music from California where it's only nine o'clock." I thanked them for an unforgettable night and Dorothy for the dance. Most of all, I thanked them for the invitation to be with Doey for the holidays. We said goodnight, and Brindy followed us to the library. I flipped the radio switch on and turned the dial to NBC's Blue Network. Static gave way to the sound of music, coming from the dining room of the Hotel St. Catherine, on Santa Catalina Island, just off the coast of Southern California.

I returned to Doey and sat down on the sofa beside her. As I put my arm around her, she placed her head on my shoulder and started to hum along with the music playing, "More Than You Know". I smiled and felt so loved and content. The music provided a background that marked the end of a perfect day.

Early the next morning I dressed and walked down to the kitchen. Anna was busy putting something in the oven. She looked up, and with a big smile said, "Edward and I are happy to welcome you home, Mr. Wynn. Come in. Did you and Doey enjoy the dance last night?"

"Yes, we did, Anna. You and Edward have helped make it very easy for me to become a member of this family. In time I hope to earn the love and respect the family has for you and Edward."

"You already have that, Mr. Wynn . . . Edward will be here soon. He's tending to the fireplaces. We have heat from an oil system that keeps us warm, but Miss Dorothy likes to see logs in the fireplaces burning. They add heat to the rooms, and beauty to the cold winter days."

The sound of Edward saying "Merry Christmas" echoed as he entered the room. Anna poured some coffee in a silver thermos and set it on a tray. Edward picked it up and together we walked to the morning room where he poured me a cup.

"It looks like we will have a white Christmas," Edward remarked. "We already have plenty of snow, but we will get more. This is Doey's favorite time of year; she loves Christmas, and has made every day in this house Christmas for us. She may belong to Miss Dorothy and Mr. John, but she also belongs to Anna and me, and now to you. Take good care of her, and come back as often as you can."

He picked up the *Chicago Tribune* and handed it to me. I took the paper from his hands and read the headlines. The daily story of war was spread across the paper's front page.

Like a ray of sunshine on a dark day, Doey walked in and said, "Good morning, darling."

"It's a wonderful morning," I said, as I took her in my arms and harvested the first kiss of the day. We stood at the window watching snowflakes add their bit to cheer a dark somber day.

Dorothy walked in with John and asked, "What are you two up to?"

"I'm glad you asked, Dorothy. Your daughter was trying to make me kiss her. She got lipstick on my collar. I was only trying to defend my honor."

John picked up the newspaper and with a wink and a smile said, "It looks to me like you lost." He read the headline and shook his head as if surprised, and laid the paper on the table.

After breakfast, John said, "Christmas Eve has always been a time when Dorothy plans something special to do in the New Year. Dorothy why don't you tell them what we have planned?"

Dorothy continued, "In June, Doey will have completed her first year of law school. The New York World's Fair will be going on and we would like for you, Wynn, to be our guest for the summer. We're sure that Doey would like that. After the fair, we will go to Terre Haute, then to Macatawa, Michigan where we will spend the rest of the summer. It will be an all-expense paid tour. We hope you can join us."

This could only be a dream. I looked at Doey. She smiled and said, "Please, say yes."

I was stunned and said the only word that would fit the occasion: "Yes!"

Edward called us for breakfast. It was the day before Christmas, a day I should be with my family and friends in Florida, but the need to be with Doey was a major change in my life, and a strong conflict to be reckoned with.

"John and I are going to his office for a Christmas party," Dorothy said. "It's an annual affair that includes lunch. John thinks that we have to make an appearance, but we will be home by one. Anna will have lunch for you, and if you go out, tell Edward where you are going. Have fun and be safe."

"We will," I replied. We spent most of the day in "Club Brooks" in the basement of the house. Doey played the piano and sang, and to add a little musical color, I added a few notes with the clarinet. We played pool, read a few chapters of Dickens *A Christmas Carol*, and quoted soliloquies from Shakespeare's plays and Poe's "The Raven." Edward came down with lunch and set it on the table before the fireplace. My life was on a fast track. Less than a month ago Jane and George were here. Today I'm alone in the house with Doey.

Doey broke the silence and asked, "What's on your mind, Wynn?"

"You," I replied. "I will never grow tired of looking at, or thinking of, you. I can't believe that you have chosen me to be with until the end of time."

"Yes," she said, "but, never forget, forever with you is such a short time."

"Doey, my darling, there's a place called 'the other side of beyond' and that's where time is endless. One day we will go there." With a kiss and a happy smile, one more vision of Doey was recorded in the memory album in my mind.

When we finished lunch, we went upstairs to the living room. "Look!" Doey said. "This is our first tree." She was pointing to two new ornaments on the tree. In old English scrolls, these words were written: "Wynn and Doey's first Christmas tree 1939."

"This is a good reason for me to kiss you, Doey."

"You don't need a reason," she replied.

We walked to the window and looked out at a beautiful Christmas scene. The sun spread a blanket of soft sunlight over the snow. We could see the passing tracks of two deer that we spotted among the trees on the hill. They were foraging for their breakfast.

Edward came in to tend to the fire and before leaving said, "Dinner will be at eight. At eleven we will go to the Episcopal Church for the Christmas Eve service. After that, we will return home and it will be very early Christmas morning."

"Thank you, Edward," I said. "I'm familiar with that routine. My parents did the same. We went to church, and after the Christmas service, my sisters and I would sit on the floor around Mother's and Father's chairs, and listened to the story of the first Christmas. I yearned for snow, but the closest we ever got was cold weather."

I turned the radio on and dialed through the static until I came to a reporter reading the news. It was more of the same, so I turned the radio off, and said, "That's a glance at our future."

"One day," Doey said, "you will be somewhere in the world fighting for our right to live. If I pass the tests, I will be flying in the safety of our country, protected by two oceans."

"This is Christmas Eve," I said "Don't let what may be, spoil our day."

That evening we went to church where the minister began by reading the story of the first Christmas. An aura of peace and goodwill surrounded the overflowing congregation, many of whom found the time to attend church only once a year.

Along the way home, soft lights and the muted sounds of peace on earth surrounded us. Edward led the way and opened the door. We entered, the door closed, and it was Christmas Day. "Even wonderful evenings like this must end," John remarked, as he and Dorothy said goodnight.

Anna yawned and Edward said, "Tomorrow will be a busy day."

Before leaving, Anna said, "Mr. Wynn, this will be your first Christmas with us. You are our Christmas gift."

"Thank you, Anna," I replied as I put my arm around her. "You and Edward have made my entrance into this family very easy."

As they left the room Doey and I moved to the sofa before the fire and sat down. "Doey," I said, "I'm living the impossible dream. Four months ago I didn't know that you existed. Now here we are and that impossible dream has come true. If, for any reason, you should leave me, know this, you will always be my dream come true. There can be no life without you."

Doey replied, with a voice filled with love, "Thank you, my darling. There can only be a dark unending future without you. We belong together. Wherever you may be, always come back to me."

We sat there with hearts and minds overloaded with grim possibilities. We spoke words of love that assured us that there would be a happy ending. We got up from the sofa and stood before the window looking at the ground covered with a carpet of December snow. The branches of trees on the hill hung low with snow and ice crystals. In the sky a full moon cast its glow of beauty over the land.

"Tomorrow," I said, "which is actually today, will be a good time for a sleigh ride."

"Yes," Doey remarked, "but for now, it's time for us to go to bed and log a few hours of sleep." Arm in arm we walked up the back stairway to the hall leading to our rooms.

"Where's Brindy?" I asked. Brindy heard his name and answered with a few scratches on the door. "That's one lucky dog." With a kiss goodnight, another perfect day had ended.

It was Christmas day! I stopped by the kitchen to say Merry Christmas to Anna and Edward. Edward said, "Breakfast will be served in the dining room and afterwards we will gather in the living room to see what Santa left under the tree. Miss Dorothy and Mr. John are in the library. You may wish to join them there."

"Thanks, Edward."

I walked into the library. John and Dorothy were standing at the window looking out at nature's picture of the day. I was deep in thought, thinking how a few weeks had changed not only my life, but the lives of Doey and her family.

"Where's Doey?" I asked.

"It's your day to watch her," Dorothy said.

"I do the best I can," I replied, "but her room is out of bounds for me, and there are times like this that I must defer to you."

I heard a voice say good morning. It was Doey with Brindy close on her heels.

"Good morning, darling. Your mother and father tell me that they will be gone for a few hours today and I am to take care of you. That won't be a problem. I plan to do that for the rest of my life." She kissed me and said, "We will take care of each other."

As we sat in chairs facing John and Dorothy, I said "Doey found the beautiful ornaments on the tree that mark our first Christmas together. We expect to have many more trees, and we want you and John to be with us every Christmas."

Brindy searched the room for predators, found none, and curled up at Doey's feet. Edward came in and announced that breakfast was ready and hearing that magic word, Brindy showed us the way to the dining room. We stood in a circle by the buffet holding hands. John thanked God for the food we were about to receive and asked God to watch over Doey and me for the years to come. "Amen" resounded around the circle.

Anna's magic in the kitchen produced a breakfast that a professional chef could only dream of. She was a good cook and she was a treasured member of the family. After breakfast John said, "Let's go to the library and talk about your trip to Florida." There, Dorothy and John gave us a gift—airline tickets to St. Petersburg, Florida, and then back to Durham.

Chapter 32

Florida-Durham 1940

The next morning we said Happy New Year, as we kissed Dorothy and Anna goodbye. Doey and I got in the back seat of the station wagon, John settled in the passenger seat beside Edward. Dorothy and Anna stood like a pair of bundled up Eskimos waving from the door step.

The airport was bright with Christmas lights. We checked in at the counter for the six-thirty flight to Atlanta. I asked about the weather report and a terminal forecast for Atlanta, where we would change planes for Tampa. We would encounter some rain and winds aloft that may cause a little bumpy ride, but that's what seat belts are for. The flight confirmed the weather report. In Atlanta we changed planes for Florida and somewhere over Georgia, we outran the rain. The land below basked in the early afternoon sunshine, and high above us, cirrus clouds added their beauty to an early afternoon sky.

Mother and Irene were at the airport to meet us. After the hugging and kissing was over, I got so confused that I kissed Doey by mistake. Mom and Irene smiled. Irene drove us to the Vinoy Park Hotel where we checked in and received keys to our rooms. Mom said, "Irene and I will wait for you in the lobby. Take your time."

After a reasonable time for "prettying up" I called Doey. Together we went down to the lobby where we sat by the fire. Doey said to my mother, "I didn't know that you had fireplaces in Florida. Wynn told me that it was always spring here."

"At times, Wynn can be a little skimpy with the truth," Irene chimed in.

Mom replied, "Welcome to our family, Doey. Wynn has written many letters telling me how lovely, thoughtful, and kind you are. His lavish praise leaves no room for doubt."

"What would Red say?" Irene asked.

"I know exactly what Red would say," Doey remarked. "He would say, 'Enough of that talk. Let's just forget it or get on with something else.'"

"You know him pretty well," Mom said.

"Yes," Doey remarked. "About a year ago Wynn and I learned that Red had received the Congressional Medal of Honor, but he has never mentioned it, and when the subject comes up he would say there's nothing to talk about."

"You know Red," Irene said. "He's not much of a talker. Dad brought him home with him one Christmas Eve when I was twelve years old. He's been part of our family ever since."

Mom said, "I'll never forget the story Red told me about how he received the Congressional Medal for saving his instructor and another pilot's life. He was an aviation cadet at Kelly Field in Texas. One night, he was on a cross country flight with another cadet and his instructor. The weather was unsettled. The cadet flying on one side of the instructor started to move a little closer to the leader. A gust of wind blew him into the tail of the instructor's plane and the two planes, out of control, fell to the ground. Red could have and should have returned to the field and reported the accident, but he didn't. He reversed his course and flew back across the crash site looking for a safe place to land. There was none. He decided to chance a land and give what help he could to the downed pilots. He headed back into the wind and landed. Both the cadet and the instructor appeared to be dead, but there was a feeble heartbeat of hope for both.

"Quickly he cut shrouds from one of the parachutes, tied one of the victims to the wing of his plane, and flew back to Kelly Field. He landed and explained the incident. He was in his plane with the engine running, but was told to cut the engine and stand down until morning. He would then lead a rescue team to the accident site and the downed pilot would be rescued.

"Red's answer was to taxi to the end of the runway and take off into the wind. If the downed pilot had survived the crash, he needed assistance now. By morning it would be too late.

"The commanding officer was furious. His plane was on standby day and night for such an emergency. Quickly the colonel was airborne. At the scene of the accident, Red landed. Again he cut shrouds from the parachute and tied the second victim to the wing of his plane, while the colonel circled the scene. He watched Red take off, and take up a heading for the field.

"Red had broken one of the strict rules of flying, but under adverse conditions he said there was no choice. He did what he thought was right. The colonel flew on Red's wing back to the field. He had witnessed a heroic deed that could lead to a court marshal or a medal."

"What happened to the pilots?" Doey asked.

"Both pilots recovered and are flying today, and Red was awarded the Congressional Medal of Honor. He gave the medal to me to keep for him. It's in a bank vault."

"He's a hero, alright," I said.

Mom turned to Doey and said, "You are here to meet the family. Unfortunately, my brother and his family are at their home in western North Carolina and won't return until the week after New Years. My daughter Ruth is a lieutenant in the Army Medical Corps at Camp Blanding, Florida and will not be able to be with us. So, for the moment, it's just Irene and me. We do have a much larger family; however, they live in Miami, Virginia, Delaware, Texas, Chicago, and California."

"My family," Doey said, "live in Terre Haute, and that's all I have. There are probably a few still living in Virginia, but I have never seen them."

Irene said, "While you and Wynn are here, Mother and I are staying at the Princess Martha Hotel. We want you to come and go as you please. We would like to spend every moment we can with you, but we know the time you have here is limited. Wynn will show you the places that were important to him; places where he worked, where he went to school, and the Albert Whitted Airport where he learned to fly. We have tried to make him give it up, but we have failed. Maybe he will listen to you."

I looked at Doey and smiled. To buy time she smiled and said to Mom, "What shall I call you, Mrs. Cary, Mom, or Emma?"

"My name is Emaline, but for years people have shortened it to Emma. I would like for you and my daughters to at least know my name."

"Thank you, Emaline. It's a beautiful name. I'm the wrong person to ask Wynn to stop flying. My mother is like you. She has told me many times that flying is not for girls. Wynn took me for my first flight in the night sky, and now I'm a pilot."

"Your time with us is so short. Just seeing you and knowing how beautiful you are and that one day you will be one of my daughters is enough. From this moment you are my daughter. This is your holiday," Mom said. "I will leave my car for you to use while you are here."

"We have my car," Irene said. "We're staying at the hotel until the third of January when my leave is up. We'll see you here at seven for dinner."

We stood on the steps of the hotel and watched until they disappeared in traffic. Doey said, "I love my new Florida family."

"There is a lot of day left, Doey. Would you like to have lunch at Maggie's Diner?"

"Oh yes, I would. Is it far from here?"

"No. It's just a good walk from here. I'll give you a guided tour." We started our walk along the east margin of the Tampa Bay. "On our left is the North Yacht Basin. Next, is the Municipal Pier, it bisects the north/south

Arise My Love And Come Away With Me

yacht basin and it juts out into the bay about a quarter of a mile. If you would like, we can go out there at another time. We will pass the South Yacht Basin and then the Albert Whitted Airport. If there is time, we will squeeze in a flight over the city. Directly across the street from the airport is Maggie's."

"Everywhere I look it's beautiful," Doey said. "You grew up in a fairy tale story. By comparison Terre Haute is a drab, somber place. I want to come back for a longer visit."

"We will," I promised. "It's beautiful, but there are places in and around the city that don't deserve that praise. There are many places that reflect a wide streak of poverty."

"Let's start with Maggie's and then go to the airport." Several minutes later we stood at Maggie's front door and entered. Doey said, "It's just as you described it. I hope Maggie's here."

I asked a waitress if Maggie was in. "Yes, she's in her office." I knocked on the door, and heard Maggie say, "Come in."

Maggie was busy writing at her desk. She looked up then stood. "Wynn," she said, "I expected to see you. I got a letter from Red. He said that you would be here for a few days. He did mention something about a young lady named Doey that you would bring with you."

"This is Doey, Maggie, and Doey this is Maggie. We came for lunch. How about joining us?"

"Only if you will be my guest," she replied. I started to open the door to the dining room. "We'll get better service in here and we won't be interrupted." We talked about Red, Joe, Sam, and Col. Mulzer.

"Doey, now you know all about my past and my friends. Are you sure that you want to be part of the gang?" I asked.

"Oh yes, more than ever."

Maggie's parting words to Doey were, "From the moment that you walked into my office, I have had the strangest feeling that I know you. You look so much like my friend Sally that you could be twins."

"I remember Sally," I said, "but I don't think Doey looks like her. To me nobody is as beautiful as Doey. If I ever see Sally again I'll take a closer look. Where is she?"

"Ask Red," Maggie replied.

"What's Red have to do with it?"

"Ask Red."

"You're just a fountain of knowledge, Maggie."

"Well, you know Red." Maggie said. "He will never be accused of talking too much."

I thanked Maggie for lunch and said, "We're returning to school the day after New Years. I'll tell Red and Sam that we had lunch with you."

Doey said "Wynn's told me so much about you and his airport friends that I want to come back and spend more time in St. Petersburg. Most of all, I have enjoyed Maggie's Diner and the time that we have spent with you. We'll be back and I'll ask Red about Sally." We left Maggie's and walked across the street to the airport.

"Here's where I spent the early days of my youth, Doey. Everything but the blimp hangar has changed. Jimmy Johnson, the airport manager, keeps in touch with Red. He would like to be a flight instructor at Chapel Hill. Red told him that his job is temporary and he could be called to active service at any time. I only learned of this a few days ago. He also said the Chapel Hill Airport would soon become a flight school for the Navy. The Albert Whitted Airport that I knew is going through a major change. It will probably become a government primary flight school. I hope they let us onto the field." We were not stopped at the gate, and continued onto the hangar office, where we rented a plane.

We lined up on the east west runway and took off into an east wind, circled the Municipal Pier and rolled out on a heading that would take us to the Gulf of Mexico. "On our right," I said, "is the Vinoy Park Hotel, and on the left is Maggie's place." We continued to climb on course to a thousand feet. "That's Central Avenue below us. It's the dividing line between the north and the south of the city. In the distance you can see the Gulf of Mexico." Along the way I pointed out prominent places that we would visit at another time. "We're flying the same course that Red flew when he gave me my first ride in an airplane."

At the Gulf's shore I banked right and descended to five hundred feet. I flew along the shore of the Gulf to the city of Clearwater, where we turned east and climbed back to a thousand feet and leveled off. In the distance, across the western shore of the bay, we could see Tampa and St. Petersburg. We started a slow letdown to St. Petersburg, where we lined up for a landing. On the ground I said, "We just flew around the world I knew when I was ten."

Doey said, "Except for the night we flew in the full moon, this is the best flight that I have ever had." We checked the Hobbs meter and paid for our time in the air, then walked back to the Vinoy.

The Don Caesar Hotel, the "Pink Palace" on the Gulf of Mexico, was our destination for lunch, where we would meet Irene and John Eicher. Sam Miller drove and Mother was by his side. In the back seat Doey and I sat holding hands.

Doey's eyes looked and blinked like a camera that had just recorded a picture worth keeping. "Wynn," she said, "I think we've discovered 'the other side of beyond.' Your hometown is beautiful. You have seldom, if ever, mentioned your life here. After the war and we are settled in our careers, I would like to come back and spend the winters here. I want to know your family and your friends as you know mine; and if I haven't mentioned it, I want you to know that I love you."

It was January 2, 1940. We said goodbye to Irene and John Eicher at the Vinoy Hotel, where we had breakfast. Sam and Mother drove us to Eastern Airlines in Tampa, where we stood in the departure lounge waiting for the announcement to board Flight 7 for Atlanta with connections to Durham, North Carolina.

"Mom," I said, "it's true. You can go home again, but you can't stay. Our visit has been ever so short. I promise, at the first opportunity, we will return."

Doey said, "Emaline, if you don't mind, I would like to call you Mom."

"Yes. You are my third daughter, and Mom is a better name for a close family member to use." Doey placed her arms around her and said "Thanks Mom, I'll write. We love you."

The loudspeaker announced our flight. Sam and I had a few words, and Doey kissed him on the cheek and said, "Thank you, Sam, for taking good care of Mom, and being such a wonderful host."

When the wheels of the plane broke the bonds of earth, we silently said, "Arise my love and come away with me." In the early evening we stepped from the plane in Durham where Carolyn and Harry were there to meet us.

Harry said, "We have a choice for dinner, Danziger's, the Carolina Inn, or the hot dog stand at the bowling alley on Franklin Street. We all agreed that Danziger's was the best choice. "Okay," Harry said, "I'll call for a reservation."

Campus life resumed with studies and rehearsals. We played for two fraternity functions in January and February. Harry booked us to play at the Sigma Chi House for their Valentine's Day dance. Doey and Carolyn were disappointed that we couldn't take them along, but we told them that we would make it up to them.

As February was coming to a close, we played at the Inter-Fraternity Sadie Hawkins Dance. Every guy was hoping to get asked to the dance by his sweetheart.

Time moved quickly as the war continued to occupy our thoughts. The headlines read:

"GERMANS OCCUPY DENMARK, ATTACK OSLO;
NORWAY THEN JOINS WAR AGAINST HITLER;
CAPITAL IS REPORTED BOMBED FROM AIR"

Chapter 33

Winston-Salem Flight

Harry, Carolyn, Doey, and I were returning from a flight to Winston Salem, about 100 miles west of Chapel Hill, where we had lunch. Harry would not accept our offer to pay for lunch or flight time.

We stopped in the weather bureau to get a briefing of the latest route and terminal report for the Chapel Hill area. The weatherman said that a low, fast moving front was passing through the area, and that we could expect rain and headwinds along our flight path. The rain showers, heavy at times, would be intermittent, and except for the wind gusts, the weather over Chapel Hill should be clearing. We thanked the weatherman and moved on to the plane.

Harry said, "Wynn, you have logged more weather time than any of us. I'll sit in back with Carolyn." He handed me the key to the plane.

Doey and I did a walk around inspection of the plane and found nothing to report. I opened the left door to the plane and told Doey to get in. The aircraft had dual controls, and a 350-horse power engine. I handed her the checklist. Doey looked at me and said, "I'm in the wrong seat. I can't fly this plane."

"How do you know you can't? You haven't tried." She went through the checklist with very little prompting. All systems go.

She started to get out of the plane, but I said, "Stay where you are, Doey." I walked to the right side of the plane and climbed into the co-pilot's seat. I handed her the key and said, "I'll be your co-pilot. Take us home."

Arise My Love And Come Away With Me

Doey looked at me and said, "No, Wynn, the pilot's time is yours to log."

"No, I'll log co-pilot time. Take us home." She gave me her "thank you" smile and became the pilot in command. She scanned the instrument panel and found the plane fit to fly. She waggled the ailerons of the plane to get the towers attention and received a green light. At the blast fence she checked the magnetos. The light from the tower was still green. At the runway she paused and once more glanced at the tower. Then she taxied into position and lined up with the white strip that centers the runway. The tower light remained green. Runway 9-5 Left was hers. Quickly she released the brakes and pushed the throttle to the fire wall, releasing the 350 horses in the engine. Faster and faster they ran down the runway to a point where a little back pressure on the yoke broke the bonds of earth, sending us into a darkening and windswept sky. Doey and I silently said, "Arise my love and come away with me."

We had gusty crosswinds that threatened to push us off course. Doey met every threat with a counter correction that kept us moving along the flight path to Chapel Hill. She searched her mind for an alternate airport and settled on Lewisburg. If for any reason the Chapel Hill Airport was closed, that would be her alternate.

She looked at me and grinned like a circus clown. There couldn't be a better flight test. Spikes of cold rain played a tune on the roof, and a darkening sky limited visibility. The plane bucked and yawed to stay on course. She made constant corrections, with a touch of the left rudder, the left wing tipped into the wind. We arrived about twenty minutes late. Doey entered the five mile circle around the tower at a 45 degree angle and waggled the wings to alert the tower, asking permission to land. The restless wind chased the wind sock around the post, limiting our landing to a runway of choice, runway 9-0 Right. Doey rocked the wings to acknowledge the green light and made a cross wind landing. The rain had stopped. The weather front was moving south. We cleared the runway and taxied to Hangar 2. She switched the engine to idle cut off and watched as the prop sucked up the last few drops of fuel before coming to a stop. We were home.

"Good flying, Doey," I said. "I think it's time for you to get an instrument rating."

Harry stopped in operations long enough to close the flight plan. The girls and I walked on to the parking lot and were in the car when Harry arrived.

"Watch for cops," Harry joked. "I will probably exceed the speed limit." Once more luck was with us. When we turned into Franklin Street, luck seemed to say, this is as far as I go. We heard the siren. "Damn," Harry said, "we don't have time for a lecture." He pulled to the curb and turned off the engine.

Clarence, the campus cop, stuck his head in the window and said, "Oh, it's you, Harry. Let's go see the sergeant. I'm sure that you know the way. In case you have forgotten, just follow me." A few minutes later we were lined up in front of the sergeant's desk and waited for his canned speech. Harry knew the drill and his fertile mind was busy gathering the words he would use in answer to the many questions he would be asked.

Like a silent motion picture, words and actions of another time moved slowly across my mind as I recalled my first time before the sergeant's desk. Could the bottle I slipped under his desk still be there? I had to know. I slipped my hand under the desk and into the hiding place. My fingers touched the smooth glass outline of the bottle. It was still there. Carefully, I removed it and dropped it into my coat pocket. The sergeant finished his lecture on crime and we were dismissed. After we got in the car, I handed Harry the bottle and said, "I believe this belongs to you."

"Where did you get that?" Harry asked.

"From under the sergeant's desk," I replied.

All he said was, "You have the talent of a cat burglar." We laughed and continued on to drop the girls at home.

Chapter 34

End of Junior Year

My junior year at college was coming to an end. We played our last gig of the year; Helen Lind sang her last song and all members of the band expected to return for their senior year.

It was final exam time, and a hush fell over the campus as students put music and parties on hold, and struggled to recall enough knowledge stored in the "must remember" nook of their minds, to eke out a passing grade.

I hadn't talked with Doey for several days, so I called and asked if she survived finals.

"I haven't received my grades yet, but think I passed," she said. "And you?"

"I'm good for another year," I replied. "I didn't call to discuss unimportant things. I called to say I love you, and invite you to meet Red and me for lunch at the airport."

"What time?"

"Today at noon, or sooner," I said. "I'll be in Red's office."

"I'll be there," she replied. "I love you, Wynn. The only reason that I'm giving up a Tri Delta luncheon is to be with you." Again she said, "I love you," and hung up.

I was sitting behind Red's desk swiveling back and forth. Red was in the chair in front of the desk. He closed the book, which he had been reading, and placed it on the table beside the chair. "You've had a good year, Wynn," he said. "You have successfully completed your junior year. You have a band, an Instructors ticket, and I believe you have Doey. I know that your mother is proud of you, and so am I."

"You have been a member of our family for many years, Red, and ever since my dad died I have looked to you for guidance. You have never let me down."

"Enough of that," Red said. "Now bring me up to date on your trip with the Brooks' family to the New York World's Fair."

"I don't know all the details. If you have questions, ask Doey. She knows more about it than I do. Her parents must think that I'm in love with their daughter, which of course I am."

"You have a full life," he said. "I hope the war in Europe gives you another year before you are called to participate, but don't count on it."

"What about you, Red?" I asked.

"I think that I'll be okay here for a while. Col. Paul Mulzer has a reserve commission and has already been called. You remember him. I too have a reserve commission in the Air Force, and could be called any day."

"But you have a job here," I said. "You are already involved with the military."

"True," he said. "But anyone can do this job, and I feel sure that before the war ends, they'll find a more useful place for me."

While waiting for Doey to appear, we killed time playing cards. Red was dealing and I had already accused him of cheating. Red said, "Just because I won the last two games you accuse me of cheating. Thanks for the compliment. Now say some more nice things about me," he said with a smile.

We heard a knock on the door. "That's probably Doey," I said as I got up and opened the door. Except for a few words from the clergy, the beautiful golden-haired girl that stood beside me was mine. "Come in," I said, and pointing to the chair behind the desk said, "please be seated. You have the answers to the many questions that Red and I have regarding our summer plans with your parents."

Doey replied with a grin, "That's my secret. I'll let you in on it as it happens."

Red smiled and said, "You two get out of here and have a fun afternoon." We spent the afternoon walking around campus, talking about our plans for the summer.

When I got back to the Fetzer House, it was as quiet as a will o' the wisp strumming a guitar without strings. I laid down on my bed, thinking about an orderly past that was prologue to a future filled with so many unpredictable problems; war prefaced every thought.

Doey and I had successfully completed our junior year at our universities. Red asked us and Doey's parents to have lunch with him at Danziger's. It was, in a way, a celebration for successfully completing our junior year at UNC and Duke.

When we were seated, a waiter came to take our orders and passed the menus around. He gave the wine list to Red and said, "May I bring you something to drink? I will return in a few minutes to take your order."

John said, "No wine for Dorothy and me. We have a long way to go tomorrow. Until we get to New York, we are teetotalers, and coffee will be just fine for us."

I looked at Doey. "Iced tea," she said.

"Coffee," I said.

Red said, "Coffee, please." The waiter left us while we selected our meals. Red turned to me and said, "So you're not going home?"

"Well, no, not right now. I am going home two weeks before school starts in September, but there's a veil over the future. We are all facing a time that only a genie or a crystal ball knows the answer."

Dorothy said, "We invited your mother to go with us, but she was expecting your sister Ruth home from Camp Blanding for a visit before being sent to some unknown place overseas. She knows that we will be leaving tomorrow to visit the World's Fair in New York, and after that we plan to go to our summer cottage for the rest of the summer. I dread the day when Wynn and Doey leave us to face the unknown."

Red said, "I talked with Wynn's mother yesterday. She is the absentee hostess for this luncheon. She wanted to be here, but couldn't. Not only will Ruth be home, Irene will be with them for a few days before returning to Atlanta to finish her nursing assignment. She has enlisted in the Army Medical Reserve and will probably end up at some army medical post. Today they are all here at the table with us in spirit."

The waiter had just set our drinks on the table. John picked up his cup, raised it, and said, "To Emma and her valiant daughters. They will be foremost in our hearts and prayers."

John continued, "It's been a long time, Red. I told you that we would meet again. I didn't know then that it would take this long. I do remember the last thing that you said to me. It will be your privilege, you said, to spend a little time and get to know what I consider to be a perplexing problem, or words similar. I'm sure you understand."

"Oh I do," Red said.

"What's he talking about?" Dorothy asked.

"Nothing much," Red replied. "It was just a little something that I had an answer for. Imagine me, a pilot giving advice to a lawyer. I'm not sure that I know what he's talking about either."

Dorothy then asked if we had seen Harry and Carolyn. "Yes," I said, "Harry, Carolyn, Doris, and Bob Lovell had dinner with us at Danziger's last night. Jack Palance had already left for home, and we were served by a more liberal waiter, who apparently was not fearful of the Federal Alcoholic Control Board's edict, so we all ordered a drink.

"Doey and I ordered a Vermouth and soda. Not because we wanted it, but to show our independence from a government edict that prohibited responsible youth from drinking. It doesn't seem right that male students could be drafted into the army to defend and maybe die for the country, but they could not drink or vote. We knew that we were bending the rules, but still, it seemed reasonable."

Our luncheon, mostly soup, salad, and sandwiches, was served with talk of the recent past that had a vague reference to Doey and me. Talk of war, by silent consent, had no place in the conversation. Try as we did to put a positive spin on the days ahead, the future loomed up to crowd our minds with 'what if's' and words that boded nothing but harm and evil. We could not escape the promise of war.

Doey's voice brought closure to the luncheon meeting. "What plans do you have for the summer, Red?"

"I'm going to Florida for a week to visit Wynn's family, then on to Maryland where I'll be until school opens in September."

"Have a good summer, Red. You have been a wonderful friend and teacher. I look forward to knowing that you will be a part of my senior year, and for years to come. We will be leaving in the morning. Wynn and I will be back by the second day of September to start our senior year," Doey said.

Red paid the bill and we walked out to the parking lot where we stood talking. Red was an important part of our life. Once again we thanked him for hosting a luncheon for my mother. Dorothy said that she would call Emma and thank her and Red for being such a good substitute host. Red got a kiss from Doey and Dorothy. John got in the way, and by mistake, I was so confused that I kissed Doey.

Red said, "I saw that."

"It was an honest mistake, Red. I wasn't going to kiss you." John and Dorothy smiled. "I was only trying to shake your hand, and ask why you were going to Maryland." I smiled and looked very sober and contrite.

Red said, "I'll borrow a few words from one of Doey's favorite sayings, and say 'It's none of your business!'" Red smiled and said, "I wish all of you a good safe summer. See you in September." We watched as Red's car grew smaller then faded from sight.

John had reserved three rooms at the Carolina Inn where we would spend the night. Doey said to her parents, "We would like to use the car. We will pick up Wynn's baggage from the Beta House where we will meet Carolyn and Harry, then go somewhere for dinner. We won't be out late. We will be in the lobby in the morning at 6 a.m. ready for the day." We drove Dorothy and John back to the Carolina Inn.

Carolyn and Harry were waiting for us at the Beta House. We picked up my luggage and put it in the trunk of John's car. It was a short drive to the Fetzer House where we spent the last minutes of our junior year on campus with Carolyn and Harry. Phil and Helen were in the living room, waiting for Helen's father who would take them to Hendersonville, a small town in the mountains of western North Carolina, where the Lind's had a summer home. Phil would be their summer guest.

"It's been a good year," Carolyn said. "I hope that our 'campus family' all have a safe summer and meet here again in the fall."

"It has been a memorable year," Harry agreed.

Helen said, "I always dreamed of singing with a band, and thanks to Wynn and Harry my dream came true."

Doey said, "Thanks to you, Harry and Carolyn, I came to a dance at UNC without a date, and Harry introduced me to Wynn. It's nice knowing that I am a member of the Fetzer family."

Mr. Lind arrived a short time later and left with Helen and Phil. Then there were four of us. We left our cars and walked across the campus to

Franklin Street, entered Danziger's, and sat down at a table in a dimly lit corner of the restaurant. Without Jack Palance there was no one to broker our illegal order for alcoholic drinks. No matter. We were in a solemn and pensive mood and even the food was of little interest. Harry said, "Let's go to Egan's and get a beer." His plan got instant approval.

We walked down Franklin Street to Egan's. The dimly lit room revealed many empty booths and a silent Wurlitzer jukebox. I walked over and put a couple of nickels in the slot and randomly punched the play buttons without looking at the music selections. The machine came alive with a Tommy Dorsey number, playing Frank Sinatra's latest hit, "Everything Happens to Me."

Harry said, "Let's sit at the bar." There were three students sitting there sopping up the suds from UNC white and blue mugs. Joe Egan stood behind the bar smiling and fielding their questions and answering with sage advice and witty conversation.

Joe saw us as we approached and moved down the long bar to greet us. "It's good to see you, Harry. I thought that you would be long gone by now."

"We're not leaving until in the morning and thought we would end our last night on campus here," Harry said. "Joe, you know Carolyn, and the beautiful girl sitting next to her is Doey Brooks, and I believe that you know Wynn Cary."

Joe said, "Yes, I know Carolyn. You go to that other school. I don't know where it is but I believe it is called Prince, or Count . . . or . . . I can never remember the name."

"You're close, Joe" Carolyn said. "It's Duke."

"Ah yes, Duke. That's the place where they make cigarettes, isn't it?"

"Doey," he said. "I have seen you here often with Wynn Cary, but I have never had the pleasure of meeting either of you. I'm always busy behind the bar." He reached across the counter to shake hands with me, and continued, "Don't tell me that you have all graduated and this is a farewell visit."

"Oh no," Doey said. "Carolyn and I attend the Duke school of cigarette manufacturing. I'm majoring in tobacco blending and Carolyn's in their school of cigarette dispensers. We still have a year before graduation." This was said with such a straight unsmiling face, that it almost made one think they were hearing the truth.

"Yes," Joe said. "I did read in the *Police Gazette* that old Washington Duke left his money to some grammar school, to make sure his name was never forgotten; it's now called Duke."

"Joe," Harry said, "we are trying to make sure that the police in Chapel Hill will never forget that once you ran a bar here. We would like a beer, and not in the white UNC cups. Please use the standard mugs and draw four beers from the keg behind you."

Joe frowned and said, "Now, Harry, I thought we were friends. Didn't I come to your rescue, when the campus cops were threatening to take you to the dean's office when you were a freshman? Now why don't you and Wynn and these lovely ladies go over to one of those nice booths where the lights are dim and I will send four beers."

"That's great, Joe, but they better be in beer mugs or we will pour the beer over the dance floor."

"You wouldn't," Joe said.

"Oh, wouldn't I?" Harry replied.

"Yeah, I guess you would," Joe said.

"Four beers, in beer mugs, coming up," he whispered, and then with a voice loud enough so the students sitting at the end of the bar could hear, "Your I.D.s clearly show that you are twenty one, and school is out so I don't see where you are in violation of any government or college laws."

Joe said to Harry, "You really wouldn't have poured beer on the dance floor, would you, Harry?"

"No. Of course not, and I do remember that you got me released from the campus cops. I still owe you, Joe."

Someone had put a nickel in the Wurlitzer and Artie Shaw was playing his version of "All The Things You Are." We finished our beers and I asked Joe how much we owed.

"Nothing," he said. "It's on the house."

We thanked Joe for the beer, and Harry said, "We'll see you in September."

Joe responded with, "Have a safe summer."

We stepped out into a night lit by a Carolina full moon. We crossed Franklin Street and paused for a moment before Silent Sam and sang a few bars of "Hark the sound of Tar Heel Voices." We also joined Doey and Carolyn and sang a bit of, *Duke we our voices raise to all thy praises untold.* We passed the Davie Poplar tree and stopped at the Old White Well for a drink of pure Carolina water. Ten minutes later we stood by our cars at the Fetzer House. We hugged and kissed the girls goodbye. Harry and I clasped hands. Harry said, "Have a good summer."

I nodded and replied, "Let our next meeting be the day before school starts in September, at Orville's and Wilbur's. The last ones there pay for lunch."

"We will be waiting," Harry said. "Bring money." Doey stood by the window of Harry's car talking with Carolyn. Harry and I had a last few words. Doey and I watched as their car turned the corner into Franklin Street, and disappeared. Then there were two of us.

"It's a beautiful night," Doey said. "It reminds me of the night we first flew in the moonlight. It was the night that I found my love, only I didn't know it then."

"It was a one-sided affair, wasn't it? I was already so in love with you, that had you asked me for the moon or a star, somehow I would have found a way to get it. That, of course, will never happen. But one night, far into the future, we will fly to the other side of the moon and stars, and on to the other side of beyond. But before this summer is over we will fly again in the light of a full moon."

Chapter 35

Washington D.C.-New York City

Doey and I sat in the back seat of the Buick and watched as the scenery and miles raced past our window and piled up behind us. John and I shared the driving. Every fifty miles we changed places and became the driver in command. Late in the afternoon we arrived in Washington, D.C. and pulled up in front of the Willard Hotel, the crown jewel of America's hotels, where we would spend the night. The hotel, two blocks from the White House, has been the gathering place for important men and women who have kept the world turning since the days of Abraham Lincoln.

After checking in, John said "Let's meet here in the lobby at seven for dinner. I think that we can all use a little rest after a long day on the road." That gave us a little more than an hour to rest. Doey and I spent most of that time talking on the phone.

"What a waste of money," I said. "All we need is one room. Mine is big enough for two."

"And so is mine," she said, "but only if you are that other one."

"With you, Doey, there will never be another one. When you have 'prettied up' and are ready to go down, call me." We exchanged "I love yous and hung up. At seven we were in the lobby waiting for our host and hostess. We sat in the dining room and we discussed our day and the plans for the day to come.

"I know that we planned to be in New York tomorrow," John said, "but that has changed. Dorothy will explain."

223

"I read the booklet on the desk in our room. It was filled with descriptions of walking and guided tours to so many of the historical places that to pass them up would be a mistake. I suggested to John that we should stay here for another few days. There is really no hurry to get to New York, and if he could make the changes in hotel reservations, we would change our itinerary.

"I have talked with the hotel," John continued, "and we will be here for two more days." Doey and I gave our loud approval. Doey's parents had been here before and we knew that the change in plans was for us.

After dinner, we left our host and hostess in the hotel's ornate lobby to rest, read papers, and listen to the nightly broadcast of Edward R. Murrow from London. With his signature sign off, "Good night and good luck," Murrow's fifteen minutes of air time was over. The war moved on, washing over the land of Europe like a wave.

"Where are we going?" Doey asked.

"There's still a lot of daylight," I said. "Let's just walk and gather a few memories."

"You're the guide. Lead on, my love." We walked past the White House and turned towards the mall. I had previously told Doey of my trip to Washington with the Boy Scouts many years ago. With this skimpy knowledge, and with the aid of a map, I kept us from becoming lost.

During the next few days, we did a lot of sightseeing and soaked up all that the sites could teach us. The city, so rich with history, beckoned the mind to partake in the education of our country. Each day was full and our nights were spent eating at some of the finest restaurants in town. As the sun set over the Potomac on our last night there, the sky turned the most beautiful shade of orange. We were grateful for the time we shared, but we were anxious to get to New York.

The last leg of our tour took us through the Lincoln Tunnel and to Central Park South where we parked in front of the Plaza Hotel on 59th Street. We were assigned three rooms on the seventh floor.

Our transportation to the fair would be by subway, that wonderful method of transportation that was one of the many experiences new to me, yet so ordinary to Doey. I absorbed everything like a sponge. There was not much that I could learn about manners. I had learned from the very best teacher, my mother. She also taught me to listen to and appreciate classical music. I could converse with a graduate student from Julliard without feeling inferior. From my father and Carolyn Parker, my high school English teacher, I learned to read and enjoy the classics and could quote several soliloquies from Shakespeare's plays. This gave me courage to dare to be in love with a girl that I had thought to be out of reach.

I was preparing to take a shower and dress for an evening on the town when my phone rang. It was Doey. "Mother and Daddy want to hang around the hotel, have an early dinner, and retire for the night," she said. "Mother said you and I should dress semi formal for a night on the town."

"What a waste of time!" I replied.

"Mother said she knew that she and Daddy couldn't keep up with us anyway, so she said to just be careful and enjoy the evening." Doey turned to me and asked with a smile, "What would you like to do?"

"I would like to start by kissing you."

She broke in to say, "I can arrange that, but what else can we do?"

"Is there anything else?" I quipped.

"Inn on the Park is just next door, where we can drink and dance. It might be a good place to start; and if they ban kissing, we might walk down to the Famous Door on 52nd Street. It's called Swing Alley, and like the song says, 'Anything goes.'"

"Call me when you're ready. I'll meet you in the Palm Court in five minutes."

"I'll be in the hall in two minutes," she said.

"I'll be outside your door in one minute."

In the elevator going down, I put my arms around Doey and started to kiss her. On the third floor the elevator stopped. The door opened and an elderly couple entered. The gentleman said, "Pardon us. We seemed to have entered at an unfortunate time."

"No," I said. "The young lady had something in her eye. I looked very closely and couldn't find it, and not to waste the moment, I kissed her. What else could I do?"

"You're a lucky young man," he said. "The young lady is beautiful. I think you did the right thing." His lady smiled in agreement. When the elevator reached the ground floor, Doey and I stepped out.

A few minutes later we entered the Inn on the Park. Charlie Barnet and His Orchestra were softly playing "Cherokee." We found a table and ordered a Vermouth and soda. At ten we left and were on our way to the Famous Door in Swing Alley. The sign above the door was so drab and ordinary that I thought it must be the back entrance, and maybe it was.

Cautiously I opened the door that let smoke and a couple of drunks out. The sound of music filled the room and couples danced and swayed to the beat of a drum. Count Basie played piano and led his twelve-piece orchestra through sounds imported from Harlem. Slowly we inched our way through the darkness looking for a vacant table. When we were opposite the dance floor, the place was so densely packed that we lost control of direction and became part of the music-loving mob.

I turned to Doey and said, "Would you like to get out of here and go somewhere else?"

"No, please let's stay."

"Good answer," I said. We were standing by a vacant table, but from the cigarette smoking in the ash tray and drinks for two on the table, it was clear that the table belonged to dancers who would shortly return.

"Sit down, Doey."

"This table is taken," she replied. "If we sit we would be claim jumpers."

"You have been reading too many western novels. When the owners of this claim come back, let me do the talking."

"I wouldn't have it any other way," she replied. "They will just tell us to move on."

"Want to bet?" I said.

"Sure, what's the bet?"

"If I win, we can share the claim on this table. If you win, we will take the ferry to Ellis Island and climb to the crown of the Statue of Liberty, on a day and time of your choice." I moved the chair out, and she sat.

"That sounds like a winner to me," she replied.

"Oh! There's more to the bet than that. If you lose, you will go up to the bandstand and ask Count Basie to play us a song and then go to the microphone and invite me and the co-holders of this table to dance with you."

On the bandstand Count Basie and his musicians had found new ways to arrange seven notes, with a few sharps and flats, and had come up with a cool sound. A voice said, "This is our table. We were just dancing."

"I'm sorry," I said. "We have been walking so much tonight, that my friend here needed to sit down." I placed my hand on Doey's shoulder as she attempted to rise. She looked at me and winked. "Take your time," I said to Doey, and went through the motions of trying to help her up.

The man at the table looked at me and said, "Please, sit down. My name is Jim Bell, and this is my wife, Betty."

"Yes," Betty said, "please join us."

"That's very considerate of you," Doey said, "but we must go. If we may intrude upon your kindness for just a few minutes, we will be on our way."

"Please stay," Betty urged. "We're from Idaho and this is our first time in New York. We have heard of the Famous Door on the radio, but never dreamed that we would actually be here to see, hear, and dance to live music."

"This is Doey Brooks and I'm Wynn Cary. Doey has been to New York several times, but this is a first for me. I'm from Florida and she's from Indiana." Jim and I shook hands. While we were talking, a waitress came to the table to take our order.

"The least I can do to repay your kindness is to offer you and Betty a drink. We don't have time for a debate so why not let me win this one?"

I wanted to ask Doey to dance, but we had closed the door on that opportunity by telling a lie about Doey's feet being too tired to stand. However, we did get a table and an opportunity to meet Jim and Betty.

Betty said to Doey, "I'm so glad that you have had time to rest. You really should dance at least once, just to be able to say that you have danced at the Famous Door to the music of Count Basie."

I said to Jim and Betty, "I would like to ask Doey to dance, but first I must tell you that I made up the story about Doey needing a place to sit and rest her feet from the long walks that we had taken. That was just to get your sympathy and a table, and now if you don't ask us to leave, I'll ask Doey to dance."

"No harm done," Jim said. "I may use that same approach next time we need a table."

We danced several times, just to assure ourselves that we would always remember we had danced to the music of Count Basie at the Famous Door. Close to midnight, we thanked Jim and Betty for their hospitality and took the memory of our evening with us back to the Plaza Hotel. On the seventh floor we lingered before room 721 and talked about tomorrow and forever. With her key, I opened the door, and handed it back to her.

Doey said "One day, we will come back to New York for a visit and stay in this very room."

"We could do that now," I replied.

"Yes, we could, but I would have to break the promise that I have made to my parents, and so would you."

"Thank you, my darling. One day we will come back and we will stay in room 721." To our goodnight routine I added another kiss and said, "That's to build a dream on."

"Until morning," she said, and softly closed the door.

Chapter 36

Statue of Liberty

The next morning my mind was filled with thoughts of a life with Doey. I was living the impossible dream. Today, I hoped to make my dream forever our dream. After showering, shaving, and dressing, I called Doey.

She said, "I was about to call you."

"I need a hug and a kiss to start our day. I need to be with you."

"Look no further." She said. "Hugging and kissing will be my pleasure." We met in the hallway outside her door.

I took her hand in mine. My eyes were filled with the image of a beautiful girl. From the top of her golden hair and sparkling blue eyes, her tantalizing body was covered with a short sleeve, blue blouse and a white skirt; her long, slim sun-tanned legs reached for the floor, where the dancing feet of one young American stood in penny loafers. She was my dream come true.

How could she be in love with me? I had nothing to give that she didn't already have. The love and devotion that I offered her already existed in her life. From Carolyn and Harry I learned that Doey had been offered love and devotion, with a life of wealth as great as the one she already knew, and had turned them down.

I bless the name of the one, who first said, "Love is blind."

I held her close and kissed her cheek and said, "Awake or asleep, you are the most beautiful dream that I have ever had."

Arise My Love And Come Away With Me

"Thank you, my darling, and you are the only man that I will ever have in my life."

"Now, it's time for us to go down and discuss our day with my in-laws."

We met John and Dorothy in the lobby before going into the dining room. Dorothy and Doey were walking ahead of us. John slowed our walk to let Doey and Dorothy get far enough ahead so they couldn't hear our conversation. "I want you to have this," he said. It was a twenty dollar bill. "It might come in handy."

I said, "John, that's very generous, but the invitation to join you and your family is much more of a gift than anyone could expect. I think of this as a long summer date with Doey, and that makes her my responsibility. I assure you that I will take good care of her." I returned the bill to him.

"Did you enjoy your evening on the town?" John asked.

"Yes, we did," I replied. I started to relate our evening, but was interrupted by the waiter, who enjoyed bringing all conversation to a halt while he had his moment upon the stage. He collected the information needed to fill our order and our day began.

"You asked about our evening on the town. We went to the hotel next door where Charlie Barnet and His Orchestra play nightly. After treating our feet to the rhythm of big band music for an hour or so, we walked down to 52nd Street, where we danced to the music of Count Basie's Orchestra."

Dorothy said, "It reminds me of the days when John and I could dance until dawn and still have enough energy to see us through the following day. We now carefully plan our nights to include a following day of leisure. We will go together to the theater to see *Tobacco Road* and, of course, to the Waldorf Astoria for dinner and end the evening in the Starlight Room. How does that sound? Let's plan to meet here at eleven a.m. and we can go to the fair."

"Doey and I plan to go to the Statue of Liberty this morning, then to the fair. We will look for you, and for sure, we'll be here in time for the theater."

"That's a good plan," Dorothy said. "John and I were there several years ago. Life isn't complete without seeing New York from the crown of the statue. Doey has her camera, so be sure to take some pictures."

"We will," I said. Before breakfast, I had called the concierge and booked two tickets on the earliest ferry. After breakfast we picked up the tickets and took a cab to the harbor.

There were only nine people with us on the short ferry to the Statue of Liberty, where a government guide met us. Many of our ancestors had sailed by this spot, searching for a better life.

At the conclusion of the tour, we were asked to line up by the door at the base of the statue where the climb to the top would begin. For what I wished to accomplish, it was important to be at the end of the line. I figured that would increase our odds of being alone. We took time to read and re-read Emma Lazarus's poem on the side of the statue:

"Give me your tired, your poor,
Your huddled masses yearning to breathe free,
The wretched refuse of your teeming shore.
Send these, the homeless, tempest-tossed to me.
I lift my lamp beside the golden door!"

A short time later, Doey and I stood at the crown window atop the Statue of Liberty. "Doey," I said, "we have come together with a strong mutual love and here we are, a little more than six months later, standing atop the Statue of Liberty. I have brought you here for the final answer to a very important question."

Doey looked up at me and with a soft voice said, "What is it, Wynn?"

"Are you absolutely as certain that you want to marry me as I am to marry you?"

"Oh yes, my darling, you know I am," she replied.

Arise My Love And Come Away With Me

I removed the engagement ring from my pocket and slipped it on her finger. Total silence surrounded us. She looked up and started to cry. Through the tears she smiled, and with a voice no louder than a whisper said, "Wynn, my dearest love, I'll be the best wife that you will ever have."

"And you will be the only wife I will ever have," I replied. Just as I started to seal a pledge of our lifetime together with a kiss, I heard a soft female voice say, "Oh! Pardon me. I seem to have arrived at an awkward moment."

"No," I replied. "You have arrived at precisely the right moment. My name is Wynn Cary and I have asked this beautiful young lady, whose name is Doey Brooks, if she would please change her name to mine and marry me, and she said "yes!" If you would be good enough to take our picture, we would greatly appreciate it." She readily agreed and I handed her our camera.

"I'm Mary Jason and this is my husband Tom." Tom and I shook hands and Mary started snapping pictures. During our conversation, three more people arrived to share our moment. I kissed Doey again, and looking at her smiling face said, "Hello, Mrs. Cary."

Hundreds of names and dates covered the walls of the statue. I looked for and found a small space, just above the window of Liberty's crown, and wrote our names and the date. Our small group of instant friends cheered.

Doey said, "One day we must go home and finish carving our names on the stable wall."

"We'll do that," I said, as we started down the small steps to the bottom of the statue. To myself I thought, "Did I dream this day, or is it real?" Those moments found a place in my heart and mind where good thoughts and memories live forever.

As close as we had become, the ring drew us even closer. It is the knot that binds us together. It is a visible symbol to the world that Doey has found her "wing man," and together we will fly through the winds of life, and fold our wings, only when God gives the word.

There will be one more ceremony, with ancient words that will satisfy the clergy, families and friends, but the commitments and words we live by, we had already said. We needed nothing more.

Chapter 37

New York World's Fair

Walking together had a new meaning for us. On the way to the fair Doey's eyes seldom left the ring on her finger. The diamond reflected a rainbow of colors as it caught the rays of the sun.

It was a warm day in Manhattan. We window shopped along the way to the subway near 42nd Street and Madison Avenue. Doey drew glances and a whistle or two from young men. At the subway I bought two tokens for twenty cents and ten minutes later we were standing on the Bowling Green Plaza, an entrance to the fair's amusement center.

Most of the afternoon was spent looking at exhibits featuring "The World of Tomorrow" and sorting through a quarter of a million people looking for Dorothy and John. At four-thirty our feet pleaded for rest. We took the hint, and public transportation delivered us back to the Plaza Hotel, where we found Dorothy and John in the Oak Bar. They also suffered from that dreaded disease, known as "fair foot." We sat at their table and compared our day.

Doey did all she could to draw attention to her ring. She placed both elbows on the table with her chin in her hands and wiggled the fingers on her left hand. "Doey," her mother said, "it's not polite to put your elbows on the table."

John said, "Is that a ring you got at the fair? Is that what you're trying to show us?"

The light in the bar was so dim that the ring couldn't reflect its beauty. "Oh no, I got the ring on my way to the fair. Wynn gave it to me at the top of the Statue of Liberty."

She removed her elbows from the table and placed her ring hand on the table before her mother, who gasped and said, "Oh Doey, what a beautiful engagement ring! John, this calls for a champagne celebration."

Dorothy turned to me and said, "Wynn, I'm so happy for you and Doey that I could cry." Immediately she searched her purse for a hanky and started dabbing at tears in her eyes.

John gripped my hand and said, "Congratulations, Wynn. It takes a strong and dedicated man to join this family and manage my daughter. Dorothy and I knew at Thanksgiving, when you and Doey shared your plans for a life together, that you two would be constant achievers. The ring is beautiful. Welcome to the family."

"Thank you, John. I'm honored."

John said, "I have planning to do. Let's get a little rest. Dress for a formal evening out and, Doey, don't forget your ring."

"Not a chance," she said.

In the lobby we paused long enough for Dorothy and John to see and admire the brilliance of the reflected light from a lump of coal that, over a million years or more, had morphed into the hardest substance on earth, a diamond.

We walked Doey's parents to the elevator. Then Doey and I returned to the Palm Court and shared words of the day that made this moment, a benchmark from which we measured time to come.

At seven-fifteen my room telephone rang. It was Doey. "Mother just called and said we are to meet in their suite as soon as we're ready."

"Yes, my favorite girl, I am ready. For the rest of my life I'm on standby status just waiting for your call. I'll be at your door in twenty seconds."

Doey said, "I'll be at your door in ten."

Quickly, I put on my coat and opened the door. Doey was standing there in a beautiful pale green formal dress. Around her neck was a dark green jade necklace with a matching bracelet. On the finger of her left hand she wore a sparkling diamond. The only thing lacking was a corsage, but I could get that in the flower shop in the hotel. I was thankful that John told us before we left Chapel Hill that there may be need for formal dress.

"Doey, I thought John said seven thirty."

"He did, but I think that he may have found time to arrange what he and mother think is important to us." We walked a few doors down the hallway to their corner suite and knocked on the door.

Dorothy opened the door and we entered into a two-room suite that faced Central Park. The beauty of a moonlit night was an extension of the tasteful decor of the room. From the bar, a record player turned a recording of "Bewitched, Bothered and Bewildered." In the center of the room, a table with hors d'oeuvres and a white orchid with a hint of green along the edge of the petals was in a vase.

"Come and sit down beside me on the sofa," Dorothy said. She was wearing a long deep purple dress with a strand of pearls that hung low around her neck. Her slim waist was girded with a narrow golden belt. On the third finger of her left hand gold rings encrusted with diamonds were evidence that she was a married woman. On her right wrist was a gold bracelet. She led Doey to the sofa by the window.

"Sit down, dear. I want to see your beautiful ring and tell you how much your father and I adore you. From the day you were born you have been our life. We knew that every birthday brought you closer to the man, who, somewhere in the world, was looking to claim you for his wife. It was inevitable that one day you would leave us. When you were fifteen you started dating. We watched from the sidelines, and never encouraged or discouraged anyone you chose for your friend. We were always there hoping that one day you would find the right man who would love and care for you, as you would for him. We just want to tell you that we know that you have found that man."

"Mother, I never had a doubt that you and Daddy were there for me, and I assure you that I never looked for a man. I was content to wait until the right one found me. From the moment that I met Wynn at a dance where he was playing, my wait was over. I knew then, that one day he would ask me to be his wife. Every moment that I'm with him is precious. Very soon, the military will take him from me. There is no comfort in knowing that more than a million women, with men in the Air Force, will be losing an estimated fifty thousand men and their futures to the war effort. That means that Wynn will have only one in twenty chances of coming back to me. I try to smile and never let him know my doubts, but I'm not brave, Mother. I live a scared and frightened life. I know the coming year is all the time we have. My only hope is that we will be able to finish our last year of college. Beyond that, hope will be nothing more than looking for life at the end of a dark and frightening road."

Dorothy put her arms around her daughter. "My darling, from the moment that I learned you were flying, fear has been my constant companion. And now, my fear and panic include Wynn. Together we will share our feelings and support each other."

"Thank you, Mother; I will have the easy and safe flying. Wynn's the one who will fly in harm's way. We will support each other."

The long dark road faded, to be replaced by a memory worth keeping. Their suite was elaborately decorated to fit our festive occasion. I said to John, "How did you arrange this on such short notice?"

"It was no problem. All it took was a phone call to the right hotel office and they did the rest. They asked a few questions, like what are you celebrating, what theme you want carried out, and do you want dinner served. I told them to bring the champagne and the theme would be airplanes and angels." Thin streamers of white gauze, like contrails, marked the pathway of two airplanes that had merged, hung from the ceiling. Two angels in white flowing robes flew just above and to the right in an echelon right formation.

"To celebrate this important night in your lives, I have arranged for you and Doey to go to the top of Rockefeller Center to the Rainbow Room for dinner and dancing. This is not what Dorothy and I planned to do, but in many ways it's better. Where and when did you have time to buy a ring?"

"I bought the ring before Doey and I went to Terre Haute for Thanksgiving, but I left it at the jewelers, thinking that I would give it to her for Christmas. That was my original plan. Of course, that changed when you and Dorothy invited me to accompany you to the World's Fair. That's when I got the idea that the crown room of the Statue of Liberty would be the right setting for such an important place for us to remember."

I sat on the sofa beside Doey, and John sat down in a wingback chair facing Dorothy. The waiter brought the platter of hors d'oeuvres and placed it on the table in front of the sofa, and returned with a tray of glasses and a bottle of champagne. "Is there anything else that I can do?" he asked John.

"No, Leon, nothing more. You have created a wonderful setting for this occasion and in such a short time." John signed the bill that I'm sure carried a generous tip for the waiter, who thanked him and left the room.

John stood and opened the champagne. The cork flew from the bottle, hit the ceiling, and fell to the floor. He poured champagne into the glasses and handed one to each of us. He raised his glass and said, "This toast is for the two people we love most in this world, our daughter Doey, and our son-in-law to be, Wynn Cary. May your lives be long and healthy and your days always be filled with love and understanding."

He walked a few steps to the bar where the record player was and turned it on. The room was filled with the soft sound of "I Love You Truly." John returned and I was rewarded with a moment that I will never forget. I stood and took Doey's hand. We were oblivious of anything or anyone. For a few moments we were alone with thoughts of our future. I wrapped her in my arms and whispered in her ear. "Doey, we will have a beautiful long life together. I don't know how I can, but I know that I will love you even more then." I thanked John for his beautiful words, and wondered if I could ever hope to provide Doey with this lifestyle that she had always known as normal.

Shortly after eight, Dorothy said, "It's time for you to leave for dinner."

"Before you leave," John said, "you may want to pin this orchid on Doey's dress."

He placed the orchid in my hand. I pinned it on Doey's gown and said, "Yes, thank you, John. I had planned to stop at the flower shop in the lobby for a corsage, but I wasn't thinking of an orchid. You think of everything."

He placed a billfold in my hand and said, "This is part of what Dorothy and I had planned for our evening with you and Doey, but the announcement of your engagement with such a beautiful ring changed that. It is now your obligation to do what we had planned. You have made our day. We plan to go out and celebrate, too. We will see you in the morning for breakfast."

Dorothy said, "We love you, Wynn. I am so happy to know that you have joined our family." There was nothing more to say except "thank you." I expected that the billfold contained money. I had come prepared to pay our way for anything Doey wanted, and whatever was in the billfold I would return to John. That was the plan I made before knowing how expensive the Rainbow Room could be. I was not surprised, however, to find that I was not ready to move in the orbit of the well-to-do.

We arrived at the top of Rockefeller Center and entered The Rainbow Room. Yes, they had our reservation, and we were led to a table by a window where we could see New York spread out before us. I was thankful for the Arthur Johnson Clothing Company and for the formal wear that at least made me look like I belonged. I thought of John's story and the memories he and Dorothy had of this very room. Doey and I would also remember this night. Eddy Duchin and His Orchestra were still playing here. Together they wove a pattern of remembrance that creates lasting memories for dancers to take with them to paste in the album in their mind.

Our memory included good food, champagne and dancing the night away. At midnight I paid our bill and we took our memories of the Rainbow Room with us, and left knowing that one day we would return.

"Let's go to the Inn on The Park," Doey said.

"You read my mind," I replied.

We walked along singing our song and entered The Inn on the Park. Between dances and a couple of kisses, maybe more, we ended our night and walked next door to the Plaza, where we boarded the elevator for the seventh floor. I opened the door to Doey's room; we walked in and closed the door. Doey said, "You shouldn't be in here."

"Do you want me to leave?"

"No," she said, "but I don't want to be the one who breaks a promise."

I held her close in my arms and said, "I don't know how long I can keep that promise. You are young, desirable, beautiful, and mine. With or without a church service and some lines on a paper, we belong together. I have no right to ask you to break a promise to your parents. You are my dearest love and with deep sorrow and frustration I will meet you in my dreams, where broken promises go unnoticed."

"Thank you, Wynn. I do love you more than life." A passionate goodnight kiss was ours to build a dream on.

The next morning we met John and Dorothy in the Palm Court to compare evenings and plan our day. "Did you enjoy your evening on the town?" John asked.

"Yes we did," I replied. "Your generosity was more than welcome. When we got the check for the evening, your gift saved us from an evening of dish washing. I know that the father of the bride is to be expected to pay for an engagement party, but somehow it didn't seem right for you to pay and not be there to enjoy it."

I laid the wallet on the table before him and said, "We used only part of it, which I intend to return. You have trusted me with Doey's future and I'm reluctant to tell you, Doey, that we can't look to your father to support us beyond our means. I do promise that you will always have everything you need. It may take a little longer to give you what you may want. And, John, you are the most generous and caring man I know. I hope that I never disappoint you."

"Wynn, you've reacted as I expected. I doubt that you will ever disappoint me. Would you like breakfast?"

We all agreed that breakfast was a good place to start. While waiting for our waiter, John said to me, "A Broadway play is on our list of things to do while we're in New York. While Dorothy and I were out last night, I picked up tickets to four plays that are drawing rave reviews from standing-room only crowds. The plays are, *Outward Bound, Tobacco Road, The Little Foxes,* and *Life Boat.* They are all matinees, beginning each afternoon at two o'clock. I apologize for not asking sooner, Wynn, and you and Doey may have something else planned, but the plays now may serve as a convenient break in the day to rest our feet and be entertained at the same time."

"John, give us a moment to consider this." I turned and said to Dorothy and Doey, "John has my vote, how about yours?"

Doey agreed. "I cast my vote for Daddy's plan."

Dorothy said, "He's my husband. I'm supposed to honor and obey. I vote for his plan."

"Democracy wins again, John. You have a landslide mandate to lead. I do have a suggestion that you may consider. That is, we go together to the fair where Doey and I will make our itinerary as we go. At eleven we'll meet you and Dorothy at the Trilon and Perisphere and return to the hotel for lunch. Then we can go to the theatre."

"That's a good plan," John said. "Let's do it."

At the Fair we stood before the theme center—DEMOCRACITY, where we would start and end our day. Piercing the sky 700 feet above the earth, like some giant three-sided obelisk, the Trylon, the symbol of the Fair's lofty purpose, adjoined a huge hollow globe 200 feet in diameter called the Perisphere.

Never before in history had man undertaken building a globe of such tremendous proportions, eighteen stories high! It was as broad as a city block. Its interior was more than twice the size of Radio City Music Hall. To describe these structures new words were coined: Trylon, from "tri," the three sides of the structure; and "pylon," indicating its use as the monumental gateway to the Theme building; and Perisphere, from "peri," meaning "beyond, all around, about."

Here was the magnificent spectacle of a luminous world, apparently suspended in space by gushing fountains of liquid reds, blues, and greens, over which clung a strange ethereal mist. An ingenious arrangement of mirror casings on which eight groups of fountains continuously played, made the supporting columns invisible. At night, powerful lights projected cloud patterns on the globe and, drenching it in color mist, created the startling illusion that it was revolving like a great planet on its axis.

We entered the Perisphere at its base and mounted the longest moving electric stairway in the world. Silently we were swept upward and delivered to the entrance fifty feet above the ground where we stepped onto one of two revolving balconies, which formed huge rings seemingly unsupported in space. The platforms turned in opposite directions and took six minutes to make a complete revolution, the show lasting just that time.

As the interior of the Perisphere was revealed, one saw in the land beneath the sky, "Democracity," a symbol of a perfectly integrated futuristic metropolis pulsing with life, rhythm, and music. Here was a city of a million people with a working population of 250,000, whose homes were located beyond the city proper in five satellite towns. Like great arteries, broad highways traversed expansive areas of vivid green countryside, where homes were located. The highways also connected outlying industrial towns with the city's heart. The daylight panorama stretched to the horizon on all sides.

After gazing at the model for two minutes, dusk slowly shadowed the scene. The light faded, and the celestial sky gleamed with a myriad of stars. To the accompaniment of a symphonic poem, a chorus of a thousand voices reached out of the heavens, and there, ten equal distant points in the purple dome, loomed marching men . . . farmers, stamped by their garb, and mechanics with their tools of the trade. As the marchers approached, they represented the various groups in modern society. All the elements, which must work together to make a better life possible, would flourish in such a city as lay below. The symphony rose to a loud mingling of discordant sounds. The figures assumed mammoth size and the music subsided. The group vanished behind slow drifting clouds. Suddenly, a blaze of light climaxed the show.

Standing in front of the Trylon and Perisphere, Doey said, "That depicts a wonderful future, but Hitler won't let it happen." For a few moments we stood there. Doey gripped my hand and asked, "Wynn, how close are you to getting your instructor's rating?"

"Three hours flying and a test," I replied. "Why do you ask?"

"I don't want you to fly in combat. I'm sure Red could help you get a job instructing."

"The French," I said, "have already given up, and unless the British wake up, the war will be over before we graduate and Hitler will have won." To myself I thought, I don't believe that, but it was the only thing I could think of. We walked along slowly, almost passing a gift stand that sold bracelets and medallions.

"Let's stop and look at the medallions," Doey said. "They only cost thirty-five cents, and I want you to have one. The sign says they are 12 carat gold, but I'll bet that in a couple of days they will begin to look like a tarnished brass pipe."

Featured on one side of the medallion was an imprint of the World's Fair, Trylon and Perisphere. On the other side was the print of a Ryan single-engine monoplane, like the one Lindbergh flew to Paris in 1927.

Arise My Love And Come Away With Me

"The original medallion," the barker said, "was designed by Tiffany, and made of 18 carat gold for Charles Lindberg's wife, Ann. For ten cents more, we will engrave any word or words, up to ten letters on the back."

"We get all of that for only thirty-five cents?" I said. "Wow! Such a deal! We can't pass that up Doey. I think that you should have a medallion to go with your ring. What would you like engraved on the back?"

Doey knew exactly what she wanted, "AMLACAWM." That was the first letter of each line of the poetry we silently said when our plane rotated, "Arise my love and come away with me."

I printed the words in the line for the engraver and ordered two medallions. To Doey I said, "Now that we are absolutely, no fooling, bet-your-life safe flying, let's get on with our long life together."

In a few minutes the engraver handed me both medallions with the necklace attached. I put one in my pocket and slipped the other one over Doey's head, where it settled around her neck and swung like a long string of pearls.

Doey lightly kissed my cheek and said, "Next to my ring, the medallion is the best gift I have ever received." We entered the amusement center, and in the distance we could see parachutes floating down from a tall tower.

"Wynn," Doey asked, "have you ever used a parachute?"

"No," I replied. "I did wear one for a few minutes when I soloed, but if I had needed it I would have hit the ground before the parachute had time to open. We were flying too low for the chute to do any good."

From where we stood we could see the parachute tower, where eleven parachutes were safely drifting down from a 250 foot tower. Doey remarked, "I know that it won't be anything like the real thing, but I would like to float down from the parachute tower just to say I have."

After standing in line for a few minutes, we were seated together below one of the eleven parachutes. A cable pulled us up to the summit of the tower. An automatic release started the drop and we floated gently to the ground. Vertical guide wires prevented swaying and a metal ring kept the parachute open at all times, while shock absorbers eliminated the impact at landing.

"I wish it was that easy," Doey said, "but I know that it's nothing like that. I hope we never have to make a parachute let down, especially if the plane is uncontrollable and someone is shooting at you."

"Yeah, that would make a difference. Just keep control of your plane and stay out of the way of people with guns."

"Oh, Wynn, please do that and come back to me."

I knew where she was going with that statement, so I gripped her hand and said, "This is a day for fun. What's next on your itinerary?"

"The Theme of the Fair is to honor the 150th anniversary of George Washington's birthday. Let's go to the Theme building and pay our respects. After that, I'm sure that you would like to go to the Congress of World Beauties. It's a show that features sixty beautiful girls in a dance routine under the direction of Earl Carroll and Billy Rose."

"Why would I want to see them when I'm holding the hand of the most beautiful girl in the world right now?" We went to the Theme building and paid our respects to George and Martha.

"Do you think they are now living on the other side of beyond?" Doey asked.

"I'm sure they are."

We skipped the pageant of sixty beautiful girls and substituted The Crystal Palace of 1939, a museum of amusement dedicated to the changing modes and manners of the last 100 years. It presented the highlight attractions of the past American Fairs in the manner of an old-fashioned family album, with the various period exhibits appropriately designed.

Pretty girls, popular songs, fashionable costumes, ballad singers, and barkers were representative of the recurrent forms of Fair entertainment. Changes in taste, costumes, scenic design, and technical methods were illustrated in the two theatres housed in the Crystal Palace itself. One of these was designed as a 19th century music hall and presented attractions and personalities, which had proved sensational to Fair visitors from 1853 to 1892; while on the second stage, the evolution of 20th century entertainment was shown.

Particular emphasis was on the personalities of the great Fairs. The first American Exposition in 1853 introduced General Tom Thumb, the renowned midget; Jenny Lind, of nightingale voice; and the Siamese twins, all closely associated with the name P.T. Barnum. The Philadelphia Exposition in 1876 presented "Couchette," the female baritone. Sandow, the strong man, appeared at the Columbian Exposition in Chicago in 1893, a fair which also presented the famous "Beef Trust," a daring group of buxom chorus girls. On the same occasion, the world famous belly dancer, Little Egypt, performed.

"Have you seen Stella?" was a laugh-provoking greeting at the Panama Pacific Exposition of 1915 in San Francisco, referring to a fantastic painting of a woman who seemed to be alive.

All the facts mentioned above were part and parcel of the Crystal Palace of 1939. The building was an exact, smaller scale replica of the famed Glass Palace of 1853. Philip Gelb, artist and designer, conceived the theme slogan of the fair Palace: "Yesterday and Today at the World of Tomorrow."

Within this glass and iron structure were many other attractions. The tin type photographer was on hand to portray visitors as they would have looked in 1853, 1856, 1876, 1893, and 1915. The mustachioed soda fountain clerk dispensed soda delights of bygone eras; the Saturday night scrub in the tub was shown; and the printed program was in the form of the *Police Gazette*. As a finale to this nostalgia, which included dramatic and colorful parades, were glimpses of the amusement attractions of tomorrow.

At eleven thirty we joined Dorothy and John at the base of the Trylon and returned to the Plaza, where we had lunch and compared our views of the fair. John said, "Let's meet here at one. We'll take a cab to the Play House Theater to see *Outward Bound*. That gives us plenty of time to shower, rest, and dress."

After we refreshed, we met in the Palm Court. John looked up from the notes he had written on the back of a hotel envelope and said, "We are going to the Playhouse Theatre at 117 W 48th St."

Inside the theatre, we followed the usher down the center aisle to the third row. We had good seats, the first four seats on the aisle. As the curtains slowly parted, the lights in the theatre began to dim, and the light on stage rose, revealing mostly elderly people gathered in the salon of an outward bound ship. The passengers were somewhat confused about why or where they were going. Slowly they come to know that they were dead and outward bound to a destination unknown.

Outward Bound was a beautiful play. Between acts there was a break allowing the audience to move about and visit the lobby, where drinks could be had at greatly inflated prices. The Brooks' family had seen Broadway plays several times. For me it was another wonderful new experience.

Back at the Plaza we sat in the Palm Court critiquing a play that we could find nothing to criticize. We arrived at a decision and gave the play, on a scale of ten being best, an eleven.

"What's next?" Dorothy asked.

John said, "I suggest we have dinner in the Waldorf Astoria's Starlight Room and dance to the music of Kay Kyser's Orchestra. Did you know, Wynn, that Kyser's band started at UNC and a few of the musicians are alumni of the university? I thought that you and Doey might approve."

"Oh! We do," Doey replied. She looked at me for agreement. I looked at John, nodded, and said, "It's a good plan, John; we will be pleased to tag along . . . and listen to the music of a fellow Tar Heel."

"In the meantime, what do you and Doey plan to do?" Dorothy asked.

"We plan to walk down Fifth Avenue and visit St. Patrick's Cathedral, and window shop along the way. If you like, we would love to have you join us," I said.

"Thanks for the invitation, but Dorothy and I plan to go for a carriage ride in Central Park. Why not join us?" John remarked.

"Thanks, Daddy, but we plan to do that before we leave New York."

"Let's meet here at seven and end our day in the Starlight Room," John said.

Doey smiled and replied with, "We'll be here at seven."

Chapter 38

St. Patrick's Cathedral

In the near distance we could see one of the most beautiful Gothic structures in the world, St. Patrick's Cathedral, and each step took us closer, until we stood before the portals of that magnificent structure. On the right as we entered was a high table containing dozens of lighted candles.

Doey said, "Let's light two candles, one for your family and one for mine." Doey selected two of the larger ones and lit them. I remember reading in the bible about the gift of the widow's mite, and dropped a bill in the cash box for what I believed we could afford. No words were spoken and silently, as if by plan, hand in hand we walked down the long aisle and knelt before the altar. We were guided by a single mind. Doey took my hand in hers and whispered, as tears streaked her lovely face, "Wynn, my darling, you are the only love that I have ever had or will have. I have only the vaguest thought of what has brought us here. My only belief, at the moment, is that we do have a guardian angel."

"I believe that," I whispered. "Without you, Doey, there would be no other future in my life." We made the sign of the cross and slowly, deep in thought, walked to the exit.

Back on the street we both wanted to find a place where we could sit and talk. We found a small table at a nearby café.

"Doey," I began, "our actions were not as strange as you think. We both belong to the Episcopal Church where, as children, we learned to kneel at the altar and make the sign of the cross. Lighting a candle, I think, belongs to the Catholic religion. I believe that just being in St. Patrick's Cathedral and

Arise My Love And Come Away With Me

lighting a candle brought a hidden desire for us to speak of our love in a church. It brought forth our desire to remind God of something He already knows. I think He was reminding us of your promise to your mother. I will not be the one to cause you to break that promise—however, I want you to know that it will be the hardest promise that I will ever be asked to keep."

For a few moments Doey was silent. She then said, "Wynn, I need you near me, to feel your touch in the night; to wake up beside you in the morning. I need to feel, that in every way, you belong to me. We have a year of school left and a war that is sure to keep us apart for who knows how long. That is totally unacceptable. We could be separated for many years." Her voice dropped to a whisper. She paused then said, in a soft voice, "Maybe forever."

"Yes, my dearest love forever is a long, long, time. I totally agree, but let's not worry your mother by mentioning it now. Let's wait until we get back to Terre Haute. For now, let's go back to the hotel where we can find a place to seal our vows with a few kisses. It's impossible to stop after kissing you once. What we have spoken of may require a dozen, maybe more. When we run out of time we will meet again at our home on the other side of beyond, where nothing will ever keep us apart."

"Do you really believe that there is such a place?" she asked.

"Do you believe there is a Heaven?" I answered.

"Yes," she replied.

"There are many names for Heaven," I said. "We know that it's beyond the moon, beyond the stars, and on other side of beyond. When we retire from life, we will go there. My only hope is that we make the trip together. Those are just a few more hopes and promises that need to be sealed with a few kisses. All that's needed is a place in which to seal them. Let's go," I said.

We entered my room, where we were alone. I took Doey into my arms and kissed her knowing that her will to resist now belonged to me. From this moment on I would break the bonds she had with her parents, who trusted me with her life. Our deception could only last a short while before our physical love had reached the point of no return. The last shreds of youth were gone. We were two thinking, reasoning young adults. The quality of our future life depended upon our action of the moment. Only we would know of the frustration it took to be responsible. Today our love affair had moved to a new level; a level that required lies and quick thinking to survive. Could I destroy that love and confidence her parents had showered on me, and maybe even how they think of Doey?

I kissed her once more and said, "Doey, you may not believe this, but I love you too much to destroy the faith and trust your parents have in me. Come, I will take you to your room." She gave a long sigh, full of disappointment. At her door I said, "Call me when you are ready to go down to the Palm Court, my love."

I got back to my room just as the phone rang. It was Doey. "Wynn," she said. "I need to be with you now. Please let's go find a place where we can be together and talk."

"Yes, we do need to do that. I know just the place."

A few minutes later we entered the Oak Bar and found a table in a far corner. The room was cool with just enough chattering people that we could talk quietly without disturbing or being disturbed by those at the next table. I ordered cold drinks and we settled in.

Doey said, "I thought that you knew of a quiet room where we could talk."

"No, I said that I know just the place. A proper place in a hotel to talk about a problem such as the one troubling us is best discussed in a dark bar filled with other people.

"You and I are faced with a big, big problem. We are blessed with a complete sense of mutual understanding. When you speak to me, I listen and understand every word you say. When I speak to you, you listen. That's how important you make my words sound. What are we going to do with all of this compatibility? We can satisfy our need to be together, as we were on the brink of doing, but only at the expense of you violating the promise that you made to your parents. I know that we are living a final test with them. They accept the fact that we have already declared a life together, and nothing can change that. They love you so very much that they want to be sure. They may have some lingering doubts about me, but they will always be there for you, and so will I. More than anything, I want them to know this. I love you too much to take a chance that some words left unspoken can, in any way, change their love for you, or their trust in me. I do believe that even if we give in to our desires, they will know that we are living with a broken promise. It will never be your fault. I will be blamed, and should be. I do know that you would still be my wife, but in time, our actions of today may then be yours alone to explain. That may or may not be; but I love you so much that I can't let that happen. Do you understand?"

Doey studied my face with her attentive blue eyes, and then solemnly nodded.

"Now, I think it's time for us to get ready to meet your folks for dinner."

A while later we followed John and Dorothy into the Waldorf and entered an elevator that whisked us up to the Starlight Room, where our evening of dining and dancing to the music of Kay Kyser would begin. His orchestra was playing and Ginny Sims was singing "I Concentrate On You."

Doey said, "Let's dance. We can eat anytime."

"Yes, I agree. We can't dance to Kay Kyser's music whenever we please. Dorothy, if we're not back by the time the waiter comes, would you please order for us, anything will do. Surprise us."

"I will," she said, "but you may be disappointed."

"That's a chance we'll take."

We danced by the orchestra and paused. It was the end of the set and we returned to our table. We all enjoyed the dinner and then danced until the band finished for the evening.

Chapter 39

Terre Haute—Macatawa

The next morning, our ten days in New York and the World's Fair became history. We stood beside the Buick and watched as the doorman supervised the packing of our bags in the car. John stood with a road map in his hand talking to the doorman. I helped Dorothy into the car and Doey and I got in the back seat. John finished his talk with the doorman and passed some money around. He took his place behind the wheel and pointed the car toward the west. We crossed the George Washington Bridge, and were on our way home.

It was a beautiful sunlit day filled with songs and laughter. We sang the "Beer Barrel Polka" and all of the old songs that came to mind, including "Down by the Old Mill Stream" and "Sweet Adeline."

On the second day, John called Edward telling him the approximate time of our arrival. Late in the day we topped the hill that once belonged to great grandfather Brooks, and together Doey and I said, "Back home again in Indiana." A few minutes later John turned into the circular driveway and we were home.

Before we could get out of the car, the door to the house opened and Anna and Edward were there to greet us. After dinner, Doey, Dorothy, John, and I sat in the library relaxing and talking about the recent past and the future. I got a warm glow just thinking about the years to come with Doey, and the promise of a long life together.

The radio was tuned to CBS for the war news. John turned the volume up just as the announcer was saying: "Representative Martin Dies from Texas, speaking from Madison Square Garden, warned an enthusiastic U.S. to stop its aping of Europe. He pleaded for tolerance. A crowd of 10,000 cheered his plea for national solidarity and urged a fight on all alien nations."

At ten o'clock John yawned and Dorothy said "It's been a long day. It's time we call it a night." Doey stood and kissed her parents goodnight. I stood beside her and I wished them pleasant dreams. They disappeared through the door to the back staircase to the upper floor. We sat down on the sofa and turned the radio to listen to music from the west coast. The announcer was saying, "Good evening, ladies and gentlemen, from the Marine Dining Room of the Hotel St. Catherine, on Santa Catalina Island just off the coast of Southern California, out in the blue Pacific, CBS is pleased to bring you the music from the Benny Goodman Orchestra." We talked about tomorrow and planned what we would do.

"Do you play golf?" she asked.

"No." I said. "I play the clarinet." She laughed. "I'm not a golfer. I have an old hand-me-down bag of clubs, and bragging rights in knowing Walter Hagan and Bob Harlow, whose brother Richard is the football coach at Harvard. Mr. Harlow was the first president of the PGA and manager of Walter Hagen."

"Walter Hagen? You know him?" Doey asked excitedly.

"Well, sort of," I replied. "I'm better acquainted with Bob Harlow, but I think that Hagen tolerated my friend Eldon, Bob Harlow's stepson, and me as he would a couple of inept caddies. My exposure to fame only lasted through nine holes. Eldon and I lied about our scores and I still ended so far over par that Bob Harlow suggested that we go to the clubhouse for lunch. Mr. Hagan and I were greatly relieved, but for different reasons."

Doey chuckled and said "Let's call it a night." At the head of the stairs, Doey and I whispered "goodnight." She turned right toward her room, and I turned left towards mine. My mind evaded sleep, and for a while, I counted more dreams than a heart can hold of a life with Doey.

The next morning, Ann Ellis called Dorothy and asked us to go with them to the club. She told her that we had just returned from New York and needed a few days rest before going to Macatawa. Ann understood and said that they were going to the lake on Monday and we would get together there.

We joined Doey's parents at breakfast. Anna showed off her skills as a cook and served Eggs Benedict, Canadian bacon, toast, jam, an assortment of Danish, and a breakfast beverage of our choice.

"And, what do you have planned for today?" Dorothy asked.

"Wynn plans to give me a lesson," was Doey's reply.

"What kind of lesson?" I asked.

"Flying," she said.

"Flying? I thought we were going to play golf."

"Oh, we will. After that we're going to fly."

At the first sound of the word flying, the day frowned and took refuge behind a cloud that had drifted over the sun. The smile on her mother's face was replaced with sorrow. In the lexicon of her mind, there was no word for flying.

Doey, like a debater, was using the word to make her case. She didn't come close. Quickly, I looked at Dorothy, who was obviously agitated. She looked me in the eye and said, "Be very careful, Wynn."

"I will," was my weak reply, knowing there was no way I could reassure her.

Doey asked her father if I might use his clubs. "Of course," he said. "We're about the same height, the clubs should be fine."

I thanked John and said, "You are too generous. Really, rental clubs at the club would be okay, and I wouldn't like to take the chance of damaging yours."

"No, no," he said, "I insist. You can't hurt my old clubs." I didn't tell him that golf was not my game, and the few times that I had been on a course, I mostly just walked around holding what I believed was the right club.

Edward brought Doey's and her father's clubs to the door and stood waiting, while Doey took a last minute look in a hall mirror. I looked over her shoulder and the two mirror reflections merged.

"What are you looking for?" I asked. "You can't improve on perfection." A crooked smile and a wink was her answer.

"I'll drive," she said. "The main road to the club is temporarily closed for repairs, so from here to the club is a monkey puzzle. If you make a wrong turn, we may never see home again." I opened the door to the driver's side and she slipped behind the wheel.

We played our nine holes of golf and I'm sure she let me win. Later, in the club's bar, we had lunch. She knew many of the members of the club and kept introducing me as an expert who once played with Walter Hagen. "Cool it, Doey. I barely knew which club to use when I ended up in the sand trap. I played a lousy game."

Many of the people who came to our table to greet Doey were close friends of hers and her family. "Will you be returning to Macatawa?" was a frequently asked question. The younger members asked about Duke University and what she was studying.

After the first interruption, I took a sip of tea and said to Doey, "Please don't involve me in your answers. Let's just say I'm someone you met at a dance. Someone who gave up a summer of doing nothing, and accepted your mother and father's unbelievable invitation to see the New York's World's Fair, and will be spending the summer with you at their summer home in Macatawa, Michigan."

When we left the club I asked, "Were you serious about flying?" She had come to a stop before entering a road, with a sign that indicated that four miles down the road, on the left, was an airport.

"Yes," she said. "I would love to have the support of both my parents, but I'm afraid that's not going to happen. You saw Mother's reaction when I mentioned flying. She takes every opportunity to discourage it. I love her dearly and want to please her, but when she came to Chapel Hill and watched me solo, I knew from her reaction that I had lost her support. I hope, in time, she might relent. I can only hope."

"I think that most mothers take a dim view of flying, especially when their own child is involved. For three or four years my mother reacted the same way as yours. I'm sure she hasn't changed, but reluctantly she has come to terms with something that won't go away."

At the airport's operation desk, it was evident that Doey had been here before. She was greeted by name. She introduced me to the man at the desk. "This is Stan Wilson," she said, and turning to me, said, "This is Wynn Cary. He has a private license and since time is so short, I thought seeing Terre Haute from the air would be the quickest way to show him our town."

"A wonderful plan," Stan said. "I'll need your license number to complete the form." I already had the license in hand and passed it over the desk to him. It took less than a minute to fill in the blanks. I signed in the space indicated and passed it back to him. The Hobbs meter in the plane would record our time, which we would pay for by the hour or fraction thereof. Doey had her private license, so we split the hour in the air.

Doey taxied the four seat monoplane to the blast fence, held the breaks, checked the magnetos, then taxied to the runway and held short. She got a green light from the tower and taxied into position and held. The light from the tower indicated the runway was hers. At the point of rotation we silently said our token of safety and broke the bonds of earth. She flew for the first thirty minutes and I flew the second thirty minutes. We flew over the town and up and down the Wabash River. We even broke a government flight rule and flew through some inviting low flying clouds. We returned to the airport and landed.

At the checkout desk, Doey signed for the flight time and the bill would be sent to her father.

"Are you home for the summer?" Stan asked.

"No, just passing through. We're leaving tomorrow for Macatawa," Doey said.

"You and Wynn have a good summer," Stan replied.

Chapter 40

Brooks' Summer Home

The Brooks' house, a two-story white cottage that fronted on Lake Michigan, was built in 1893, the year the Chicago World's Fair opened. It was a year-round cottage, built to survive winters that sometimes lingered on into spring.

Doey kept her Star Class sailboat, named *Stardust*, at the local boat yard on Black Lake, a short sailing distance from Lake Michigan. We started most mornings with a swim in the lake or a sail along the coast. When the moon was bright, we sailed in its shimmering rays of light, coming all the way from heaven. The moon was called a lover's moon. In November it would be a harvest moon and in the war, I was to learn, it was a bomber's moon. In a game of pool or sailing I was Doey's equal. It's not possible to live in Florida for twenty-plus years without learning how to sail, or live in a fraternity house and not learn to shoot pool. Sometimes, in the evenings, we drove down to Saugatuck for dinner and dancing at the pavilion.

Even though we were having such a wonderful time, the war news loomed over us like the darkening sky, just before a storm. The Battle of Britain had begun on August 8th and the news was not good.

"Churchill asked a Second Lieutenant, who was guarding a pier on the south coast, what his mission was. 'My mission', the Lieutenant said, 'is to run back from the pier and telephone my command post when the Germans are sighted. The command post is in a golf club. I have to use a pay telephone', he remarked. 'The safety of England depends upon my having the *right change when the Germans arrive.'"*

Arise My Love And Come Away With Me

After a few weeks, we said goodbye to Macatawa. Anna and Edward would stay for a few days to clean and close the house that would not be opened again until spring. For the many years they were with the Brooks family, love and respect, not money, had formed an unbreakable family bond.

We packed our memories of a summer that could never again be repeated, and headed for Chicago. At the Midway Airport, I said goodbye to John and Dorothy. John and I shook hands. Dorothy put her arms around me and with a big hug and a kiss said, "You were a wonderful guest, Wynn. You came to our home as Doey's guest and left as Doey's companion for life. I know that one day soon, Doey will bring you back to us. Take good care of yourself and Doey. You now have two homes and a place in our hearts. We love you, Wynn."

"You and John have been very generous and just to say thank you, is hardly enough. I am deeply indebted to you and John for including me in your summer plans. I will take good care of Doey. She is my life. We will see you again soon."

They sensed that I would like to have a private moment with Doey and returned to the car leaving Doey and me to say goodbye. Our minds had already labeled the summer a spectacular success, and we were moving on to a future of aviation and a lifetime together. With proprietary confidence, I reached for her hand, held her close in my arms, and brushed her lips with a kiss.

"That wasn't much of a kiss," she said.

"It's just the warm up," I replied.

Her beautiful golden hair hung loosely around her shoulders and lovely face. Her eyes were as blue as the sea on a bright summer day and sparkled like the ring on her finger. She smiled and said, "We did have fun this summer, didn't we?"

"Yes, we did. I learned so much. Your lifestyle is more than I ever imagined life could be. I can never thank you and your parents enough for inviting me to be your guest for a magnificent summer, which included the New York World's Fair and a summer at Mac." I used the word Mac for Macatawa that was commonly used by the homeowners. "We'll meet in two weeks," I said to a dream dressed in a light blue blouse that clung to the tantalizing, mature figure of the girl I loved. Around her neck, on a golden chain, hung the thirty-five cent medallion we bought at the New York World's Fair. The engagement ring was a symbol marking the beginning of a committed life together.

"Two weeks is a long time," she said. For a few minutes we spoke more of our summer. I was sure that it was a time that neither of us would ever forget. I carefully locked the yesterdays away in my mind and started a new chapter that would bring us a step closer to a lifetime together.

"It's time to go," I said. I put my arms around her and drew her to me. I looked down at her lovely face. Her eyes were closed and we were just about a kiss apart. With no time for hesitation, I pulled her closer and our parting kiss was one to remember. I knew that I had a dream and a future worth keeping.

From the entrance to the airport I turned and waved to her. "I'll call you when I get home!" She smiled and threw me a kiss.

Chapter 41

Start of Senior Year

At the end of two weeks at home, I returned to Doey and Chapel Hill on September 2, 1940, for my senior year. The soft winds of summer lingered on into fall. After checking in at the Beta House, I called the Tri Delta House at Duke University and asked for Doey. She wasn't in. I left a message and headed for the airport.

Sam Hughie was in charge of operations. He looked up as I approached. "She's here," he said.

"Who's here?" I asked.

"Doey!" he said. "Doey Brooks; she's looking for you. She's in there with Red, probably filing a complaint against you."

"Me? I hardly know her. I just came by to see Red and the rest of you misfits. Who did you say was in there with him?"

"Doey Brooks, you jerk. Last term you got weak in the knees and turned red in the face whenever her name was mentioned. Boy, something weird has happened to you over the summer."

Sam got up and shook my hand and said, "Welcome back, Wynn. Do you have your instructor's ticket yet?"

"No, I'm sorry to say. I was busy all summer with more important matters, but I'm here now hoping to stay out of the draft until I log a few more hours. When the war comes, a pilot with an instructors rating will be sure of a job."

"Yes, you will surely have a job," Sam said. "What would you like to do?"

"I would like to fly with the Air Force, but I would probably have to start over and learn flying the Air Corps way. Have patience, I tell myself. The military will make the choice."

"With your education and flying experience you may go through Cadets in grade. That's only a guess. I'm sure that Red will be glad to see you, and I'm sorry you struck out with Doey."

"Thanks, Sam." I knocked on Red's door and heard "come in." Red was sitting at his desk talking with Doey. "I just arrived, and with nothing better to do, I came over to rattle your cage. I didn't expect to find Doey here."

Red stood and held out his hand. "It's good to see you and Doey, Wynn."

Doey turned toward me and winked, then said, "Did you enjoy our summer at the Fair and Macatawa?"

"It was tolerable," I replied. What was she up to? I didn't have a clue, but played along. "You know as well as I do, Doey. You ruined what could have been a nice summer." I shrugged, and threw my hands in the air to show indifference.

I looked at Red and then Doey, and said, "We ran into one of my old girl friends, Betty Moran, at the top of the Empire State Building. We kissed. It was just to say hello. Maybe I did hold the embrace a little too long and people were beginning to talk. There was a whistle or two. The whistle was probably for Betty. She is good looking, isn't she? But that didn't mean a thing." I paused, looked at Doey, and then continued.

"Yeah, I suppose that I shouldn't have kissed her. She got lipstick all over my mouth and collar, and we did carry on a conversation longer than necessary. I know that it was thoughtless of me leaving you out of our talk,

Arise My Love And Come Away With Me

but just because I left you standing there, while I walked with Betty to the down elevator, where we stood talking, it couldn't have been more than ten or fifteen minutes. Betty looked up at me, like . . . well, like maybe like she had something in her eye. I looked carefully, but didn't see anything. I didn't know what to do, so I kissed her again. What else could I do? While standing there the elevator door opened. She entered and said 'I'll see you in Chapel Hill in a few weeks' and as the door was closing, she threw me a kiss. Now I ask you, Red, did I do anything wrong? Doey was so upset that she ran off and left me standing there. Her thoughtless action ruined the entire summer."

"Interesting," Red said. "Would you like to hear my version of what happened to you during the summer?" Without waiting for an answer he continued. "You went to the top of the Statue of Liberty." He paused, and then continued. "Doey, why are you trying to hide the engagement ring that Wynn gave you? Hold it out so that I can give you my appraisal."

Doey held out her hand and said, "We were going to tell you as soon as Wynn arrived."

"Red," I said, "how do you know all this?"

"Easy," Red replied. "Your mother told me. She has always thought of me as family, and as a family member I'm entitled to know these things. That's wonderful news and I appreciate your coming here to tell me."

"You are a member of the family, Red, and we did come here to tell you," I replied.

Red said, "I'm glad you're here for another semester, and I didn't believe a word of what you and Doey were saying."

"I'm sorry," Doey said. "My attempt at levity is a few words short of the way Wynn would have handled the information. You may be sure that we wanted you to know."

"Wynn," she said, "you did tell me that I could mention the highlights of the summer to anyone in our family. That qualifies you, Red."

"Yes," Red replied, "and I promised Wynn's mother not to say anything until you give the word."

Doey moved closer to me and put her arm around my waist and said, "Wynn and I are engaged." She held her left hand out to display the diamond ring on her finger. It sparkled with a rainbow of colors, reminding me that I owed the jeweler a few more dollars before the ring legally belonged to her. Doey continued, "We think that it's best for now not to let the students or universities know."

"I'll keep your secret," Red said. "We will have a quiet celebration later. We're about through here, and I'll need more time to talk about your summer, but for now I have some work to do." He got up and started to leave, then turned to say, 'Harry and Carolyn are waiting for you at Orville and Wilbur's."

I looked at Doey and said, "I forgot."

"So did I." She turned her ring around so the diamond didn't show and said, "If we had met Betty, you wouldn't have kissed her, would you?" She waited for my answer.

"You'll never know," I said with a grin. "It's just 11:30. Let's go."

We walked into Orville and Wilbur's. Sitting at our favorite corner table by the window were Carolyn and Harry. When they saw Doey and me approach, Carolyn closed the book that she had been reading and laid it on the table.

Harry said, with a big grin, "We have been waiting for lunch. Did you bring money?" He stood and shook hands with me. Carolyn and Doey were already deep in conversation. Harry sat down next to Carolyn. I sat next to Doey and we all started to talk of our summer.

"Harry, have you been sitting here all summer just to win a bet and get a free meal?" I asked.

"Well, not all summer. We did manage a few days off and went to the California World's Fair in San Francisco."

Arise My Love And Come Away With Me

Carolyn picked up Doey's left hand and said to Harry, "I told you that they would make a beautiful couple."

"Show them your ring," Harry said to Carolyn in a whisper.

Carolyn laid her hand on the table beside Doey's. The rings were identical. "Where did you get the ring, Harry?"

"The same place you bought Doey's. Carolyn liked it so much, that's what I bought." The rings had a fast moment of glitter before they were hidden from sight.

"Congratulations, Harry," I said. "You and Carolyn also make a beautiful couple."

"We've waited all summer to tell you," Carolyn replied.

Harry changed the subject and said, "I have reserved a table for four at eight o'clock tonight at Danziger's. I went to the restaurant's office and talked with the head man, Sam Gilmore, and told him that the dinner was for a very special occasion. I requested a bottle of Dom Perignon to be served at our table, number 4 in the corner, and we would like to have Jack Palance serve our dinner and wine. Sam told me that 'If you and your guests are not students and have proof that you are 21, we don't have a problem. However, if you don't, you know the government and the university will not permit you to have alcohol in any form. That's the law. We can't serve alcohol to those who can't meet those specs.' I told him that there is also a government law that restaurants tolerating rats in the pantry is a no, no! I said I know that they are doing everything they can to control the problem. There are other dining places where we could go, but they have the same problems. We don't go there. We like it here. Rats may still be prowlers, and if they are, and I think they are, no one will learn of it from me. I want you to know that we appreciate your effort to solve the problem. I want you to know that I and my friends learned at home, under the guidance of our parents, that an occasional glass of wine with our dinner is okay as long as its sole purpose is not used to bring out the need for what may become a habit. I assure you that the friends I will bring here will never upset the decorum of the room, as many of your adult patrons have by letting alcohol be the only purpose of

267

their drinking. If the word got out that you have rats prowling the premises, it will never come from me, but it may be repeated by some of my friends. I can't control their thinking.

"Sam gave in and said, 'Harry, you win. But the first time that you and your friends lose control of your drinking, and I hear one complaint from the other diners, I will have to ask you to leave. And don't forget, I know your father and I suspect that he will be on my side.'

"Yeah, I know him too, and maybe you're right."

There was no denying it, Harry was smooth.

With lunch over, Doey asked Wynn, "Are you going to fly today?"

"Yes, the planes now have two-way radios and I'm anxious to try them out. Why don't you come with me, Doey?"

"Yes, thank you. I think I will," she said.

Chapter 42

The Plan

The day for us was over. Harry found the highway to Chapel Hill and we headed back to the Fetzer House. On the way Harry told me that he was thinking about the future of the band.

He said, "It has been on my mind for the past couple of weeks, and I have come up with a plan that I would like to discuss with you before tomorrow morning's meeting with the band. I discussed the problem with Professor Gilmore, who among other duties is our ear to the chancellor's office. He listens to the Student Union requests, and, if in his opinion it is valid, he will pass it on to someone who is on speaking terms with someone in the chancellor's office for approval. He assured me that our band could play one dance a month in the gymnasium. The dance would welcome all students of the university, and there would be no charge for admission; however, he would need to get approval for us to use the radio system.

"He said he would talk to someone in the chancellor's office and have an answer after the holiday, and maybe even today. I'll go to his office as soon as it opens and hope for the best. In the meantime, I need your help in developing a plan for raising the money to pay the band. I think I may have one." By the time we got to Chapel Hill, we had a plan that was so bizarre that no one but Harry could have thought of it. My only contribution to the scheme was to listen and laugh. We parked at the Fetzer House, left our bags in the car, and headed for bed.

Saturday morning by nine thirty, Harry and I had arranged the chairs, music, and stands in the living room of the Fetzer House, and waited for the band to assemble. When they arrived a short time later, I stood in front of the band and asked for their attention.

"Harry has a meeting this morning to ask for permission for us to play in the gym. To play there, we must have the approval of the university's front office. However, there is a rule that may be too high a hurdle for us. The rule is: If we play for a dance there, the music must be free, and the dance must be open to the entire student body. Harry is trying to find a way to keep within the rules and still earn money to pay the band, so I think we should listen to his plan. You're on, Harry," I said and sat down.

Harry stood up and with his usual confident smile, along with his gift of gab, he began to make sense of what, at first, seemed to be an impossible scheme, then paused, and said, "We will hold a raffle." Again he paused, waiting for a reaction.

Helen said, "What will we raffle, Harry?"

"Good question," Harry said. "I was just coming to that. We will hold a raffle . . ." Again he paused to collect the right words.

And again Helen said, "The raffle, Harry, what will we raffle?"

"Tickets, and provide them to any male member of the student body. The ticket will have spaces for the name of any girl who is a registered member of the student body. There is a line on the ticket for you to sign your name, and the name of the girl for whom you are voting. You may vote for any girl and as many times as you like. Each vote will cost 25 cents. In the event that more than one person votes for the same girl, the winner of a dance date will go to the man who cast the most votes.

"An independent committee, selected by the student body, will audit the results. For example: The men in the band may cast as many votes as they like for Helen. But it's a sure bet that Phil Clay will win with the most number of votes for Helen.

"There will be a raffle, two for each of the next seven months beginning in November and finishing before the end of this school year. For our first raffle, it is my hope that we can depend on all members of the band to participate. The band needs the money and publicity. And Helen, if you can accept this program, I can assure you that you will not only be known as the 'Queen of Swing,' but known by every student on campus.

"At the first raffle and dance you will sing 'I Ain't Got Nobody (and Nobody Cares for Me.)' One at a time, a member of the band will come up and say, 'I care, Helen,' and ask you for a date. When the last band member is seated, the music goes on. Then someone on the dance floor will yell 'I care, Helen. How about a date?' Then another voice from the crowd will yell 'So do I, Helen', and the auction will begin.

"The girls who receive votes must agree to abide by the rules and participate. Those who don't want to play the game may opt out. Money collected for the raffle will be held by the Inter-Fraternity Council and be used to pay the band for playing.

"At the beginning of each dance in the gymnasium, we will start by inviting the winning couple of the last auction to come to the bandstand, where we will acknowledge their win. The photographer from the school newspaper, 'The Daily Tar Heel,' will take their picture. It will be on the front page of the paper the next day. In addition, they will receive a dinner for two at Danziger."

Helen said, "I opt out, Harry. I am not for sale at any price. What else can we raffle?"

"Good question," Harry said, "I was just coming to that." He paused, trying to find an answer, and said "We need you, Helen, to make it work."

"That's not much of an answer, Harry," Helen said. "What, in detail, do I have to do that's so critical to making your plan successful?"

"Helen, just give me time to lay out the entire plan, and then I promise to be patient as you tell me what you won't do."

"The plan Harry, what's the plan? I'll be quiet and listen," she said, "but I don't think that I'm going to like what you have to say."

Harry said, "We are going to raffle you to the highest bidder, and at each weekly Inter-Fraternity Council dance we will auction another . . ." Harry was stopped by the hush that fell over the room.

Then Helen's quiet voice filled the room and with conviction she said, "I'm not for sale to anyone for any price! Everyone on campus now thinks it's their duty to play some kind of joke on me, or make crude, obscene remarks. The last time I walked across the campus, as I passed, Silent Sam's gun went off. It was loud enough for everyone to hear. The person who lit the firecracker that made the sound, I'm sorry to say, is in this room."

Bill Reeder stood and said, "I lit the firecracker, Helen. It was done in fun. Now I know how thoughtless it was, and I apologize to you and the band. My hope is that my stupidity can be forgiven, and I can assure you, Helen, that everyone in the band is in love with you and would never do anything to harm you. It's you and your voice that has made us a better band."

"Thanks, Bill, for saying that. I, too, am in love with everyone in the band. I know that you meant no harm. I'm afraid that every time I pass Silent Sam someone will say something that I would not like to hear."

Harry replied, "I'll walk with you, Helen." A chorus of voices from the band members said, "So will I."

"That won't be necessary, fellows. It's good to know that I have seven brothers to look after me, but I'm sure that I can make it on my own. Now I know you're kidding, Harry. What's your real plan?"

"I'm not kidding, Helen, that's it. We need a way to earn money to support the band. We are playing well, but we can't survive playing only for the Inter-Fraternity dances. Over a short time we have increased the band from the original four to six. Then Helen and I joined. We now have eight to support on the meager budget that the council cannot afford to pay. We can continue, but you know that the minute we charge the student body to pay to come to our dances, we will have to join the musician's union and pay dues. At best, we only have 10 months before graduation, if that long. The unknown factor is the war. It is more than possible that some or maybe all of us will be called into military service before we graduate. The choice for the little time we have is to continue as is, or follow the plan that we should at least consider. There may be a better one; however, let's discuss it now and get on with the future.

"The crucial question is how can we survive without charging more for our music? Believe me, Wynn and I have spent many hours looking for a way to survive, and keep our amateur standing. If you are in favor of our plan, it will need your complete faith and help to make it work. I have already talked with some members of the band, and I'm assured of their support for a plan that depends mostly on blind faith. After band practice stick around and we will talk. Then if you don't agree, we will change our approach. Now I have an appointment at the chancellor's office and I can't be late. Wynn, the band is yours," Harry said, as he excused himself.

"Thanks, Harry. Good luck with your meeting. Bring back good news. We will be waiting."

"Bill," I said, "take care of band practice. I need to have a talk with Helen. We'll be across the hall. What I have to say won't take long."

We sat on the steps in the hall and I said, "Helen, you are more to us than just a member of the band. There is not anyway that we would embarrass you. When Bill Reeder lit the firecracker, to him it was meant to be a harmless joke on you, his band sister. He never gave a thought to what you or others might think, but if he had heard one crude or obscene remark, he would be in the dean's office explaining why the person who made that remark was in the medical clinic being treated for a black eye. We all back you and your position completely. I know that you will win more than enough votes to honorably win the first contest. Personally, I don't see any possibility of you losing. You have earned the love and respect of the students. You are an icon, the Queen of Swing. Everyone knows who you are, and after you sing for a wider audience, you're sure to win.

"Harry told me that he was prepared to assure you that you would receive the votes necessary to win. For the moment that's all I can say. If I were you, I would tell Harry that you want to help the band, and whatever the outcome, abide by the rules. Tell him that you need no help from anyone, other than those votes that are legally obtained. I know that the band and Phil will be voting for you. I hope that we can leave this conversation here."

"Thank you, Wynn, for your support and the band's. I had already decided to tell Harry that I am willing to enter the contest and abide by the rules."

We could hear the band softly playing "It's Always You." "That song needs a singer," I said.

"Thanks for the talk," she answered. "Let's go."

Before the band practice was over Harry returned to tell us that our gig in the gymnasium would be broadcast over the university's radio network. "Now," he said, "if you will excuse us, Helen and I will have our conversation."

Helen said, "Harry, I have had time to think and there is no reason to talk. I will join the contest and do everything that I can to win; but win or lose I will abide by the rules and not ask for help from anyone. I do appreciate your good intentions, and I love you and the band's effort to help me. I want to win for all of you, but I must do it alone."

"Alright Helen, the band and I will be standing by to help in any way we can. Don't forget that we are running for the same honor. When you win, we win. To have a winning singer, we have a winning band."

As soon as practice was over, I called Doey to tell her about our good fortune. Doey said, "Harry talked with Carolyn not more than twenty minutes ago. He told her that you received permission to play in the gym in November. That's wonderful news, darling."

"Yes, some of that is true. It was Harry's gift with words which has made it possible for us to play there. Without him, we would still be playing only for the Inter-Fraternity dances. The opportunity to have a band at all was his idea. All the moves in the right direction we owe to him. Helen Lind was also a joint effort by Harry and Bob Lovell. The band's progress really belongs to them. I just show up on time, play a few tunes with them, and go to Egan's."

"Well, yes, but without you, there wouldn't be a band for Harry to promote."

"That may or may not be true, but I love you for saying it. Why don't you and Carolyn get ready and Harry and I will pick you up for dinner."

We picked the girls up and went to Egan's. We sat in the corner booth and the jukebox was playing the new recording by Ray Noble and His Orchestra, "A Nightingale Sang in Berkeley Square" written by Eric Maschwitz and Manning Sherwin. As the song ended, Doey squeezed my hand and whispered, "Oh Wynn, the words to that song remind me of the night we met. Let's play it again."

"Gladly my love," I said as I took her hand in mine and led her to the dance floor. The words touched our hearts and told our musical story . . .

> "That certain night, the night we met,
> There was magic abroad in the air,
> There were angels dining at the Ritz
> And a nightingale sang in Berkeley Square.
>
> I may be right, I may be wrong,
> But I'm perfectly willing to swear
> That when you turned and smiled at me
> A nightingale sang in Berkeley Square.
>
> The moon that lingered over London town,
> Poor puzzled moon, he wore a frown.
> How could he know we two were so in love,
> The whole darn world seemed upside down.
>
> The streets of town were paved with stars,
> It was such a romantic affair,
> And as we kissed and said goodnight,
> A nightingale sang in Berkeley Square."

As the evening drew to a close, we kissed and she whispered, "This is our song."

Chapter 43

Harry's Wrong Way Flight

In the weeks that followed, with Red's help, I studied the FAA Manuel that contained the hundred or more questions that might be asked on an Instructor's Rating Test. I was fairly sure of the flying requirement, but the answers to the questions that might be asked were in the manual.

The day arrived when Red closed the FAA manual and slid the book across the table to me. "Schools out," he said. "Take the test."

Five days later I joined three other pilots in the ready room, and with a government inspector watching our every move, I groped my mind for answers that I hoped would match the questions. After more than an hour, I signed my name to the test and handed it to the inspector. "Good luck," he said.

Two weeks later I received a letter from the FAA. I had passed the written and flight requirements. I expected Red to offer me a job, but he didn't. We both knew that I was enrolled at Chapel Hill to learn. I was ready for the war that was coming, and now it was time for me to give full attention to solving the economic—as well as the military—problems of the world.

On Thursday, Carolyn and Doey had classes all morning, but they were free to join us for Harry's final flight test for his private pilot's rating. Sam Hughie, his instructor, stood by the plane, a BT 17 Basic Trainer, on the ramp at Hangar 2 giving his instructions. Carolyn, Doey, and I stood by listening. The flight was the last test before the FAA approved or disapproved of issuing Harry a private pilot's license. Carolyn asked Harry if he had a good luck charm to ward off danger.

Arise My Love And Come Away With Me

"Yeah," he said. "It's the label off of a bottle of beer I had last night at Egan's."

"Oh, Harry, for once can't you be serious?" she replied.

We stood by the runway and watched as he took off. When his plane faded from sight, Sam went to his office and we slowly walked to Red's office. I knocked on the door and heard "Come in." Red was behind his desk. He looked up and said, "What can I do for you?" I started to speak, but he cut me off.

"Whatever it is, make it brief. I have some work to do," Red said.

"We just watched Harry take off to fly for his private license. We wanted to hang out here for a while and chat with you."

"Find another place to hang out," Red said. "I don't have time to talk now. Come back in about an hour. We can talk then until Harry returns, and together we'll go to the runway and watch our hero land."

"Sorry for the interruption," I said. "We'll be back." We walked over to the terminal and sat down by the newsstand.

"What will Harry do on this flight that's so different from the other flights he's made?" Carolyn asked.

"Harry will fly a triangular course to two other airfields, where he will land, go to their Base Operations and have his logbook signed, then take off and fly home. When he lands here, Sam will sign his logbook and Harry will become a private pilot. Red will report Harry's accomplishment to the CAA in Washington, D.C., where his private pilot's flight test will be recorded, and a certificate of competency will be sent to Harry. His name will be added to the Bold Eagles Scroll that's on the wall in the Pilot's room at Orville and Wilbur's," I said.

"Let's go to Orville and Wilbur's," Doey replied. A few minutes later I was sitting at the pilot's round table. Doey and Carolyn were slowly walking around the room looking at the new pictures and items of interest on display.

After a cup of coffee, and forty-five minutes of random chatter, we returned to Red's office. Sam was there with Red talking and listening to the radio receiver, which was tuned to tower frequency. A few minutes later we heard Harry's voice calling the tower. "Foxtrot to Tower; Alpha Charlie Bravo in range."

"Roger, Alpha Charlie Bravo, continue downwind. You're number two to land."

A few minutes later Harry's voice broke radio silence and said, "Foxtrot Tower, Alpha Charlie Bravo in range, over the fan marker, landing with Exray."

"Tower clears Alpha Charlie Bravo for runway 1-8."

Red said, "Let's go and watch Harry land."

We stood by the runway watching as Harry's plane appeared. Sam, Harry's instructor, exclaimed, "My God, he's landing the wrong way!" Quickly the tower called all traffic with an emergency notice. "All traffic. Repeat, all traffic, Emergency. Runway 1-8 closed to all traffic."

We watched as Harry's plane flew past the tower and on to the west. "How could he have done that?" Sam said. "He knows better!" We watched as his plane gained altitude, then pulled up into a half loop and rolled out on top. He had gained a little altitude and reversed the course. The assigned runway was dead ahead. He dropped the nose of the plane and side slipped along the flight path to the threshold, where he gently raised the nose of the plane, throttled back, and the wheels of Alpha Charlie Bravo gently touched the ground and rolled out.

As Harry made his way back to Hanger 2, we were waiting. In my mind our flying days were over. I ran the possibilities of censor through my mind. I hoped that Harry would have a good excuse for what he did. Red was in charge of flight training and would have to record the incident to the Air

Force in his next report. At the very least, Red would carry an unsatisfactory report in his 201 file. If he learned of my involvement in showing Harry that illegal maneuver, my hope of flying for the Air Force would be doomed.

Slowly the plane came to a halt. Harry powered down and switched the engine control to idle cut off. The prop turned a time or two and stopped. Slowly he stepped from the plane. Red was furious. Sam was speechless. Harry was smiling. He knew the maneuver was illegal, so close to the ground, and this time he had pushed the envelope too far.

Red said in a soft voice, dripping with venom, "Would you care to explain that illegal maneuver?" I shut my eyes and prayed.

"What did I do wrong?" Harry said. "I didn't notice I was going the wrong way until the tower told me to go around again. I took the only way I knew, at that moment, of reversing my course."

"How did you learn that maneuver?" Sam asked.

"I read it in one of the private flying manuals."

"Yes," Sam replied. "It was there to warn you of the illegal maneuvers that you must not attempt without an instructor." Harry and Red looked at me.

Harry took a deep breath and said, "I received no advice from anyone. I knew it was wrong."

Red replied, "You didn't have a lapse of memory; you showed no concern for the people on the ground, your instructor, the flight program, or the tower whose job it is to keep flight order within five miles of the airport. You were showing off. I should dismiss you from the program. How will others in the program react knowing that they too can break the rules of flight and get away with it?"

"Sam, see me in my office when you're through here," Red remarked.

Red turned, looked at me, and said, "I don't know how he could have done that, but I have a suspicion."

"We need to talk, Red," I said.

"Later," was his reply, "but not now." He walked to his office.

Sam and Harry walked back to the debriefing room. Doey, Carolyn, and I decided to stay out of the way and continued on to the terminal, where we stood by a window looking at the office area of the field. Sam and Harry went into the debriefing room and closed the door. What seemed like an hour was less than thirty minutes. We watched as Harry and Sam emerged and stood there talking. We couldn't hear what Sam said to Harry, but they parted with troubling looks. Sam nodded in our direction, turned, and walked to Red's office. We left the terminal and quick-timed it back to the debriefing room.

I put my arm around Harry's shoulders and asked, "How did it go?"

"I knew it was wrong," he replied. "I could have gone around, but I had permission to land. The runway was mine until I landed. Once committed, I acted upon an urge to fly a maneuver that I was taught by someone whose name I can't remember."

"Thank you, Harry, but I think that we're both in trouble. I still have to answer to Red."

Harry said, "I'm really sorry, Wynn. This is entirely my fault. Don't worry. Cheer up! I don't need a private license. I have a plan. I know I was wrong, but I know that I can fly. You will probably get off with a lecture."

"You have surely proven that you can fly," I said. "I think that Sam and Red are very aware of your ability, but they have to go by the book of regulations. You and I will probably be grounded and get one of Red's vitriolic official slaps on the wrist with a wet noodle and carry a blot on our official record, but I think we will, in some way, survive. I didn't believe what I said. "For now, let's take the girls to Durham and go home."

Arise My Love And Come Away With Me

Four solemn, dispirited students pulled up before the Tri Delta House and stopped. Carolyn kissed Harry and said, "I know that you and Wynn are worried. It might be best if Doey and I stay on campus tonight."

"No," Harry said. "I'll be here on time. You and Doey be ready."

I got a quick kiss from Doey, who said, "I don't know how you can be involved in this, but if you're in trouble, so am I. I'm sure that Harry will find a way out."

I replied, "I'm not worried and neither is Harry." The car started to move. Harry smiled and threw them a kiss.

He looked at me and said, "I'm sorry, Wynn. I don't think that we've heard the last of this."

"You said that you have a plan, Harry, what is it?"

"I'll be grounded," he said. "I know I won't get my private license. I believe the thing to do is to resign and go to Canada and enlist with the Canadian Air Force."

"Damn it, Harry, that's the dumbest thing that you have ever come up with. You are just feeling sorry for yourself. You're a good pilot, and they know it. Cut them a little slack." We sat there in silence watching the familiar sites along the road disappear behind us.

Early Monday morning Harry and I went to Red's office. I knocked on the door. "It's open, come in," Red said.

We entered and stood before his desk. "Good morning, Red. Harry and I would like to talk with you."

"I expected that I would see both of you this morning. What have you to say?" Red replied.

"Yesterday I asked to talk with you, Red, but you said later, not now. Now, I would like to say what I would have said yesterday when you had a suspicion that someone had taught Harry the maneuver. If you suspected me, and I think you did, you were right. I did go through the procedure twice, with Harry as a passenger. I was merely repeating a maneuver that I have watched others do. I should have had the sense to know that I was endangering his life. I am not an instructor in anything. I'm not even legally in the flying class. I did say, without Harry's asking, that you must always be sure that you have enough altitude to complete the routine before you run out of altitude and hit the ground."

Harry broke in to say, "It's a very easy routine to fly. I learned only by watching. Wynn had nothing at all to do with my actions. I was grandstanding for the girls. I did do wrong, and the fault is mine. Whatever the consequence may be, I will take it with me. I will turn in my resignation today."

"You will do no such thing," Red said, with a strong voice that rolled like thunder. "Both of you will stand before the flight class and apologize to Sam Hughie. The class must realize that the rules of flight are made by experts in the field. At this moment there are students who watched in awe as you put on a show. They will point you out as someone to look up to. You broke the rules and got away with it. They will try the same maneuver without instruction, and some may die, but you will go merrily on your way not knowing the stupid unthinking part that both of you played in their death. We are not in business to please the girls. Our job is to turn out the very best pilots that we can."

I started to speak and Red said, "Wynn, until we have a talk and I am satisfied that you understand the rules of this government funded program, you are not to fly with or discuss flight maneuvers with anyone in the flying class program. Do you understand?"

"Yes I do, Red."

"You and Harry are dismissed."

At 8:30 the next morning we stood before the class. We spoke in solemn voices admitting that what we had done was wrong. We apologized to Red and Sam. In detail, I explained why any maneuver that ends close to the ground must be carefully planned, or you might end up digging a hole in the

Arise My Love And Come Away With Me

ground that will destroy the plane, and more than likely, your life. I told them only a certified flight instructor is qualified to give you information that's made to keep you safe. I looked up in time to see Red and Sam, walking out the back door of the classroom.

Harry was regarded by the class as a hero, and I was the one who got Harry into trouble. In a few days the dark cloud that we survived under drifted by, and once again there was peace in our time.

On October 10th, Red and Sam invited Harry and me to have lunch with them at Orville and Wilbur's. We were back on friendly terms with them, although neither of us was permitted to fly. We ordered lunch and while waiting, Sam took a letter out of his jacket pocket and handed it to Harry saying, "I almost forgot this. It's a copy of the one Red received from the FAA. They have finally decided what to do with you. You may want to be alone when you read it."

So this is why Sam and Red invited us to lunch, Harry thought. I did the wrong thing and now I'm paying for it. He had already told me that he had scrapped the idea of joining the Canadian Air Force. The cost of leaving Carolyn was a price too high to pay for breaking the rules of flight. He would delay, in any way he could, to have even one more day with her. Harry had decided he would stay in Chapel Hill and take his chance with the draft. There was bound to be another way to fly. The exuberant Harry that challenged every rule of life had lost to the rule of flight.

He took a deep breath and opened the letter. For a moment he sat there in stunned silence and then passed the letter to me. I scanned it and looked at him. His smile became a grin. He turned to Sam and said, "You and Red may never know what you have done for me. I want you to know how deeply I appreciate your friendship. I may never know how you squared things with the FAA, but you have my word that I have learned an important lesson."

Red said with a grin, "Let's eat before we all start to cry."

The old Harry we knew was back. He now had his private pilot's license. After lunch, Red and Sam went back to work. Harry and I stood by his car in the parking lot. "You drive, Wynn." We got in the car and headed for the Fetzer House.

On October 16, 1940, students at UNC went to Woollen Gymnasium to register for the draft. We signed our names to a list that ultimately would contain more than twelve million. There was no doubt that we had crossed a point of no return. After registering, we returned to class, but from that moment on our world had abruptly changed. The reality we knew was gone, and we knew we could never go back. Reality can exist at one time and in one place only. Maybe we would find it in another place and in another time. This thought brought with it the realization that there might not be another place or time. Hundreds of thousands of men and women would find their place in a small plot of ground marked by a white cross. The survivors would come home to wait for a time when the next demented despot rattled his sword and unleashed the dogs of war.

Chapter 44

The Nightingales

We played our last fraternity dance before starting our gym gigs. When the sounds of the last musical notes of "Goodnight, Ladies" were played, we joined the patrons of the dance and headed for Egan's. Bob Lovell, Harry, Helen and I sat in a dark booth drinking that special drink in the UNC mug, all except Helen, who had a Coke.

"Harry, for a couple of weeks you've been thinking about a new name for the band. What progress have you made?" Bob asked.

"Yeah Bob," Harry said, "everyone in the band has been thinking. We have considered every name from Wynn Cary and the Misfits to The Carolina Blues, but nothing seems to fit."

"Well," Helen said, "the most requested number that we have played for the past month has been "A Nightingale Sang in Berkeley Square." What about Wynn Cary and the Nightingales or the Chapel Hill Nightingales?"

"We're getting close," Harry said. "Are there any more suggestions?"

I replied, "What's wrong with just The Nightingales?"

Everyone had their say and with a show of hands, our band became The Nightingales. To celebrate, Harry ordered a round of drinks and we raised our cups exclaiming, "To the Nightingales!"

At midnight, Egan's closed and four happy people singing "Hark the Sound of Tar Heel Voices" headed for home. We walked across campus stopping to pay our respects to Silent Sam, a bronze statue of a Civil War hero. Who he was, was not clear, but it is reasonably certain that he was not a Yankee. Silently he had guarded the campus for more than a century. He had tenure. It is said that he'd fire his gun whenever a chaste maiden passed by. I couldn't vouch for the truth of that, but girls did pass him every day and I have never heard a gun fired.

Helen said, "Don't look at me? Maybe his gun doesn't work."

Bob escorted Helen home and Harry and I continued to the Fetzer House.

Chapter 45

Rehearsal

The next day the band gathered at the Fetzer House for rehearsal for our big dance at the gym. "Our upcoming gig," I said to the group, "requires careful timing. We will be patched into the university's radio network, where we will play for exactly fifteen minutes. Your timing must be to the second. There can't be a second of dead air. Our moment of fame will be in your hands."

Harry said, "That evening at 7:30 p. m. the doors to the gym will open and the dancers will start drifting in. At 8:00 p.m. I will introduce The Nightingales to a background of soft music that will slowly increase in volume until the introductions are finished. We will open with our theme song, 'A Nightingale Sang in Berkeley Square.' We may be treading on the toes of the Musician's Union and be fined for playing this song."

I told Harry that the song was protected by a copyright, and that we could be fined for using it. "If we use it," Harry said, "and we get fined for infringing, I will pay the fine."

"No," I said. "We will pay it." From the moment we played it and until we graduated we were never challenged. Our luck was holding.

Harry quickly looked around the room and said, "Where's Helen?"

Phil said, "That's what I wanted to talk with you about. Helen has a temporary problem with her voice. It's raspy and not much louder than a whisper. This morning she went to the clinic. After a throat examination the doctor said that he was reasonably sure that her vocal chords should return to normal. She wants you to know that she will be ready to sing."

Harry threw his hands up and said, "This is not our day, Wynn, what's next?"

"It's a good question, Harry. You solved all the financial problems of getting us the gym gig. My job is to provide the music. Helen has our good wishes for a quick recovery and we can only hope that she will be ready." I was groping for an answer that made sense, but there didn't seem to be one. Then I remembered when Doey played the piano and sang several songs for me. "Luck is with us, Harry. I happen to know a good singer, and she is here with us tonight. Doey, will you help us?"

"Yes, Wynn, you know I will. If you have a copy of the words and music, let me have them for a few minutes, and then we can run through it with the band."

I knew Doey's key and said to the band, "Key of F, fellows."

As the band began to play and Doey began to sing "Somebody loves me. I wonder who, I wonder who it can be . . ." When the music ended, Doey got a standing ovation.

Harry said, "I didn't know you could sing, Doey. Let's play it again and I will record the time." I raised my hand and, on the down beat, Harry punched the start button on the time clock and The Nightingales began to play. As the music started, Harry ran through the speech he would give.

As the music ended, we moved on to the next item on the list to rehearse. Phil Clay and Jack Palance sat on the sofa. "Have you run through the raffle story?" I asked.

"Not yet," Phil replied.

"Do I get a starring part?" Jack asked.

Arise My Love And Come Away With Me

"Your part, you broken down boxer, is more than you deserve, but you will get star billing for just showing up," Harry replied with a grin.

At six thirty, I said, "It's time to quit. Go home, or do whatever you have in mind. I think we have a winner. Don't do anything stupid like getting sick or run over by a bus, and take good care of your ten fingers. We have no replacements for any of you."

Harry and I took Doey and Carolyn to the Carolina Inn for dinner. While waiting to be served we talked about the gym program. "If all goes well," Harry said, "we will celebrate at Danziger's. If the program for the evening does not go well, we may go to Big John's Hotdog Stand at the local bowling alley for dinner and entertainment."

"What we need is a better frame of mind," I said. "When we finish dinner, let's go to Egan's." A few minutes later we walked across the campus and were seated in a dark booth at our favorite dispenser of beer in a UNC mug. We ordered three beers and a Coke for Doey.

At eleven-thirty our day was about to wind down. We left the dimly lit booth at Egan's and walked back across a darkened campus to the Tri Delta House. The filtered light from a waning moon and stars were growing dim. We kissed the girls goodnight and watched as they faded from sight as the door closed behind them.

A few days later, Doey called to tell me that her parents would be coming to our gig. "Daddy would like to come and hear The Nightingales play and asked if you would make reservations for two rooms at the Carolina Inn, one room for my parents and one for me and Carolyn. He invited Red to join us for dinner and the dance. Can you make the reservations?"

"Sure. I'm very pleased to know that Red is coming. If you or I called him, he would give us at least a dozen reasons why he couldn't accept our invitation. I'm glad your father has more influence."

Permission to play in the gym and air the music over the radio network was more than I ever dreamed possible. Next I called Red. Our talk of twenty minutes or more included John's invitation to dinner and the dance that followed. "Doey and I will be at the airport Sunday, Red. We'll see you then. Don't change your mind. Bye for now."

Chapter 46

Our Big Night—Gym Gig

The day of the dance was upon us. Harry and I had an early breakfast, and then met the band members at the Fetzer House to run through the numbers to be played tonight. Harry drew the drapes across the windows. He stood in front of the band. "We have a lot to do and the next few hours are all the time we have. In addition to Helen, we now have nine musicians. Bill Reeder held two sessions with the new members, Jim Kaley and Morris Livingston, who will be with us tonight for the gym gig. They were recruited from the student body by Bob Lovell. If all goes well, they will become permanent members of the band."

Helen had regained her voice and the band never sounded better. When the last notes were played, I said, "The lights will slowly dim and go out. A spotlight will be focused on the extreme left corner of the stage. As the light begins to grow brighter, Helen will be standing alone on stage left. She will be wearing a black silk evening gown with accessories that features a design for cleavage that will draw attention." Helen was amply endowed and needed nothing more to draw attention.

"The band will begin to play and Helen will sing, 'Nobody loves me.' As she sings, one by one the band musicians will come to her and say, 'I love you Helen. I care.' That's your cue, Phil. You stand and loudly say with feeling 'I care, Helen. Will you marry me?' You take a step or two towards Helen. Jack will grab your arm, and you and he will share your eight to ten seconds of fame trying to be the one to reach Helen."

I turned to Jack and said, "The dean of the acting school will be there tonight to hear what you have to say and how you act. You know the importance of timing. Don't let your bit with Phil go more than ten seconds. Break a leg!"

"As Jack and Phil are scuffling to be the first to reach Helen," I continued, "Bill Reeder will be the last musician to walk up to Helen, but before he can speak, Helen will say 'Do you also love me, Bill?' To which Bill will reply 'Heck no! I've got a girl. She's gone home for the weekend. I just wanted to ask if you would like to go to Egan's with me after this is over.' She will say, 'Yeah, let's go.' And she will take his arm and they disappear into the dark. I think we'll do well. Now remember its formal dress, so wear your tux and be on time."

Harry said, "As the song ends the lights are brought to full bright. I will be revealed standing before the microphone. The timing will be close. The band will play our theme song and we will be on the air. I will introduce the band to the listening audience. The band will play and Helen will sing. After our allotted fifteen minutes of air time, I will then sign off and the winner of the raffle will be announced."

The practice ended and Harry and I went to the gym to set up the ten new music stands, a gift from the fraternity council, that I was reasonably sure were paid for by Harry. The stands were white, trimmed in Carolina Blue. Across the face of each stand was our name, The Nightingales.

"Everything looks good, Harry. Thanks for the stands." We drove back to the Fetzer House and I borrowed Harry's car so that I could take Doey to pick up her parents at the airport.

At a quarter of six, we met in the lobby of the Carolina Inn. John and Dorothy were seated by the lobby's fireplace. All invitees were accounted for. Doey, Dorothy, and Carolyn looked stunning in their long evening gowns. Each adorned an orchid furnished and pinned on by John. Harry and I would be working with the band later and our dress code for the evening was formal. Red and John were looking important in their dark suits.

John said, "Our table is waiting, shall we go in?" We were seated at Fungus's table.

Arise My Love And Come Away With Me

"Good evening," Jimmy said. "Welcome to the Fungus Café." He passed the menus around the table. "May I get you something to drink while you peruse the menu?" He handed John the wine list.

Dorothy said, "Jimmy, I believe you know everyone at the table except the gentleman sitting next to me. He is Major Hederman. He's in charge of the government flight schools at Duke and Carolina Universities."

"I'm very pleased to meet you, sir."

Red nodded and said, "I'm pleased to meet you, Jimmy."

Jimmy continued, "I'm happy to make your acquaintance, Major. I'm considering enlisting in the Air Force. If you can make me a general, I'll quit now and join up."

All Red said was, "Keep your day job, Jimmy."

Jimmy turned to Doey's father and said, "Thank you, Mr. Brooks, for again choosing the Fungus Café for your dining and listening pleasure."

Starting with John he took drink orders. When he got to Harry he said, "How did this bum get in? To whom does he belong?"

"The bum belongs to me," Carolyn laughed.

He moved on to me and said, "I'm glad to see you back, Wynn. Do you have a place in your band for a triangle player?" Last on his list was Doey. "Welcome back, your Majesty. I hasten to be of service." The drinks, food, conversation, and soft piano music combined to make the night one to remember.

"If you will excuse Harry and me, it's time for us to move on to the gym. Take your time. We have reserved a table near the bandstand for you." Harry and I thanked John for dinner.

293

At the gym, Harry checked the lighting and the spotlight to be used. The new bandstands were in place. Helen was going through the music to be played.

The musicians, wearing tuxedos, took their places behind music stands. Bob Lovell and his drums were elevated two feet above the floor, on a separate stand. He caught my eye and grinned. I stood before them as they waited for the down beat for the music to begin.

The dancers began to arrive. The tables near the bandstand were the first taken. Harry saw Carolyn and our guests enter and walked up the aisle to meet them. I stood before the band watching the clock on the wall tick off the last few seconds to eight. I counted one and two and three and four. The band came alive with "Hark, The Sound of Tar Heel Voices." Everyone stood and sang the alma mater.

The gym lights dimmed and went out for only a few seconds. Then a bright spotlight framed Helen standing before a microphone at the left side of the orchestra. She was wearing a long black formal with a spray of small red roses at the left shoulder. Again the light grew dim, and the band filled the room with the sound of our theme song. Helen picked up the beat and softly, with feeling, sang "A Nightingale Sang in Berkeley Square."

Harry stood at the right side of the orchestra before a microphone, and said, "Good evening, ladies and gentlemen of the listening audience. I'm speaking to you tonight from the Woollen Gymnasium, on the beautiful campus of the University of North Carolina at Chapel Hill, where from out of the night, Wynn Cary and The Nightingales play for your dancing and listening pleasure, featuring the pleasing voice of that beautiful Queen of Swing, Miss Helen Lind, singing the beautiful ballad 'It's Always You.' My name is Harry Woods."

The revolving mirrored light hanging from the ceiling cast a touch of romance, and the dancing feet of young America crowded the floor and gave their approval of the music and entertainment. After 15 minutes of air time, Harry stepped to the microphone and signed off. Our moment of fame was over.

At the end of the first set of music and a five minute break, Harry stood before the mike to announce the winner of the first raffle for one of the girls entered in the contest. After the crowd settled down, Harry said, "Wynn Cary lost by the flip of a nickel to be the bearer of the good or bad news of the raffle tonight. The man who wins the date with Helen Lind is . . . Phil Clay!" The crowd cheered as Phil kissed Helen on the cheek.

John, Dorothy, and Red were having a good time enjoying the music. During a break, I returned to their table and whispered to Doey, "Tomorrow night the moon will be full. Let's fly."

Her eyes lit up and she said, "I'm ready, let's do it."

The evening ended and the band was given a rousing round of applause. Doey's parents looked proud and clapped in agreement. "Wynn," John said, "your band is terrific. I hope you continue to play as long as you can. Music is such a wonderful way to escape the reality of the world."

"Thanks, John. We all love to play and, hopefully, we can continue until we are called to duty."

Doey and I left and went by the airport to reserve Red's Stinson for the next night. This became a regular routine for us whenever there was a "Doey's moon."

Chapter 47

December 1940

It was the 11th of December. Doey and I had survived the midterm exams, and to celebrate, we had lunch with Carolyn and Harry at Orville and Wilbur's. Over lunch we talked of the Christmas break and which dance we should attend. Duke offered Benny Goodman's Orchestra, and UNC countered with Artie Shaw and His Orchestra. We had a stalemate. Harry and I would always vote for UNC, while Carolyn and Doey would cast their votes for Duke. In fifteen minutes we had a problem without a solution.

Harry said, "The way we're voting, we will always end up with two votes for Duke and two for UNC. At the moment there are no planes in line waiting for takeoff. Let the first of five airplanes in line for takeoff vote for us. If it's a monoplane it will be a vote for Duke. If it's a biplane, it's a vote for UNC. Do we agree with the plan?" We all nodded in agreement. The first plane to taxi for takeoff was a biplane. Harry and I cheered. The next four planes to take off were monoplanes.

"What time shall we be at your door?" I asked Doey.

"Seven thirty," she replied with a grin.

At 7:30 p.m. Harry parked the car at the Tri Delta House. A rising "Doey's moon" and bright stars hung in the night sky. Orange, yellow, and red leaves on the ground were a reminder that winter was just a week away.

We entered the Student Union Building and left the cold outside. We could hear the toe-tapping music of the Benny Goodman Orchestra and the lilting voice of Martha Tilton singing "And The Angels Sing". At the cloak room we traded our coats, hats, and mufflers for a handful of claim tickets, and entered the ballroom where the decorations alone put us in the holiday spirit.

Doey handed me her flat evening purse that easily slipped into my pocket. We placed our dance programs on the table. It was the equivalent of staking a claim for a Virginia City silver mine. However, like days of old, claim jumpers lurked in the background.

We followed Carolyn and Harry to the dance floor. Doey took my hand in hers. I pulled her close and we moved in time with the music. Her head rested on my shoulder and her eyes were closed. I pulled her closer and whispered in her ear, "Doey, I love you." To which she squeezed my hand in response. Martha Tilton's voice filled the room with words of our song. We suppressed the moments of thinking about a future, which remained out of focus, and settled on the now.

We bumped into Carolyn and Harry. Carolyn said, "We're going to take a break and see if we still have a table."

"We'll go with you," Doey said. The song ended and Harry led the way back to our claim. The table was still there.

Doey reminded me that the last time we were here we ordered hot coffee and walked out to the terrace. We retraced our steps from that night and I said, "How could I not remember? Two of the most important events in my life occurred that night. First, we put an end to Joe Riddle's attention to you. Then we walked to the terrace where I kissed you and said I loved you. For the first time you believed that I meant it, and we sealed our forever together with a kiss. Then you said, 'What took you so long to say that?'"

When we returned to the dance, our hearts and minds were beating and thinking as one. Carolyn asked, "Where have you been all this time?"

"On the patio," I replied.

"In this weather?" she asked.

I put my arm around Doey and from Irving Berlin's song, quoted, "I've got my love to keep me warm."

"Harry, you never say nice things to me, like Wynn says to Doey," Carolyn remarked as we left for home.

Chapter 48

Holiday Dance

Our fall semester was coming to a close. Thanks to Harry, who made it possible, and the student body, who made it profitable, our gym gigs were successful. The holiday dance would be our last before everyone left for Christmas. The gym was decorated with festive holiday trimmings and students were dressed in their best evening wear. The mood was joyous and fun. At midnight the sound of our theme song filled the air and the night of music, dancing, and singing were over.

When the last note was played, Harry and Carolyn left for Egan's to get a table for eight. Bob Lovell said, "Egan's will be crowded. You and Doey had better hurry. I'll take care of the band. Jane and I will meet you there. Save us a place."

"Thanks, Bob," I said, "but Doey and I have something to do and we'll be a little late." We left and started walking to the Fetzer House. Along the way she squeezed my hand and said, "What is it, Wynn? All evening you've looked worried and acted in a way that I don't understand. Is it something I've said or done?"

"No dear. Let's wait until we get to the Fetzer House and then we'll talk." We walked down Fetzer Lane to a house bright with lights and a night filled with music, singing, and laughter. I was hoping for a place with a lot less noise. We walked to the back of the house where Harry's car was parked. I opened the door and we got in.

"Doey," I said, "there's a problem that's confronting us and it needs an answer." Doey held her breath, looking concerned. I continued, "Yesterday

I received a letter from your mother. She expects me to spend the Christmas holidays with you in Terre Haute. The problem is I can't do that. I told my mother that I would be with *her* for Christmas. I can't break that promise for the second time."

Before I could say another word, Doey replied, with a look of relief, "Our mothers knew that we were faced with this problem. They both wanted us to be with them during the holidays and they have solved our problem for us. I will go home with you for Christmas, and you will go home with me for New Years." There was a long pause and then she continued, "Wynn, I also got a letter from Mother yesterday. Apparently she didn't tell you that she had talked with your mother. I am so thankful that they know our problem. We may never have an opportunity like this again. Soon the military will take us, and the war may never give us another opportunity to be together. I remember what Jane said when she and George faced a similar problem. She found the words in the Bible. To George she said—and now I say much the same words to you—'*Where you go, I will go. Where you live, I will live. Your people will be my people. Where you die, I will die, and there I will be buried.*' It's not an exact quote, but it does say how I feel. I hope that you will come home with me to Terre Haute for New Years."

I wrapped my arms around her and whispered in her ear, "I do love you, Doey. Let's go." We walked into Egan's, where I took her into my arms and we danced to a tune that cost someone a nickel. When the dance ended, Harry, Carolyn, Doey and I arrived at our table at the same time.

Harry said, as he picked up his beer mug and took a couple of swigs, "Where have you and Doey been?"

"Band business," I replied. As we started to sit down, I noticed a paper in front of Harry's drink. "What's that for?" I asked, pointing to the paper.

Harry said, "When we came back to the table after a dance, I found that someone drank my beer. Before the next dance, I wrote in big letters on paper from my note pad 'I SPIT IN MY BEER' and placed my mug on the edge of it." Harry sat down beside Carolyn and took a big swig of her beer. "The message worked. The beer is still here." He took another big swallow and set the mug down.

There was something written under Harry's words of warning. The dim light in the room made it difficult to see what it was. I picked the paper up and read the answer to Harry's message 'SO DID I. I knew that you were too cheap to buy your own beer, so I spit in your date's beer also.'"

"Yes," I said, "your warning to the beer thief certainly worked. The beer is still here. However, you should have read the message the beer thief left." I handed Harry the papers. He read them and quickly looked around the room. A couple of tables away Jack Palance, his date Melinda, and a couple that we didn't know were laughing.

Harry said, "Excuse me for a moment, Carolyn. I'll be right back." He got up, and with his beer mug in hand, walked to Jack's table and said, "Excuse me, Jack. You left some beer in my mug and I've brought it to you. You may as well finish it." He poured the beer into Jack's mug, which added a little more than it could hold. Beer ran down the sides of the container leaving a ring of suds on the table. Without a moment of hesitation, Harry reached for the silk handkerchief in the breast pocket of Jack's coat and sopped up the suds. For a second or two, Jack and his friends sat in stunned silence. Then they roared with laughter.

Harry looked down and said, "I really didn't spit in my beer."

Jack picked up his mug that was still dripping and took a few sips and said, "I didn't spit in your beer, either." He stuck out his hand and said, "Friends?"

Harry clasped his hand in his, smiled and said, "But Carolyn did."

Jack looked at his beer in puzzled silence and set the mug down. "Harry, I want you to meet my friends Linda Hogan, Judd Towne, and you know my date Melinda." With a theatrical swing of his arm, he pointed to Harry and said, "This derelict is Harry Woods. After you shake hands with him, count your fingers. Harry, you win this one. You never learned how to lose, did you?"

Chapter 49

Spring Semester 1941

Our holiday went off without a hitch. Both families were pleased. At the beginning of January, Doey and I returned to the twilight time of reality. The world we knew was slowly slipping away. Like the leaves of autumn, the empty chairs in the classrooms were our barometer of the changing times.

"HITLER SEES VICTORY IN 1941, DISAVOWS WORLD CONQUEST . . . . 2 ITALIAN TRANSPORTS SUNK . . . . HITLER TELLS US NOT TO INTERFERE . . . . WILL TORPEDO AID SHIPS, HE SAYS."

The young people of America were caught in the net of war-time propaganda. The attrition of peace gave way to a life of excitement and despair. There was no option, no turning back. Our future was war. We still had five months of our senior year to go, with some assurance that we would be permitted to finish the year before being included in the draft.

The military had recently installed a radio system called the SCR 522 that permitted air to ground communications between pilots, tower, controllers, and GCA (Ground Control Approach). This system aided in helping pilots stay on the glide path when landing at a field where the weather had slipped below minimums. It was especially helpful when landing in the rain on a dark night at a strange field, and finding that head winds along the way had caused the engines to use more than their allotment of fuel. When in range of the field call GCA, whose call sign is "Darkie," and once contact was made, the GCA controller would talk you down. The last contact would be from the controller, who would say, "Check and set your gyros. You are on the glide path. Ground control approach, out." In other words, stay on course, trust your instruments.

I called a meeting of The Nightingales at the Fetzer House. To my pleasant surprise, all members had returned from the holidays. Everyone had a story to tell, but they ended their tales with comments of the war and the uncertainty of being called to duty.

I turned to the band and said, "In five months our senior year ends. Okay, guys, enough talk, let's tune up." After the sounds of the instruments were tuned to the vibrating A key of the piano, I turned to Helen and said, "Let's start with our theme song, "A Nightingale Sang in Berkeley Square"—and sing it pretty."

After two hours, our lackluster rehearsal finally came to an end and it was time to move on. Harry reminded us that our first gig of the season was on February 14th. I told the members of the band that we would have another rehearsal before then and that we must "play each note with feeling or we'll be run out of the gym." Everyone laughed, but agreed to be ready by the dance.

Almost every day Doey and I talked on the phone. It was early in the evening of a cold, seventh day of February. The phone rang at the Fetzer House. Harry answered and handed the phone to me saying, "It's that girl again!"

After a few moments of conversation of assurance that our love was intact, I said, "What now, my love?"

"Daddy just called to tell me that he and Mother were coming on Wednesday the thirteenth. They would like to come to our Valentine dance on the fourteenth. They would also like to invite Carolyn, Harry, and Red to be their guests for dinner at the Carolina Inn."

"Please tell John that it's a done deal, my Valentine. I'll take care of the details. Wear your ring and medallion. It's time to let everyone know how much we mean to each other."

"I will. I love you," she replied.

We ended our telephone talk with a few words of love, romance and we sang a few words from our song. Then I handed the phone to Harry and said, "That other girl would like to speak with you."

Harry picked up the phone and said, "Hello, beautiful." He and Carolyn talked for another twenty minutes. When he hung up, I said, "I never heard such drivel." Harry threw his book at me.

Saturday the eighth of February, I walked over to the Carolina Inn and reserved two rooms; one room for John and Dorothy, and one room for Doey and Carolyn. Bill Reeder and the band were in place playing the last few notes of "I'll Never Smile Again."

The band had been practicing and sounded great. The cobwebs from the holidays had disappeared and the band was in top-notch form. Harry had briefed them on the Valentine night dance at the gym. Once more we ran through the new numbers. When the echo of the last drumbeat faded, I said, "That's a wrap. You never sounded better. And, Helen, you are everyone's Queen of Swing. You make us look and sound good."

On Sunday, Doey and I met Red at Orville and Wilbur's for lunch. It was then that we learned that the airport would soon be taken over by the Navy.

"What happens to you and Sam Hughie?" Doey asked.

"We'll both be reassigned," Red said. "When and where, I don't know."

"More and more students are leaving to join up before the draft gets them," I said. "Doey and I have been assured that we may finish here before we're called. It's a dim life to look forward to." The start of a cheerful day had ended.

We thanked Red for lunch. As we walked out, we stood in the Round Table room and I asked Red what plans he had for the rest of the day. His reply was, "I plan to do a little flying."

Arise My Love And Come Away With Me

We watched as Red walked the short distance to the field, where his red and blue Stinson stood on the tarmac. Moments later he taxied to the runway and was cleared for takeoff. As we watched, the plane faded into the distance on a north east vector.

"Where's he going?" Doey asked.

"Ask Red," I replied.

The Valentine's dance was upon us. Harry and I picked up the girls for dinner with Doey's parents. The girls looked beautiful in their gowns and we looked smart in our suits. After dinner we went to the gym, where Harry had arranged for a table near the band for John and Dorothy.

As the band began to play, I could see Dorothy and John walk to the dance floor. They looked like a couple of kids moving in time with the music. Harry was an attentive "second" date to Doey, making sure she got a chance to dance. The dance floor was alive for the next three hours. As the evening drew to a close, we realized that we were truly a success.

Time seemed to move quickly. Midterms came and went, as did the spring fraternity and sorority events. We played every few weeks, but the reality that our college days were drawing to an end was apparent.

Doey was ready to get her private license. On Saturday April 19th Doey arrived at the airport at 9 a.m. I met her at the entrance and we walked together to Red's office. When we entered the office, Red and Jim Harley, the FAA flight inspector, were talking shop.

"Where are your parents, Doey?" Red asked.

"Daddy knows about the flight, but he couldn't bring Mother. She gets too emotional. She doesn't like to watch me fly, so Daddy said he would find the right time to tell her."

"Well, you know the routine, Doey." Red said. "Fly to two airports, have operations sign your log book, and come home. We will hear your arrival when you call the tower for landing instructions. Good luck!"

"Thanks, Red," Doey replied. We left the office and headed to the flight line where Cub Bravo 8-5 was waiting for her. I stood and watched Doey get in the plane and get ready for flight. It was a beautiful clear day with just a few clouds in the air—a perfect day for flying. Doey silently said, "Arise my love and come away with me," as she took off and I waited patiently for her to return.

About an hour had passed when I saw her plane in the sky. After two circles of the field she called the tower for landing instructions. "Bravo 8-5, the tower clears Bravo 8-5 to runway 1-8R. Follow the Cessna downwind. You are number two to land."

Doey acknowledged and watched the Cessna turn base, then final and line up for approach. Her headset came alive with "Bravo 8-5, you are cleared to land." She descended along the base leg and turned for final approach. She reduced power and brought the nose of the plane up. The wheels of Bravo 8-5 gently touched the ground, rolled out, and taxied back to where Jim Harley, Red, and I stood. The plane's propeller turned a few times, sucking the last few drops of fuel, and stopped.

Red went to the plane and opened the door. Doey was smiling as she stepped from the plane. She passed the test for her private license. Jim came up next to her and said, "Congratulations, Miss Brooks. Your license will be in the mail within a week. In the meantime, you may use this signed pink copy of your license to fly."

I couldn't wait for Red and Jim to leave. When they finished congratulating Doey, they left for his office. I quickly pulled Doey into my arms, kissed her, and said, "You are now a private pilot, Doey. If you have time, I would like to be your first passenger."

She smiled and said, "It will cost you a few more kisses. Can you afford it?"

"Gladly," I replied.

Doey and I continued to fly, giving us plenty of practice for the assignments that were to come. I was flying bigger planes and I felt that Doey needed to gain more experience in something other than a Cub.

Doey and I went to operations, where I signed a flight plan for a Beech Craft, and we returned to the hangar. After a preflight check, I called, and we listened to information Charlie, the ATIS hourly report of weather and altimeter settings for the airport. Next, I called Ground Control who cleared us to runway 9-0 left and hold. At the blast fence I held the brakes and powered up to check the magnetos. There was no drop in rpm's. I called Chapel Hill tower and said, "Tower, Bravo 7-5 holding short 9-0 left, ready for takeoff."

The tower responded, "The tower clears Baker 7-5 into position and hold."

I taxied into position, lined up with the white stripe that divides the runway, and called the tower, "Bravo 7-5, in position for takeoff."

"Bravo 7-5, you're cleared for takeoff."

The gang bar advanced the twin engine's power to the limit. At rotation, Doey and I recited our line of poetry and we headed for the practice range. Our routine included recovery from stalls and spins at take offs and landings, and other maneuvers required for check out of the BT 17.

I looked at my watch. "It's ten minutes to ten," I said. "Red told me that you would be flying the Boeing BT 17. Compared to the Cub that you have been flying it looks intimidating, but it's not. You just go along for the ride. It will do the rest."

After each maneuver, Doey became more confident. It felt like she had been flying forever. We spent happy hours in the air, sharing our mutual love for each other and for flight.

Chapter 50

End of Senior Year

Today, unlike most, was somber. It was June 5, 1941. Graduation ceremonies at Duke and UNC were over. My mother and Doey's parents sat together in the lobby of the Carolina Inn talking of the immediate future.

Their plans were simple. At six in the morning, Doey and her parents would leave by car for Terre Haute. Mother and I would leave Chapel Hill by train for Florida, and the last two years of our days in Durham and Chapel Hill would silently slip into the past.

Two days earlier, we attended graduation ceremonies at Duke University, where, for the first time, we met Harry and Carolyn's parents. Doey was now ready to take the bar, and Carolyn had earned a degree in political science. The following day the scene would move to Chapel Hill, where Harry and I would receive our academic rewards.

After breakfast in the dining room, we all moved to the lobby where Doey and I excused ourselves and left our parents to become better acquainted. We left the Inn at eleven o'clock, knowing that today was the end of the only life we shared. Aimlessly we walked the paths leading to places of learning. My head was filled with images that I would relive, in memory, many times in years to come.

We turned down Fetzer Lane and stopped at number 126, and stood before the silent house, which in the past had always reverberated with sounds of music and laughter. Doey and I were the first to arrive. We opened the door and silence met us. From the moment we entered, melancholy ruled the day. Without planning, our Fetzer family slowly began to appear. No plans had been made for a meeting, but like salmon swimming upstream to spawn, a common element of memory beckoned each of us home. Within twenty minutes all members of our Fetzer family arrived: Harry, Carolyn, Helen, Phil, Bob and Jane. We spoke of a dark and evil future that promised nothing more than a round trip ticket to war. If you didn't survive, you got free transportation home in a body bag.

As a group, we had shared most things worth keeping. Our conversation moved to the present, when Phil asked if anyone knew where Red and Sam were.

"Yes," I said. "Red is a lieutenant colonel in England. Why he's there and what he's doing, he couldn't say. Sam's flying with the U.S. Ferry Command. Every day he's in a different part of the world. Last I heard he was on his way to India."

"I'm glad to be getting out of here," Harry said. "The Chapel Hill we knew is gone. Students have been leaving every day to join the military. The airport we knew has been taken over by the Navy. If you're not in the Navy Aviation Program, the field is off limits." For more than two hours we relived our college days.

Bob Lovell closed the door to the past, saying, "It's time for Jane and me to move on. Our parents are waiting for us at the Beta House to drive us home to Mt. Airy."

After getting their goodbyes and hugs, Bob and Jane left. And then there were six. We stood on the porch and waved to Helen and Phil until their car turned right and disappeared into the Franklin Street traffic. For the last time Harry and I clasped hands.

"Write," I said.

"I will," he replied. We kissed the girls, and spoke of an abiding friendship that would last forever. Doey and I walked with them to their car and watched as they faded into a splash of afternoon sunlight. We closed the door on the past and walked away in a pensive mood.

The deep booming sound of the bell in the Moorhead Tower rolled across the campus, tolling the time of day. It was two o'clock. We entered the Inn and found our parents, seated in an almost deserted lobby, talking. They had eaten lunch, and had just returned from a long walk in the arboretum. Now they were ready to go to their rooms for an afternoon nap.

Mother had just told Dorothy and John a story from my early past. I heard Dorothy say, "He did that?"

"Yes he did," Mother replied. That brought forth another round of laughter.

"Am I the 'he' that you were talking about?" I asked.

"Yes," John said. "Now I know that you will be a good member of our family."

"John, whatever you were laughing about, please don't any of you tell Doey."

"We won't," Dorothy said, as she held out her hand with her fingers crossed.

John said, "We have asked Emma to cancel the train trip to Florida and go with us to Terre Haute. We were about to go up to our rooms for a nap."

I put my arm around my mother and said, "Let's go to Terre Haute, Mom. It may be the only opportunity we will have to all be together for a long time."

John said, "Let's have dinner in the Fungus Café. Give me your tickets and I will take care of your travel plans."

Mom, with a dazed look said, "That's the easiest answer to a question that I have ever had to give without saying a word." We walked to the elevator with them and watched as the door closed. Then Doey and I entered the dining room and settled at a table near the silent piano.

"Your father is a wonderful and thoughtful host, Doey. I had planned to take Mother home, stay for a couple of days, then head to Terre Haute and you. We will now be together until the military needs us." We ordered hamburgers and a Coke.

"What's next?" I asked.

"Let's go to Egan's," Doey replied.

"Good choice, Doey." I put the check for lunch in my pocket and left money on the table, including a tip.

We walked across the campus to Franklin Street and entered Egan's. Joe Egan was behind the bar talking with a group of college students. When he saw us seat ourselves at the bar, he said, "Welcome, Wynn. What can I do for you and Doey?"

"Two beers please, Joe," I replied.

"You have been hanging out with Harry and Carolyn. You are even beginning to sound like him. I suppose you want the beer in beer mugs."

"Yes," I said. "That would be nice, and I promise that I won't pour the beer on the dance floor."

"Two beers in beer mugs, coming up," he said. "By the way, where are Harry and Carolyn?"

"They left a couple of hours ago. Harry decided to join the Air Force before he's drafted, and within a few weeks, Doey will join a group of women pilots, delivering airplanes to military bases."

"What about you?" Joe asked.

"I'm already in an aviation cadet program. I'm just waiting for their orders of when and where to report." Doey and I had our drinks and a few last words with Joe. I slipped a dollar bill across the bar to pay.

Joe pushed it back, saying, "It's on the house, and the very best of luck to you and Doey."

"Thanks, Joe."

We walked back across the campus, down fraternity row, and stopped at the Beta House. A few of the brothers were still there. There was no need for introductions since Doey had been there several times. We were greeted by Brother Bob Evans, president elect for the coming year.

Bob said, "Doey, I see that you're still hanging out with that bum Wynn. Why not forget him and marry me?"

"Bob," she replied, smiling, "if you were the last man in the world, maybe I would give it some thought."

Bob said, "Oh, thank you, Doey. Thank you. The flame in my heart for you was about to flicker and go out. Thank you for the encouragement." He took her in his arms and bent her backward. The kiss that followed brought silence to the room. Even the sounds of the pool balls stopped clicking and the players stood watching from the doorway.

"Thanks, Bob," I said with a smile. "Now, why don't you go play in the traffic?" I turned to Doey and said, "I'm going up to my room to see if I've overlooked anything worth taking. In the meantime, stay away from these sex fiends. I won't be long."

There was nothing in the room worth keeping. When I returned I heard the clicking sound of pool balls. Doey, with pool cue in hand, was about to put the eight ball in the side pocket. She took careful aim. The cue ball gently tapped the eight ball which rolled into the pocket. The game was over. Doey smiled, returned the cue to the rack, bowed and said, "Thank you, gentlemen, I enjoyed the game."

Back at the Inn we walked up to Doey's room, and with her key I opened the door. She took my hand and said, "Come in."

"Thank you. I intended to." We entered and closed the door behind us. "You invited me in, so you speak first," I said.

"No. I would prefer to listen to what you have to say and then I will talk," she said.

"First, I would like to say how very much I love you. In every way, I know that we belong together, and to please your mother, we are now to wait until the war is over before announcing our wedding plans. I intend to speak with her tonight and tell her that we are already as married as we need to be. I will ask her to release you from your promise to wait until after the war. Then she can arrange the biggest wedding in the history of Terre Haute that will please her and her friends, the minister, and members of the local church. I know that what I ask is somewhat out of sequence, but so is a war that could keep us apart for a very long time. I hope that you can freely join me in that request."

"Wynn, my darling, we continue to think alike. It's impossible that you can love me more than I love you and yes, tonight we will talk with Mother. She is the one who will have to wait until after the war for a lavish wedding party. Let's freshen up and meet in the lobby."

I wrapped my love in my arms, kissed her and said, "When you are ready to go down, call me."

At six forty-five my phone rang. It was Doey. "I'm ready."

"I'll be there in five minutes," I replied.

"Five minutes is a long time," she quipped.

"Then I'll be there in two minutes," I answered and hung up.

In the lobby our parents were gathered around the radio listening to the war news from London. "On June sixth Hitler began his war on Russia. Now their army is on the march from the Arctic to the Black Sea. London has ousted the Rome Consuls and warned the U.S. not to interfere." There was a pause, then, "This is Edward R. Murrow reporting the war news from

London . . . Good night . . . and good luck." Without a break in time, the CBS announcer said "Listen to Murrow tomorrow." The voice of Kate Smith then filled the room with her theme song, "God Bless America."

Doey and I sat on a sofa facing our parents. Dorothy said, "When I listen to your mother talk, I'm listening to you. You both have a gift of words, with a slight southern accent."

"Thank you, Dorothy," Mother said. "We grew up in a part of Florida where people from the north settled many years ago. The school teachers are mostly from the north, and that accounts for only a hint of a southern accent in our speech."

"We're going to the movies to see Greta Garbo's latest picture," John said. "Why not go with us?"

"You will enjoy it," Doey said. "Wynn and I saw it last week with Carolyn and Harry, in Durham."

"What are your plans for the evening?" John asked.

"First," I said, "you will not need a car. We will walk with you across the campus to Franklin Street. When we cross the street we will be standing in front of the theater."

"Then what will you and Doey do?" Dorothy asked.

"We're going to the Beta House," I replied. "If any of our friends are still on campus, they'll be there."

John said, "If you're not at the Inn when we return from the movie, we will see you and Doey at five thirty in the morning. We want to get an early start."

"If you need us," I replied, "we will probably be here or out for a walk around the campus." I kissed Mother and said, "Behave yourself, and enjoy the picture."

314

Arise My Love And Come Away With Me

We had no thought of doing any of that. As soon as our parents left for the short walk across the campus to Franklin Street and the movie, we took the elevator up to Doey's room. At the door, Doey turned to me and said, "Do you remember that night in Terre Haute, when we were standing outside my bedroom door? You opened it and I said 'I wish that I could invite you in and one night I will'. Well, this is the night!'"

She took my hand and we entered the room. I locked the door behind us. We turned off the lights, leaving one dim desk lamp on. There was no place for youth and innocence in this room. We eagerly lay down on the bed and held each other tenderly. Touching, kissing, and breathing together as one. We caressed each other and whispered our love, and I wished we could stay like that forever.

Then Doey slowly disentangled herself from me and said, "Wait, I want to do something special." She sat on the side of the bed, picked up the phone, and called room service. "We would like a bottle of champagne and two glasses please." After discussing names, vintage, and pedigrees of the wine, she found one she liked. Fifteen minutes and the same number of kisses and caresses later, the wine arrived. Doey added a tip to the chit and signed her name. Before we could uncork the bottle, her phone rang. It was her father.

"I just wanted you to know that we are back," John said. "The movie was sold out so we walked down Franklin Street to Egan's. We were curious to know where you and Wynn spend your leisure time. We even met Joe Egan. Mother and I had a glass of wine and Emma had a Coke. I introduced myself, Mother, and Emma to Joe and told him that we were here for our daughter's graduation from Duke and Mrs. Cary was here for her son's graduation from UNC."

Doey rolled her eyes and shook her head in disbelief, as her father continued talking.

"Between giving attention to patrons at the bar he returned to talk with us. When we got up to leave, I started to pay the tab, but Joe said, 'Now that I know Mrs. Cary is Wynn's mother and that you and Mrs. Brooks are Doey's parents, there is no charge. I owe them. The dance crowd flocked here after every dance that Wynn played for. I can't charge you. Thank them for me. Wynn was the pied piper; the music man. Wynn and Doey, Harry and Carolyn are not customers, they are my friends. I'm very glad to meet you. I hope you will come back'."

John continued saying, "I tried calling Wynn. I want to give him the train reservations for tomorrow. Do you know where he is?"

"Yes, Daddy, he's here," she said. "Thank you for taking care of the train tickets." She handed the phone to me and laughed. What else could she do?

"Hello, John. We'll be right down. We do need to talk about tomorrow." I hung up. I had been to Doey's room before, but I never felt the need to tell them, but now I did. I hope they were not suspicious of my conduct with their daughter. I felt greatly relieved that we did not break her promise to her mother. Now they knew that we were alone and together here in her room at nine o'clock at night. Yes, Doey was their daughter, but she was also, except for a few lines on a paper, my wife. It was time to let our parents know that we were responsible adults and that we would live our life our way.

"Don't uncork the champagne," I said. "We'll be back."

We stepped out of the elevator and from a lobby window we could see light from a full moon. "It's a 'Doey's moon,'" I said.

"It is beautiful," she replied. "It's a good night to fly."

Our parents were seated in a secluded corner of the almost deserted lobby. The light from the Carolina full moon added a touch of beauty to the evening. John stood and greeted us like he already knew what we would say. There were two chairs before the sofa where they sat. John pointed to the chairs and said, "Come and join us." Doey sat down.

I stood, and to John I said, "Thank you, John, for taking care of our travel plans."

"I'm glad to do it, Wynn, and I'm very happy that we're all going home."

I turned to the others and said, "I have one more bit of information to share with all of you. When Doey and I were in New York we felt the need to go to St. Patrick's Cathedral. Without a spoken word, plan, or reason, slowly and quietly we walked down Fifth Avenue to St. Patrick's. Inside the door on the right was a table of lighted candles. Next to them was a supply of various sizes of new candles. Doey picked up two of the larger ones. I lit them and placed them on the table. Silently we walked down the aisle to the altar, and kneeled. No words were spoken, and no priest or minister was present. We were alone with our thoughts. After a few minutes we got up, made the sign of the cross, and walked out. My silent feelings were of Doey, and what she means to me. We walked away with a spiritual feeling that we had said our marriage vows. Doey experienced much the same emotion. In a few weeks Doey and I will be inducted into military service. There will not be time for us to have a formal wedding. We are responsible young adults anxious to get on with our lives. We thought you should know this."

Doey stood and put her arms around me and whispered, "Oh, Wynn, I hope you know how very much I love you." Mom and Dorothy dabbed at tears in their eyes.

John stood and said, "Once more, Wynn, welcome to our family. Now if I may be excused for a few minutes, I have a party to plan. Wait here. I'll be back in a few minutes." Several minutes later he was back. "Follow me."

He led us to a room that was big enough for twenty. The room was paneled in dark wood and tastefully decorated. Prints of eighteenth century ships hung on the wall. Dark tables, comfortable chairs, and a fireplace added a touch of luxury. A Tabriz carpet lay on the floor. It was a cozy room that looked like a picture of an English Gentleman's Club. There was a bar and piano, and five people. John said to Doey, "While we wait for the hors d'oeuvres and champagne, why don't you play and sing your song to Wynn?"

Doey and I walked to the piano and sat. In a low whisper she said to me, "I'm not sure that I can sing. My throat feels like I'm catching a cold." She looked at me, smiled, and began to sing and play, *"That certain night, the night we met, there was magic abroad in the air, there were angels dining at the Ritz and a nightingale sang in Berkeley Square. I may be right, I may be wrong, but I'm perfectly willing to swear, that when you turned and smiled at me, a nightingale sang in Berkeley Square."* She stopped singing, sneezed, and then spoke the final words. *"The moon that lingered over London town, poor puzzled moon, he wore a frown. How could he know we two were so in love, the whole darn world was upside down. The streets of town were paved with stars, it was such a romantic affair, and as we kissed and said goodnight, a nightingale sang in Berkeley Square."*

She turned to me and said, "One day we will go to Berkeley Square and hear our bird sing."

"Yes," I said, "we will." Our audience of three applauded. The waiter had just brought a tray of hors d'oeuvres and a bottle of champagne. The party took a turn for the better.

"Play another song?" John said.

Dorothy said, "Doey, are you alright?"

"Yes, Mother," she replied. "I'm just a little tired from all the day's activity." Through the evening, Doey pretended to feel better than she actually felt. Dorothy and I recognized it as the onset of a cold.

Dorothy said, "It's been a wonderful evening, but tomorrow will be a long day of travel. For now, let's take the memory of this night home, where it will be continued in Terre Haute."

Doey said, "Thank you, Mother."

On the third floor we stood together for a few moments talking about the evening. John said, "It's time we turn in. Be sure to call the front desk for a wakeup call."

Doey and I walked down the hall to Mother's room. "Sleep well." We hugged her and watched until she walked in and closed the door. Doey coughed and sneezed, and said, "I'm sorry, Wynn. I'm thinking of the song 'Everything Happens to Me.'"

"Never apologize for feeling bad, Doey," I replied. We could see Dorothy standing before her door holding something in her hand.

"Where are you going, Mother?" Doey asked.

"I was waiting for you," she said, and handed me two small bottles of medicine and a box of aspirins. "See that she takes this, Wynn. Doey, you will be better by morning."

I took Doey to her room. She gave up the act of feeling good and took the medicine. "I'll be fine by morning. Oh, Wynn, we must be living under a black star." She turned her head away as I started to kiss her, and said, "I'm tempted, but a hug is all that I can offer. I don't want our first night together to be remembered for a cold and a sore throat. Tonight is not our night, but our night will come. I promise."

"Goodnight darling. I'll be with you in my dreams, and I'll call you in the morning."

Early the next morning I called Doey, who said that she was feeling much better. In the lobby Mother, John, and Dorothy were talking about us. They were all concerned about the development of Doey's cold. I told them that I took Doey to her room and gave her the medicine Dorothy provided.

"This morning when I called her, she said she was ready to go home." They gave me a curious look.

John said, "Let's eat and get this show on the road."

We checked out of the Carolina Inn. All of our baggage had been carefully packed into John's Chrysler station wagon. Dorothy was in the front seat and Mother shared the back seat with an overflow of handbags containing law and economic books that would remind Doey and me of our college years. John got behind the wheel and was ready to roll. We wished them a safe trip home and waved until they turned north on Franklin Street.

I called Edward from the Inn to tell him of our travel arrangements. "Doey and I will be leaving Chapel Hill by train at seven thirty this morning.

We'll call you when we arrive, and take a cab home. Mr. and Mrs. Brooks have already left. My mother is with them. She will be their guest for a few days." I took a moment to ask how he, Anna and Brindy were.

"Anna and I are fine," he said, "and Brindy spends his days by the front door waiting for Doey to find her way home. Without her, the home is just a house. It will be nice to have Doey and you home again." We said goodbye and hung up.

We left our college ties to the past and walked to the Chapel Hill depot, where we boarded the train for home. It was a long, trying trip for Doey. Her cold and sore throat had worsened. I was at the point of asking the conductor if there was a doctor on the train. "Please don't bother," Doey said, "I will be fine once I get home."

We had lunch and dinner in our room. Doey's selection from the menu was nothing more than soup and hot tea.

Chapter 51

Doey Gets Pneumonia

That evening we arrived in Terre Haute. I called the Brooks' house and after the third ring Edward answered. "We're at the train station," I said. "Has Mr. Brooks arrived?"

"No," he replied. "Mr. Brooks is taking his time. They will be here about one o'clock tomorrow. He told us the wonderful news that you and Doey are engaged, and without his permission, or yours, Anna and I have a plan that I hope you and Doey will approve. I will be at the station to pick you up in thirty minutes."

"Thank you Edward, but we'll take a cab home. We'll be there in thirty minutes or less. Doey's anxious to talk with Anna and you." We said goodbye and hung up.

When we arrived home, Edward and Anna, holding Brindy on a leash, were standing by the front door. Quickly they came to us.

"Welcome home," Edward said. "Leave your baggage in the car, and come in." Edward and I shook hands.

"Doey is not well, and maybe needs a doctor," I said. Edward and Anna showed immediate parental concern. Doey belonged to them and Anna immediately took charge. She put her arm around Doey, who said, "All I need is a little rest. I need to lie down."

"Rest easy, baby," Anna said. "I'll see that you get whatever you need." She turned to Edward and said, "Call Dr. Leland." I picked up Doey and carried her to her room and placed her on the bed. Brindy lay on the floor next to her bed. Soon Edward arrived with our baggage. Anna said to me, "As soon as she is comfortable, I'll call you. Why don't you and Edward wait in the library?"

While waiting, I asked Edward who Dr. Leland was.

"Dr. Leland is the best of the best. He and Mr. John met at the University of Chicago when Mr. John was a freshman. Dr. Leland was in his second year in the medical school, and Mr. John pledged the Sigma Nu Fraternity. That's where they met and they have been friends ever since."

Thirty minutes later, Anna came to the library and said, "She's had a warm bath and is now in bed. Dr. Leland called to say he will be here soon. She's asking for you, Mr. Wynn, go to her."

I ran up the stairs into her room. I bent over the bed and said, "I'm here, Doey."

In a whispering voice, she opened her eyes and said, "I'm so sorry, Wynn. It's no time for me to be sick."

A few minutes later, Dr. Leland arrived. He was a tall thin man with a mop of unkempt brown hair that had specks of white at the temples. After asking Doey a few questions he said, "Open your mouth as wide as you can."

With a tongue suppressor and light he checked her throat, then her blood pressure, and with his stethoscope, checked her lungs and breathing. He then said, looking at us, "She should be in the hospital where she would receive around the clock treatment."

In a weak voice Doey whispered, "Wynn, I don't want to go to the hospital. Don't let them put me in the hospital. Where's Daddy? He will tell them what to do. Oh, Wynn, I feel so bad."

Dr. Leland gave her a shot in the arm and in moments she relaxed. In a couple minutes all we could hear was raspy breathing. Dr. Leland's diagnosis was pneumonia. "I would like to have her in the hospital where she would get the medical attention she needs, but Doey can be very hard to convince, once she makes up her mind. For now all we can do is let her sleep."

We walked down to the library and joined Edward. Dr. Leland asked, "Where are John and Dorothy?"

"Mr. and Mrs. Brooks were in Durham for Doey's graduation. There wasn't room in the station wagon for Doey and me, so we took the train. It was not a pleasant trip for her. By the way, my name is Wynn Cary. I'm a friend of the family."

Edward turned to Dr. Leland and said, "Mr. Wynn and Miss Doey are engaged to be married."

"Congratulations, Mr. Cary," Dr. Leland said. "I have known John and Dorothy since our freshman days at the University of Chicago. I was best man at John's wedding. When I became a physician, John and Dorothy were my first patients. I delivered Doey and have been their family doctor for many years."

"Thank you, Dr. Leland. Use your magic and assure me that Doey will be alright."

"Doey's a strong young lady and if she gets proper attention, I feel sure that you'll be standing before the Episcopal minister, eagerly waiting for her to come down the aisle to claim you. When do you expect John home?"

I looked at my watch. It was twenty minutes to midnight. "Depending on the time that he's going by, he could be here by ten or eleven in the morning."

"I will be here in the morning at eight o'clock with a registered nurse. We will have three nurses for around the clock care. I will ask John about the hospital, but I think that we already know the answer to that." He turned to Anna and gave her instructions for the night.

Anna thanked him for coming and assured us that she would be watching over Doey all night. I walked to the door with Dr. Leland then returned to the library. Anna had already returned to Doey's room.

Edward said, "I'll make a pot of coffee and take it up." I went up to Doey's room and told Anna that I would be there through the night and, if she were needed, I would call her.

"No," she replied. "Mr. Wynn, she's my baby and I can't leave her."

"Neither can I. She's my life," I replied. All night we sat there not knowing what we could do.

At about five a.m., Edward came in with a pot of coffee and two bowls of mixed fruit. Anna had fallen asleep in her chair. Edward gently awakened her and said, "Why don't you and Wynn lie down and sleep? I will watch Doey and call you, if needed. Dr. Leland and a nurse will be here in a couple of hours."

After much persuasion, Anna picked up a cup of coffee and a bowl of fruit and said, "I'll be in the bedroom, just a few steps down the hall. If she needs me for anything, call me."

Edward said, "Wynn, your room is just the other side of this wall and you need some rest. Go and I will call you when she wakes up."

"Thanks Edward, but I'll stay until the doctor and nurse come."

"I understand, Wynn. If I may, I'll stay with you."

At eight o'clock Dr. Leland arrived with a nurse, whose name was Betty Fox. They asked several questions about Doey and how she was during the night. After the debriefing Dr. Leland said, "The nurses will be in charge of the room at all times. They will tell you when it's convenient for you to enter and when you should leave. Before entering, wash your hands with soap and hot water, and wear a mask. You will find them on a table by the door to her room. When you leave, drop the mask in the can with a lid. Keep your visits to a minimum. As Doey begins to improve, your visits can be a little more frequent and longer. The nurse on duty will keep you informed of Doey's condition at all times." Dr. Leland left us saying that he would return in a few hours to discuss Doey's condition with Dorothy and John. We all had the feeling that the worst was yet to come.

Edward received a call from John stating that arrival would be about midday. He asked if Doey and I were there, and Edward said we were anxiously awaiting their arrival. Minutes later Dr. Leland arrived with a nurse named Christine Bright, and went up to see Doey.

From the morning room window Edward and I had a view of the road. A few minutes past one, Edward said, "I see the car. They're almost here." We were standing by the front door as John entered the driveway and parked next to Dr. Leland's car. Edward and I went out to meet them. They were a tired-looking, but happy, group of travelers. I opened the car doors and helped Mother and Dorothy out.

John joined us and said, "Is this Dr. Leland's car?"

"Yes, it is," I replied. "He's here because Doey is sick."

Dorothy said, with a touch of panic in her voice, "Where is Doey?"

"She's in bed. The doctor assures me that she will be up and about soon. Before you go to Doey he asks that all of us wait for him. He would like to talk with us before anyone goes into her room. I told him that we would be waiting in the library."

As we entered the house, we met Dr. Leland coming down the stairs. John and Dr. Leland shook hands and after a few solemn words, John introduced Mother to Dr. Leland and led the way to the library.

There was a moment of silence and then Dr. Leland spoke. "Doey has pneumonia. I believe that we have caught it in time. How soon she will recover will depend in part upon your understanding the seriousness of her illness. It can be fatal and it is contagious. With John's permission, I have arranged to have three registered nurses here around the clock. The alternative is to take her to the hospital."

After a few minutes, Dr. Leland had answered all the questions. "John," he said, "after you and Dorothy wash your hands with soap and hot water, we will go in together. I have placed a box of masks on the table so you can cover your nose and mouth. Always be sure you wear one when you enter the room. The nurse on duty will be in charge and she will tell you when it's convenient for you to enter. No discussion is necessary. If she tells you that it's time to go, just remember that she is acting in Doey's best interest. Anna, Edward, and Wynn already know the rules."

Anna excused herself saying, "I'm so glad that you're here, Miss Dorothy."

Edward stood and said, "Mrs. Cary, your room is ready." We followed Edward up to the west wing where Mother would stay.

Dorothy turned to me and said, "Before Dr. Leland leaves, I will call you. I'm sure you will want to hear what he has to say."

Mom sat down and removed her shoes. "Wynn, I have come at the wrong time. I should go home."

"No, Mom, you are here at the right time. Dorothy will need someone to talk to. If I had any idea that you were in the way or here at the wrong time, I would tell you. Fate has put you here at the right time."

Like a snails' race on a hot summer day, time oozed on. By the second of July, Dorothy and I stood by Doey's bed and watched as she took a few steps around the room with her nurse. On the evening of the fourth of July, I carried Doey downstairs, placed her in a wheel chair, and rolled her into the morning room, where the family had gathered to watch the fireworks display through the window. The nurse sat in a chair to the left of Doey. I was on the right, holding Doey's hand. She was weak but kissable. I was anxious to get her alone, but more dark and less people would be needed before I could hold her close and tell her how much I loved her.

On the tenth of July, Dr. Leland made his last visit. All evidence of illness had been erased from Doey's room and John returned to his office to take care of whatever lawyers do to stay busy. The next day we said goodbye to the day nurse. Doey was feeling much better.

Chapter 52

Terre Haute 1941

On the 15th of July, Doey said, "Wynn, there's a full moon tomorrow night. Let's go to the club for dinner and then go fly. I want to fly with you once more before you leave me."

"Are you sure that you're up to it?"

"Oh, Wynn," she said, "there's such little time for us. Please, I want to fly in the high, un-trespassed sanctity of space with you again. Yesterday you got a letter from National Airlines telling you to report next week. That gives us less than a week before you leave me."

I told our parents that Doey and I planned to go to the club for dinner. John asked, "Doey, are you sure that you're feeling up to it?"

"Yes, I am," she replied. "After breakfast I would like to show Emma our horse, Buckshot, and the stable with the names on the wall. Wynn wants to finish carving our names and then I plan to rest and maybe take a nap before we leave for dinner." She looked at me and said, "What will you do?"

"I'll watch you sleep," I said with a grin.

Dorothy said, "After Emma sees the stable, we are going into town to shop. We'll be home for lunch."

"Have fun and be careful," I said. It was obvious to me that they had planned the day to give Doey and me some time alone. After Mother saw the horse and names on the wall, Dorothy came to the stable and said, "It's time

Arise My Love And Come Away With Me

to go." We watched as they got into Dorothy's car and headed over the hill to town. We were alone at last. I finished carving our names on the wall. Only the date was left to be finished.

Doey said, "Wynn, I need to lie down and rest for a while." We returned to the house.

"Let's go up to your room, Doey. I'll read a book and watch you sleep. If I am gone when you wake up, I'll be in my room, just on the other side of this wall."

"One day we will tear the wall down and have one big, beautiful room."

"We'll do that, Doey. Now sleep. We have a dinner date." I kissed her and settled down to watch and read. I had no idea how long I had been sleeping, or what room I was in. The book had fallen to the floor. I was brushing a fly from my face. Slowly I opened my eyes. The fly was gone. I looked at the bed. It was empty. There was evidence that it had been slept in and the bathroom door was open. Doey was gone. I started to get up, but an arm holding a feather appeared from over the back of the chair. Quickly I grabbed it and pulled Doey into my lap.

"I thought you were going to watch me sleep?" Doey quipped. "I slept for more than an hour, and for the past thirty minutes, I've been watching you sleep." Once more she brushed my face with a feather. "Get your clarinet, Wynn, and let's go down to the basement and play a few tunes."

"Doey, are you sure that you're up to it?"

"Oh! Yes, I am. I've never felt better."

"I'm so happy to hear that. I was thinking that you would need a few more days," I said.

"Wynn, we don't have a few more days. You will be leaving me soon, and I don't know when I will see you again. Monday you leave for New Orleans. In a couple of weeks I will leave for Willow Run to join the Henry Ford Aviation Operation. Let's pretend that tomorrow is the first day after a declaration of peace. Let's go to the basement and celebrate with the sound of music."

Doey sat at the piano playing chords, while I warmed up the clarinet by running the chromatic scale and playing a few notes of Chopin's Clarinet Concerto. We played Duke's and Carolina's alma maters and then our song. Doey began to sing. At the end of the song we heard Edward say, "That was beautiful. Would you like lunch served down here?"

"Yes, Edward. That would be nice. When our parents arrive ask them to join us," Doey replied.

We continued playing songs from our college days and we heard John say, "Do you know 'Only Forever'?"

"Yes," I answered. "If you can hum it, we can play it."

For Dorothy we played "I'll Be with You in Apple Blossom Time" and "Down by the Old Mill Stream."

Very softly I said to Doey, "Let's give your left hand a work out with a little boogie and end with our song." As we finished playing, there was a standing ovation. I took Doey by the hand, and together we bowed, and not knowing what else to do, I kissed her. Edward came in with lunch.

We sat at the table talking about the war and what Doey's and my part would be. Doey started to cry and said, "Please, no war talk. We already know what our part will be." The magic spell of music was gone. Doey excused herself from the table and we left. Three loving, caring people were left to reflect upon the last threads of our youth that were about to break.

Early that evening, with Brindy leading the way, Doey and I walked down the front stairway and into the library. Mom and Dorothy were playing gin rummy. John was reading the newspaper and listening to the news. Edward was behind the bar mixing drinks. Doey and I were dressed for a night out. "We're going to the club for dinner and maybe to the airport," I said. "Doey may want to fly in the moonlight, but if the sky is totally overcast, we may just come home."

Mom and Dorothy looked at each other and shared a moment of panic. Dorothy said, "There will always be a moon, darling. There will be other times to fly in the moonlight."

Doey stomped her foot and said, "Mother, you just don't understand. Don't any of you understand? In three days Wynn will leave me, maybe forever. Three days is all the time we have."

John got up and put his arms around us and said, "Your mothers do understand. They have nothing but the worry they live with every moment that you are out of their sight."

"I'm sorry Daddy. I apologize for letting my emotions run rampant with feelings that we all must live with." She kissed our mothers, smiled, and said, "Edward, I would like a Coke, please."

I looked at Doey and said, "Make it two, Edward."

He poured our drinks and sat them, along with a box containing flowers, on a table between our chairs. "Your mothers," John said, "bought the flowers when they were out shopping today, and wanted to be sure you got them before leaving for dinner."

Doey smiled and said, "Thank you, Emma and Mother." I added my thanks and Doey pinned the rose bud and sprig of fern to my coat lapel, and I pinned two small red carnations in a bed of greenery to Doey's gown. We finished our drink and again thanked our parents for just being who they are. John walked to the table where the record player sat and pushed the "on" button as we walked out of the room.

The light from a full moon lit our way to the club. Small clusters of puffy white clouds completed a picture of a late summer evening. As we arrived at the club, we sat in the car for a few moments looking at the western sky where a big harvest moon added beauty to the starlit sky. "Let's fly!" she said.

Thirty minutes later we stood before the operations desk at the airport. Doey signed for a plane, a Stinson. We taxied to the blast fence, held the brakes, pushed the throttle of the engine to the fire wall, checked the magnetos, taxied to the runway and held. "If it's okay with you, Wynn, I'll fly the first leg and you fly the second."

"Whatever," I said. "As long as I get to kiss you, I'm yours to command."

"If you don't kiss me, there's no point in going," Doey said, as she waggled the ailerons and rudder indicating that Alpha Charlie was ready to fly. She got the green light from the tower indicating the runway was hers. At lift off, we silently said, "Arise my love and come away with me." Doey eased Alpha Charlie into a gentle climb. Off to the left we could see the lights of the club growing dim.

"Lift the nose, Doey, and head for the moon." We were at five hundred feet and climbing. At a thousand feet she leveled off and trimmed the plane for level flying. In every way she was a pro. She was my love. She was my life. "The moonlight goes with your hair," I exclaimed. She engaged the automatic pilot, and I pulled her gently into my arms and we flew on.

"Wynn," she said as she scanned the sky and the control panel, "this may be our last flight together for a long time. I will remember it and you, whenever I fly. My heart will always be with you. Take care of it and come back to me."

During a long lingering kiss I kept an eye on the sky around us and whispered, "I'll be back." We flew on through the moonlit night. Our hearts were beating with love and our minds were harboring grim thoughts. All too soon our time in the air was over. I reversed our course with a wingover and headed for the airport, and landed.

We returned to the club and entered. Dodd, the maître d', welcomed us. "Doey," he said, "did you and Mr. Cary enjoy your flight in the moonlight?"

"How did you know we flew?" Doey asked.

"Your father called to check up on you and to satisfy your mothers."

"Our mothers," I said, "are fearful of our flying, and they must know where we are at every minute. I'm afraid that will never change."

"Vince will be very happy to see both of you. He will do everything he can to brighten the end of your day. I'm glad you are feeling better, Doey."

"Thank you, Dodd. You and the club members have been very kind asking about my health. I believe that I received cards and flowers from everyone in the county."

"When the staff and club members knew that you were ill there was a lot of praying for your recovery. Your letter of appreciation to staff and club members is posted on the bulletin board. Around here you are a very special person. We are pleased to have you and Mr. Cary with us tonight."

"Thank you, Dodd, for your kind words," Doey replied.

We were escorted to our table near the bandstand, where Vince met us with a big smile. He said, "Welcome back, Doey. Your father made our day when he told us that you and Mr. Cary would be with us tonight. He also said something about flying. I'm not sure that I understand that. Are you flying somewhere tonight?"

"No, Vince. We have finished flying for the night."

"Do you have a plane?" Vince asked.

"No," I replied. "We rented one for the evening. Mr. Brooks just wanted to make sure that we didn't drink before flying. We would never do that."

Vince left us to peruse the menu. A short time later he returned to take our order. I looked at Doey and asked if she would like a Manhattan. She shook her head and softly said, "No, I would like coffee."

For dinner we ordered New York steak medium and a selection of whatever. Our minds didn't linger on food. We were not in a festive mood. Even the music was only background for a conversation which carried no hope of extending the time we had together. Soon we would be hundreds of miles apart, and in a few months, maybe a continent apart. There was no guarantee that we would ever be together again.

The music and dancing was for another time. We pushed the food around on our plates and spoke of a future that dissolved into parallel courses—a future that ended with nothing more than a faulty dream. Soon we would enter a new life, where a faceless, nameless someone would enter our names on a schedule that would move from clipboard to clipboard recording our readiness for war duties.

"Let's go home," Doey said.

I asked Vince for the tab. "There is no tab," he said as he handed Doey a paper box.

"This is for you, Doey. I had the chef make a special dessert for you," Vince said. He placed the box on the table before her. "Take it with you, Doey, and when you are feeling better, I will expect you and Mr. Cary to return."

I slipped Vince a tip, which he refused, saying, "Thank you, Mr. Cary, but this is my night to welcome a lifelong friend home."

Doey kissed Vince on the cheek and softly said, "Thank you, Vince, for remembering a moment in my youth. We will be back."

On the way out we were stopped by several club members who welcomed Doey's return after her illness. In the foyer we said a few words to Dodd and were on our way home. A hint of moonlight filtered through dark clouds and lights from the car showed us the way home.

I parked in the driveway. We sat there for several minutes in silence. Then Doey said "Wynn, we will remember this as the night we crossed the Rubicon. There is no turning back. Our generation is committed to a life of killing. When we kill enough to stop the spread of Hitler's evil empire, our government will release us to help the world recover what it has lost."

"Doey, you sound as if you believe that when that war ends there will be world peace. I don't believe the world will ever live in peace. When this war is over, no one really wins. New alliances will be plotting the next war. From the beginning of recorded time there have been wars and the world has recovered. I'm afraid that time, money, and science will probably find a way to destroy the world, and a dead planet will orbit the sun." Soft sprinkles of rain began to fall as we sat there in silence. "Let's go in, Doey."

I opened the door to the house. Brindy was there to greet us. From the library we could see our doting family was waiting. As we approached I heard John say, "They're home!" We walked into the library and were met by smiles and questions. "Did we fly? How was the dinner? Who did we meet?"

Doey said, "Yes. We did fly and then we went to the club." I thanked John for the champagne, but declined saying we didn't drink it, and told our mothers the music was beautiful, but we didn't dance. The music was no more than a background sound, for a solemn night and our answers were accompanied by smiles that were forced.

John said, "It's good to see you and Doey smile again."

Mom stood and hugged Doey and me and quietly said, "Is something bothering you? Your answers to our questions are almost, but not really the truth, are they? If what bothers you is none of my business, I'm sorry to intrude, but anything that affects you and Doey also affects us."

Doey said, "Yes, Emma, we do have a problem. It has nothing to do with how Wynn and I feel for each other. The facts are that Wynn and I must say goodbye so soon. We may never see the life we planned together. It's that simple. We know our lives apart could be devastating. Wynn leaves me Sunday morning and we enter a life in which we have no say." Doey looked at me and with tears threatening to fall, whispered, "God please help us."

Mom put her arms around us and said, "I'm sure that God heard your plea for help and as sure as the sun rises in the morning, you will have the help you asked for."

"My darlings," Dorothy said, "sit down and try to relax. I will bring you cups of hot chocolate to go with what Vince made for you. Just know that wherever you and Wynn go, you will always have our love and concern."

Dorothy returned carrying a tray containing a plate with a peanut butter and jelly sandwich, cut in half, and two cups of hot chocolate. In their eyes we were children again, but the tie that binds was a slip knot that released us. We were the adults and they were our children. They looked to us for assurance that we were alright, and that we would always come home to them.

For Doey and me the last few days and nights were separated by short blurs of sunlight. We tried to make every minute a memory worth keeping. For lunch the next day I carried a picnic basket of food up the hill. Just over the rim of the hill there was a place among a stand of oak trees known only to Doey and me. We spread a blanket on the ground. I set the basket down and Doey came into my outstretched arms. We spoke of Harry, Carolyn, Red and Sam and wondered where they were. Our thoughts returned to the present where untouched food lay. We repacked the basket and walked back to the rim of the hill and stood there. My eyes recorded the peaceful scene and stowed it away for future viewing. Doey was doing much the same. She looked at me and placed her hand in mine. Slowly we returned down the hill for home.

The next day we took Dorothy's car and roamed aimlessly around the countryside, ending in the city. We stopped at the Malt Shop, where we had sandwiches and coffee. After lunch we drove home and parked. The precious time moved on and briefly paused on Sunday. For the last time we attended church services with our family.

Monday morning I awoke with soft rivulets of rain running down the window panes. I picked up my bag and walked down the back stairs to the kitchen. Doey and Brindy were there. Mom was talking to Anna. Quickly she got up and moved to my side. "May I join you?" she asked.

"Of course you may," I said as I put my arm around Mom.

"Thanks. Let's join Dorothy and John in the library," she replied.

After breakfast John said to me, "It's time to go." Our mothers, Anna and Brindy stood in a line at the front door, and like a military inspection I moved before them collecting kisses and hugs along the way. Doey, John, Edward and I got into the station wagon and headed to the airport, where I would board a plane for New Orleans.

We entered the terminal where I signed in, checked my bag, and paid for my one-way ticket. We then walked out and stood in the shadow of the morning. The loudspeaker announced the arrival of Flight 3 for New Orleans and stops along the way. John and I hugged and shook hands. "Take good care, Wynn, and come home when you can." Edward spoke his variation of the same words, and we clasped hands.

John said to Doey, "We will wait here for you."

Doey and I walked into the dark side of morning. I wrapped her in my arms and said, "I love you, Doey Brooks."

She kissed me and said, "There's no way that you can love me more than I love you." Her face was wet with tears. I kissed her again. She responded saying, "Wherever you may go, always come back to me."

Over the loudspeaker we heard that the plane was ready for boarding. Slowly we left the dark behind and walked, hand in hand, to the plane. John reappeared and stood beside Doey and said, "I'll take good care of her, Wynn. Come back to us."

I kissed Doey and said, "Thanks, John, I'll be back."

From the window of the plane I watched them walk back to the gate entrance to the field. They turned and waved until the plane taxied out of sight.

Two weeks later Doey received a letter telling her to report to Henry Ford Operations in Dearborn, Michigan for training. The manufacturing plant was called Willow Run, located between Ypsilanti and Belleville, Michigan.

Henry Ford manufactured B-24 Liberators and repaired a few AT-11 aircraft for the U.S. military. Doey trained in the military manor of aviation procedures, where she and many other capable women became members of the WAF (Women's Air Force). Her main duties were to deliver planes from the manufacturer to military installations throughout the United States.

We did not see each other again for a whole year.

Chapter 53

New Orleans

I went to New Orleans to work for National Airlines. It was September 21, 1941. Our government had requisitioned two National Lockheed Electra planes to transport war material to military bases along the east coast with daily stops from Key West to Miami, Tampa, Orlando, Jacksonville, and west with stops at Tallahassee, Mobile, and New Orleans where the crew would spend the night. At 6 a.m. the crew would repeat the same stops in reverse order, back to Key West from New Orleans. I was the third man in the crew. My job was to see that the cargo was loaded in a way that maintained the correct weight and balance for the aircraft, so that it could fly safely.

There were times on every flight when the captain would let me fly co-pilot. However, I was not permitted to be in the co-pilot's seat on take offs or landings. On each flight, the co-pilot of the plane, when airborne, would trade places with me so I could gain flight experience. The captain was not an instructor and I didn't have a commercial license, so I suppose it was illegal.

After a few flights, I became one of the radio operators for the line. At 6 a.m. each morning, at the beginning of a shift, I would broadcast: "Jacksonville Operations advise that Operation New Orleans is on the air." We would notify them of all passengers whose destinations were somewhere along the route to Jacksonville, and which passengers would continue on to other destinations. This gave the passenger reservation office the information they needed to reserve space on flights continuing on from Jacksonville.

I also learned to read weather reports, including barometric pressure, in flight weather, and terminal forecast. Our shifts were eight hours long. My job was temporary, but it was a link between ground and air. It was something anyone could do, but I needed an income.

On Sunday, December 7, 1941, Japan bombed our battleships in Pearl Harbor, Hawaii, and President Franklin Roosevelt finally had a reason to declare war. I received a letter giving me seven days to report to Maxwell Field in Montgomery, Alabama for induction into the Air Force.

"U.S. DECLARES WAR, PACIFIC BATTLE WIDENS . . . . 1,500 DEAD IN HAWAII . . . . MANILA AREA BOMBED . . . . HOSTILE PLANES SIGHTED AT SAN FRANCISCO . . . . U.S. NOW AT WAR WITH GERMANY AND ITALY . . . . JAPANESE CHECKED IN ALL LAND FIGHTING . . . . 3 OF THEIR SHIPS SUNK, 2D BATTLESHIP HIT . . . . JAPANESE POUNDED IN LUZON, WARSHIPS CHASED . . . . RUSSIANS ROUT NAZI ARMIES ON MOSCOW FRONT . . . . HOUSE GETS BILL TO REGISTER ALL MEN 18 TO 64."

I wrote to Doey to tell her that my days at National Airlines were over. For almost six months, she had been flying airplanes from manufacturers to somewhere in the country where they were needed. I called her base to tell her that I was now officially in the war and that I would call and write again when I knew where I would be stationed.

At Maxwell Field, I trained on all the planes necessary to fly the B-24's. Since I already had a great deal of flying experience, I was able to move through the military training at a quick pace. I became a second lieutenant and would go through cadet training. I was sent to Selma, Alabama for primary training. After checking my civilian log book and a flight in a PT 17 trainer, I was on my way to Harlingen, Texas for advanced training. After several weeks there, I was ordered to Thunderbird Field in Arizona. There, I completed my training and finally became a legitimate U.S. Air Force pilot.

Although Doey and I had not been together for almost a year, we wrote each other constantly. When I received my orders to report for deployment in San Diego, I was given a ten-day leave. I quickly contacted Doey in hopes that she could find a way to meet me there.

Chapter 54

San Diego

Somehow Doey was able to trade missions with another pilot and meet me in San Diego before I shipped out. I stood near the runway and watched as the military DC3 landed and taxied up to the terminal. Eagerly I watched the cabin door open. Doey, in her WASP uniform, was the third to emerge, and when she reached the bottom step, I swept her into my arms and our three days and nights began.

We took a cab to the Coronado Hotel where I signed the hotel register and got the key. At the door of room 743, I opened the door, set Doey's flight kit and parachute inside, picked her up, carried her across the threshold, and said, "I love you, Doey Brooks. Will you be my wife?"

"Yes, you know I will, Lieutenant Cary. I will make you a wonderful wife. Do you require proof?" she asked with a mischievous smile. "Please say yes."

"Yes, my darling. If we live to be a hundred, our love will be the same. There is no way that it can improve."

I carried her diamond wedding ring on a chain around my neck with my dog tags. I removed the ring and slipped it on her finger; kissed her, and softly said, "Hello, Mrs. Cary." It was Friday, July 15, 1943 the night Doey became my bride.

I drew the curtains across the windows until the room became a shade of lovers' dark. She used the time to remove her blouse. Within a few minutes we stood looking much the same as Adam and Eve would have looked without the fig leafs. She pressed her beautiful body to mine. After a lingering kiss, for a moment I couldn't believe that Doey really belonged to me.

She gave me her only remaining gift of love. I pulled her close, picked her up, placed her on the bed and lay down at her side. We explored the hidden places of our bodies that were off limits by the strict conduct of our time. The moment our passion reached a climax, we crossed the last boundary of the restricted love life we had known, into the unbridled sex life of matrimony.

We had no license signed by a clerk in the marriage bureau or a paper with a fancy scroll of words bearing the signature of a minister of the Gospel to place somewhere in a drawer to prove that we were married. I do have a license from our government to kill humans, and in three days and two nights, I could possibly be on my way to becoming a professional killer.

We spent the next two nights exploring the pleasures of married love. I cradled Doey in my arms. We lay there side by side bound by the tender action of a love that we had never known. It completed the meaning of "forevermore." For a few moments I lay there thinking of our future.

Doey said, "Wynn, have you ever loved another woman as you have just loved me?"

"Doey," I replied, "how could I have known about love? I didn't know what love was until I met you. The answer to the second question is, yes. I have known several girls that I have slept with, but with whom I had never experienced love." She snuggled closer and drifted off to sleep. There was not enough time to count all my blessings. I just lay there with Doey in my arms. At last, my love and future lay beside me. Could life get any better?

A ray of sunlight found the slit in the drape and awakened me. For a moment I lay there with my eyes closed. I reached for Doey, but she wasn't there. Was last night only a dream? If it was a dream, it was a dream, come true.

Doey appeared in the bathroom doorway wearing a white bathrobe with the label Coronado Hotel and said, "Good morning, darling. Are you as sure as I am that we belong together?"

"Don't even harbor a doubt," I replied. "We have a strong commitment for a long, long life together." The soft pleasing essence of a Paris perfume surrounded her. "Come back to bed." She slid beneath the covers and found me ready, willing and able.

At noon, Doey borrowed a Jeep from the ferry command. We drove along the waterfront and found a little café called The Sunrise. Outside we sat on the patio, under an umbrella, having the first meal of our "married" life. We watched as a gentle breeze chased little waves from across the bay to the shore. A Pelican stood on a post at the water's edge watching and waiting for the leftovers. In the sky, gulls were showing off flying skills that were not taught in flight schools.

After brunch we drove north along the coast to the town of La Jolla, where we bought bathing suits and swam in the little cove at the base of the bluff. In the early afternoon we went to the Playhouse Theater, where a new actor, Gregory Peck, was soon to be discovered by Hollywood.

Like planes in flight, our days and nights went flying by. All too soon it was time to pack our bags and return to an uncertain future. We checked out of the hotel and went to the airfield to meet Doey's co-pilot, Betty McClure.

Betty, Doey, and I walked around the AT 11 checking the plane's fitness to fly. I was hoping to find something wrong that would delay takeoff. Nothing was found. Betty took a picture of Doey and me, and then entered the plane to wait for Doey, where together they would go through the check list.

We stood by the plane she would fly to San Antonio, Texas. At the last minute she removed the wedding ring from her finger and placed it in my hand. She looked up at me and said, "Wynn, my darling, take good care of yourself, and my wedding ring. I want you to keep it until we meet again in Terre Haute. Without you, there can be no future."

I held Doey close and said, "Be very careful, darling. I'll be back. A long beautiful life is waiting for us. The minute I know where I'll be, I'll send you my APO address."

"Don't worry about me" she replied. "I will be fine dear. It's you that will be flying in harm's way. You must come back to me!"

A long kiss ended her three-day leave. I stood watching as she and Betty ran through the check list. Doey started engine two and then engine one. She held the brakes and powered up to check the magnetos. Both engines were ready for takeoff. She looked out the window smiling, threw me a kiss, released the brakes, and the AT11 began to roll. At rotation I silently said, "Arise my love and come away with me." When the plane faded from sight, I wondered when we would see each other again.

Chapter 55

Off To War

My ten day leave was up and I reported for duty as a Second Lieutenant. I joined the officers and men of the 410th United States Air Force, along with many others, and boarded the Victory ship *John Paul Jones* in San Diego, California for a cruise to the beautiful South West Pacific.

A little more than three weeks later the *John Paul Jones* slipped into a dock in Australia, where its cargo of tired and seasick Air Force men off-loaded their gear and stepped ashore into a place with no name.

The beautiful South West Pacific of my dreams was not beautiful. To make up for that, they did have one million flies and yes, they did have a few sheep; maybe a few less than there are stars in the sky. Disappointed? Yeah. This was just the beginning of our "reality" check and our inoculation into war. The next morning, our regimen of the 410th—now clean, showered and shaved-stood in a large Quonset hut watching as Colonel Andrews and a captain walked down the aisle and mounted the steps to the stage.

Col. Andrews' opening remark was: "Welcome to the war. We are in northwest Australia, in a place with no name. We will be here a few weeks and then move north to enter the war zone." After whistles and cheers from the audience reduced to a whisper, he introduced Captain Bill Kyle, saying, "Capt. Kyle is a veteran of the war. He has logged eleven missions. He will be with us until we finish our allotted time here, and then fly with us to our next assignment."

With a nod from the colonel, Capt. Kyle said, "Good morning, gentlemen. I have been re-assigned to your unit and will be with you until we enter the fighting war that rages not far north of us. For you it will be the beginning of a long road that leads to Tokyo, where the war will end. Those of us who make it there will return home and pick up the pieces of our lives that no longer fit. I hope that we can all go home together."

For three weeks we walked, talked, ran miles in the sun, and listened to lectures. We became a band of brothers. One day, while running, we heard the sound of far away engines. We stopped and watched as six B24's dropped their gear, and one by one entered their final approach, landed, and taxied to a strip along one side of the hanger. It was a beautiful scene. I wondered which one would become the *Nightingale*.

Capt. Kyle quickly became known as Bill, and bonded with our group. We gathered for our afternoon lecture. Col. Andrews addressed the men saying, "At o six hundred, we will say goodbye to this beautiful oasis in the sun, scorpions, and flies; I know that you will miss the odor of the sheep." A friendly roar of agreement filled the air. "This day is yours, and as Edward R. Murrow would say, 'Good night and good luck.'" We stood, watching as Col. Andrews left the room. I spent the day reading and writing letters to Doey and Mother.

The next morning the *Nightingale* and the other B-24's lifted their wheels, and like a flock of geese, followed Col. Andrews and Capt. Bill Kyle to a base near Hollandia, New Guinea. Once again we had the following day to rest. The next morning we gathered in the ready room. We heard a loud, drawn out "Ten Hut!" I looked at my watch. It was 4:30 a.m. A moment of quiet followed. We watched as Col. Andrews and another colonel walked down the aisle and mounted the two steps to the podium. Col. Andrews introduced a man that I recognized from my youth, Col. Joe Bailey. My mind snapped back to my days at the Albert Whitted Airport in St. Petersburg, Florida, where I met Red Hederman and his flying partner, Joe Bailey. In memory, I relived many days of those long ago moments that crowded my mind.

When Col. Bailey said, "I am the commanding officer of the base that you will now call home. Welcome to the war, gentlemen. Tomorrow you will fly your first mission. I will fly with you. We will assemble here at O-six hundred." Joe was always economical with words, straight to the point with

Arise My Love And Come Away With Me

no embellishments. We stood and watched as Cols. Andrews and Bailey left the room.

Late in the afternoon I was told to report to Col. Bailey. His first sergeant ushered me into his quarters and said, "Lt. Cary reporting as ordered, sir." He saluted and walked out. Joe was seated at his desk writing. He looked up as I saluted. Joe greeted me with a big smile and said, "Hello, Wynn. It's been a long time."

"It's been several years, sir," I replied.

"We can speak in private of our past without strict protocol," he said, "but in public we need to be careful." For the first time we spoke of [ZG] meaning St. Petersburg, our code that any of my friends would know. It identifies the place where I first met Joe, Red, Sam, Maggie, and Sally.

"Red and I keep in contact. Did you know the he and Sally Weatherford are married? He's in England flying with the Eighth Air Force and Sally's at home in Maryland. The colonel sent a letter to me and said that he also sent one to you" Joe said.

"Joe, I did get a letter from Red. It had been opened and censored. The last page was missing and there was no APO address. If you have his address, I'd like to have it."

"Of course," Joe said. "You will fly your first mission tomorrow. There will be an element of six. You will be my co-pilot. Be alert and don't speak of our past acquaintance with anyone." I nodded as he continued. "You will be treated as any other member of the group. At 6 a.m., the pilots, co-pilots, navigators and bombardiers will meet in the ready room for an orientation mission. Each element of four will be led by an experienced pilot. Their job will be to get us from here to there and back safely.

"To help ensure our safety, sixteen P38's from the 49th fighter group will join us as we near the target. As we leave the target, our P38 fighters will be there to shepherd us home. I'll see you at briefing. My advice to you is to keep alert, and there is no place in flying for alcohol. That about covers it, Wynn."

347

"Thank you for the advice, Colonel, I assure you that I don't drink and I will keep alert." Our time together was up. I saluted him and walked out. In my hand was a letter to Col. Joe Bailey, from Red. I went back to my bunk and read the letter. I decided to write to Doey as I promised.

My dearest love,

I have arrived at a place that I can't find on a map, so I have given it a name. I think the Devil lives here so I will call it Hell. I am told that any letter with APO 727 on the envelope will find me.

I have spoken many times to you of Joe, Red's partner. I met him when I was ten years old. We were both surprised to meet again here in Hell. It was good to see an old familiar face. We fly our first mission tomorrow. I know that I have a job to do. God willing, everything will be okay.

I love you, my darling. I feel you close to me and that will keep me safe.

Wynn

With the briefing over, we drew our flight gear and we were on our way to fly our first mission. Across the dark, damp summer sky, six planes formed up on the colonel's wings and headed northwest to an island, where we would drop our cargo of death, ending the lives of Orientals whose only fault was believing that their Emperor is a direct descendent of God, and to die for the Emperor is a God-given privilege. We hoped to fulfill that privilege. Like a signpost in the sky, our planes left a contrail that pointed straight as an arrow to our target. We were now on their radar, and a swarm of Zeroes, Japanese fighter aircraft, arose in angry objection to bar our way.

At the Initial Point, referred to as IP, we became a target for guns on the ground. The Zeroes, not wanting to be included with us as the target, withdrew and took a position outside the danger of ground fire. They waited for us to fly clear of the target area before resuming their threat. Our planes were under constant attack. On the ground or in the air death seemed my servant.

It seemed like an eternity. Our first mission was over and all survived to live another day.

Doey and I corresponded regularly. She was occupied with flying planes throughout the United States and over to our British allies. This war was being fought on many fronts. It was like a see-saw, going back and forth making advancements and suffering losses. So many people were dying. Several of my fellow pilots were lost during our missions. My flight group was transferred to a base in the Dutch East Indies. For two years, we waged a war that seemed to have no end.

"PRESIDENT ROOSEVELT IS DEAD . . . . TRUMAN TO CONTINUE POLICIES . . . . 9TH CROSSES ELBE, NEARS BERLIN . . . . TRUMAN ASKS WORLD UNITY TO KEEP PEACE . . . . 7TH IN NUREMBERG . . . . SOVIET PUSH REPORTED . . . . NAZIS LOSE 905 PLANES, MOSTLY AGROUND."

Chapter 56

31st Mission

It was April 19, 1945, the day of our thirty-first mission. We awoke with the splatter of rain dripping from a dark sky. At 6:30 a.m. we finished a breakfast of powdered eggs and something alive with weevils, and headed for a briefing that would, once more, take us in harm's way. Long ago our thoughts of home and a free life had flickered out, only to be replaced with a tired spirit that had no place in it for hope. Occasionally, the face of a young new replacement would show up to fill the vacancy left when Fate randomly tapped someone on the shoulder and said, "You'll do." Then Death would cast the dice and say, "Read 'em and weep."

The briefing of the mission was a repeat of yesterdays. The weather to and from the target would be wet according to the meteorologist's best guess. For the local area we could always count on low nimbus rain clouds split by thunder and lightning, or torrential rain followed by a blazing hot sun. It was weather ideal for mosquitoes, alligators, and spiders. Occasionally our meteorologist would receive a weather report from a far away base or a submarine that had surfaced to recharge its batteries. The weather they reported could be for an area several hundred miles away, and could provide only scant help in plotting a weather map that could be relied on. On the wall was a map of our area of responsibility. A chord stretched from our base to a target, almost five hundred miles away.

To me, the navigator was the most important man in our crew. His mind had already begun our mission for the day. Using the first letters of the acronym, "Can Dead Men Vote Twice," he began to calculate the day's mission. This acronym was nothing more than an easy way of helping a sometimes forgetful mind in finding true course. "C" referred to compass course, "D" referred to deviation, which measures degrees east or west of the magnetic pole. "V" was for variation, and "T" was used to give the "true" course. Through rain, turbulence, and drift, he, like a coursing hound with nothing more than a scent, could find a place that was nothing more than a dot on a map, or the IP. That is where the bombardier took over and, with the use of the top secret Norden Bomb Sight, maneuvered the plane into the proper position, where our cargo of death and destruction would be dropped to do the maximum harm.

From take off to landing we would be flying over miles of Japanese-held land and water, defended by Zeroes. This time, we would have a force of 36 B-24's flown mostly by the 5th and 13th Air Force pilots on temporary duty with the British Air Force based at Moratie. We would bomb the southern islands around Leyte, where MacArthur, whose mission was unknown to us at the time, would mark the beginning of the end of the war in the South West Pacific. The war in the Pacific would continue until the second A-bomb was dropped.

Jeeps sprinted around the field delivering crews to waiting planes. Crew chiefs and pilots had brief discussions of their planes' readiness to fly. Yesterday we had 12 B-24's on the mission; today 36 were scheduled to fly. Each would carry ten men and 12 bombs, each bomb weighing 1000 pounds, that's 432,000 tons of munitions. That should be enough to end the war, but it won't. The rest of the briefing was straight out of the book. It included an en route weather report put together by the best guesses the meteorologists could determine. But, with no weather reporting stations along the way to aid in plotting a weather map with meaning, it was really nothing more than a hunch.

I flew the *Nightingale* to the IP. The bombardier took over, maneuvered into position, and said the words that we all wanted to hear, words that we came almost six hundred miles to hear, "Bombs away!"

We lost seven planes and 70 good men on that mission. *Kansas City Kitty*, a plane with nose art of a beautiful girl in a provocative pose, piloted by Capt. Kyle, flew echelon right on Col. Bailey's wing. My element of three flew echelon left and just above the colonel's position. I tucked our plane's right wing in a little closer to the formation and had just scanned the sky and the planes around us. I saw a brief flash as a lone Zero streaked across our formation leaving holes in the right wing of the *Nightingale*, and sending *Kansas City Kitty's* left wing with number four engine still attached, spiraling towards the ground, twenty thousand feet below, followed by the doomed B24 and her ten-man crew. No help could be offered. We had a mission to fly. We were still more than 100 miles from Apache, our home base. Capt. Kyle, his crew, and his plane would be added to the long list of departed friends to be remembered.

By the omission of chatter on the intercom, I knew the crewmembers, like me, only had thoughts and prayers, giving thanks to God and asking for the few more hours that it would take the *Nightingale* to land us safely back at home base. Somewhere over the Mindanao Sea, my companion Death left me. Only for awhile he seemed to say, "I have business that can't wait. It's far across the sea. Wait for me, I shall return."

For the first time I felt that I would survive the war and live to see Doey and home again. When the wheels of the *Nightingale* returned to the soil of our island, it was a tired, dispirited crew that deplaned and made their way to the debriefing room, where questions concerning the mission were asked and answers were given. Then our tired crew, who long since had moved beyond the breaking point, headed for sleep, where we would continue to thank God and pray for a long stand down. There wasn't an atheist in our crew.

When I walked into my quarters, I saw four letters on my cot. The tired desolate feeling that obsessed me clung like a second skin. At the moment I wanted nothing more than a long undisturbed sleep. I would read the ones from my mother and Doey's mother and save the ones from Doey to read when I awoke. I picked up the letters from Doey and slipped them under my pillow. If I received more than one letter, I always saved Doey's for the last. I could then read and re-read them without being distracted by not knowing what was in the other letters. So I opened the letter from Mom.

My dear son,

Yesterday, I received a call from Dorothy. Her first words were so frightening that I asked her to calm down and speak slower. I immediately jumped to a conclusion that something had happened to John.

Dear God, Wynn, the call was to tell me that our beloved Doey was dead. She died on a street in London, from a Nazi buzz bomb attack. Please dear, dear Wynn I know what this terrible news will do. Please be careful, dear, and know how very much I have loved Doey since the moment we met and waited for the day that she would become part of our family. I have prayed for you and Doey from the first time we met in Florida.

You must not lose your faith in God. I love you, Wynn. Please stay well and come home to me.

Love,
Mom.

I then opened Dorothy's letter and quickly scanned it, hoping to find that some terrible mistake had been made. It was almost a copy of Mom's letter that left no doubt that Doey was gone. I sat there, on the cot, shaking and trying to make some reason out of the fearful hand I had been dealt. My mind traveled every line of hope, only to find there was no hope. My life and dreams of Doey had abruptly ended. My mind rejected any thought of going home after the war was over. I was alone with memories of the past and faced a future without Doey's love. That's impossible. There could be no future.

Death, my companion, had been the only winner in this war. I thought that I stood between him and the ones I loved. If he chose anyone for his evil empire, it should have been me. When I felt his absence, I thought that I had won. Now, death was what I wished for. Now I knew that I would live in his shadow to be tormented by a memory full of hate, which would only end when he gave the word. "Almighty and caring God, where are you?"

Jim O'Neal, my co-pilot, came in and spoke to me. I had no voice for the spoken word. I looked at Jim and tried to speak. Uncontrolled shaking and words with no meaning made it impossible to answer. Instead of speaking I handed him Mom's letter. Silently he read the letter, then came to the cot and sat down beside me. He folded and returned the letter and removed two small bottles of brandy, which were given to crewmembers after briefings, from his pocket. Each bottle contained about two swallows. He opened one, handed it to me, and said, "Drink it!"

Ordinarily I would have refused, but the bars of my will to live were down, so I drank it. Jim opened the second bottle and said, "Drink!" I had no will to refuse so I drank again. He removed my boots and turned me so that I could lie down. "Sleep," he said, and drew the mosquito netting around me. My frantic, panicked mind struggled with sanity—and lost. The last thing I remembered was when my boots came off. At six a.m. I awoke and lay there thinking the dark and frightening thoughts of yesterday. Slowly my mind focused on the now, trying to recall what the order of this day was. Did we have a mission to fly? If so, I had missed the briefing and would have a lot to explain.

I remembered the mail and my hand moved under the pillow in search of Doey's letters. There were still two to read. I sat up and with trembling, hopeful hands, opened one of the last letters that I was to receive from my Doey.

> *Dearest Wynn,*
>
> *When you receive this letter, I will be back from a wonderful short trip to BS. Even though I did not hear our bird sing, I think he is somewhere safe, and when this war is over, together, we will find him.*
>
> *Today, I will return to the land of Brindy, and within the week will return to Able-1. I have the easy assignments, and you live in harm's way. Please don't let me become one of your worries. You are every minute in my prayers, and on my mind. You are my life. Take care of it, and take care of my ring. I need you, my darling. I need more than the memory of those three beautiful days and nights in San Diego.*
>
> *All my love,*
> *Doey*

In letters, we wrote in our own special code. I am in [Brindy] meant that she had arrived in Scotland, [EZ] meant London, [BS] meant Berkeley Square. She would return to *Brindy* and from there would be flown home with other ferry pilots to [Able-1], the United States.

The last letter carried a postmark that was later than either of our mother's letters, which would indicate that Doey was still alive. Quickly I opened Doey's letter with the latest postmark, and read.

Dearest Wynn,

I arrived in the land of Brindy, and while waiting for a return trip to Able-1, I had time to come to E2 and look for the place where our bird sings. For a couple of days, I have reveled in the luxury of having nothing but you to fill my mind with love, and dreams of our time to come.

Please, darling, without you, there can be no dream of tomorrow. I will write again before leaving for Able 1. When we run out of stars to count, you will still have all my love.

AMLACAWM,
Doey

From her relief pilot Betty, I later learned that Doey had accepted the mission to co-pilot a plane to Scotland, which had no military markings and was consigned to a location in Scotland. This was the only flight they had flown overseas. Since their return flight was not for a few days, Doey and Betty had gone to London.

They had spent the night at The Ritz Hotel on Piccadilly. The next morning, while having breakfast in the dining room, Doey wrote her last letter to me and slipped it in a small handbag that carried a few personal items and a book of crossword puzzles. She checked out of her room, but left the bag, along with her travel kit, at the concierge desk and asked him to hold it until she returned from Berkeley Square. She and her co-pilot would be leaving at ten o'clock for the American Air Force Ferry Base in Scotland, and would pick the bag up then. She inquired about Berkeley Square and asked if it was far enough to take a cab or should she walk.

"The cabs, Miss," he said, "are very unreliable, and Berkeley Square is only a ten to fifteen minute walk from here. Will you need transportation when you return?"

"Yes," she said. "There will be two of us. I will only be gone a short while. I should return in less than an hour. We will then be going to Victoria Station."

"Thank you, Miss. I will take care of your travel kit and travel transportation for two."

Upon hearing the buzz bomb, Doey quickly left Berkeley Square and was on her way back to the Ritz Hotel. She heard the air raid warning, but was unfamiliar with the procedure or the way to the nearest bomb shelter.

When the engine propelling the bomb, starved for fuel, stopped, the buzz bomb dropped its nose and headed for the ground. A building was shattered and the young life of Dorothy Doey Brooks instantly ended with the earth-shaking blast of the bomb. Germany made a last desperate attempt to turn the war in their favor, by releasing a buzz bomb attack on London, but it was too little and too late.

Two short weeks later, on the night of May 8, 1945, Edward R. Murrow, chief of CBS European correspondents, broadcast these words from London. "This is London. Tonight it is a city of song, celebration, and thanksgiving. There are fireworks and parties. Air raid shelters are as remote as covered wagons. Many words have been spoken and much drink has been consumed. Even the searchlights are staggering across the sky. The churches have been crowded. London has been somewhat hysterical and still is. And in the mist of all the celebration, there have been many men and women with tears in their eyes.

"The organized killing has ended in Europe. The young men and women of many nations have suffered, sacrificed, and achieved victory. The coming months and years will reveal what we shall do with that victory . . ."

This marked the first day of world peace in Europe, and the countdown of peaceful days would go on until the next despot rattled his sword and dared his neighbor to step over the line he had drawn in the sand. The war was over in Europe. However, in the Pacific, Death marched on and seemed to say, "Only a few more souls to harvest, then I will rest."

Chapter 57

Japan to Seattle

I was promoted to captain and was sent to Okinawa to assume command of the 35th Fighter Control Squadron. On the morning of August 6, 1945, at 2:45 a.m., the order to use a force that would end the war in the Pacific—the world's first operational atomic bomb—was underway. The plane was the B-29 Superfortress *Enola Gay*, piloted by Colonel Paul Tibbets. It took off from the runway at Tinian, an American airbase in the Marianas, a location as close to Japan as the giant Boeing bomber could get.

Hiroshima was the target and at 8:15 a.m., powered by four, 2,000 horsepower engines, the *Enola Gay* dropped its payload, *Little Boy*, a 12-foot-long, 28-inch-diameter bomb. Its explosive power equaled 20,000 tons of TNT, all in a single bomb that weighed about 9,000 pounds. The plane made a sharp dive to the right following the release, and 43 seconds later, the bomb exploded at 1,890 feet above ground. The force of the explosion chased the *Enola Gay* from the target area, while a mushroom cloud rose 45,000 feet in the air, three miles above them. They flew away in silence, shocked by the devastation below. The cloud was visible for more than an hour as they flew back to the base. The Japanese were given the ultimatum to surrender unconditionally or face further atomic attacks. Three days later, a second atomic bomb was dropped on Nagasaki. That was the final blow—Japan surrendered.

We all waited for our orders to ship out. Our regular briefings became more jovial. On the morning of our departure, the sergeant made a plea for compliance to a military order that all military watches would be placed in a box on the table before boarding the ship for home. A major in our group raised the sleeve of his left arm, and pointing to his military issued watch said, "Without our watches, how can we possibly find our way home? We would like a time hack."

"Hold it one moment, please," another major said, pointing to his government-issued watch. "I'm sure that all you men would like to leave Japan with the correct time." Several moments of silence passed while the group readied for their last military time hack.

The sergeant looked puzzled and then a big grin spread across his sober face. He looked at his watch and said so that all could hear, "The time, sir, in fifteen seconds, and on my count, will give us the exact time." When he started the reverse countdown, he was accompanied by every voice on the dock. We all joined in. The sergeant saluted the major and said, "Is there any other way that I may be of service, sir?" He paused for a moment waiting for the laughter to subside, and said, "I shall report that all watches were casualties of the war. Now that you have complied with all of the items on your checkout list, I wish all of you a pleasant trip home." He turned the sailing briefing over to Colonel John Bennett, made a perfect reverse turn, saluted, and walked away taking the first layer of war remembrance with him.

For some, the healing of war and the transition to civilian life had started. For most, it would take a little time, and a few would never find the life they had left. They would live out their days lost in a frightening past.

Col. Bennett moved front and center to address our group. He spoke in a tired but passionate voice. He was about six feet tall, slender, and ramrod straight. His hair had a tinge of gray at the temples. The ensigns on his shoulders placed him in the signal corps. He reminded me of John, Doey's father. The ribbons on his chest spoke of long service. He was maybe forty, but looked sixty.

For the last time, as a group of soon-to-be civilians, we stood at attention and listened to our last orders for the day. Col. Bennett then wished us a pleasant trip home, and said, "You may now board the SS Liberty Ship *Gaucho Victory.*"

My military exile in Japan was over. For more than two weeks *Gaucho Victory*, for most, was a joyful exciting cruise. For me, I was returning to uncharted waters without a rudder. Reality ruled the moment. We were going home. I was part of that unhappy transition and would almost give my life not to have been. For more than two years I had lived a life where fate was the supreme ruler. I dreaded living a life that the war years had shattered. The thought that thousands of others faced a similar condition, or worse, was no consolation.

Dimly, through a misty evening fog, Seattle's lights could be seen. The ships intercom came to life with, "This is the captain speaking, welcome home. We are in the Seattle, Washington Harbor. Unfortunately, there is no space at the dock tonight. We will remain at anchor until seven a.m. and then move to our assigned position at the dock. Please consult the orders that were delivered to your quarters during the night, or you may obtain them from the purser's desk after nineteen hundred tonight. The crew and I thank you for a job well done. Welcome home, and good luck."

As soon as I could, I called Dorothy and John to tell them of my travel plans to Terre Haute. Their answer to my question of whether or not it would be convenient for them was more than re-assuring, as I expected it would be. There was pent-up grief in their every spoken word. They passed the phone from one to the other; they both spoke at once. Dorothy was crying; hopelessly, John made every effort to remain calm. In a moment of silence I told them that I would be leaving Seattle at ten in the morning. I would be discharged from the Air Force at Fort Sheraton, Illinois, but I didn't know the time of arrival or how long it would take.

"I'll call you from Fort Sheraton. When I get my discharge papers, I'll take the train from Chicago down to Terre Haute. I'll see you soon and please don't concern yourself with transportation. I know the way to your house."

We took a few sad moments remembering Doey and what might have been. They knew how much I loved her. John's controlled voice, laced with sadness, said, "We love you, Wynn. Doey brought you into our family, and there will always be a place for you here. Please call me when you get to Fort Sheraton."

"Thanks, John. You and Dorothy gave me Doey to love and care for, and I failed the mission. I encouraged her to fly, and I'm so terribly, terribly sorry. I'll call when I arrive."

I hung up and for a few moments stood there thinking dark thoughts. War was the world I knew and all I was fit for. I should be back at our base, in the East Indies, to start our thirty-second mission. But the war was over, and there would be no more early morning briefings. My plane, the *Nightingale,* would share the uncertain future of the ten men who flew to hell and back with her, 31 times. I thought of John and Dorothy, and what tomorrow would bring.

September 1946 I was in charge of one of the twelve railroad cars filled with homeward bound airmen. My job was to maintain order. There was to be no drinking, no rowdy behavior, no fighting, and no gambling.

The moment the doors closed and the train began to roll, the party started. The dice came out and the corks began to pop. Through the din of noise and laughter, the faint strum of a guitar could be heard adding *arpeggios* to enhance a tenor voice singing "Sentimental Journey." As the singing went on the decibels in the car decreased to *fortissimo*, bringing sound down to a point where even a legally deaf man would say thanks. For the better part of two days and one night the train provided a beat of its own. The wheels click-clacked over the rails and the train whistled at every town along the way.

John and Dorothy met me at the train. Dorothy put her arms around me and softly said, "Welcome, dear Wynn, we have come to take you home."

John took my hand and put his arm around my shoulder and said, "We have talked with your mother and she knows that you will spend some time with us before going home." He hesitated, and with the back of his hand wiped tears from his eyes. "We know the love and the plans you and Doey had, but God had other plans. Why He had those plans, we may never know."

John picked up my B-4 bag and led the way to the parking lot. Hand in hand Dorothy and I followed. John Brooks was fifty-five years old. His once dark brown hair, which I remembered, was now mostly gray, and tired blue eyes gave evidence of the sorrow and despair that had touched his life. He wore a long-sleeve shirt with a button-down collar, light gray slacks, a dark blue sport coat and a light blue tie. Black shoes clad feet that no longer moved with a purpose.

The car, a four-door Buick, was the same one that provided our transportation to the World's Fair in New York, the summer of 1939. Memory took me back to those long ago days that will forever span the short lifetime that Doey and I shared.

Like looking through a prismatic glass, each vision of her was highlighted with bright sunlight and colors . . . sounds of music . . . dancing to tunes I helped provide for weekend dances . . . and the nights we headed for the moon and flew among that broad band of luminous stars that seemed so clear and near, called the Milky Way. Each day or night had brought us closer to the life we planned.

John spoke, and like a fade out in a movie, the visions of long ago faded back into the memory held in my mind. "You and Dorothy sit in the back and I'll drive," he said. We stood in silence for a moment until John spoke again. "Would you like to stop at the cemetery on our way home?" The question, of course was mine to answer, and nothing to me was more important.

"If there is a florist nearby, can we stop for some flowers?" I asked, as I opened the door and helped Dorothy into the car.

At the cemetery John stopped at the gate. A soft spring breeze moved among the clouds creating a dance of light and shadows among the tombstones. The towering elms moved their leaves in concert with the shadows, adding their touch to nature's beauty.

John led the way along a path through a garden of flowers to Doey's grave. Along the way Dorothy paused and gripped my hand. She looked up at me. There were tears in the eyes of her pale face. She trembled and with a soft voice told me why I would not see anything but a white cross. "There was a marker, but I didn't like it, and when I knew that you were coming home, I had the marker removed and ordered a replacement. John and I like the new wording on it and I'm sure you and Doey will too. The new marker should be in place in a day or two." My mind held thoughts too grim to be expressed.

"Wynn, we love you as Doey did. In a letter she told us about her last meeting with you in San Diego. That was more than two years ago and now there will be no joyful homecoming for her and a dreadful one for you," Dorothy said.

I was pleased to know that Doey had told her parents about our time in San Diego. They caused me to remember the ring that I gave Doey in the Crown Room of the Statue of Liberty, and together we relived that day and added it to the memory of the weekend at the Coronado Hotel in San Diego.

From where we were standing we could see John. He was on his knees; his lips were moving, processing thoughts that were too private to be trusted to sound. I could only surmise what thoughts were coursing through his troubled mind. I realized that the hopeless loss that I lived with was big enough to be shared. Did it help to know this? Not really. But I did know that Doey's loss was shared by her family and mine. Maybe some logic, in time, would support that thought, and make it easier to bear; but for now I carried the loss alone.

Before moving on, I took a few moments to look at Dorothy, the woman I had come to love as Doey's mother. She was fifty-five years in age, and about five feet seven-inches tall. I was looking at an older Doey. She had the same slim build; her golden hair framed a still beautiful face, with eyes as blue as a summer sky—eyes, that now looked tired, vacant, and bewildered. Dorothy and I moved on to join John.

We stood in silence at a gravesite marked only by love and a white cross. I tried to believe that the mangled body turned to ashes, that were once my beautiful Doey, was not there, but the cross was there to remind me that once a beautiful girl flew the skies like an angel.

"I'm here, Doey," was all I could say, as I stooped and placed the flowers at the foot of the cross. We spent another few minutes standing, letting our minds run rampant with silent thoughts. Finally, John said, "Shall we go now? We will come again when the new marker is in place."

We started to leave, but I couldn't move. "Please," I said, "I would like to stay a little longer. I would like to be alone with her for awhile."

Dorothy replied, "Take your time; we will wait for you in the car."

I dropped to my knees and arranged and re-arranged the flowers. Tears backed up behind my eyes and began to flow. "The war is over and I have come for you, Doey. I brought the wedding ring with me. You are mine. I will leave the ring with your mother, and I will always treasure the few nights we had together, so very long ago, in San Diego. Rest easy, my dearest love. We will meet again; and we will fly again. I talk to you every night; and I love you so. When the doors of my mind open to the past, you will always be there. Rest easy, my darling."

Dorothy and John said nothing when I opened the rear door of the Buick and got in. No one spoke. Dorothy took my hand in hers. John pointed the car in the direction of home, and three hopeless, heartsick people moved through a vacuum with minds haunted by the past.

At the top of the hill I could see Doey's home. With the mental image of her by my side, and as tears threatened to fall, I silently thought, "Back home again in Indiana."

John stopped on the circular driveway in front of the door and got out. I helped Dorothy out. They stood there waiting for me as I walked around to the trunk of the car to get my bag. "Don't bother with that," John said, "Edward will get it." I was already at the back of the car so I grabbed the bag, and together we moved toward the front door. The door opened before we got to the steps and Edward walked out to meet us.

"Welcome, Wynn," he said. "It's so very good to see you home again." He took my out-stretched hand in his and placed his other one around my shoulders, and again said, "It's so very good to see you again."

"Thanks, Edward," I replied. "I'm glad to be home." We walked into the house and Edward closed the door behind us.

"Take his bag up to Doey's room," Dorothy said. "It's his now."

Edward moved to the stairs. With one hand on the stair railing he turned and said, "Wynn, for several years we have talked about you and prayed for your safe return. For years, Anna and I have considered you one our family."

"Thank you, Edward. I think of you and Anna every time I think of Doey and her parents, and that's all the time."

"Thank you, Wynn. You have belonged to our family for a very long time." He turned and walked up the stairs.

"Come and sit down, Wynn," Dorothy said. "You must be tired after such a long trip." She led the way to the library where John was already seated and trying to look at ease. I sat in the chair opposite him and tried to think of something to say.

Dorothy asked to be excused for a few minutes, and John was trying so hard to act like his old self. He had a smile on his face that didn't go with the dull look in his eyes, and a voice that trembled when he asked questions about the past that I found impossible to answer. An awkward silence prevailed in the room. It was a troubling time for both of us. It was a moment that faded when Dorothy returned with Anna who was carrying a tray of cold drinks, and set them on a low table in front of the fireplace. Before Anna left the room she came to me and said "Wynn, for more than three years I have prayed for your and Doey's safe return." Her voice dropped to a whisper and said, "I just didn't pray hard enough." With tears in her eyes she took my hand in hers and kissed it. As she turned to leave, she said, "Lunch will be ready in twenty minutes."

I looked around the room and asked, "Where's Brindy?"

Dorothy replied, "Wynn, Brindy was very sick and we had to put him down. It was sad to let him go because he was such a loved member of the

Arise My Love And Come Away With Me

family. Doey was at Boeing in Seattle at the time and she couldn't make it home in time to be with him. We wanted to tell you, but Doey insisted that you lived too close to death to tell you about Brindy. She said she would tell you when you returned home." Tears welled up in her eyes and sadness permeated the words as she spoke. "Brindy is buried in the oak grove just over the top of the hill. Doey said you would know the place."

After lunch I excused myself and went up to Doey's room that now, I was told, was mine. When I first entered the room, I noticed a large photograph of Doey and me on a table, which was new to the room. I knew without looking further that the picture would take me back to a time that should be joyfully remembered, but it would only add to the uncontrollable grief that would undermine the small progress that my mind had reluctantly accepted. *Please God, no more surprises.*

I realized that to retain what little sanity I had, I would have to forget the past, and forgetting the past seemed impossible. I might as well have said, remove my soul and take my eyes. There was nothing more to see or touch. Take the music and memories of a soft moonlit night, when we flew among the stars, or sailed the warm summer waters of a lake, bright with a path of moon-mist all the way to heaven. And take those beautiful planes we loved, that once belonged to peace, which now can only be remembered as an instrument of killing. Must I spend what's left of my life looking for an elusive past? And yet, I suppose that I was one of the lucky ones, who made it back with no more than a badly scarred memory and a lost soul. I did not have to search my memory to find friends or acquaintances who, if still alive, would count me as one of the lucky ones. Lucky?

On the table below the picture lay Doey's wings and the medallion which we had purchased at the New York World's Fair. My emotions were about to become uncontrollable. They had reached a point where another glance at the past, and they would end in visible and audible grief. The world behind me was more real than the world that I faced.

There was nothing harder to bear than a need for what was gone. It's painful when the past seems so far away and equally hurtful when everything lost crowds close around you. I was a stranger in the real world, lost and helpless. I was a stranger desperately trying to wake up from a nightmare.

365

There was no awakening. There was no recovering what had slipped away. There was only remembering. I removed my wings and World's Fair medallion and laid them beside hers. With emotional control that I didn't know I had, I was able to rejoin my almost-in-laws, and together we would share a common future.

Thomas Wolfe was a great writer from the University of North Carolina at Chapel Hill, with wisdom beyond his years. Among the literature he left was the novel *Look Homeward, Angel*, in which he states that you can't go home again, and it's true. Of course, you could go home again, but you couldn't stay. You would constantly be chasing a past that had vanished, and it would take a lot of mental gymnastics to put that behind you. For now, I couldn't see the possibility of ever doing that. It might take some part of every day, for the rest of my life, to come to terms with the past. I had every intention to try, but first I had to leave the past, including a life that might have been, to a lasting memory of what once was.

At 7 p.m. Edward called us to dinner and said that Anna had prepared a feast for my homecoming. It was truly a feast, but a cold plate of government-issued Spam or K rations would have done as well. I made sure that Anna knew how much I appreciated her effort.

John sat at the head of the table. I helped Dorothy into her place at the foot of the table, and I sat down, in what had been Doey's place, between the two. We pushed the food around on our plates and searched our minds for something to say.

When dinner was over, Dorothy excused herself and announced that she was ready to retire, and tomorrow we would return to the cemetery to see if the marker had been replaced. John and I moved to the library and settled in for an evening of useless talk. John asked me if I would like a brandy. I really wasn't much of a drinker, but I realized that he was filling dead air with sound, and replied, "Yes, please." John poured two shots of Napoleon brandy into each of the snifters, and added a dash of soda. Without a word, he handed me a glass and sat down.

"Wynn," he said, "it's important for Dorothy and me to keep you in our life. Except for what's happened, you would have been our son-in-law. You *are* our son-in-law. For more than two years, my law firm has expanded into Chicago, and we have plans for an office in London. We have added eight new lawyers. With my partner Joe Bennett's agreement, Doey became a new full partner. Her name has been added to the firm, which now is known as Brooks, Bennett and Brooks. Doey, of course, knew about the expansion of the firm, but held off her decision to join until after you came home. She wanted your approval, and whatever it may have been, that's what she would have done." Mentally I stored the words in Doey's memory nook in my mind.

"John, you and Dorothy will always share my love for Doey. Of course she would have had my approval."

"There is a ring," he continued, "that Dorothy keeps on a gold chain around her neck. It's the ring the British government found on Doey's finger when she was killed. They sent us her wings and ring along with her ashes." He paused to gather his thoughts. "Doey told us about the ring and her last visit with you in San Diego."

"I know about the ring that Dorothy has, but did she tell you that there is a wedding band that goes with it? I have the ring with me, and when I go, I will leave it with her. I told Doey on our last day together, that after the war we would meet here in Terre Haute, where I would place the ring on her finger. In every way she was my bride. It was her choice to wait until after the war to get married. In spirit she will always be with me, and I know that she would want us to be a close family. I will see you and Dorothy as often as possible."

John's voice seemed to be a little stronger, and surprisingly, we had taken the first step toward the future. We retired for the evening, but my fitful night was haunted by the past.

We were lost in a vortex of impenetrable storm clouds, their glowing red anvil heads, linked like a string of beads, spread across the horizon making it impossible to fly around or climb over. Lightning bolts and claps of thunder filled the sky. Furious winds roamed the realm of Zeus, arbiter of human destiny, who watched over the battlefields of the sky and chose those souls worthy to abide forever in Valhalla.

The Nightingale's wings were flapping like a seagull looking for a haven from the vengeful storm. Our target for today lay on the other side of the impossible pass. St. Elmo's fire danced around the propellers giving off a flickering blue light. I lowered my seat and turned the cockpit lights up and reached to turn off the autopilot before the violence of the storm could overpower the system. It was too late. The control panel had vanished; nothing was there. I was alone. The lights flickered and went out. Vertigo was in control, and Valkyrie, the Norse God of Odin, who kept tabs on those who were about to die, smiled.

With a heart beating like a drum and with a sound of despair . . . I softly said, "Oh, Doey . . . oh Doey," my companion Death returned to lead the crew of the Nightingale into the Pantheon of forever.

Red appeared and like an echo in a dream, his words kept saying, "Rest later! Rest later! It's time to fly! Forget what's outside the plane. Keep your eyes on the instruments. Trust your instruments, and don't let this plane fall into a stall or spin. Carrying fifteen thousand pounds of bombs and tanks full of fuel, through a turbulent sky, needs a pilot, not a quitter. Wake up! Sleep is for another time."

A crack of light appeared along the horizon, and as seconds passed we left the dark behind and entered a sky filled with scattered planes. Faintly I heard an echo repeating my name. Dimly I could see raindrops falling softly against a window. I was hallucinating. Our quarters, a Quonset hut, didn't have a window. My mind led the way into another dimension. I must be dead.

I lay in a bed; my pajamas were soaked with perspiration. I trembled with uncontrollable movements. My mind struggled with reality . . . and lost. I awoke in Terre Haute, Indiana. John and Dorothy had replaced my crew. They stood on either side of the bed assuring me that I was safe and the war was over, but it wasn't . . . the war would be with me for many years of my life. Dorothy re-made the bed with clean sheets and asked if I had another pair of pajamas. John brought me a shot of brandy and watched as I drank it.

It was 3:25 a.m. by the clock on the dresser. I assured John and Dorothy that I was okay, and that they should go back to bed. After much persuasion, they did. I took a shower, dressed, and went downstairs to the library, where I was alone with memories of a distant past. On the mantle of the fireplace was a picture of Doey and me, standing beside the plane after her solo flight. My mind raced back to that place of promise, and ran rampant with memories and questions that had no answers.

At random I chose a book off the shelf and sat down to read. At six-thirty Edward gently spoke my name, and I opened my eyes to the present. In the fireplace, long orange and yellow flames licked the logs sending pale smoke swirling up the chimney. On the table beside my chair lay the book, unopened.

"Good morning, Edward," I said.

"Good morning, Wynn. May I get you some coffee?"

"Yes, please."

"I went to your room," Edward said. "Mr. John told me that you had a difficult night. He will be down shortly. Breakfast will be served at seven."

Edward left the room and I was again alone in a place that Doey had called home for twenty-three years. The house faced south across a bend in the Wabash River. I watched as a crack appeared along the horizon that let the darkness out. The cold rain of last night had ended, and rays of the sun cast a feeble light across the land. More rain was in the forecast. It would not be a good day to remember.

Dorothy and John came into the room and sat down by the fireplace. We exchanged good mornings and struggled for a meaningful conversation that failed. We knew that we were reacting to a common post-war trauma . . . death of a loved one. For now, there was only room in our hearts for Doey.

At 7:30 a.m. Edward came to the library door and announced breakfast. We responded to habit, and without a thought or a spoken word, we arose and followed Edward into the breakfast room. Our conversation centered on our visit to the cemetery and my plan to leave the next day for Florida. It took only minutes to cover plans for the day. At eight o'clock, with breakfast over, we moved into the library where we drank coffee and stared at the flames in the fireplace.

"I would like to call my mother to tell her that I'm here. I should have called when I arrived at Fort Sheraton, but she knew that I was coming here first. If I may, I'll use the phone in Doey's room," I said. "I plan to leave tomorrow, so I would like to go back to the cemetery today and spend some time with Doey."

There were tears in Dorothy eyes and John just shook his head and said, "I know you must go, but please . . ." his voice trailed off to a whisper, then nothing.

I excused myself and went up to Doey's room and called home. I could hear the phone ringing. I let it ring six times and was about to hang up when I heard Mom's voice say, "Hello."

"You sound out of breath," I said.

There was a long pause and then Mom said, "Oh, Wynn. Oh, Wynn. Thank you, God! Thank you! Oh, Wynn," she said, in a trembling voice no louder than a whisper. "You're home. Oh dear God, you deserve a better homecoming than what you have."

"I'm in Terre Haute, Mom, with Dorothy and John. They are inconsolable. Doey died and the British government had just released her ashes and returned them last week. What little progress they had made has vanished. They are going through the same torment all over again. We are just three people adrift in a sea of sorrow."

We talked for another fifteen minutes, mostly to assure her that the war was over and that I was in one piece and in good health. I inquired about my sisters, Ruth and Irene. "Ruth returned a few days ago. After three years in England and France she needs a long rest . . . and Irene is still in the Orient, I believe the Philippines," she said, as she began to cry.

"Mom, I can't leave them now. I can't leave Doey now. I'm going back to the cemetery today. I'll be home in a day or two. I'll call you before I leave."

She wanted to know more about Dorothy and John. Between sobs she said, "Wynn, I can only imagine what torment you, Dorothy, and John are facing. Please tell them for me that Doey will always be my very dear daughter. I loved her as one of my own, and there will always be a place in my heart for her, and for them. I will stay in touch."

"I will tell them, Mom. I love you, and I'll see you soon. I'll call you again later today. I must go now." I waited a moment for her to hang up. Once more she said, "I love you, Wynn." I heard a click, and my first spoken words to home, in more than two years, were nothing more than words of hopeless despair. I hung up the phone and sat there for a few moments, not sure of what my next move should be. I was incapable of making decisions.

I carried Doey's wedding ring, along with my dog tags, on a chain around my neck from the weekend we shared in San Diego to this moment, where a future for two could only be a tortured dream for one. Carefully, I removed the ring that had been with me from the moment Doey and I parted in San Diego, more than two years ago, and dropped the dog tags into a side pocket of my B-4 bag.

When I returned to the library, I found Dorothy and John discussing the plans for the day. Other than a decision to visit the cemetery, there were no other plans. "Dorothy," I said, holding out the ring, "this is Doey's wedding ring. I told her that when the war was over we would meet here and plan our wedding. I wanted for us to be married before I left for the Pacific. She accepted the engagement ring, but wanted to delay the marriage until the war was over. I put the ring on a chain with my dog tags that I wore around my neck until this morning. I removed the ring and I know that Doey would want you to keep it for us."

Dorothy said, "Wynn, you are very thoughtful, but don't you think you should keep it?"

"No, Dorothy," I said. "The ring can only be a keepsake to remind me of a future that is not to be. In my heart I carry every picture of Doey and every word that we ever spoke. In time, I pray that the bad memories will be lost, and the good of our lives will always be there."

Dorothy removed the golden chain from around her neck and slipped the wedding ring onto the chain. She replaced the chain around her neck and started to cry. John had a sad, vacant look in his eyes, and I suppressed tears. It was Sunday and I could hear the far away tolling of church bells.

John called the cemetery and asked if the replacement marker was in place. He was told that it wasn't, but the engraving was complete and it would be delivered and installed some time tomorrow.

I told John and Dorothy that I would leave tomorrow, but would like to go to the cemetery today, if it was convenient for them. They said they had planned for us to go, and if I would like, we could have lunch in town and later on in the evening we would have dinner at their club. They were planning and thinking for today and tomorrow. It was a good sign.

Chapter 58

Cemetery

At the cemetery we spoke lightly of the past and talked of Doey as if she were standing there with us. I realized that what we said, and how we said it, was a sham. We were trying so hard to invite normalcy back into our lives.

I do believe that Doey's spirit was there, trying to tell me to get on with my life. In my mind, she seemed to say, *"Come fly with me and be my love. We can fly beyond the limits of life. I know what's behind the other side of beyond. I have been there. When the time is right, I will take you there. You will always be my love. I'll take you to that place where forever is never too much time. Come fly with me and be my love again."* My mind heard what I wanted to hear. I turned my doubts over to faith, and I had to trust in a decision that I could live with.

"Tomorrow," I said to John and Dorothy, "I plan to go home, but before I do I would like to be alone and spend some time with Doey. I have rented a car, and will stop at the cemetery before going on to the airport."

John said, "We'll take you to the cemetery, and we'll wait in the car for as long as you like, and then take you to the airport."

"That's a very generous offer, John, but I can't let you do that. I don't know how long Doey and I will talk, and I really can't ask you and Dorothy to wait for us. I do appreciate your offer, but know this, I will always be here for you and Dorothy, as Doey would have been. You tell me that I am your son-in-law. Please know how proud I am to know that. Every day, for more than two years, the constant thought of Doey sustained me. Her spirit was with me on every mission. Just knowing that she would be waiting when I came home helped me stay out of harm's way. The thought of her kept me and the crew of the *Nightingale* safe. For revenge, death found Doey on a street in London, and took her into his quietness. I'm so, so very sorry. He should have taken me.

"Since being here, I have learned that we can't measure time by a day or a year. Our time is measured by infinity. Doey has told me that we will meet again. If I am to believe that, I must trust in God. We have a lot to come to terms with, and when I leave, I will take the memory of her with me. For more than two years she has lived in my heart. She will always be with me. I will never be alone again."

John listened, and then quietly said, "This too, will always be your home, Wynn. Come back to us."

"Thank you, John. I will."

From the cemetery we toured the city and county, visiting scenes out of Doey's past. There was the grammar school where she played the part of an angel in a Christmas play, and not far down the street was the high school where she graduated and gave the valedictorian speech. After the obligatory tour of town we went home to await our eight o'clock reservation at their club.

Arriving home John said, "Dorothy would like to lie down and rest awhile, and I think that I will join her. We want you to feel at home." He paused for a moment and again said, "This is your home, Wynn. We hope that you will come home as often as possible." I assured him that I would.

I went up to Doey's room, which now Doey's and mine, and called home. The phone rang twice and was answered by my sister Ruth. I immediately recognized her voice and said, "When did you get home?"

"A week ago," she said.

"Where were you?" I asked.

"England and France," she replied. "Where are you?"

"Terre Haute," I replied.

"Mom's letters always contained a page or two about you and Doey," she said. "She loved her from the moment they met in Florida. She thought, even then, that when the war was over, you and Doey would come home to a wedding celebration that would last a lifetime. I'm so very sorry about your loss, Wynn. I know how much you loved her, and what you meant to her, and her family."

"Thanks, Ruth. Have you heard from Irene?" I asked.

"She's still in Manila, but should be coming home soon. When are you coming home?" she asked.

"I'll be home late tomorrow or the next day. It depends on when I can get a flight," I replied. "How's Mom? Is she there?"

"Yes, she's here. She's changed, Wynn. The war has been tough on her. I thought that three years in England and France was difficult duty, but when I look at her I can see that her life of worry and service on the home front is very close to claiming her as a victim. She's had the four of us to worry about, but the loss of Doey has been more than she can handle. Doey was her third daughter. I know that you and Mom may never fully recover from her loss, but Irene and I know about war, and what it can do to survivors. We will always be close and do what we can. I would hate to wake Mom up since she's just gone to sleep, unless you want me to."

"No, please let her sleep. Tell Mom I called, and give her my love. Has your friend Art returned from the Pacific?"

"No" she answered. "He's been flying with the Pacific fleet for almost three years. He's in Honolulu now, but should be home within a few weeks. With the flying he's done, he hopes to get on with an airline, but knows there are thousands of pilots who will come home with the same idea. I'm glad you called, Wynn. It's been a long time."

"I love you, Ruth," I said and hung up.

Chapter 59

Country Club and Our Last Meeting

That evening we went to the Terre Haute Golf Club for dinner. Most members knew of Dorothy and John's loss, and surrounded us with their thoughts and kindness. Among those who expressed their feelings were George and Jane. They came to our table and spoke in voices of genuine sorrow. Jane said all the right words to Dorothy, John, and me.

George said, "Wynn, I want you to know that I have nothing but admiration for you, and I want nothing more than to be your friend. Our home will always be open for you. Come soon and stay as long as you can."

"Thank you, George," I said. "I have always thought of you and Jane as good friends. I know that it's a comfort for Dorothy and John to know that your parents live just across the road from them. I didn't know that you and Jane live in the neighborhood, too."

"Oh, yes." He lowered his voice and said, "Jane and I have been a respectable married couple since the week after Pearl Harbor. I was in the Naval Reserve and got an immediate call to report for duty. Until I was discharged last August, Jane was living with my parents. We now have a house of our own with a large mortgage. We are just three blocks away from my folks and the Brooks' residences.

To Dorothy and John he said, "I have known you since I was a child. Doey and I shared our youth. My thoughts for you and John will never change. Jane and I will always be a close neighbor. If you need us, just think our name and we will be there."

The next morning, a bright sun inched its way over a cool morning sky. Edward, accompanied by Anna, brought my bag down from my room and put it in the trunk of the rented car. I thanked Edward and Anna for the care they gave Dorothy and John, and told them how much I appreciated their friendship.

I put my arms around Dorothy and looked down into a beautiful face that needed a happy smile to go with it. She searched for a pleasant smile and came up with one that didn't go with the sad look on her face. I wrapped her in my arms, kissed her cheeks, and said, "Dorothy, if John or you ever need me, I will be here to care for you just as Doey would have. Doey will always be with me as I will always be with you and John. I do love both of you."

I clasped John's hand, and said, "I'll go home for a few weeks and then return to my home here in Terre Haute. In the meantime, I will keep in close touch. You have my mother's phone number. Please use it at any time of the day or night. I will only be a few hours away. You are my family."

The new words on Doey's marker were probably something special to Doey and her family. I had asked Dorothy what the new wording would be. She said, "It's just something that comes to mind when John and I think of Doey. It's just a little something that reminds us of her . . . and of you."

She was already close to tears when Edward said, "Excuse me for one moment please. Wynn, you left your flight jacket lying on a chair in your room. I thought you might want to take it with you."

"Thank you, Edward," I said. "Yes, I'll take it." Again he apologized for breaking in on my conversation with Dorothy. The moment that Dorothy and I shared was gone.

My Terre Haute family of four stood watching and waving as I left the circular driveway and headed for the cemetery. On the way I stopped at the florist and bought a dozen tulips.

At the cemetery I parked near the gate, turned off the engine, and sat there looking at a scene of beauty that harbored nothing but grim thoughts. I left the car and walked along the familiar path through the garden of flowers leading to Doey's grave.

I walked up the small hill that sheltered her grave from sight. A breeze played among the leaves of the elms. Their branches spread like a benediction over her grave. I could see the top of the white cross. It seemed to rise out of the ground as I approached. When I stood before the cross and looked down at the marker, I was not prepared for what I saw. Instantly tears began to blur my vision. What small recovery that I made from losing her was gone. I sat down at the foot of her grave, and over and over I read the words on the marker. Each reading brought with it a memory of the past that now could only remind me of death and a white cross.

Dorothy "Doey" Brooks
1912-1945
Arise My Love and Come Away with Me

To the end of my life I will never believe that the box of cold ashes that are buried there was Doey. She is not there . . . she lives beyond the moon and on the other side of beyond.

One day I will go there and we will fly again.

Epilogue

To me Doey will always be that beautiful blue-eyed, golden-haired girl, standing by an airplane on the ramp at the Chapel Hill airport. She is still 23 and I am 93.

Many years ago, and what I believed would be the last time, I drove from Chicago down to Terre Haute with my wife Gloria. It was a cool day. The sky was filled with stratus clouds on a background of sunlit blue. I could see what looked like a D.C.10, flying northward through a sky of stable air. It was probably a commercial plane heading for Chicago's O'Hare Airport.

I stopped at a familiar florist along the way and bought three bouquets of tulips. At the cemetery I got out of the car and said to Gloria, "I don't know how long I'll be."

"Take your time," she replied. "I'll be waiting for you."

I entered the gate of the cemetery and walked along the path to Doey's grave. The same old elms waved a greeting, and flowers along the pathway were showing off by nodding in the soft spring breeze. My heart began to beat in time with the silent movement of my lips, as I hummed the words of our song, "A Nightingale Sang in Berkeley Square."

The war was over, leaving only fading memories of our college dreams. Each year, on Doey's birthday, I returned and placed tulips upon her grave. This, the last time, I sat down beside her and we spoke of many things. I said, "This may be my last visit, Doey. For the past week I have been in Chapel Hill looking for places where I found you. Once more, we flew in a moonlight dream and listened to the chimes of midnight again. You are always close to me. You share a permanent place in my heart with another, and one day, we will live forever, beyond the moon and stars, in that beautiful valley, in a place on the other side of beyond.

"The airport we knew is gone now, Doey. The Ready Room, where I first saw you from afar and knew, even then, that I was in love with you, and that one day you would become my wife, is no longer there. The old campus that we knew is as we remember.

"Silent Sam, the Davie Poplar tree, the white old well, the Carolina Inn, and the bell in the Morehead Tower, which still sends its booming sound across the beautiful campus, are still the same, and as beautiful as when we left.

"On Franklin Street, Danziger's and Joe Egan's are gone; leaving only memories of you, Carolyn, and Harry. Only the shadows of your smiles are left to remind me that once we were students there. You and Carolyn from Duke University and Harry and I from UNC. We were there with youthful dreams of tomorrow. We pledged a love that we would share for a long life together. It was a life that sadly deprived us of a future.

"You, Carolyn, Harry, Red and Sam live in a fragile memory that marks the time of those long-ago airport and college days."

Doey's parents, Dorothy and John, rested peacefully beside her. I was sitting at the foot of the marker on Doey's grave. The bronze letters on the marker, "Arise my love and come away with me," had aged with a patina of gray and a touch of dark green, much like the color of hanging moss on a southern oak. For almost an hour, I continued my silent talk with Doey and her parents. Silently they responded to every thought or word which needed an answer.

When I left the cemetery, I passed close to three people visiting what appeared to be a new grave. I recognized the desperate look of grief in their vacant eyes. I wanted to stop and tell them that God never saddled a person with more grief than they could handle, and in time they would be able to live easily with the past. Of course they wouldn't believe me.

At the gate, on impulse, I turned to look one more time at a scene that had become so important to my life. For the first time I realized that in my heart and mind, there was no longer room for hate.

My final words were to Doey, and as a tear or two threatened to fall, I said, "Doey, I love you." And like an echo far away, "A Nightingale Sang in Berkeley Square."

It was not easy to ask God's forgiveness. I had carried a hatred of war, a lost trust in the Almighty, and the senseless evils of man, too long to easily change them for peace. "Let's go home," I said to Gloria, as I got in the car.

"I'm glad I came with you," Gloria replied.

For more than sixty, happy years, she had been my wife. On October 8, 2007, my dearly beloved Gloria died. I am now alone, spending the waning days of my life writing a story of a time that was.

Col. Richard "Red" Hederman died in 1948 and is buried in Arlington National Cemetery.

Col. Joe Bailey, my friend and Squadron Commander in the Air Force, met death somewhere over the Molucca Sea, leading a squadron on a mission to Balikpapan, Borneo, in the South West Pacific.

Capt. Harry Woods, a P 51 pilot and college roommate, lost his life on an escort mission to Hamburg, Germany in 1944.

Carolyn Perry Woods, Harry's widow, died in Florida. She was 81. Her son, John, and daughter, Doey, and I, their godfather, were with her at the end.

*   *   *

When the earth is bright, in a full moon's light, in memory you're with me still. Our love, like the "Littlest Star," will always shine for us. Wherever I go, you are with me. Our love will never die. Now I have the memory of two loves to warm my heart. Somewhere in time, the light of the world that I know will dim and go out. I will instantly awaken and be with the two loves of my life, in that beautiful place, on the other side of beyond.

Acknowledgements

I want to thank a few of my "Number One" girls for inspiring me to write a story about long ago and far-away places.

Thank you to Michelle Beaulieu for her invaluable assistance in the creative process and reassuring me that I had a story to tell, and Linda Swarzman for being my frequent sounding board and confidant.

Most grateful thanks to Melinda Thomas, my editor, for her extreme patience, enormous dedication and encouragement in bringing my story to publication.

Special thanks to Bob Berner for always listening.

I love you all!

CPSIA information can be obtained at www.ICGtesting.com
Printed in the USA
BVOW021749250712

296134BV00002B/163/P